USA TODAY bestselling author **Heidi Rice** lives in London, England. She is married with two teenage sons—which gives her rather too much of an insight into the male psyche—and also works as a film journalist. She adores her job, which involves getting swept up in a world of high emotion, sensual excitement, funny and feisty women, sexy and tortured men and glamorous locations where laundry doesn't exist. Once she turns off her computer she often does chores—usually involving laundry!

Clare Connelly was raised in small-town Australia among a family of avid readers. She spent much of her childhood up a tree, Mills & Boon book in hand. Clare is married to her own real-life hero, and they live in a bungalow near the sea with their two children. She is frequently found staring into space—a surefire sign that she's in the world of her characters. She has a penchant for French food and ice-cold champagne, and Mills & Boon novels continue to be her favourite ever books. Writing for Modern is a long-held dream. Clare can be contacted via clareconnelly.com or at her Facebook page.

A BABY TO TAME THE WOLFE

HEIDI RICE

CINDERELLA IN THE BILLIONAIRE'S CASTLE

CLARE CONNELLY

MILLS & BOON

First Published in Great Britain 2022
by Mills & Boon, an imprint of HarperCollins*Publishers* Ltd,
1 London Bridge Street, London, SE1 9GF

www.harpercollins.co.uk

HarperCollins*Publishers*
1st Floor, Watermarque Building,
Ringsend Road, Dublin 4, Ireland

A Baby to Tame the Wolfe © 2022 Heidi Rice

Cinderella in the Billionaire's Castle © 2022 Clare Connelly

ISBN: 978-0-263-30087-1

06/22

MIX
Paper from
responsible sources
FSC® C007454

This book is produced from independently certified FSC™ paper
to ensure responsible forest management.
For more information visit www.harpercollins.co.uk/green.

Printed and Bound in Spain using 100% Renewable Electricity
at CPI Black Print, Barcelona

A BABY TO
TAME THE WOLFE

HEIDI RICE

MILLS & BOON

To my son Luca, who will never read this book,
but whose childhood obsession with wolves
and his gala performance in a Year 6 production
of *Little Red Riding Hood* as the wolf led to my
love of this particular fairy tale and thus—eventually—
to my decision to write this story. I owe you one,
my gorgeous boy—which unfortunately
does not include a share of the royalties,
just in case you were wondering!

PROLOGUE

Katie, I need your help! It's an emergency!

KATHERINE MEDFORD WRAPPED the large black trench coat around her red velvet cape to shield it from the spitting rain as she shot out of the Tube at Leicester Square while reading her sister Beatrice's eighth text in a row.

What was the problem this time? That Katie would have to fix? Because she was already late for her booking. And unlike Bea, who had their father Lord Henry Medford's considerable financial largesse to rely on, Katie could not afford to lose this job or the twenty-pounds-an-hour commission. The phone began to buzz. Katie's thumb hovered over the 'reject call' button as she dodged pedestrians along Charing Cross Road, en route to the children's bookshop where she was supposed to be reading fairy tales to an audience of four-to five-year-olds in ten minutes and counting.

But, as she went to press her thumb down, the image of Bea from years ago aged fourteen, tears streaking down her cheeks, her face a sodden mess of confusion and fear as Katie was marched out of Medford Hall by their father, tugged at Katie's chest. She sighed and clicked the 'accept call' button as she broke into a jog.

'Bea, what's the problem?' she said breathlessly, the corset of her costume holding her ribcage in a vice. 'I'm late. I don't have time for this, unless it really is an emergency—'

'It's Jack Wolfe,' her sister said, getting straight to the point for once and mentioning the billionaire corporate raider Katie had never met—because why would she, they hardly moved in the same circles. But she knew her sister had got engaged to him a week ago because of the pictures of Bea and her new fiancé all over the Internet.

An irritating ripple streaked down Katie's spine.

Wolfe had been hotness personified in a rough, un-tamed, wildly charismatic way wearing a perfectly tailored tuxedo. The mysterious scar on his cheek which marred his chiselled features and the tattoo on his neck—just vis-ible above the pristine white dress-shirt—made him look even more darkly compelling next to Bea's bright, willowy blonde beauty. Katie would almost have been jealous of her sister, except she didn't have to meet Jack Wolfe to know he had to be a man like her father.

No, thanks. One overbearing bully is all I need in my life.

'He's invited me for dinner tonight at his penthouse on Hyde Park Corner, just the two of us,' her sister rushed on. 'And I'm scared he's going to want to take our relation-ship to the next level.'

Katie stopped dead in the street, her heeled boots skid-ding on the rain-slick pavement. Her fingers tightened on the phone as she registered the panic in Bea's voice.

'What do you mean, you're scared?' Katie gentled her tone to contain her own panic. 'Has Wolfe done something to frighten you, Bea?'

Wolfe was well known for being a rough diamond, with the looks of a fallen angel to go with his stratospheric rise from an East End council estate to the high-flying busi-ness circles in which her father moved. But Wolfe was also a big man, tall and strong, with a muscular physique that filled out his tux to perfection.

And that was without even factoring in the scar and the tats. How exactly had he got that scar which the tabloids had been speculating about for years? Was he violent, aggressive, dangerous?

Her own breathing became ragged as she was thrust back to a time long ago when she'd still been a little girl, hazy half-formed memories lurking on the edges of her consciousness. She swallowed down the wave of humiliation that those stupid nightmares still had the power to wake her up on occasion, struggling to escape something she couldn't see but knew was right there, ready to hurt her if she let it. She evened out her breathing... *Don't go there. Focus on Bea.*

'No, Katie, don't be silly. Jack's not like *that*,' Bea replied with more conviction than Katie felt. 'He'd never hurt me.'

'Then why are you scared of being alone with him?'

Bea huffed out a breath. 'Because he'll probably want to have sex and I'm not sure I'm ready. To be honest, I'm pretty sure I won't ever be ready. He's just a bit too much for me. He's ridiculously smart, and he can be very witty, and he's exciting to be with, but underneath all that there's an intensity about him. I have no idea what he's thinking. He's so guarded, it's like a super power. He's way too deep for me. You know how shallow I am.' Bea's manic babbling finally stopped.

There were so many things to unpick in what Bea had confided, Katie didn't even know where to start—not least because she absolutely did not want this much information about Jack Wolfe. But perhaps the most astonishing thing was the two of them hadn't had sex yet. While Bea was pretty flaky, she had dated before. And Jack Wolfe didn't strike her as the kind of guy to remain celibate for months while dating anyone…especially someone he'd asked to marry him. The guy oozed sex appeal. He could probably give a woman an orgasm from thirty paces.

So not the point, Katie.

'You're not shallow, Bea,' Katie said, because she hated it when her sister put herself down. That was their father talking.

'Whatever,' Bea said, sounding exasperated. 'But I still don't think we'd be a good match,' she added. 'At all.' She huffed. 'I'm worried I'll fall in love with him and he would never love me back.'

Say, what now?

'Then why on earth did you agree to marry him?' Katie asked, walking briskly again as she remembered the children who were sat in a bookstore eagerly waiting for Little Red Riding Hood to put in an appearance. She was glad Bea wasn't in an abusive relationship. But she did not have time to debate her sister's confusing love life right now.

'Because Daddy insisted I say yes,' Bea murmured sheepishly. 'Jack has loaned Daddy some money on generous terms. If Daddy finds out I've broken it off, and if Jack changes the terms, he'll be furious…'

Katie's pace slowed again. She might have guessed their father had engineered this situation. Why couldn't Bea just stand up to him? But she knew why. Bea was scared of their father's temper tantrums, and with good reason… 'Surely you must know you can't marry Jack Wolfe if you don't love him, Bea?' Katie said softly.

'I know I have to break it off, but Katie, it's the pressure. Jack is very hot, but I'm sure he plans to seduce me tonight. And I'm not sure I'll be able to resist him. And once we've slept together it will be that much harder to dump him. I don't want to hurt his feelings.'

Whoa... What the...?

'Bea, you're not serious? Jack Wolfe has built a fortune on being an absolute bastard. His business strategy is to chew up smaller companies and spit them out. You said yourself you don't think he could ever love you. If the guy even has feelings, I'll be astonished.'

'Everyone has feelings, Katie,' Bea countered gently, making Katie wonder if her sister's airhead act *was* actually an act. 'Even Jack.'

'Do you think he has feelings for you, then?' Katie asked, the stupid ripple turning to a deep pulsing ache in her chest. What was that even about?

'No.' Bea sighed. 'He's very attentive. But he's not at all romantic. He pretty much told me he only asked me to marry him because he thinks I'll make a good trophy wife.'

Oh, for the love of...

'Bea, he sounds worse than Father,' Katie said, exasperated. At least Henry Medford had pretended to love their mother once. 'You shouldn't have let Father bully you into saying yes.'

'I know...' Katie could hear her sister's huff of distress even over the blast of a taxi horn. 'Which brings me to why I rang,' Bea added, her voice taking on a desperate tone that Katie recognised only too well, because it was usually the precursor to Bea asking her to do something outrageous or ridiculous or both. 'Could you go to Jack's place tonight at seven?'

'Why would I do that?' Katie asked. Did her sister need moral support to tell Wolfe the engagement was off?

'He's flying in from New York,' Bea said, bulldozing over Katie's question. 'But I told the doorman, Jeffrey, to expect you so you can wait for him in his penthouse—which is spectacular, by the way,' Bea added, her tone segueing neatly from desperate to wheedling. 'If you're there instead of me when he gets home, you can tell him I'm not going to marry him and I won't have to worry. Then I can tell Daddy *he* broke off the engagement.'

Katie stopped dead again. So shocked she didn't know what to say. Bea had asked her for huge favours before. Favours she'd almost always agreed to because she wanted Bea to be happy, and she knew her sister had a massive problem standing up for herself—thanks to their broken childhood.

Katie had always been there to stand up for Bea when her sister's courage or determination had failed her. But this was…

'You have got to be joking!' Katie cried. 'I can't turn up at his place unannounced to dump him on your behalf. I've never even met the guy.' But even as she said it she felt the little frisson of something… Something electric and contradictory and wholly inappropriate rippling through her tired, over-corseted body. The same something that had rippled through her when she'd studied the photos of her sister and Jack Wolfe together a bit too forensically. 'Plus I won't have time to change out of my Little Red Riding Hood costume,' she added a little desperately. She lived in north North London and she was supposed to be reading fairy tales until six. Assuming, of course, she hadn't already been fired for being late. 'I won't do it, Bea. Absolutely no way…'

But even as she said the words the corset cinched tightly around her thundering heart and Katie could feel her fierce determination not to make an absolute tit of herself slipping out of her grasp.

Bea was her sister and if there was one thing she would always be prepared to do, it was her sister's dirty work. Because Bea had been there for her when she'd needed her most.

And there was also the matter of the ripple that was still playing havoc with her senses at the thought of a brooding, overbearing billionaire who was the very last guy on earth who should inspire a ripple in a smart, grounded, totally pragmatic, tycoon-despising woman like herself.

Perhaps she needed to meet the man to discover exactly how overbearing, arrogant and annoying he really was, and sort out this ripple once and for all.

CHAPTER ONE

JACK WOLFE GLANCED at his watch as the chauffeur-driven car pulled up outside the Wolfe Apartments on Grosvenor Place.

Five past three in the morning. Terrific. Only eight hours late.

He rubbed grit-filled eyes as he dragged his stiff body out of the car.

His contact lenses were practically bonded to his eyeballs, and he hadn't slept a wink on the plane. Normally he'd never take a commercial flight but, thanks to an engine problem with the Wolfe jet at JFK, he'd had to fit his six-foot-three-inch frame into a bed built for a skinny ten-year-old.

He checked his phone as he walked into the building and sent a half-hearted nod to the guy on the desk. He'd had no reply from Beatrice, but at least he'd managed to text her from JFK before he'd found another flight and postpone the dinner he'd had scheduled for last night. So she wouldn't be waiting in his apartment.

He stepped into the private lift that would whisk him to his penthouse on the top floor of the building and frowned at the floor indicator. Weird he wasn't more devastated about being forced to postpone tonight's dinner date. Perhaps it was time he addressed why it had taken him so long to fit seducing his fiancée into his schedule.

He liked Beatrice, a lot. And, as soon as he'd begun dating her, he'd marked her out as a perfect candidate for his wife. As tall and beautiful as a supermodel, she had a slightly kooky and admirably non-confrontational temperament which meant they had never had a disagreement. She didn't have a paying job, which meant there would be no conflicts of interest when it came to time management in their marriage—he was, after all, a workaholic.

And best of all, because of her father's position and her aristocratic lineage, she had the class and the social connections he needed to finally break down the last of the barriers still closed to him in the City of London and, more importantly, on Smyth-Brown's board—smoothing the way for the takeover he had been planning for years. So he could finally destroy the man who had destroyed his mother's life.

There was just one problem in his arrangement with Beatrice, though.

Sex. Or, rather, the lack of it.

She'd been hesitant to become intimate at first, especially after she'd accepted his proposal. There was no rush and there was a fragility about her which reminded him rather unfortunately of his mother.

There wasn't much of a spark between them. But that hadn't bothered him either. He was an experienced guy with a highly charged libido. He'd lost his virginity as a teenager to a woman twice his age—and he'd had a ton of practice since at satisfying women.

The only problem was, after building towards the moment when he would finally make Beatrice his, he really hadn't been anticipating last night's dinner as much as he'd expected—in fact, it had almost begun to seem like a chore. He'd never dated any woman for longer than a few months, so he had been planning to suggest that they conduct discreet affairs once their sexual relationship petered out. But he really hadn't expected to feel quite so jaded before their sex life had even started.

His brow lowered further as the private lift glided to a stop on the fourteenth floor of the building. The bell pinged and the lift doors swished open. Thrusting his fingers through his hair, he stepped into the apartment's palatial lobby area and dumped his luggage next to the hall table.

He was being ridiculous. Seducing his fiancée wouldn't be a chore, it would be a pleasure, a pleasure which was long overdue. He was simply exhausted right now, and frustrated at the prospect of having to delay their first night together for another couple of days at least. He'd never had to be this patient before. Apparently there *was* such a thing as too much anticipation.

The ambient lighting gave the strikingly modern hall furniture a blue gleam, but he resisted the urge to request the main lighting be switched on. His eyeballs were so damn sore now, they felt like a couple of peeled grapes. No wonder he wasn't in the mood to jump Beatrice or anyone else.

Dragging off his tie and shoving it into his pocket, he headed into the open-plan living area. Floor-to-ceiling windows looked out onto Wellington Arch and the faltering stream of traffic making its way around Hyde Park Corner and up Piccadilly, the dawn creeping up to illuminate Green Park.

Calm settled over him, as it always did when he had a chance to survey how far he'd come from the frightened feral kid he'd once been. He adored this view because it was a million miles away from where he'd started in a squalid, one-bedroom council flat on the other side of London, ducking to avoid his stepfather's fists.

Rubbing his eyes, he walked deftly through the shadows towards his bedroom suite. He entered the bathroom from the hallway and finally managed to claw out his sticky lenses. He was all but blind without them and, after taking a shower in the dull light afforded by the bathroom mirror, he took the door into the bedroom.

Darkness was his friend, always had been, because he had once had to hide in the shadows.

Not any more.

The heady scent hit him as he closed the door to the steamy bathroom. Something spicy and seductive. Had Beatrice come into the bedroom before getting his message his flight had been delayed until tomorrow? When she'd never been in his bedroom before.

But it didn't smell like Beatrice. She had an expensive vanilla scent. This scent was far more arousing. Fresh and earthy—it smelled like ripe apples and wildflowers on a summer day. A wave of heat pounded south and made him smile. Even if he was so shattered he was having scent hallucinations, the instant erection proved he wasn't becoming a eunuch.

His groin continued to throb as he found the huge king-size bed in the darkness and dropped the towel from around his hips.

He climbed between the sheets, his exhaustion still playing tricks with his sense of smell. He closed his eyes, enjoying the deliciously erotic scent and the satisfying warmth in his crotch as his bones melted into the mattress. His mind plummeted into sleep and he found himself in a summer orchard, the ripe red apples heavy on the flowering fruit trees, the scent of earth and sunshine intensifying.

Warmth enveloped him. The sound of a light breeze

through the orchard matched his breathing, deep and even, and impossibly sensual. The ache in his crotch throbbed. A sigh—soft, sweet, hot—rustled through the trees and stroked his chest and shoulder as he lay in the sun.

He stretched, turning into the electrifying caress, wanting, needing, more. His searching hands found silky hair, satin skin. He plunged his fingers into the vibrant mass and pressed his palm over velvet-covered curves, the tart apple freshness surrounding him in a cloud of need.

His arousal hardened and the vague thought shimmered through his mind that this would have been the best wet dream he had ever had... But why was his dream woman clothed? And what was she clothed in, he wondered, as his fingers encountered rigid ribbing. At last he found the plump curve of a breast through soft cotton, the nipple pebbling as he plucked it.

The last of the fatigue melted away, his appetite intensifying, energy sparking through his body like an electrical current as he began exploring sweet-scented flesh with his lips, his tongue, his teeth. He nipped and nibbled, kissed and sucked, locating a soft cheek, a tender earlobe, a graceful neck and a stubborn chin... Gasping breaths feathered his face, urging him on.

His mouth finally landed on full lips to capture shuddering moans as voracious and needy as his. Fingertips, firm and seeking, caressed the taught muscles of his abs, sending the electrical sparks deep into his groin. His hands sunk further into the mass of curls and the delicious apple scent became even richer. He held his angel's head to take the kiss deeper, the summer sun warming his naked skin, shining off the plump red fruit and through the vivid green canopy overhead.

A wave of possessive hunger flowed through him as the stiff length of his arousal, so hard now he could probably pound nails with it, brushed more velvet. Was that a thigh? A belly? More damn clothing?

The earthy, erotic apple scent, the heady sobs and those caressing fingers ignited a firestorm that finally centred where he needed it the most.

'Yes.' He groaned. But then suddenly everything changed.

'Wait… Stop…' a groggy voice whispered close to his ear. Then snapped loudly, 'Get off me.'

The panicked cry sliced through the sensual fog like a missile, hurtling him out of the summer orchard and back into the dark apartment. He yanked himself back in the darkness, letting go of the mass of curls, hideously aware the warm, soft, body of his dream woman had gone rigid and become far too real.

'What the…?' He growled, the pain in his groin nothing compared to the sickening, disorienting feeling clutching at his ribs. 'Are you really here?'

'Yes, of course I am!' came the hissed reply. Palms flattened against his chest, probably to push him off, but he was already rolling away, brutally awake now, his head throbbing, the painful erection refusing to subside despite his shattered equilibrium.

A barrage of questions blasted into his muddled brain all at once.

Had he just molested a woman in his sleep? And what the hell was she doing in his bed? In his bedroom? At three in the morning? Because this definitely was not Beatrice.

A dark figure scrambled out of the bed and a switch clicked.

'Argh!' He swore viciously, as the sudden glare turned his eyes to fireballs.

He threw his arm over his face, to stop his retinas from being lasered off, and yanked up the sheet to cover the still-throbbing erection. But not before he caught a blurry glimpse of wild russet hair and bold, abundant curves trussed up in a red and black outfit worthy of a lusty tavern wench in a gothic novel.

Was that a corset? Turning her cleavage into the eighth wonder of the world?

Horror and guilt gave way to shock and outrage as awareness continued to spit and pop over his skin like wildfire. Whatever she was wearing, it wasn't doing a damn thing to calm the inferno still raging in his crotch.

'Dim the lights,' he demanded of the house's smart tech system as his mind finally caught up with his cartwheeling emotions and his torched libido.

Was this some kind of a sick prank, or worse, an attempt at blackmail?

'Who are you?' he demanded as his temper gathered pace.

Whoever she was, it was not his fault he'd touched her. Kissed her. Caressed her... Good God, begged her to stroke him to orgasm... Shame washed over him and the erection finally began to soften.

He cut off the thought of what he'd almost done. He'd been virtually comatose. And he was the one who was naked. And he'd stopped the minute he'd woken up enough to figure out what was going on.

And this was *his* bed, in *his* place.

The lights dipped as requested, the only sound her laboured breathing and his thundering heartbeat as he slowly lowered his arm. He waited for his flaming eyeballs to adjust to the half-light. He couldn't see her properly, his myopia turning her into a series of fuzzy, indistinct shapes. But somehow, even without being able to make out too many details, he could sense her vibrant, vivid beauty—not classy and fragile like Beatrice's but raw and real and way too sensual. The earthy, spicy scent tinged with the ripe aroma of a summer orchard still permeated the room. Not a hallucination, then, but the smell of her.

Other memories flashed back to torment him. The feel of her lush curves—satin and silk against his fingertips—the taste of her still lingering on his tongue—heady and sweet and more addictive than a class A drug.

He thrust clumsy fingers through his hair.

'What the hell are you doing hiding in my bed?' he demanded when she didn't speak, letting every ounce of his outrage and frustration vibrate through the words. 'In the middle of the night…disguised as a Victorian hooker?'

'I'm not dressed as a hooker. This is a Little Red Riding Hood outfit!' The inane reply stumbled out of Katie's mouth, her whole body still vibrating from the shock of Jack Wolfe's touch. Firm, forceful, electrifying. Her mind still reeled from being catapulted out of heaven and into hell in one second flat.

Unfortunately, her body had not got the memo—that she was now in the most compromising, mortifying position she had ever found herself in in her entire life—and that was saying something for someone who had earned a living as a children's entertainer for the past five years.

Her nipples were hard enough to drill through steel and the weight in her sex felt like a hot, heavy brick throbbing in time to her frantic heartbeat.

She'd been fast asleep, dreaming of him… Or so she'd thought. But now her panicked gaze devoured the man himself.

Jack Wolfe, in all his glory.

The snapped photos had not done him justice. Sitting up in his bed with a sheet thrown over the mammoth erection she'd had in her hand only moments before, Jack Wolfe was a smorgasbord of hotness laid out before her on thousand-thread-count sheets.

Her shocked gaze took in every inch of him in the softened lighting. The muscular chest, the broad shoulders, the swirling tattoo of a howling wolf which flared over one shoulder blade and across his left pec—only partially obscured by the sprinkle of chest hair that surrounded his nipples and arrowed down through washboard abs.

She jerked her gaze back up before it could land once again on the tent in his lap.

His eyes narrowed, or rather squinted, and she had the weirdest feeling he couldn't quite see her. His glare didn't alter as she took in the full masculine beauty of his face.

All sharp angles and sensual lines, his bone structure was perfectly symmetrical except for a bump on the bridge of his nose. And the livid scar which sliced through his eyebrow and marred his right cheek. His eyes were a startling, pure almost translucent blue with a dark rim around the edges. And horribly bloodshot.

She noted the other signs of fatigue: the bruised shadows under his eyes, the drawn lines around his mouth. Sympathy and guilt joined the tangle of emotions making her stomach pitch and roll. But at least it went some way to stem the flood of sensation.

'I don't give a damn who you're disguised as,' he finally snarled, the sharp tone cutting through the charged silence with the precision of a scalpel. 'I want to know what you're doing in my bed waiting to jump me in the middle of the night!'

'I… I fell asleep.'

'Well, duh…' The sneer broke through her shock and shame to tap into her own indignation—which had completely malfunctioned in the face of his extreme hotness. However hot he was, she was not the one who had initiated Kiss-mageddon. Even sound asleep she'd known that was him. His firm touch skimming over her curves, cupping her breasts, tightening her nipples to…

She swallowed.

Focus, Katie, for goodness' sake.

'I didn't jump you…you jumped me,' she managed.

He scraped his fingers through his hair, pushing the short, damp waves into haphazard spikes. 'Fine, we're even there,' he said, the growled concession surprising her a little. Even naked—*especially* naked—he didn't look like the type of guy who backed down often. 'But I still don't know who the hell you are or what you're doing in my penthouse dressed as a porno version of Red Riding Hood!'

Porno…? What the…?

'This costume's not pornographic. It's not even revealing!' she all but yelped, her own outrage finally coming to the fore. *Of all the…* 'I wear this outfit to read fairy tales to four-year-olds and I've never had any complaints.'

His burning, bloodshot gaze skated over her and drowned her outrage in another flood of unwanted sensation. *Drat the man.* 'I expect their fathers enjoy the show even more than they do.'

She sputtered.

But then she glanced down at her costume. Okay, it had become a bit dishevelled during their dream clinch. She hooked the corset at the top, which she'd loosened before taking a quick nap in what she'd thought was a guest bedroom after getting Bea's text telling her she was off the hook and Jack wouldn't be coming home until tomorrow afternoon.

Wrong again, Bea.

There were no personal items in this room, not even any toiletries on the bathroom vanity… Who lived like that? she thought indignantly as she yanked up the cotton chemise under the corset so it more adequately covered her ample cleavage.

It seemed her quick nap had turned into a deep, drugging sleep before he had so rudely awakened her with his hot, firm touch and his voracious…

Seriously, Katie, focus, already.

She struggled to control the burn of humiliation. And arousal. Not a great combination at the best of times. She had to leave ASAP, now she'd finally gathered enough of her shattered wits to think coherently. But she still had a message to deliver.

'I'm here on behalf of your fiancée, Bea Medford,' she said, even though he was still glaring at her as if she'd ruined his night instead of the other way round.

'How do you know Beatrice?' he demanded, the frown on his forehead becoming catastrophic.

She opened her mouth to tell him, then snapped it shut again as her common sense caught up with her panic. The less this man knew about her identity, the better. He might have her sued or arrested. Even if he'd kissed her first, she was the one who had been in his bed, sound asleep at stupid o'clock in the morning. 'Bea wanted me to tell you,' she continued, ignoring his question. 'She's breaking off the engagement.'

The words dropped into silence and a dart of anguish pierced her ribcage. She hated to be the bearer of bad tidings, even to overbearing, staggeringly hot and arrogant billionaires.

But the pang dissipated when she noted his reaction. He looked mildly surprised, supremely irritated but not remotely devastated. And his glare—which was still directed squarely at her, as if *she'd* been the one who had just dumped him by proxy—hadn't dimmed in the slightest.

'I see,' he said. 'And she didn't come and tell me this herself *why* exactly?'

I know, right?

Katie quashed the disloyal thought. She was on her sister's side—*always*.

But it was impossible not to feel at least a little pissed off with Bea when she had to blurt out, 'She doesn't love you, and she didn't want to hurt your feelings.' She left out the bit about Bea's fear of succumbing to Jack Wolfe's all-powerful seduction techniques, because she had no desire to stroke his already over-inflated ego. Again.

Forget thirty paces. The man had almost given her an orgasm in less than thirty seconds while she'd been sound asleep.

Wolfe's glare intensified. 'Duly noted.' He growled without so much as a flicker of emotion.

So Bea had been right—Jack Wolfe certainly did not have feelings for her, at least not feelings that could be hurt. Katie's heartbeat took a giddy leap. She squashed it like a bug. Why should she be pleased by evidence that he was a heartless, manipulative bastard?

This man had proposed marriage to her sister without giving a hoot about her. When Bea was the sweetest, kindest, most beautiful woman on the planet…give or take the odd episode of unnecessary drama and the fact she was too much of a coward to do her own dirty work.

'Although that still does not explain why you were hiding out in my bed in the middle of the night, disguised as Little Red Riding Hooker,' Jack added, snapping Katie out of her revelry.

Little Red Riding…?

She stiffened at the insult, ready to fire something equally insulting back at him, but the scathing retort got caught in her throat when his glowering gaze raked over her outfit again. And what she saw in it triggered a new wave of heat.

'Tough,' she managed, her throat as raw as the rest of her. 'That's all the explanation you're going to get.'

So saying, she turned and grabbed the boots she'd left by the bed.

Time to stop bickering and run.

She heard his shouted demands—something about staying put and giving him a proper answer to his questions—as she sprinted out through the bedroom door.

She wasn't particularly athletic but, now her flight instinct had finally kicked in big time, she raced through the living area faster than a championship sprinter, grabbing her red velvet cape and raincoat en route. The lift doors were open, the lift waiting for her—*thank God*—and she made it inside and stabbed the button before she heard the crash of footfalls. The doors slid closed on the sight of two hundred and twenty pounds of enraged, spectacularly fit male sprinting towards her, wearing nothing more than a pair of hastily donned boxer shorts and an enraged expression.

She tugged on her boots as the lift dropped to the basement, then raced out of the building's garage. It was only once she jumped aboard a passing night bus heading towards North London that the adrenaline high caused by her narrow escape diluted enough for her to breath properly.

She was retiring as a children's entertainer as of tonight and finally moving out of London. She had enough money saved now, just about, to move the fledging bakery business she'd launched a year ago to the next level.

Her Welsh grandmother had left Katie a cottage in Snowdonia in her will—because she had always been proud of Katie for breaking free of her father's control. Angharad Evans had always despised Henry Medford after the way he had treated her daughter, Carys—Katie and Bea's mother. The mother Katie barely remembered.

The old cottage in the heart of the forest needed some work after being empty for years, but the beautiful forest glade where the smallholding was situated was like something out of a fairy tale, and satisfyingly remote. And the online business Katie had been building for over a year would be even better there, reducing her overheads once she'd invested in a new kitchen.

It was way past time she started making a life for herself that she loved. Instead of one where she was just squeaking by—and humiliating herself on a regular basis. And, if moving out of London and going into hiding in rural Wales also meant avoiding Jack Wolfe's prodigious temper, his hot body and any fallout from tonight, so be it.

CHAPTER TWO

One month later

'WHAT DO YOU MEAN, I can't drive to Cariad Cottage?' Jack Wolfe stared incredulously at the old farmer, who was staring back at him as if he'd lost his mind.

Maybe he had. Why hadn't he been able to forget the woman who had ruined all his best laid plans four long weeks ago now? So much so he'd finally hired a private detective to find her. And rearranged a ton of meetings first thing this morning to make a six-hour drive to the middle of nowhere just to confront her.

'Not in that, boyo,' the man said in a thick Welsh accent, glancing at the Mercedes Benz EQS convertible Jack had liberated from his garage at five o'clock that morning when he'd finally been given an address and discovered Little Red Riding Hooker was his ex-fiancée's older sister.

'You'd need a tractor, or a quad, maybe,' the farmer added. 'Or you could walk. Take about an hour—maybe two.' He glanced down at Jack's shoes. 'But there's a storm heading in.'

What storm? There had been no mention of a storm on his weather app. The sky above the treetops on the edge of the forest was startlingly blue, not a cloud in sight. Perhaps the guy was a friend of Katherine Medford—and was trying to head him off.

Well, you can forget that, mate. He had a score to settle with Miss Red.

He intended to get payback, not just for the broken engagement—which was now threatening to screw up the Smyth-Brown takeover—but for all the sleepless nights in the last month when he'd been woken from dreams of apple orchards and scantily clad wenches to find himself unbearably aroused.

Somehow, he'd become fixated on the woman. And he didn't like being fixated on anyone or anything. It suggested a loss of control he would not tolerate.

She owed him.

'Fine. I'll walk,' he said, tugging up the collar of his jacket and opening the muscle car's boot. He toed off his designer loafers and stamped on brand-new walking boots. He threw the car keys to the farmer, who caught them one-handed.

'There's two hundred in it if you keep an eye on the car for me until I return,' he said.

The man nodded, then asked, 'You want me to send one of the lads with you for an additional price? So you don't get lost.'

'No, thanks,' Jack said. 'I won't get lost.'

He had envisaged this meeting in his mind's eye over four whole weeks and six long hours of driving. He didn't want company.

The farmer didn't look convinced. Jack ignored him and strode off along the rutted track into the shadow of the forest, the earthy scent of lichen and moss lightened by the fresh, heady perfume of wild spring blooms.

The storm hit forty-five minutes later, by which time his feet were already bloody from blisters, his face had been stung to pieces by midges and the phone signal had died, leaving him staggering about in the mud, trying to keep to the track.

The only thing still driving him on in his cold, wet, painful misery was the thought of finally locating Little Miss Riding Hooker again and wringing her neck.

Katie inhaled the lush, buttery aroma of chocolate and salted caramel as she lifted her latest batch of brownies from the oven.

She wiped floury hands on her apron. Only two more batches and she'd be ready to load the quad bike and drive her orders to the post office in Beddgelert. She frowned at the rain hammering against the cottage's slate roof and battering the kitchen windows. That was if the spring thunderstorm which had begun an hour ago ever stopped.

Heavy thuds broke through the sound of hammering rain.

Someone had come to visit? In the middle of a storm? How odd.

Dumping the apron, she headed towards the sound which was coming from the cottage's front door. Probably stranded hikers. It certainly wasn't locals, as they knew to come to the kitchen door.

Poor things, they must be lost and completely soaked. She'd treat them to a cup of hot cocoa and ply them with cookies until the rain stopped—she had to take advantage of every sales opportunity at the moment, given the woeful state of her finances. Who knew installing an industrial-grade kitchen in an off-grid cottage would be so expensive?

The thuds got more demanding as she rushed through the cottage's candlelit interior. The second-hand genera-tor had died an hour ago. Thank goodness for her wood-powered Aga or her whole afternoon would have been a wash-out.

'Open the door.' The gruff, muffled demand sent a frisson of electricity through her. The memory flash—of a taut male body, translucent-blue, bloodshot eyes and a furious frown—was not wanted.

That was four weeks ago—in another life. Stop obsessing about your disastrous encounter with Jack Wolfe.

'Just coming!' she shouted as cheerfully as she could over the hammering.

Impatient, much?

But, when she flung open the heavy oak door with her best 'come buy my cookies' smile, the memory flash flared as if someone had chucked a gallon of petrol on it. And her smile dropped off a cliff.

'Mr Wolfe?' Her numb fingers fell from the door handle as shock reverberated through her system hot on the heels of the five-alarm fire.

Was the man of her wet dreams *actually* dripping a small lake onto her doorstep, his arms clasped around his waist, his broad shoulders hunched against the cold, his dark hair plastered to his head while he wore a designer business suit so drenched it clung to his muscular physique like a second skin?

Or was she having an out-of-body experience?

'*Mr?* Really?' he said, or rather growled, in that gruff tone that had a predictably incendiary effect on her abdomen. 'Let's not stand on ceremony, Red. After all, we've already shared a bed.'

What?

Horrified realisation dawned.

This is not a dream, Katie. Shut the stupid door.

But, before the shock and heat could recede enough for

her fingers to get the message, Wolfe had figured out her intention and thrust his foot forward.

The door slammed on his muddy boot. He swore profusely.

'Blast, sorry...' She cringed. She hadn't meant to injure him. *Much.*

He shoved the door open and marched—or rather, limped assertively—past her into her living room, trailing mud, rainwater and his injured dignity with him.

The muscle in his rain-slicked cheek, gilded by candlelight, twitched like a ticking bomb. But before she had a chance to ask what on earth he was doing in the middle of North Wales, hiking in a thunderstorm—in what looked like an extremely expensive and now totally ruined designer suit—he shivered so hard, his clenched teeth rattled.

And her shocked arousal got bowled over by a wave of sympathy.

While taking pity on him would have been a stretch because—even drenched and freezing, and with several nasty-looking midge bites he still had an aura of ruthless command which would have impressed Attila the Hun—she did not want the surly billionaire catching his death in her cottage or stomping any more mud onto her grandmother's handmade rug.

'There are towels and a shower through there,' she said, pointing towards the downstairs bathroom. 'Take off your suit and drop it outside so I can dry it by the stove. I'll find you something to wear,' she finished with more authority than she felt.

His scarred eyebrow arched and his sensual mouth curved into something halfway between a sarcastic grin and a suggestive sneer. 'You want me naked again so soon, Katherine? I'm flattered.'

He knows my name! Bea, you're a dead woman.

'Oh, shut up,' she managed, flustered now as well as panicked and confused and inappropriately turned on. 'Don't worry. I promise not to even *look* at your dignity this time. Let alone touch it.'

So why are you talking about it, you muppet?

Perhaps because she'd thought about it far too much in the past month.

Heat flared in his now laser-focussed gaze as it raked over her. 'Shame,' he murmured with a rich appreciation she did not have one clue what to do with.

She made a hasty retreat up the stairs to locate something dry for him to wear from the sack of her grandmother's old clothes that she'd recently washed to take to a charity shop in Bangor. Something that would cover his dignity and salvage what was left of her sanity.

Some chance.

She's stunning. Even more stunning than I imagined.

Jack allowed the thought of Katherine Medford's glorious curves in flour-dusted jeans and a worn T-shirt, her shocked emerald eyes, her pale, freckled skin and wild, red hair warm him as he peeled off his sodden clothing, dropped it outside the bathroom door and stepped into the snug shower cubicle.

The water pressure left a lot to be desired, but the heat was welcome as another shivering fit hit him. As he thawed out, his mind began to engage with something other than the visceral shock of Katherine Medford's unusual beauty.

Her cottage—its whitewashed stone and bright-blue gingerbread trim beckoning him out of the storm like a beacon—was cosier and more comfortable than he had expected from the detective's report on her finances. Thunder crashed outside as he dried himself off with one of the fluffy towels neatly folded on the vanity. The smell of apples from her shampoo reminded him forcefully of the erotic orchard he had visited nearly every night for a month in his dreams.

He dragged on his damp boxers, the only item of clothing which had survived the journey. And scowled down at the burgeoning tent in his shorts.

Behave.

She was everything he'd remembered and more—especially now he was wearing his lenses and could see her more clearly. But the resultant effect on his libido and his self-control was not good.

And worse was the way her saucy, sparky attitude affected him. Since when had he found defiance arousing? She'd slammed the door on his foot! And yet, as soon as he'd got inside the house, the thought of chastising her had taken second place to the thought of feasting on her full lips.

He sighed, rubbing his hair dry.

Time to get real. She might look harmless, but he already knew she wasn't. She would not get the better of him. *Again.*

'Here. It was all I could find that looked big enough.' He turned to see a toned arm appear at the door holding a…? He scowled and tilted his head. What was that? It looked like a piece of purple towelling with…were those pink ruffles?

'Great,' he murmured, lifting it from her outstretched fingers. 'Thanks,' he said, not sure he should be all that thankful. The arm immediately disappeared back behind the door.

'Would you like some hot cocoa?' the disembodied voice asked.

'I'd prefer coffee,' he said. Coffee was the least he was going to need to wear the monstrosity she'd handed him.

He shrugged on the worn frilly towelling robe. It was tight across his shoulder blades and only just covered his back-side. He looked ridiculous in it, but it was warm and dry and smelt of laundry detergent, with a hint of her. He'd worn enough second-hand clothing as a kid to appreciate comfort over sartorial elegance any day.

'I'm sorry, I don't have coffee,' she said, sounding al-most apologetic.

'Cocoa it is, then,' he said, then caught another whiff of the delicious aroma which had enveloped him when he'd first stepped into the cottage. 'And a slice of whatever it is you're baking,' he added, his stomach grumbling loudly as he realised he was starving.

'The brownies are not for sale,' she said. 'They're al-ready on order.'

'I'll give you fifty quid per brownie,' he said, not joking.

He heard an astonished huff which made the goose pim-ples on his arms—and a few other things—stand to at-tention.

'Okay, sold,' she said, not sounding all that grateful for his generosity. 'But don't think I won't bill you,' she added with a sharp tone that made him smile. He knew the value of something all depended on what someone was prepared to pay for it. And her mercenary zeal was something he could appreciate.

'There's ointment in the cabinet for your midge bites,' she added. 'It'll stop them itching.'

'How much will that cost me?' he asked wryly.

'It's free… For now, but don't tempt me.' The door began to close before she added. 'I've lit a fire in the liv-ing room, so you can sit in there once you're decent until the cocoa is ready.'

His smile sharpened as the door snapped shut, his usual

confidence when it came to women, and especially this woman, finally returning full-force.

Decent? Is that really what you want? I don't think so, Red. Not from the way your eyes darkened as soon as you spotted me on your doorstep.

Maybe she had a more volatile effect on him than any woman he'd ever dated, but that didn't have to be a bad thing. When was the last time a woman had challenged him? Or made him ache, for that matter, for four solid weeks—enough to have him tracking her all the way to the wilds of North Wales and trashing his favourite suit?

Perhaps his obsession with her was much more straightforward than he had originally assumed. And just as easily remedied.

After tying the belt on the ridiculous robe, he found the ammonia-based ointment in the cabinet and began dabbing it on the bites on his face and neck, surprised when the angry swelling stopped itching.

The grin widened as he touched the robe's *frou-frou* frills. No doubt Katherine had supplied him with this sartorial disaster to threaten his masculinity.

Yeah, good luck with that, Red!

It would take much more than donning a second-hand dressing gown to put a dent in Jack Wolfe's ego. And he intended to make sure Katherine Medford found that out the hard way…

He chuckled. *Pun fully intended.*

CHAPTER THREE

Katie perched on the armchair opposite her uninvited guest and watched him devour his third brownie.

How could Jack Wolfe still look hot wearing her grandmother's dressing gown? Even the lurid pink trim hadn't dimmed his forceful masculinity one bit. Perhaps because too much of his magnificent chest was now visible in the deep V of the robe's flounced neckline.

'That's a hundred and fifty pounds you owe me,' she said, just in case he'd forgotten the agreed price. Instead of looking outraged, he smiled. Or was it a smile? It was hard to tell, the sensual curve as cynical as it was amused. She remembered what Bea had said about him being impossible to read. Her sister had not been wrong. The man was about as transparent as a brick.

'And worth every penny,' he murmured, licking the last of the caramel crumble off his fingertips.

Her heartbeat, which was now beating time with the torrential rain outside, sunk deeper into her abdomen. If he was trying to intimidate her with that sexy glint in his eyes, it was definitely working.

'So, what are you doing in Snowdonia, Mr Wolfe?' she asked, struggling to keep her voice firm—which required every acting skill she'd ever acquired. 'Assuming, of course, it's not an unlucky coincidence you turned up on my doorstep?'

She'd gone over all the possible motives for his appearance—from the bad to the absolutely catastrophic—while waiting for him to emerge from her bathroom and she couldn't think of a single one that might be benign.

Bea had rung her to thank her, the day after the night of the dream clinch, and said Jack had agreed to release her from the obligation without changing the terms of their father's loan.

Lord Medford had still been angry, but at least he hadn't freaked out completely. Knowing what their father was capable of when his plans were thwarted, Katie had been grateful, and also surprised Wolfe had been so amenable. But now she knew why. Obviously, he'd been planning to get payback on the messenger instead: *her*.

'No, it wasn't a coincidence,' he said, his intent gaze causing her goose bumps to get goose bumps. He placed his plate on the table beside the sofa. The pink trim on the robe caressed his pecs. 'I hired a detective to find you.'

She might have been relieved Bea hadn't ratted her out after all if she wasn't shocked at how determined he had been to locate her. Had she really injured his dignity that much? Because, as she recalled, it had been pretty robust.

His gaze skated over her, setting off more bonfires. 'I never would have guessed you and Beatrice were sisters.'

She bristled. She couldn't help it. She loved Bea to pieces, but she knew perfectly well that when men met her baby sister—tall, willowy, serene and dazzlingly beautiful Bea—they didn't notice Katie or spot the family resemblance. Unlike Bea, Katie was short, had insane hair and was, well, not exactly slender. She'd learned over the years to embrace her curves—and her chocolate addiction. She'd never be slim or elegant—she'd failed at a ton of yo-yo diets to prove it—but she was happy with who she was now and she was healthy and fit.

'Well, we *are* sisters,' she said. 'As much as I would love not to share any genetic code with my father, he insisted on a paternity test when we were both born to make sure we were his. Because that's the kind of trusting, charming guy he is.'

The muscle in Wolfe's cheek hardened. 'You don't get on with your father?'

'"Don't get on" is a bit of an understatement,' she said, proud her father's scorn no longer had the power to hurt her. 'We don't have a relationship. As a teenager, I wanted to be an actress. He had planned for me to marry one of his business associates. So he kicked me out of the house. It was tough for a while, and the actress thing didn't pan out because I didn't have the right "look",' she added, doing air quotes. 'But I've never missed being under his thumb.'

'How old were you when he kicked you out?'

She shrugged. 'Seventeen.' Perhaps he thought she was a fool to have walked away from all that privilege. From what she'd read about Wolfe in the business press, he'd never had any of the advantages she'd been born into. But she didn't care about his opinion. No one got to judge her life choices any more. That was the point.

'That's very young to be on your own,' he said, surprising her when the fierce look on his face became almost sympathetic.

Katie dismissed the giddy blip in her heart rate. She didn't need his pity. 'I wasn't totally alone,' she said. 'My *nain* was still alive then, so she helped me out.'

'Your *nine*? What is that?' he asked, pronouncing the word in English.

'It's Welsh for grandmother.' She glanced around the cottage. 'Cariad was her home. She left it to me five years ago, when she died,' she added, then wondered why she was giving him so much unsolicited information. 'And seventeen's not that young. I was older than you were when you ended up on the street.'

He stiffened, the frown returning.

Touché, Jack. Two can play the interrogation game.

'How did you find out I was once homeless?' he asked, his tone deceptively soft but with steel beneath. She remembered what Bea had said about how guarded he was with personal information. Apparently that hadn't changed.

'I did an Internet search on you after... After that night.'

The frown deepened. 'I didn't know that information was on the Internet.'

'It's not in the UK press, but I found an article written three years ago for a celebrity website in Mexico. They mentioned the rumours about your background while saying how much money you'd donated to a charity for street kids while you were there.' She'd wondered, when she'd read it, if the story had been planted to make him look good. Apparently not, from the way his jaw clenched.

'I see,' he said, then pulled his smart phone from the pocket of the robe and began tapping with lightning-fast thumbs.

She would hazard a guess that when his phone service returned *Estilo* magazine was going to be forced to take down the article.

'So it's true,' she murmured.

His gaze met hers as he pocketed the phone, the guarded look making the blip in her heart rate pulse.

'What is?' he asked evasively.

'That you were homeless as a child,' she continued, refusing to be deflected by the 'back off' vibes.

Shadows crossed his expression and the pulse of sympathy echoed in her chest. Moments ago it would have been impossible to imagine Jack Wolfe had ever been vulnerable and afraid and at the mercy of people more powerful than himself—and even harder to believe she could have anything in common with him. But, as she watched him debate whether to admit the truth or stonewall her, it became less hard.

'I wasn't a child,' he said at last.

'How old were you?' she probed, because the article hadn't been that specific. She'd simply assumed his 'early teens' had to be younger than seventeen.

Again she saw him debating whether to answer her, then he shrugged. 'Thirteen.'

'That makes you a child, Jack,' she said, stunned he could believe otherwise.

'Believe me, I'd seen enough and done enough—*more* than enough—at that age to qualify as a man.' He rubbed the scar on his cheek and the pulse in her chest bounced.

I wonder who gave him that scar?

'And I was certainly never a victim,' he added, dropping his hand. He reached across the space to snag her wrist. 'So you can take that pitying look off your face.'

His touch was electrifying, shocking her into silence when he stood and dragged her to her feet.

He was too close to her, his big body generating warmth, the scent of him enveloping her. Her apple shampoo mixed with a tantalising, musty aroma which threw her back to that night in his bed and into that unbearably erotic dream.

'I don't pity you,' she said, shuddering when he cupped her cheek with his other hand, pushing her wild hair back from her face and hooking it behind her ear. The gesture was disturbingly possessive, but oddly tender too.

'Good,' he remarked, his gaze roaming over her face with a purpose which made her more aware of his addictive scent and the heavy weight sinking into her sex.

'But I do feel sorry for that boy,' she said boldly, ignoring the renewed ache she thought she'd tamed weeks ago.

'Well, don't be. That little bastard is long gone.' His mouth lowered to hers, his eyes dark with arousal now. 'I'm a man now, a man who always gets what he wants.'

She should push him away, tell him to let her go, but she couldn't seem to move, couldn't seem to speak, all her senses focused on his lips and the memory of them skating over her skin, igniting fires which had been burning ever since.

'And what I want now is *you*, Red,' he murmured.

It was an outrageous thing to say. They didn't know each other, they certainly didn't like each other, and it was fairly obvious he was still mad at her for what had happened with Bea…

But, even knowing all that, her heart continued to hammer harder than the rain outside as her body softened into a mass of molten sensation.

What was happening to her? She wasn't a virgin. But she'd never felt anything like this instant, insane chemistry. Her two boyfriends as a teenager had been nothing like Jack Wolfe. They had been friends, not a rich, powerful, ruthlessly driven man who was the complete opposite of sweet or generous or kind.

So why couldn't she tell him to get lost?

He framed her face with both hands. The rough calluses abraded her skin as he tilted her face up to his.

'You want me too.' His hot breath, flavoured with caramel, whispered over her lips. 'Say it.'

She flattened her palms against her *nain*'s robe, wanting to push him away. But then his ridged abs tensed beneath her fingertips.

'Tell me the truth, Katherine.'

'Yes,' she whispered on a soft sob of need.

* * *

Yes.

Triumph leapt in Jack's chest, her reluctant acceptance yanking at something deep inside. He slanted his mouth across hers, capturing her startled gasp, and threaded his fingers into her wild hair to hold her steady, releasing the tantalising scent of apples as his body ached.

The firestorm of need that had been propelling him here all along soared as her lips parted, instinctively giving him more access, and he thrust his tongue deep.

She tasted of cocoa and sin—silky, rich, delicious and even more addictive than her brownies. He explored in demanding, hungry strokes, while running his hands down her sides to capture her bottom and press her into his erection. He exploited each sigh, each shudder, scattering kisses across her stubborn jaw, biting into her earlobe, feasting on her neck.

Her kisses, tentative at first, became as fierce and furious as his. He draped her arms around his neck and drew her closer still, stoking the fire until it burned.

Feeling his control slipping, he yanked himself back and held her waist. Her eyelids fluttered open, her expression a picture of stunned arousal and shocking desire.

He let out a gruff chuckle, trying to ease the tension in his gut and calm the driving need to devour her.

'Where's your bedroom?' he asked, surprised he could actually string a coherent sentence together.

She frowned and he could see the wary confusion cross her face.

'What are you scared of, Red?' he coaxed.

Her gaze flared with outrage and a strange pressure pushed at his chest.

She really was glorious when she was mad.

'I'm not scared of *you*, that's for sure.' The fierce denial made her eyes flash with green fire. The desire in his abdomen flared.

Who would have guessed her independence was even hotter than those gorgeous curves or the fiery passion in her eyes?

'Then let's take what we both want,' he said.

It was a dare, pure and simple. A risky strategy for sure—and not something he would normally do. He didn't have to fight for what he wanted—not any more. Everything eventually fell into his lap, women most of all, because he always made sure he held all the cards.

But Katherine was different. Because he wanted her more than he had wanted any woman. She challenged him, excited him, pushed and provoked him. She already knew more about him than any woman he had ever slept with. The compassion in her eyes when she had revealed what she knew about his past had horrified him. And made him want to prove he wasn't that wild, angry kid.

No one looked at him with pity in their eyes. Not any more. He was the master of his own destiny now. And he intended to be the master of hers too.

The thought of how fixated on her he'd become should have made him extremely uneasy. But, as he watched her gaze flare with the same need and the same desperation, and felt her body soften, the fire in his gut became too intense to think about anything but getting her naked and ending this craving to finish what they'd started a month ago.

'Upstairs,' she said. 'First door on the right.'

He swore with relief, then grasped her hand in his and dragged her up the narrow staircase. He had to duck his head under an exposed beam to enter the low-ceilinged room. A flash of lightning illuminated a cosy, unashamedly feminine space. A brass-framed bed had been crammed into the small area and was covered with a home-made quilt and scattered with colourful cushions, the head-board draped with fairy lights. He flicked the light switch but nothing happened.

'The generator's out,' she said over the roar of thunder.

He marched to the window and drew the curtain, gilding the room in a watery light, but it was enough to see her more clearly, and that was all he cared about.

Untying the robe she'd given him, he dropped it on the floor, his skin burning from the sensory overload.

Her gaze darkened as it roamed over him, her breath shuddering out as it snagged on the tattoo he'd had done several lifetimes ago. He'd debated having it removed. The faded artwork had meant something to him once but seemed crude now, and vulgar on the man he had strived to become. But her avid gaze gave him pause.

How could he feel both exposed yet flattered by the desire darkening her eyes? He didn't need her acceptance or her approval.

Returning to her, he lifted the heavy fall of hair off her nape and cradled her head to tug her mouth back to his. Her hands flattened against his abs as he kissed and ca-ressed the stubborn line of her jaw. 'You're wearing way too many clothes. Yet again,' he murmured.

Katie gave a throaty chuckle. 'I know,' she managed.

'Then let's remedy the situation.' Jack grasped the hem of her T-shirt and yanked it over her head.

It was his turn to feel light-headed as he took in the sight of her magnificent breasts cupped in red lace. Dark nipples poked at the sheer fabric, swollen and erect.

He rubbed his thumb across one rigid tip, gratified when she gasped and the nipple drew into a tight peak. He slid the bra straps off her shoulders, then unhooked the lacy contraption to release the abundant weight into his palms.

He lifted them to capture the engorged nipple with his lips. Tracing the puckered areola with his tongue, he choked down a rough chuckle when her fingernails dug into his shoulders. She clung to him as he worked one stiff peak then the other, kissing, nipping, tugging, her body bowing back like a high-tension wire. She panted, her un-inhibited response even more exquisite than the feel of her flesh swelling and elongating against his tongue.

Keeping his mouth on her breasts, he released the buttons on her jeans with clumsy fingers and edged the denim off her hips enough to press the heel of his palm into the heat of her panties.

He groaned as his fingers slid under the gusset and found her clitoris, the slick nub already drenched with desire. He felt her contract around his invading fingers as his thumb caressed the bundle of nerves with ruthless efficiency. His own pain and need dimmed in the drive to make her shatter. Just for him.

She clamped down hard on his probing fingers, crying out as the wave hit with stunning force. He held her there, ruthlessly stroking until she slumped against him, limp and exhausted.

The scent of her arousal permeated the room, making his erection buck against his shorts.

I want to be inside her.

The fierce urgency joined the visceral ache. He stripped off the rest of her clothing in record time, then scooped her into his arms and laid her on the bed.

She stared at him, her gaze unfocussed, her breathing ragged, her red hair dark against the light quilt and her skin flushed with afterglow.

She was a banquet he wanted to feast upon for hours. But as he kicked off his boxers, and the painful erection sprang free, he knew the feasting would have to wait, because right now he had to feed the hunger clawing at what was left of his self-control like a ravening wolf.

He slid his arms under her knees to lift her legs high and wide and position the aching erection at her entrance.

'Hold on to me,' he grunted. Katie's hands clasped his shoulders as he thrust deep in one powerful surge.

Her sex massaged his length. So tight. And for one brutal moment he thought he would lose it. But, using every last ounce of his control, he held on enough to establish a rhythm that would drive them both towards oblivion. Together this time.

She opened for him, her body accepting all of his. His grunts matched her soft pants as she met his thrusts. The tide rose, barrelling towards him, and the pleasure and pain combined into a furious storm no less powerful or elemental than the one still raging outside.

Her body clamped down at last, triggering his own vicious orgasm. Shattering in its intensity, the climax gripped him as he soared into the abyss. But, as he crashed to earth, two thoughts slammed into him at once as he collapsed on top of her.

I didn't use a condom.
I want her again already.

CHAPTER FOUR

KATIE'S FINGERS SLID OFF the broad shoulder pressing her into the mattress, Jack Wolfe's erection still solid inside her.

But, as the halo of afterglow faded, the shattering truth settled on her chest. And felt even heavier than Wolfe's muscular body.

What had she done?

She'd never made love before with such urgency, and passion and ferocity—he'd stoked it for sure, but she'd been a willing and eager participant in her own destruction.

He groaned as he rolled off her.

She flinched, aware of the tenderness from their brutal joining and the sticky residue he had left behind.

This man had been engaged to her sister only a month ago. And, even if he and Bea had never slept together, Katie had just crossed a line—an ethical, moral line. She didn't even like the man. And she certainly didn't trust him.

Perhaps she should be grateful they'd got the hunger out of their system that had been building since that night. But her panic only increased when he shifted beside her and laid a possessive hand on her stomach. The heat didn't feel anywhere near as satisfying as it should have, but worse was that sense of connection which couldn't be real.

She shifted, attempting to scoot off the bed, but his hand curled around her hip, holding her in place.

'Where are you going?' he asked.

She was forced to look at him.

His tanned skin glowed in the turbulent light as the storm continued to batter the window. His strong features, marred by that jagged scar, looked saturnine, the unreadable expression doing nothing to contain the storm raging inside her.

'I need to wash up,' she said, horrified at the thought she hadn't asked him to use protection. She'd been blindsided by him, enough to lose not just her control but every one of her scruples and priorities. And that had never happened to her before. Not ever.

And they weren't even dating.

She grasped his wrist to lift his arm off her. He didn't protest as she sat up and scooped her discarded T-shirt off the floor. She tugged it on, feeling brutally exposed.

Bit late for that, Katie.

Thank goodness the T-shirt was long enough to cover her bare bum because her panties had vanished.

As she stood, intending to lock herself in the bathroom until she could figure out how on earth to play this situation, he said softly behind her, 'I'm sorry. I should have used a condom and I didn't. I've never done that before.'

She glanced round, surprised by the apology and by the frown on his face that suggested he was telling the truth. The heat that shot through her already overused body at the sight of him naked and still partially aroused was not at all welcome.

He threw the quilt over his lap, but the lazy movement suggested he was doing it to protect her modesty, not his own.

Not that she had any. Not any more. Not after the way

she'd thrown herself at him. And gone completely to pieces at the first touch of his lips, the first intimate caress.

'Are there likely to be consequences we need to address?' he asked, gathering his faculties a lot quicker than she could.

She shook her head. 'Not unless you have any unpleasant diseases,' she managed, so humiliated now she couldn't even look at him. She turned to stare out of the window, the sun finally putting in an appearance and making the raindrops on the forest leaves sparkle.

The cottage was in a small glade with a mountain stream at the back. One of the few memories she had of her mother was from here, smiling when Carys had brought her and Beatrice to Snowdonia to visit their *nain*. Before her mother had died and her father had forbidden them both to visit 'the old crone', as he liked to call Angharad Evans.

When Katie had arrived to clear the place out a month ago, she'd felt instantly as if she belonged here. But she felt lost now, disorientated, as if she'd become someone other than who she had strived to be—smart, independent and accountable to no one but herself. Had she also betrayed Angharad Evans' memory in the process by welcoming a man as ruthless as her father into her grandmother's old bed?

'I'm on the pill to help with my periods,' she murmured, grateful at least that by a stroke of luck an unplanned pregnancy wouldn't be a consequence. But then she wondered why she had explained the information. Jack Wolfe hardly needed to know she wasn't dating.

Perhaps that was why she'd succumbed so easily to the erotic charge which had flared without warning as soon as he'd declared an interest. It had been four years since she'd been intimate with anyone.

But, even as she tried to persuade herself her insane behaviour had been purely physical, she knew it wasn't. After all, it wasn't as if she hadn't had an orgasm in four years. She was perfectly capable of taking care of her own needs in that department. Although not even her vibrator had ever given her an orgasm—two orgasms—so intense she could still feel the dying embers threatening to reignite any minute just at the sight of Jack lounging on her bed like a well-satisfied tiger... Or rather, a well-satisfied wolf.

Wow, pathetic much?

'I'm clean,' he said, interrupting her pity party. 'I have a rigorous medical every year for my company's insurance,' he added, surprising her with his candour. 'And, as I said, I've never had sex before without a condom.'

'Good to know,' she said, trying to find the information reassuring.

'How about you?'

She swung round at the probing question. Outraged, despite the rational part of her brain telling her he had just as much right to ask her about her sexual history. 'I'm clean too,' she snapped. 'As luck would have it, I'm nowhere near as promiscuous as you are.'

He barked out a half-laugh, completely unperturbed by the bitchy response. 'Don't believe everything you read about me,' he said. 'I've become surprisingly discerning in my old age.'

The frank response made her wish she could take back the revealing reply as she recalled he had never slept with her sister. He'd been engaged to Bea for a week and had dated her for over a month. Why hadn't he seduced her sister with the same fierce focus he'd just seduced her with after meeting her exactly twice? And why should it matter when she'd stopped comparing herself to Bea years ago?

His scarred eyebrow arched and a speculative gleam

lit his eyes, accentuating the dark rim around his irises. She had the hideous feeling he could see what she was thinking.

'Just out of interest, when *was* the last time you dated?' he asked, the forthright question slicing through her confused thoughts.

Heat scalded her cheeks.

Good grief, she'd never been a blusher, but she'd never met a man who was quite so direct. Or abrupt.

'A while,' she offered, not about to tell him the truth and encourage any more probing questions. Or, worse, declare herself the loser in the game of Who's the Most Jaded Person in the Room they seemed to be playing.

'Exactly how long is a while?' he countered, undeterred by her evasive answer.

'That's none of your business, Jack,' she replied, then realised her mistake instantly when a smile that had 'gotcha' written all over it appeared.

'So it's Jack now, is it?' He lifted his arms to link his fingers behind his head as he sat back against the cushions, revealing the tantalising tuffs of dark hair under his armpits and the roped muscles on the underside of his biceps that bulged distractingly. 'Progress, at last,' he finished, the smile now full of wolfish smugness, or smug wolfishness. *Take your pick.*

Was that his real surname, she wondered. Because it suited him almost too perfectly.

'We just made love,' she said. 'Even I can see the irony in still calling you Mr Wolfe after that,' she finished, struggling to gain some semblance of control over the conversation.

'Did we? Make love? Are you sure?' he mocked. 'How quaint.' The smile took on a cynical slant, which made him look even more jaded—and hot.

'It's a figure of speech,' she said wearily, suddenly tired of the banter and the knowledge she wasn't as tough and invulnerable as she had always assumed, or at least not where he was concerned—which only made this situation more dangerous. 'We had sex, then, if you prefer,' she added, trying to regain some of her usual fierceness in the face of extreme provocation. Did he know how shaky she felt right now? She certainly hoped not.

The smile became rueful, which didn't slow her pounding pulse in the least. 'Funny, because it didn't feel like just having sex,' he said. 'I've had a lot of sex in my life and that was... Well, different.'

Had it been? For him too? Despite his vast experience?

She squashed the foolish thought. He was toying with her, seeing if he could unnerve her even more. Why was she letting him?

She dragged her fingers through her hair and tied the wild mass in a ruthless knot as she glanced out of the window. The panic retreated as she noticed the storm had finally passed. The late afternoon sunlight struggled to peek through the trees. 'The storm's over,' she said, far too aware the storm in her gut hadn't abated in the least. 'Your suit should be dry enough to put back on,' she added, the hint so blatant even he couldn't miss it. 'I'll pack you some brownies for the road free of charge,' she finished, knowing she wasn't even going to hold him to the one hundred and fifty pounds he owed her. She needed him gone now, before she lost what was left of her sanity...and her self-respect.

She headed to the door, ready to hole up in the bathroom until he'd left her bed. And she could breathe again.

But as she reached for the doorknob his gruff voice sent unwelcome sensations sprinting down her spine. 'Not so fast, Red.'

She turned. He was still lounging on her bed but his gaze had become flat and direct, the muscle in his jaw twitching. 'I'm not finished with you yet.'

'Tough, because I'm finished with you,' Katie said with a conviction she was determined to fake until she'd got him out of the house.

She instantly regretted the bold challenge when the brittle light in his eyes sharpened and he let out a rueful chuckle. 'I wasn't talking about sex,' he said, the searing perusal making it very clear he didn't believe her for a second. 'Precisely.'

Her pulse began to punch her collarbone with the force and fury of a heavyweight champion. 'Then what were you talking about?'

'I have a proposition for you,' Jack said, the silky tone underlined with cold hard steel. 'One you won't want to refuse.'

She swallowed down the lump forming in her throat and locked her knees, the arrogance in his tone as disturbing as everything else about him. 'I don't take orders from you, Jack,' she said, determined to believe it. 'Even if we did just sleep together.'

It was a very long time since she'd allowed herself to be bullied by any man. And, whatever his proposition was, she had no intention of accepting it. He unsettled her in ways she had no control over, and that could not be good. But her curiosity got the better of her when she added, 'What's the proposition?'

He lifted his hands from behind his head and placed them on the taut skin of his belly, drawing her attention to the increasingly visible bulge under the quilt. Her gaze shot back to his face as the sensation sunk like a hot brick into her abdomen. But it was already too late, because his lips curved in that sexy smile that told her he had caught her looking.

'Go wash up,' he said. 'I'll meet you downstairs in twenty minutes. We should probably discuss it when we're both fully clothed,' he added. 'I would hate to take unfair advantage of you.'

She glared at him, knowing full well Jack Wolfe would have no qualms about using any advantage, unfair most of all. But she bit her lip, because calling him out on the blatant lie would be tantamount to admitting he *had* an unfair advantage. And being clothed before she challenged him again would be the smart thing to do… Especially after all the stupid things she'd done.

'Fine,' she said, reaching for the doorknob. 'But, just so you know, the answer is going to be no.' She marched out of the room with a flourish, slamming the door on his low chuckle, satisfied she'd managed to get the last word.

As she showered off the evidence of her stupidity, she promised herself that, no matter what his proposition was, however tempting, however tantalising, however hard to refuse, she would send him packing. Because she owed it to the seventeen-year-old kid who had spent a year sofa-surfing through London and doing crummy minimum-wage jobs on nightshifts to gain her independence. She wasn't about to lose it to a wolf.

CHAPTER FIVE

'WHAT DO YOU MEAN, *no*? You haven't heard the deal yet!' Jack stared at Katherine Medford, not sure whether to be frustrated or amused by the stubborn scowl on her expressive face. Although both reactions were preferable to the fierce tug of need she caused simply by breathing—which was starting to annoy him.

'I don't have to listen to the deal. Have you gone completely insane? I don't want to be any man's mistress but, even if I was going to do something as demeaning as that, it definitely would not be with you.'

Jack let out a gruff laugh, releasing the tension in his ribs. Katherine Medford really did look spectacular when she was mad, and she was practically frothing at the mouth now. He needed to get a grip on the effect she had on him. He'd never found argumentative women a turn-on before, but there was something about Katherine's spitfire qualities that fascinated him.

Go figure.

This fascination was purely sexual, though—for both of them—which surely made her even more perfect for the position he was proposing. A lot more perfect than her sister, anyway.

'Why not me?' he asked.

He had expected pushback and had been more than

ready to counter it—after all, that was what negotiations were for. And he happened to be good at them. But her vehement rejection of his proposal was a little over the top, even for her.

'Because you're…' she spluttered, her cheeks suffused with that becoming blush which made the freckles across her nose glow. Something he'd noticed earlier when he had been lying in her bed, far too aware of her naked curves silhouetted against the window through her old T-shirt.

'Because you're *you*,' she said, as if that was supposed to mean something. 'Plus you were engaged to my sister about ten minutes ago. And I don't even like you.'

She leant against the kitchen counter where he'd found her after putting on his clothes. The trousers were trashed and the shirt hopelessly wrinkled, but at least both garments were dry.

His lips quirked. 'I'd say we just proved upstairs you like me well enough,' he said.

'I'm not talking about sex. I'm talking about everything else.'

'Such as?' Jack asked. This ought to be good. Was she a hopeless romantic? Under that guise of pragmatism and practicality? He had to admit he was a little disappointed. But he could work with that if he had too.

Perhaps it was pride, or perhaps it was the sexual obsession that hadn't faded despite their no-holds-barred antics upstairs—but whatever it was, he did not plan to take no for an answer.

She folded her arms, making those generous breasts plump up underneath her T-shirt.

'Such as shared goals, trust, enjoying each other's company,' she spat out, her brows puckering. 'Oh, and how about the biggie? Actually knowing more about you than

I could find out in a few hours of searching online or ten minutes spent in bed with you? Such as that, maybe.'

So not a hopeless romantic, then. *Thank God.* Trying to persuade Bea they actually had a future together had always made him feel vaguely uneasy. At least with Katherine he could dispense with any semblance of hearts and flowers. He had decided that marriage wasn't necessary—Smyth-Brown's board could go hang on that one. He'd find another way to appease them long enough to get his hands on the stock he needed for a controlling interest. But having Katherine as his convenient date wouldn't hurt in that regard when he got her to London. She was still the daughter of a lord, albeit an estranged one.

'You spent *hours* searching for information about me online?' Jack asked, starting to enjoy her indignation when her glare intensified. 'I'm flattered,' he mocked, pressing a hand to his heart, even though the truth was he wasn't lying entirely. He'd have preferred her not to have unearthed information he had directed his legal team to have removed but, now she had, perhaps he could use it.

'Don't be,' she said. 'I was curious, that was all. I'm not any more.'

'Are you sure about that, Red?' He snagged her wrist, forcing her to unfold her arms. And felt her satisfying shudder.

She tried to tug free. He held on.

'You really don't want to hear me out?' he coaxed. 'Find out what I'm offering in return for your cooperation? You're in a much better bargaining position than you think.' Especially now he knew how much he enjoyed having her in his bed.

Getting this hunger out of his system, out of *both* their systems, wasn't going to be as easy as he had originally assumed. But, then again, their explosive chemistry would be a good way to enjoy their time together as he finalised the Smyth-Brown takeover and ripped the company Daniel Smyth's family had built over generations to shreds.

While he wouldn't normally have given his opponent a heads-up on how much he wanted to finalise a deal—after all, that was the biggest no-no when it came to deal-making—he could be generous with Katherine to have her where he wanted her.

'I don't care about the details. I don't want to live with you, I don't even want to date you, plus my life and my business are in Wales. It's completely absurd.'

'Is it?' He glanced at the gleaming kitchen equipment he knew she'd gone into considerable debt to finance. One of the biggest mistakes of fledging businesses was to be overexposed to debt in the first year. But her rookie mistake was his gain. He'd spent twenty minutes upstairs re-reading the detective's report on the financial situation of Cariad Cakes Etc and he was more than ready now to go in for the kill.

'How about if I told you in return for your being at my beck and call for—let's say, six months…' that should be more than long enough to get this frustrating, insistent fascination out of his system. '… I would give you a hundred thousand pounds' worth of investment for your business over the next year for a ten percent share of the profits? And a ten-thousand-pound capital injection to cover your current debts.'

Her mouth dropped open, the bright, unguarded hope in her eyes making the slithers of gold in the emerald green glimmer. His chest tightened, surprising him. After all, he never got sentimental about business, and this would be—essentially—a business proposition. But even so he felt oddly deflated when the glimmer dimmed almost instantly.

'Exactly how co-operative are you expecting me to be?'

Katie demanded, the brittle, defensive edge making Jack wonder about the young girl who had been forced to leave home to escape her father's influence.

He'd only met Henry Medford a handful of times, and he hadn't liked him—the man was an arrogant blowhard whose conservative investment strategy lacked vision and originality, and he had sensed that Bea was, if not scared of her father, then certainly determined to stay on the right side of him. While he didn't do sentiment, it was Bea's tentative attitude to her father which had persuaded him not to pull the Medford loan after their break-up.

He didn't sense fear from Katherine, but he could see her fierce determination to avoid the influence of any man would have to be overcome. Or at the very least managed.

'As I said, there will be some social requirements. I prefer to date women who elevate my social standing in ways money alone cannot.'

Not entirely true. He didn't give a damn about his social standing normally. But right now dating her would be useful in his quest not to scare off the Smyth-Brown board with what an inside source had told him was their concern about his 'lower-class background'.

'As the daughter of a hereditary peer—even an estranged daughter,' he added. 'You fit the bill.'

She blinked, looking momentarily stunned. 'I'm sorry… what? Did we just time-travel back to the nineteenth century?' Her gaze darkened with pity, making his temper spike. 'We're living in the twenty-first century, Jack. No one cares about titles and lineage any more. Especially not in the City of London. I think you're totally overestimating the importance of social status in your bid for world domination.'

'As you've never come from nothing, I would hazard a guess you know nothing about what it's like to be barred or blocked from your chosen path because of things you cannot change,' Jack said tightly.

'You're right,' Katie replied, the instant capitulation as galling as the sympathy shadowing her eyes. 'Maybe you can't change your past, or where you came from. But surely you're living proof it doesn't have to matter?' The hint of pity in the words loosened the leash on his temper still further. 'For goodness' sake, Jack, you don't even have a cockney accent. Why on earth would you need to date someone like me when you're a gazillionaire?'

He'd worked hard to get rid of his East End accent, he thought resentfully, well aware of the snobbery of his early investors who had been unwilling to put their money into the hands of someone who didn't pronounce their Ts and Hs properly. But he'd be damned if he'd give her more ammunition with which to condescend to him. He'd never been ashamed of his accent, or where he'd come from. He was just aware of how it had stood between him and his goals. And, anyway, having her seen as his date was nowhere near as important as getting her to London so she would be available when he wanted her.

'Frankly, we're getting off the point. I'm not interested in discussing the reasons why I want you on my arm at social events,' he said, resenting the fact she had managed to sidetrack him and touch a nerve he had considered long dead. 'All I'm willing to do is negotiate the terms of your acceptance.'

She huffed out a breath. 'Well, I'm not willing to negotiate it. I don't want to date you for any reason.'

The provocative comment was like a red rag to a bull, triggering every last one of his competitive instincts. Even if he hadn't desired her in his bed for the foreseeable future, her refusal to negotiate was enough to make him determined to change her mind.

'I think you're forgetting I lent your father a large sum of money on preferential terms,' he said. 'If I call that in, he won't be happy.'

Her eyebrows shot up, the surprise on her face almost comical. 'Really, Jack? Are you trying to blackmail me?' she asked, obviously expecting him to be ashamed of the implication.

He wasn't. In truth, he much preferred using the carrot to the stick when it came to persuading people to do what he wanted, but he hadn't been nicknamed the Big Bad Wolfe in the financial press for no reason. 'I wouldn't call it blackmail, simply a fact.'

Her eyebrows levelled off, her breathing becoming slightly laboured, which only made her more tempting. He clamped down on the inevitable surge of lust, while acknowledging that her inability to hide her response to him was another point in his favour.

'Call in the loan if you want,' she said. 'My father can't bully me any more. And neither can you.'

The bold statement demonstrated a bravery he admired, making it harder than expected to crush her rebellion. 'I'm not sure Beatrice would agree with you.'

She sucked in a breath as the implications of his threat finally dawned on her.

Distress flickered across her features, the obvious fear for her sister making him feel like a bastard, but he ignored the knee-jerk urge to reassure her. He'd given Beatrice his word he would not change the terms of the loan. And, while he could be unscrupulous when necessary, he never broke his word.

But Katherine did not need to know that. Using her concern for her sister against her was simply a negotiating tactic. He didn't need her to think he was a good man—in fact, it was better if she knew he was not.

Even so, he found it more difficult than he would have expected to remain unmoved when she hissed, 'You bastard.'

He shoved his hands into his pockets to resist the urge to touch her again. Crushing her spirit had never been his intention, but he always played to win, and this situation was no different.

You have to say no. This is insane.

Katie stared at Jack Wolfe, the strange feeling of unreality almost as disconcerting as the sensation rioting over her skin.

She loved Beatrice dearly, but it was time her sister stood up for herself. Katie couldn't protect her from their father's temper for ever.

And didn't she have the right to protect herself? Of course, the chance to clear Cariad Cakes' debts was tempting. But if she accepted she would be at Jack Wolfe's mercy.

Oddly, though, it wasn't the thought of the arguments and disagreements yet to come that bothered her. She'd already noticed a big difference between the way Jack Wolfe approached a negotiation and the way her father had bullied her. Jack might be commanding, powerful and ruthless enough to attempt to coerce her over the loan he'd made to her father but, weirdly, she also appreciated the fact he was being so pragmatic about what he wanted. Despite his outrageous suggestion, he hadn't condescended to her, hadn't tried to seduce her and had treated her like an equal. Something her father had never done.

She pursed her lips and crossed her arms over her chest to stop the pulse of connection getting any worse. And making her give in, when she knew it would be foolish even to contemplate becoming Jack Wolfe's trophy mistress.

Jack Wolfe was dangerous—not just to her independence but her sense of self. Because beneath the ruthless businessman was a man who could cut through her defences without even trying.

'Come on, Katherine,' Jack said, obviously tired of waiting. 'Is it really that hard to say yes?' he asked, the seductive tone reverberating in her abdomen as he stepped closer.

The hot spot between her thighs throbbed at the memory of him inside her—hard, forceful, overwhelming.

'It's only six months.' He cupped her cheek, the rough calluses turning the ripples to shudders. 'By which time, we'll have tired of each other. And by then your business and your future will be secure.'

She shifted away from the tantalising caress, her bottom pressing onto the countertop. She must not get carried away again on the tide of passion that had got her into this fix in the first place.

But, instead of crowding her even more, pressing his advantage, Jack remained where he was. He thrust his hands back into his pockets, almost as if he were having to force himself not to touch her.

And something flickered across his face. Something as shocking as it was unexpected.

Yearning.

But it was there one moment and gone the next.

She must have imagined it. Perhaps it was wishful thinking—making them seem like equals when they really weren't. She cleared her throat. Looked away from him. Night had fallen outside, but a full moon cast an eerie glow over the forest glen. Eerie and, compelling. And almost magical.

Snowdonia had given her strength, purpose and a sense of wellbeing ever since she'd arrived here determined to build a new life. But there was still something missing which had nothing to do with her financial instability or the endless stress of not being strong enough to make her dreams come true.

There was a Welsh word for the feeling of something lost, something longed for, connected to their homeland, that couldn't be directly translated into English: *hiraeth*. Her *nain* had explained it to her when Katie had been a homeless teenager but, being English, and never really having had a homeland she cared about, Katherine had never understood it.

But what if the *hiraeth* her mother had felt being away from her homeland, living with a man who had never really loved her, had been something like this deep tug of yearning? A part of her being she couldn't control?

Katie let out a slow breath, her heart galloping into her throat.

She turned back to find Jack still watching, still waiting, any trace of vulnerability in his expression gone.

She unfolded her arms, raised her gaze and ruthlessly controlled the hum of arousal.

'The answer's no, Jack,' she said.

Something leapt into his eyes that looked like regret. But she knew she must have imagined it when his jaw hardened and his gaze became flat and remote.

'Very well,' he said, surprising her with the instant capitulation. But then he stroked her chin with his thumb and the brutal sizzle rasped over sensitive skin.

She stood trapped in his penetrating gaze and regret sunk like a stone into her abdomen.

'But be advised, Katherine,' he said, his tone as harsh as the light in his eyes. 'I never give anyone a second chance.'

It was a warning that should have been easy to reject, but it wasn't, the foolish urge to call him back and say yes to his devil's bargain all but overwhelming when he took her quad keys, promising to have the vehicle returned that evening.

As the front door slammed behind him, her breath guttered out, her body collapsing against the kitchen counter. But the moment of relief did nothing to disguise the hollow weight still expanding in her stomach—which made no sense at all.

CHAPTER SIX

'I'M GLAD TO SAY the nausea is perfectly natural...' The doctor sent Katie an easy smile in the cubicle office of the small surgery in Gwynedd.

'How?' Katie asked, confused now, as well as exhausted. She'd been sick for the last ten days, every afternoon like clockwork, and it was starting to seriously impact her business. Because baking cookies and cupcakes and brownies when even the whiff of chocolate or vanilla essence made you puke was impossible.

It had been over two months since she'd turned down Jack Wolfe's insane proposition to become his mistress for six months. But nothing had gone right since the moment he'd slammed her cottage door behind him. It was almost as if he'd cursed her.

Sleep had alluded her for the first few weeks—florid, forceful, disturbing dreams tormented her every night in which he demanded her complete compliance and she obeyed without question. She could still smell him—bergamot and sex—on the sheets, despite washing them a hundred times. Could still feel his lips on her breasts, feel the hard, forceful thrust in her sex whenever she woke from fitful dreams. Then she had become tired and listless, falling asleep at a moment's notice, the thought of him always there, ready to jump her in her dreams.

The phantom sickness had almost been a welcome distraction at first to explain away the general malaise that seemed to have befallen her ever since he had left. This wasn't about Jack Wolfe and his insulting offer. This was about her working herself to the bone.

But in the last week, when it hadn't got any better, she had begun to panic. She couldn't afford to take any more time off work or she would lose her regular customers. She was on the verge of falling behind on her bank loans—and if that happened Cariad Cakes Etc would go under. But, far worse than that, if she lost the business she could end up losing her home, because she'd mortgaged the cottage to pay for the refit. The only upside was she'd saved money on her grocery bill because the last thing she wanted to do was eat.

The gynaecologist sent her a bright if slightly condescending smile. 'You're pregnant.'

'I'm…' The word dropped like a bomb into the silent surgery. For several moments she couldn't even process it. 'But that's not possible. I… I can't be pregnant, I'm on the pill,' she finally blurted out round the wodge of panic in her throat.

The doctor had made a mistake. That was all there was to it.

'I see,' the doctor replied, her brows furrowing. 'Ah yes, I have it here in your notes,' she added, reading off her computer monitor. 'Well, obviously it's extremely rare for this to happen. But no method of contraception is one hundred percent effective, even the contraceptive pill.'

'But…' Katie stared at the older woman, her skin heating under the probing gaze.

'Of course, if you haven't had sex in—'

'I did, but only once. And it was nine weeks ago,' Katie cut in, horrified by the blast of heat that hit her cheeks.

'But... I *can't* be pregnant,' she said again, her voice breaking on the words even as her hand strayed to her belly. Was
this actually happening? Had she somehow got pregnant
with Jack Wolfe's baby?

Tears prickled behind her eyes as the truth blindsided
her.

If their moment of madness had left her pregnant—and
somehow, where Jack Wolfe was concerned, it seemed
more than possible—she would never be able to forget him
for the rest of her life. And she hadn't exactly had much
luck with that already.

The doctor's expression went from confident to concerned in a heartbeat. 'Miss Medford, I did a blood test,'
she said gently. 'You are definitely pregnant. What happens now, though, is of course your decision.'

Is it?

'At only nine weeks' gestation, you do have options,'
the doctor added softly.

Do I?

Why did she feel as if she didn't have a choice, then?
As if it was already too late? The sensible thing to do now
would be to have a termination. This pregnancy had been
an accident. A mistake. There was no way she could keep
her business afloat if the morning sickness and the exhaustion kept up for another week, let alone any longer.
And, even if she managed to get through the pregnancy
without going bankrupt, how was she going to be able to
run a demanding business while looking after a baby? She
couldn't afford to pay for child care, or staff—not for a
good few years yet, anyway.

But even as the fear and panic overwhelmed her she
cradled her stomach and a surge of protectiveness swept
through her. That morphed into something powerful and
unstoppable.

She breathed out slowly to prevent her frantic heart beating right out of her chest. She'd never planned to be a mother—had never even thought of it. And now was the worst possible time for this to happen—especially with a man as ruthless and powerful as Jack Wolfe.

But what terrified her most of all was the thought of having her life ripped apart once again. The way it had been when she'd been seventeen—and her father had glared at her with hate in his eyes and told her to get out.

She blinked back tears and forced herself to suck in another careful breath… And think.

You've been at rock bottom before but you made a new life for yourself. A better life. By doing whatever you had to do to survive. Why can't you do the same again?

Another breath eased out through her constricted lungs but it felt less painful this time. She caressed her invisible bump.

Okay, kiddo, Mummy's got this. Whatever happens now, we're in this together.

It wasn't until she sat on the local bus back to Beddgelert twenty minutes later, her backpack stuffed full of pamphlets about everything from pregnancy vitamins to the benefits of breast feeding, that the full impact of what she'd have to do next knocked the air out of her lungs a second time.

I'm going to have to see Jack Wolfe again.

Informing the taciturn billionaire that she was pregnant with his child was going to be tough enough. Especially as she was fairly sure he would not be pleased at the prospect. He might not even believe the baby was his.

But what choice did she have? Not only did he have the right to know he was going to become a father, but she would have to ask him for help. She'd already maxed out all her credit cards and the next loan payment was due on Friday. She could ask Beatrice for money, but that would only be a temporary fix, and if her father found out Bea was spending any of her allowance on Katie he would probably cut her sister off too.

The idea of having to travel to London tomorrow, cap in hand, and beg Jack Wolfe for a loan went against every one of her principles. Given the insulting offer she'd turned down two months ago, it would also threaten to destroy every ounce of the independence and self-respect she'd worked so hard to gain since she'd been seventeen. What made it worse was knowing she would be completely at his mercy.

After the endless battles with her father, being at any man's mercy went against the grain. And, having defied Jack once already, she wasn't even sure he'd have any mercy.

Be advised, Katherine... I never give anyone a second chance.

The rocky escarpment of Pen-y-pass disappeared behind them as the bus travelled into the lush green valley of Nant Gwynant.

Jack might be forceful and overwhelming. But what scared her most was how vulnerable she felt at the moment. If he knew she was pregnant, would he use it against her? What if he had found someone else to be his mistress? Would that be a good thing or bad thing? What if he demanded she get an abortion? He couldn't *make* her do anything, but somehow giving him the power to try scared her even more.

Of course, she wouldn't be able to hold off telling Jack about the pregnancy for very long. But why did she have to tell him everything straight away? Surely she'd be in a better bargaining position if he didn't know? Asking him to reconsider the offer of financial help for her business would be hard. Especially as she wasn't even sure any more whether or not she wanted to be his mistress.

After all, however adamant she'd been two months ago, she still hadn't forgotten the effect he had on her—not even close. But telling him about the pregnancy and throwing herself on his mercy—or lack of it—felt so much more risky.

This was just another negotiation, she told herself staunchly, but it was one she had to make work for her and her baby and her business. The last thing she should do, given what a skilful negotiator Jack was, was give him an even stronger bargaining position.

'Mr Wolfe, there's a Miss Medford downstairs in reception. She doesn't have an appointment, but she insists she knows you, and the front desk asked me to check with you first before they send her away.'

Jack's head lifted at his PA Gorinda's comment. The bump of exhilaration annoyed him. 'Do you know *which* Miss Medford?'

'No, Mr Wolfe, but apparently she's been very persistent.'

'Uh-huh,' he murmured as the bump went nuts.

It had to be Katherine. He hadn't spoken to Beatrice since she'd broken off their engagement, and she didn't have the guts to come to his office without an appointment. Katherine, on the other hand…

'I did tell them there was no way you would—'

'It's okay, Gorinda.' He cut her off. 'Have them send her up.'

Gorinda disguised her astonishment with a quick nod, like the first-class professional she was.

As Jack waited for Katherine to arrive, he got up and

paced across the office. He should have told her to go to hell. She'd rejected his offer two months ago now. He'd intended to forget her as soon as he strolled out of her cottage. To find someone else. But it hadn't quite worked out that way. Not only had he not been able to forget her, no other woman had come close to exciting him the way she did.

None of them had Katherine's vibrant hair, her lush curves, her quick wit or her sharp, intelligent emerald eyes. And not one of them made him ache.

He'd come to the conclusion that, if he couldn't have her, he didn't want anyone else. Which was infuriating.

How had she captivated him so comprehensively? When her rejection still stung, reminding him of the feral kid he'd once been…? On the outside, not wanted and never to be invited in.

He returned to his desk, determined not to let her see his agitation—or his excitement at the thought of seeing her again.

Several eternities later, Gorinda stepped into the office with Katherine. After announcing his uninvited guest, his PA left and shut the door.

He took his time staring at the woman who still occupied far too much of his head space.

In a tailored pencil skirt, a silk blouse and low heels, her wild hair pinned on top of her head in a ruthless up-do, she looked more sophisticated than he'd ever seen her. But the power suit and heels couldn't disguise her lush curves or dewy skin. Or the way the buttons of her blouse strained against her cleavage. Was he imagining it, or did her breasts look even more spectacular than he remembered?

'Hello, Katherine,' he said, his tone huskier than he would have liked. He remained seated, keeping his expression flat and direct, even as the bump in his heart rate accelerated. 'To what do I owe the unexpected pleasure?' he added, doing nothing to hide the slice of sarcasm in his tone.

Her cheeks turned a delectable shade of pink. The inconvenient arousal flowed south.

Damn, I still want her—too much.

He shifted in his seat, the sudden recollection of wrapping his lips around those hard, swollen peaks aggravating his temper, not to mention the ache in his pants.

The sour taste in his mouth wasn't far behind, though. She had to be here to renegotiate his offer. Why he should be surprised, he had no idea. But what surprised him more was his disappointment. She'd rejected him when he'd offered her a generous deal two months ago. He'd told her then she wouldn't get a second chance and he still meant it. However much he might still want her.

'Hello, Jack,' she said. 'Can I sit down?'

He swept his hand towards the leather armchair on the other side of the desk. 'Go ahead. You've got five minutes to say whatever you came to say,' he said, gratified by the flash of annoyance before she managed to mask it.

Damned if he didn't still find her rebelliousness a major turn-on.

But as she crossed the room and sat down he frowned. Had she lost weight? Because he could still recall every luscious inch of her in far too much detail and, apart from her breasts, her curves didn't look as much of a handful as he remembered. Not only that, but she moved stiffly, without the confident energy of two months ago.

As her face caught the sun streaming through the office windows, he noticed the tight line of her lips and the bruised shadows under her eyes that she'd tried to mask with make-up.

He stifled the concern pushing against his chest and forced it into a box marked 'not your problem'.

She'd probably been working herself to the bone to make a go of her failing business. But why should he care? He'd offered her a way out. And she'd thrown it back in his face.

He glanced at his watch. 'You've got four minutes now,' he said.

'I wanted to ask about the financing you mentioned two months ago.' She leaned forward, offering him an even better view of her cleavage—which had to be deliberate. 'It's been…' She sighed, the gushing breath weary. 'More of a challenge than I thought to keep up payments on my loans. If you're still interested in investing, I could offer you twenty-five percent instead of ten.'

His disappointment at the evidence that she could be bought after all was tempered by the surge of triumph. He had her where he wanted her now. But he'd be damned if he'd give her an easy ride. 'And the deal I discussed?'

'I'd be willing to do that too, of course,' she said without a moment's hesitation. 'With the six-month time limit you mentioned, obviously.'

'And what exactly would you be prepared to do for this investment?' he asked, keeping his gaze fixed firmly on the blush which was now spreading across her neck.

'Whatever you want me to do,' she said softly.

His chest tightened with anger. 'Uh-huh,' he ground out, holding on to his fury with an effort. 'And what do you envisage that entailing?'

He'd intended to pay to relocate her to London for six months, because their affair would have to be at his convenience, not hers. But if they had decided to sleep together—to get this damn chemistry out of their system—he had never intended to buy her cooperation in

that regard. But she'd never given him the chance to explain any of that two months ago. She'd simply jumped to
the conclusion he would be paying her for sex—and had
rejected him out of hand.

He steepled his fingers to stop them shaking as the fury
started to consume him. 'And if I said I didn't just want
to date you socially? That I wanted you in my bed for the
duration? What then?' he asked, finally pushing the point.

Her eyes widened, the flash of anxiety going some way
to satisfy his sense of outrage.

That's right, Red, let's see how far you're willing to go!

Her face fell, the blush blazing now as the last of the
eager hope he had glimpsed died. He'd shocked her. And
insulted her. Just as he'd intended.

But just as he was sure she would finally realise how
insulting that proposition was, to both of them, she said,
'Okay, if that's what you want.'

The anger flared, but right behind it was astonishment.
And that heady shot of arousal still throbbing in his groin.

How could he still want her when she was only offering herself in exchange for payment? Had her outrage at
the cottage all been an act?

Of course it had, he thought viciously, surprised to realise he actually felt disillusioned when he'd figured he
had lost all his illusions years ago.

He was a deeply cynical guy because he'd had to be.
He'd come from the very bottom and made it to the top.
And he'd had to fight like hell to scale every rung of that
ladder. He couldn't afford sentimentality or loyalty unless
it benefitted his bottom line.

But although he'd been angry when he'd walked
away from her—because she'd denied him something he
wanted—in the weeks since he'd been captivated by the
notion that Katherine Medford might actually be the real

deal. Someone prepared to put their dignity and self-respect before money. And status. And benefitting their own bottom line.

The sour taste in his mouth made his lips twist in a cruel smile. 'I see,' he said, letting his gaze roam over her, the perusal deliberately insulting as he got up from his desk. He walked towards her, suddenly determined to punish her for destroying the image he'd had of her... And get some much-needed payback for the snub that had bruised his ego more than it should have.

What a fool he'd been, wasting months getting hung up on a woman who didn't even exist.

He beckoned her out of the seat. She stood, wary eyes searching his face, her magnificent breasts rising up and down with her staggered breathing.

She chewed on her lip while her deep-green eyes dilated to black. Satisfaction flowed through him.

'What...what do you want?' She wrapped her arms around her waist, holding in her shudder of response, but he could see the peaks of her breasts standing to attention beneath her blouse.

Red, we both know you want me as much as I want you.

He let the cruel smile spread, damned if he was going to leave her with any pride. People had thought they were better than him his whole life. And he'd taken great pleasure in proving them wrong. She was no different from all the rest.

He leaned closer, close enough to take in a lungful of her tantalising scent—apples and earth and pure, unadulterated sin. The burgeoning erection hardened enough to brush against her belly and he heard her sharp intake of breath, felt the judder of reaction course through her body.

He shoved his fists into his pockets, determined not to touch, not to take. This time she was going to come to him.

'I want you to show me what you've got,' he whispered against her neck. 'That's worth a hundred grand of my money, Red.'

He straightened away from her.

Her expressive features tightened and resentment sparkled in her eyes, highlighting the shards of gold in the emerald green.

There she is.

His breath clogged his lungs and desire flared, crackling in the air between them like an electric force field. But, before he had a chance to register the jolt of excitement, she lifted her arms and grasped his shoulders.

Her fingernails trailed across his nape, sending arrows of sensation shooting through his spine, straight down to his groin. And then she lifted her face to his, offering herself with a boldness, a determination, that robbed him of breath before she rose up on tiptoes and pressed her lips to his in a defiant kiss.

Elemental need exploded like a firework display in his gut, and all thoughts of payback, of punishment, were obliterated by the furious juggernaut of desire too long denied.

Her lips opened on a staggered breath and he thrust his tongue deep, capturing each startled sob of her surrender. He yanked his clenched fists out of his pockets and grasped her hips to pull her vibrating body against the brutal ridge in his trousers. He ground the erection against her, each stroke of his tongue, each brush of his shaft, driving him closer to the edge.

His hands skimmed up her side and cradled her breasts. She bowed back and he dragged his mouth down to suckle the frantic beat in her neck. He fumbled with her blouse, giving a staggered groan as the buttons popped. Lifting the fragrant flesh free of its lacy prison, he traced the engorged peak with his lips but, as he trapped the swollen flesh against the roof of his mouth and suckled hard, she bucked in his arms and cried out—the shocked gasp one of pain, not pleasure.

What the...?

'Ow!'

Her distress doused the fire and he released her so abruptly, she staggered backwards. He caught her elbow before she could fall over the armchair.

'How...?' he managed, his pulse thundering so hard in his ears he was struggling to hear, let alone think.

What had just happened? One minute they had been devouring each other, and then...

She tugged her arm free, her movements jerky, frantic, her eyes downcast, her body shaking with the same tremors wracking his own. He watched her gather the remnants of her blouse. The blouse he'd torn off her.

'Did I hurt you?' he asked, his voice raw.

How the hell had everything got out of control so quickly? He'd been ready to take her right here in his office. The point he'd been trying to make—which seemed petulant and pointless now—was instantly forgotten in the maelstrom of needs triggered by her glorious defiance and the touch of her lips on his.

She shook her head, but her chin remained tucked into her chest and he couldn't see her face. She was still shaking, her knuckles whitening on the torn silk.

Guilt washed through him. He tucked his thumb under her chin and drew her face up to his. 'Katherine, did I hurt you?' he asked again.

Her eyes—that deep, vibrant emerald—were mossy with distress, but devoid of the accusation he had been expecting. 'No,' she murmured, the apologetic tone only confusing him more. 'It's just, I'm a lot more sensitive there.'

His gaze dipped to her full breasts now plumped up under her tightly folded arms. 'Okay,' he said, still trying to figure out where that cry of pain had come from.

'Oh, God,' she whispered, clasping her hand over her mouth. 'Where's the nearest toilet?'

Her features drew tight, a sheen of sweat popping out on her brow, her face turning grey beneath the impressive beard burn starting to appear on her cheeks.

'What?' he asked, the concern he'd tried to contain earlier expanding like a beach ball in his gut.

'Your nearest toilet, Jack!' Her voice rose in distress. 'Where is it?' she cried. 'I'm going to throw up!'

He pointed to the office's large *en suite* bathroom, shocked and confused now, as well as extremely turned on.

She shot out of the room so fast, an apple-scented breeze feathered across his face. Two seconds later, the sounds of violent retching echoed around the silent office.

What the hell is going on?

He walked across the carpeted floor, propped his shoulder against the door jamb, the beach ball expanding as he watched her bent over the toilet bowl, puking her guts up.

He supposed he ought to be offended, embarrassed even, that his lovemaking had made her violently ill. But he was still reeling from the sudden shift from incendiary lust to total disaster—and the feeling he'd just been kicked into another dimension without warning.

The erection finally deflated—mercifully.

Perhaps he shouldn't be surprised, given Katherine had a habit of bringing enough drama into his life to put a TV soap opera to shame. But, as he rinsed a face cloth out in the sink, confusion gave way to curiosity and concern. And a ton of unanswered questions bombarded him all at once.

Why had she come here? And, more importantly, why *now*? Because her motives didn't seem nearly as straightforward as he'd assumed. If she was really an opportunist, an unscrupulous femme fatale prepared to sell her body to rescue her business, why hadn't she agreed to become his mistress two months ago?

The gruesome retching finally subsided and she collapsed onto her bottom. Sitting cross-legged on the floor, she didn't just look tired, she looked shattered and fragile. In a way she never had before. Fragile, defensive and... guilty.

What did she have to feel guilty about?

He handed her the cool cloth, ignoring the residual buzz as their fingers brushed.

'Thank you,' she said, wiping her mouth before folding the cloth with infinite care and pressing it to her burning cheeks. 'It's okay, that's the worst of it over,' she murmured, as if this had happened before.

He crouched beside her, unable to resist the urge to swipe his finger across her clammy forehead and tuck a stray strand of hair behind her ear. She trembled, but didn't draw away from his touch. Her gaze met his at last. The guilty flush highlighted her pale cheeks.

His what-the-hell-ometer shot into the red zone and the wodge of confusion and concern threatened to gag him.

'Why did you come to me?' he demanded, his guts tying into tight, greasy knots. Was she seriously ill?

'I told you, I need money to save my business,' she said, but she ducked her head again.

'Don't give me that crap,' he said, annoyed with her now, as well as himself. Why had he believed so readily that the bold, beautiful, belligerent and stunningly defiant woman he had left behind in Wales had become some conniving little gold-digger in the space of a few months?

He grasped her chin, losing his patience as the sense of detachment, cynicism and ruthlessness which he had relied on for so long became dull and discordant. He shouldn't care why she was here, why she needed his money so badly, but he did.

'Tell me the truth. Are you seriously ill?' he asked.

She puffed out a breath. 'No.'

The relief he wanted to feel didn't come. 'Then why did you just lose your lunch in my toilet?'

The guilty flush became so vivid it would probably be visible from Mars. 'Because I'm pregnant,' she replied. 'With your child.'

CHAPTER SEVEN

'You... What?' Jack murmured, his voice rough with shock, and Katie watched his gaze drop to her belly.

Katie's still tender stomach flipped over as his knees dropped to the bathroom tiles, his balance shot, as well as his usual cast-iron control.

'It was an accident,' she said. 'I can take a DNA test once it's born, if you don't believe it's yours,' she added, expecting to see suspicion, even accusation, on his face.

When his gaze rose, though, he still looked dazed. But then two creases appeared between his brows.

She braced, ready for anger, but all he said was, 'How long have you known?'

'Since yesterday,' she replied. 'I'd been sick on and off for two weeks and it was affecting my work.' She knew she was babbling, but she couldn't seem to stop, wanting to fend off the accusations that were bound to come soon. He'd treated her with contempt as soon as she'd arrived. Which only made her more determined to hold her ground, to get what she needed before he found out how much she needed it.

But his expression remained oddly unreadable.

'It's not easy baking when even the scent of food makes you nauseous,' she finished.

'No doubt,' he said, his gaze drifting back to her belly. 'I thought you were on the pill.'

Oddly, the question lacked the cynicism she'd expected, but even so she went on the offensive.

'I *was* on the pill. But it was low-dosage and I'd only been on it for a week. Even so, the doctor said it's extremely rare.' Feeling stronger, she added an edge to her voice. 'It seems you have extremely fertile sperm.'

'Who knew?' His lips quirked, the hint of wry amusement surprising her even more. Did he think this was funny? But as he continued to study her in that unnerving way he had, as if he could see past every one of her defences, his brow furrowed again. 'Why didn't you tell me about the pregnancy as soon as you arrived?'

She cursed her pale skin as the tell-tale heat crawled up her neck.

'Because I didn't want to get the third degree about how it had happened. Or have you try to talk me into an abortion,' she said, knowing she had been right not to blurt out the truth and give him even more power to hurt her.

Anger spread up her chest to disguise the hurt as she recalled the insulting way he'd treated her. Had he even really still wanted her? Or had he simply intended to humiliate her, get her to show him how much she still wanted him, before he slapped her down?

She'd put everything into that kiss, had lost herself in it seconds after he'd responded, but had he? She wasn't even sure about that any more. Had it all been a game to him to make her go insane with lust just so he could humiliate her more when he rejected her?

'What the hell makes you think I'd try to force you to have an abortion?' he asked, surprising her again. Because he didn't look superior or in control any more. He looked furious.

'Because…' She sputtered to a stop. He actually looked really offended. 'Well, aren't you?' she managed, her righteousness faltering a little.

'Do you want to have the child?' he asked.

Emotion closed her throat. The baby felt so real to her now, even though, according to all the research she'd done in the last twenty-four hours, it was no bigger than a grain of rice.

'Yes, I do want it, very much,' she said without hesitation around the thickness in her throat.

'Then I will support your choice,' Jack answered without an ounce of sarcasm. Or even any apparent resentment.

Katie's jaw went slack. To say she was surprised by the statement would be a massive understatement. She wasn't just surprised—she was stunned speechless.

'Really?' she whispered at last. 'You're not angry?' she asked, not sure she could believe him as she struggled to contain the painful hope pressing against her chest wall.

Was this just another trick? Surely it had to be? She would have expected a man as cynical as him to feel trapped, or at the very least suspicious. She certainly had not expected him to so readily believe not only that the baby was his, but that her pregnancy had genuinely been an accident.

'I pay for my mistakes,' Jack said. 'And this is my fault, not yours. I should have worn protection and I didn't.'

Our baby is not a mistake.

It was what she wanted to say. But as she opened her mouth to protest Jack stood up and, taking her elbow, pulled her to her feet.

'I do have some conditions, though.'

'What conditions?' She stared at him, trying to decipher what was coming so she could ward it off… But as usual his expression gave nothing away.

How could he be so controlled when her emotions felt as if they were being squished through a meat grinder?

'We need to be married—until after the baby's born. No child of mine will grow up without my name.'

'You don't have to be married to me to give the baby your name,' Katie began. 'You can just put your name on the birth…' He pressed his finger to her lips, silencing her.

'You were happy to sleep with me for a hundred-thousand-pound investment in your company about ten minutes ago, Katherine. So why should marriage be a problem?'

'I know, but…'

'But nothing. We can separate in…' He paused. 'When is it due?'

'I won't know for sure until I've had the first scan,' she countered, beginning to feel totally overwhelmed again, and not liking it.

'Ball park,' he said.

'January.' She huffed.

'We can separate in February, then. I'll have it written into the contract.'

'What contract?' she asked, her voice rising. He was trying to railroad her. *Again.*

'The contract you're going to sign before the wedding in four weeks' time.'

'What?' She actually squeaked. He wanted to get married in a month? 'I haven't even agreed to marry you yet.'

'But you will. You know as well as I do, you're all out of options, or you wouldn't have come to me begging to prostitute yourself.'

'I didn't beg!' she gasped, outraged. 'You insisted.'

'And you agreed—then you kissed me as if your life depended on it. And we both went off like a couple of rockets on Bonfire Night, coming within one sensitive nipple of doing each other on my desk in broad daylight when any one of my employees could have walked in on us. So let's stop arguing about semantics.'

She glared at him but couldn't help but feel her panic ease a little.

At least he hadn't been faking his response any more than she had. She wasn't sure if their uncontrollable chemistry was necessarily a bonus in an already overwhelming situation. But it felt important that in at least one part of their relationship they were equally compromised.

'I need time to think about all this,' Katie murmured, suddenly unbearably weary, the emotional rollercoaster of the last twenty-four hours taking its toll as he led her back into his office.

She sat heavily in the armchair, the feeling of her life spinning out of control again doing nothing to ease her surprise when he squatted in front of her and placed warm palms on her knees.

'What is there to think about, really?' Jack murmured. 'This is a business deal which will give me what I need— a chance to elevate my social status and ensure the child is not born a bastard—and give you what you need—a chance to save your company and allow it to grow.'

He glanced at her stomach again. The muscle in his jaw tensed. Perhaps he wasn't as nonchalant about the pregnancy as he seemed. 'And give the child my financial support for the rest of its life.'

The child.

The impersonal description reverberated in Katie's skull—pragmatic and painfully dispassionate.

Her heart shrunk in her chest.

The baby really was nothing more to him than a mistake he had to rectify. Had she really believed he would feel any differently? And why would he?

She cleared her throat, trying to dislodge her sadness

at the realisation her child wouldn't have a father in anything other than a financial capacity.

So what?

She didn't *want* Jack to be a father to this baby. She knew what it was like to grow up with a father who thought of you as a commodity, or a burden. Why would she wish that on her own child? She needed to deal with the practicalities now. Nothing else.

'What exactly would the marriage entail?' she managed to ask. 'Would I have to leave Wales?'

He stood up and walked to the desk. Leaning against it, he folded his arms over his broad chest as he studied her. The beard burn on her cheeks from their earlier kiss began to sting as his eyes heated with something which looked like more than just practicalities.

'Yes. You would live with me wherever I happened to be, travel with me and attend public and private events as my wife when required.' He paused, his gaze skimming her belly again. 'And your condition allows.'

'But my home and my business are in Wales.'

'You'll need to base yourself and your business in London. This is a marriage of convenience,' he said, his gaze darting to her stomach again. 'But it's not going to do the business interests we talked about much good unless it appears real. I'm afraid that's non-negotiable. I'm sure we can figure out a manageable schedule for your social responsibilities as my wife.' He frowned. 'How long has the vomiting been going on?'

She blinked, the question feeling way too personal in what—for him, anyway—appeared to be a business negotiation.

Get real, Katie, that's exactly what it is. And what you want it to be.

'Two weeks now,' she said. 'But it wasn't as bad today as it has been. I think it might finally be getting a bit better.'

His brows climbed up his forehead. '*Seriously?* It's been *worse* than the exorcism routine I just witnessed?'

She let out a half-laugh, the tension in her gut easing at his horrified expression. For a split second it almost felt as if they were a real couple. But she sobered quickly, setting aside the fanciful notion. One thing she mustn't do was mistake his concern for his business priorities with any real concern for her. Or their baby. Of course he didn't want his trophy wife projectile-vomiting at inopportune moments.

'The good news is I've never been sick in the evenings,' she said. 'So social engagements shouldn't be a problem.' Of course, she usually felt exhausted by the end of the day, but he didn't need to know that yet. Hopefully the fatigue would fade too, and not having the stress of figuring out how she was going to keep her business afloat would surely help. Of course, she wasn't familiar with the kind of high-society events he was probably referring to. She would have to wing it, but she'd be damned if she'd let him know she wasn't up to the job he was offering her.

And it *was* a job. A job she was being handsomely paid for—something she would do well to remember.

He nodded. 'Good, although I doubt I'll have to make too many demands on your time. I'm not a social animal at the best of times. I'm sure we can make the marriage convincing with a few well-timed engagements...' His gaze intensified and awareness rippled over her skin. 'Especially given our extraordinary chemistry.'

Her heart bobbed into her throat and the familiar ripple shot down her spine. 'Right, about that...' Her gaze dropped away from his. 'What if I didn't want to sleep with you?'

The silence seemed to stretch out for several endless moments.

It was a lie, and she was sure he knew it. After all, she'd kissed him senseless less than ten minutes ago.

But she wasn't sure she *could* sleep with him especially while carrying his child, and not risk getting much more invested in their fake marriage than she should. Her emotions were screwy enough already.

Gee thanks, pregnancy hormones.

Sleeping with him had already had major consequences—throwing her life into complete turmoil while he seemed mostly unmoved. She didn't want to put herself at any more of a disadvantage.

He was watching her with a typically inscrutable expression but the muscle in his jaw was twitching again.

He didn't like the suggestion. But then, to her surprise, he shrugged. 'Suit yourself.'

'Really?'

'Of course,' he replied. 'Whatever we do together in private will be by mutual consent. That was always going to be the case. It was you who made that assumption two months ago that I would be paying you for sex.'

'Okay,' she said, feeling both chastised and embarrassed. As well as uncertain. She hadn't exactly received the concession she'd been asking for—a marriage in name only. And, given that his seduction techniques so far had turned out to be extremely effective…

Oh, for goodness' sake, Katie. Stop creating problems where there aren't any. Yet. So what if Jack Wolfe could seduce a stone? You can cross that bridge when you come to it. Time to quit while you're ahead.

Jack Wolfe was right about one thing: she was all out of options.

'So what's your answer, Katherine?' he asked, the negotiations clearly over.

She concentrated on the twitch in his jaw and controlled the familiar shot of adrenaline that was always there whenever he looked at her with that laser-sharp focus.

Take the risk. You need this—for your business and your baby. And, remember, he can't hurt you unless you let him.

'Okay,' she said. 'I guess we're getting married, Mr Wolfe.'

CHAPTER EIGHT

'I NOW PRONOUNCE YOU man and wife.'

The vicar's voice echoed in Katie's chest like the heavy clang of bells that had greeted her when she'd arrived at the historic chapel nestled in the heart of Bloomsbury ten minutes ago. She stared at her hand, weighed down by the gold band studded with diamonds Jack had eased onto her ring finger a few moments before.

Breathe, Katie, breathe.

She blinked and tried to release the air trapped in her lungs—which was starting to make her ribs ache under the bustier the stylist had insisted needed to be worn with the lavish cream silk designer wedding gown she had seen for the first time that morning.

You agreed to this, now you have to make it work. For the baby's sake.

Not easy, when she hadn't had a chance to draw a full breath since the moment she'd agreed to Jack Wolfe's devil's bargain just four weeks before.

The minute she'd said those fateful words, Jack had taken charge. At first she'd been too shocked at the speed he'd set things into motion to really object.

He'd been unhappy at her insistence she had to return to Wales that day. Despite her exhaustion, she'd managed to stand her ground, and had felt as if she'd achieved a major concession after she'd agreed to travel home in a chauffeur-driven SUV and return to London as soon as was feasibly possible.

After a sleepless night at Cariad—spent considering and reconsidering what she'd committed to—she'd discovered the next morning that the big concession in his office had been an entirely Pyrrhic victory. A battalion of people began to arrive at the cottage in a steady stream of all-terrain vehicles.

First had come world-renowned London obstetrician Dr Patel and her team who had explained that, with Katie's permission, her pre-and ante-natal care was being transferred to the consultant's exclusive clinic in Harley Street. After a thorough check-up, and a long chat with the highly professional and wonderfully reassuring doctor— together with an assurance that Jack Wolfe would be footing the clinic's astronomical bill—Katie had swallowed her pride and agreed to switch to her care. Perhaps Jack's high-handed decision to hire the obstetrician without Katie's input didn't have to be all bad. This was his baby too, after all. Maybe this was a small sign he was beginning to take that on board.

After Dr Patel had left, a PA called Jane Arkwright had arrived, hired to help Katie relocate her business over the next two weeks. Again, Katie had forced herself not to overreact. This was what she'd agreed to. She just hadn't thought it would happen quite this quickly. Luckily Jane was efficient and personable, and had helped to prevent Katie's anxiety hitting critical mass when she'd introduced her to a team of solicitors and accountants with a batch of documents for her to sign—including a pre-nup, a framework for what appeared to be extremely generous child support payments once the baby was born and a host of other legal and financial agreements about Wolfe Inc's investment in Cariad Cakes Etc.

Eventually, though, even Jane's capable presence couldn't stop Katie from freaking out. Why did everything have to be done in such a rush? Couldn't they postpone the wedding for a few more weeks at least?

Eventually, Katie had insisted on contacting Jack. But this time she had been unable to budge him even an inch—as his calm, measured voice had explained, everything was exactly as they had agreed. And the wedding was already booked for as soon as legally possible. Again, as they had agreed.

Yup, his decision to let her return to Cariad had been nothing more than a clever negotiating tactic to lure her into a false sense of security before the full force of his will bowled her over like a tsunami.

And so it was two weeks later, as the afternoon light fell on the forest glade, she had locked up Cariad for the next seven months and had been directed by Jane to the all-terrain chauffeur-driven SUV for the six-hour drive to London, with the moving vans following behind.

When she'd arrived in Mayfair at midnight, though, she hadn't been driven to Jack's penthouse but to a newly purchased and luxuriously furnished six-bedroomed townhouse on Grosvenor Square with a full staff—including a personal chef, a stylist and a housekeeper—ready to cater to her every whim over the following two weeks while she 'settled into' her short-lived life as Jack Wolfe's fiancée.

Jack, though, was nowhere to be seen. Katie's relief had quickly morphed into consternation, however. After all the panic on the drive down about whether or not she would be moving into Jack's penthouse, she'd been deflated to discover her new fiancé had been *en route* to New York for a month-long trip when she'd called him two weeks ago—and that he would not be returning to London until the day of their wedding.

The days that followed had seemed to accelerate at speed through a packed schedule of visits, meetings, appointments and events all expertly curated by Jane. They'd involved everything from interviews to hire her new bakery team, to endless fittings at a designer couturier in Covent Garden to supply her with a lavish new wardrobe for the role she was about to play. She'd been too preoccupied and frankly numb to spend time dwelling on Jack's absence. And too tired each evening to do anything but fall into a dreamless sleep.

In truth, the only thing she'd still felt she had any real control over when the day of the wedding had dawned was her pregnancy. Thanks to lots of helpful advice from Dr Patel, and her insistence Katie listen to her body clock and delegate where appropriate so she got all the sleep she needed, the nausea and fatigue had begun to subside. But everything else—her new home, her new business premises in Hammersmith and the team she had begun to build—had started to feel like a strange dream she might wake up from at any time.

Somehow, her life had been so comprehensively overpowered by Jack Wolfe's organised assault on it over the past month, she'd even forgotten to stress about the prospect of her wedding until a few moments ago when she'd stepped into the chapel—to see him standing at the end of the aisle with his back to her.

As if the first sight of him again since she'd been ushered out of his office four weeks before—looking tall and indomitable in an expertly tailored wedding suit—hadn't been shocking enough, the panic she'd kept so carefully at bay during the last few days began to cinch around her ribs along with the bustier as she made her way down the aisle on the arm of his COO, Terry Maxwell.

She'd been offered the chance to invite guests but, once she'd discovered Jack was only inviting a few of his key staff, she'd declined, simply inviting Jane, who Katie had discovered was a sturdy port in the storm of her new reality.

This wasn't a real wedding. And it would have been beyond awkward to invite any of her friends, and especially Bea. After all, she could still hear her sister's gasp down the other end of the phone line when she'd told her of the marriage and the pregnancy. Bea had been her usual sweet self after the shock had worn off, and had tried to sound positive and encouraging on Katie's behalf, while Katie had been able to hear the barely disguised disbelief in her voice, wondering what had happened to her sensible sister.

Katie had channelled every acting skill she'd ever acquired to sound like a woman in love and hold back the desire to confide in her sister. Jack's legal team had insisted she sign a non-disclosure agreement preventing her from revealing the truth about the arrangement to anyone but they need not have bothered. She'd made a promise. A promise she refused to renege on.

As the vicar's words declaring the marriage complete floated up to the chapel's elegantly carved vaulted ceiling, Katie forced herself to raise her gaze from the ring.

Fierce purpose flared in Jack's eyes.

Maybe the marriage was fake, but it didn't *feel* fake as his piercing gaze proceeded to roam over her face with a possessive hunger that stole her breath.

'You may kiss the bride, Mr Wolfe,' the vicar announced with an avuncular chuckle.

Katie clutched the bespoke bouquet of Welsh woodland wild flowers—ivy, daisies and enchanted nightshade. It had been handed to her by the florist what felt like several lifetimes ago. Her gaze darted to the smiling clergyman and then back to Jack.

The sensual smile touching his lips, full of knowledge and purpose, and sent the twin tides of panic and arousal rippling through her already overwrought body.

Public displays of affection had been part of their written agreement. But, when she'd agreed to that aspect of their deception, she hadn't factored in a proper wedding with a dress, a ring and a thoughtfully designed bouquet, not to mention a ceremony in one of London's most exclusive chapels, which he'd somehow managed to pull off in less than a month.

Katie had simply assumed Jack would probably want to do something basic and understated. But, when Jane had outlined the plans for the 'big day', Katie had resigned herself to going through with it, understanding that the elaborate dog-and-pony show Jack had insisted on had to be part of the push to make the marriage seem real. So why hadn't she been better prepared for this kiss?

Her lips pursed to stop the hum of sensation getting any more pronounced as Jack's gaze lowered pointedly to her mouth. Katie's eyes fixed on his face as she tried to convey her feelings to him telepathically.

Could we please get this over with ASAP?

But Jack, being Jack, seemed in no hurry whatsoever to rush the kiss that would seal their devil's bargain.

The knowing smile spread across his features, making her sure he knew exactly how the molten weight in her belly had lodged between her thighs.

She struggled to remain calm as her breathing sawed out through congested lungs and Jack took his own sweet time lifting the jewelled veil over her head. He then spent another infinitesimal age arranging the tulle with careful precision over the hairdo a team of stylists had spent hours taming into an artful chignon threaded through with more woodland flowers.

His gaze met hers at last and his thumb skimmed down her burning cheek—possessive and electric. The contact startled her, making the fire flare at her core.

She stiffened, desperate to temper her reaction, not wanting to give him the satisfaction of knowing how easily he could turn her into a mass of pulsating sensations. But she realised she had already given him all the ammunition he needed when he leant down, his thumb sliding under her chin and sending the darts of heat shimmering south, to whisper into her ear, 'Relax, Red, I won't bite. Unless you want me to.'

Before she could think of a pithy response, his lips found hers and the last of her composure shot straight up to the vaulted ceiling.

His tongue licked across the seam. Her mouth opened, surrendering to him instinctively, just as it had done four weeks ago. The lava swelled and pulsed as he explored in expert strokes. His all-consuming kiss dragged her into a netherworld of passion and provocation as her tongue tangled with his.

And every last coherent thought flew right out of her head—bar one.

More.

Jack drove his tongue into the warm recesses of Katherine's mouth, devouring the taste he had become addicted to. A taste he'd spent the last four weeks away from his new bride to control.

The fire roared in his gut, turning his flesh to iron as the kiss went from controlled to desperate in a heartbeat. He grasped her cheeks to angle her head and take the kiss deeper, to devour more of that glorious taste and her elemental response.

She kissed him back, her tongue duelling with his as they consumed each other in fast, greedy bites.

He heard the sound of the bouquet dropping onto stone tiles, then her hands slipped under his waistcoat, grasping fistfuls of starched linen. Her whole body shook as she clung to him, as if she were caught in a storm and he were the only thing anchoring her to earth.

His muscles tensed, the desire to scoop her into his arms and carry her to some dark, secret corner of the chapel all but unbearable.

'Mr Wolfe, perhaps you and your bride would like to sign the register?' The vicar's voice seemed to drift into his consciousness from a million miles away, through a heady fog of heat and yearning, then registered in his brain like a bombshell.

He tore his mouth from Katherine's. She was staring at him, her eyes glazed, her full lips red and swollen from the ferocity of the kiss. Her expertly arranged hair hung down on one side, tugged from its moorings by his marauding fingers.

She let go of his shirt.

How can she still drive me insane so easily?

He cleared his throat to dislodge the rock pressed against his larynx and sucked in an unsteady breath, far too aware of the heavy erection pressing against his boxers.

It was a good thing the tailor had insisted the wedding trousers be fitted loosely or he would be giving the whole of the congregation a clear demonstration of how much he wanted his wife.

His wife.

The thought struck him for the first time that maybe this arrangement, this deal, wasn't going to be as manageable as he needed it to be. And that was without even factoring in the problem of her pregnancy.

He'd travelled all the way to New York to get a grip on his reaction to her. The fact he couldn't stop thinking about her, had even dreamed about her, had only made him more convinced distance was his best strategy, for the time being at least.

It had nearly killed him a month ago to keep his reaction to the news of her pregnancy in check. He had never planned to father a child for the simple reason he had no clue *how* to be a father, and he knew he didn't have the tools necessary to learn.

But, as he had crouched beside her in his office bathroom, the shocking discovery of her condition had been swiftly followed by another, even more disturbing, revelation.

While he didn't want to care for this child in anything other than a financial capacity, he did care for Katherine Medford. Enough to want to protect her and her business. Enough to want to mitigate the ravages of what he'd done to her body. Enough to ensure this child had his name. In the weeks since, he'd persuaded himself that the visceral reaction had to come from a need to be a better man than the man who had sired him.

Katherine had simply triggered that knee-jerk reaction with her suggestion he might try to bully her into a termination. At first he'd been furious at the whispered comment, but he'd come to accept that had to be why he had been so determined to get her to agree to this marriage. And why he had been so focussed on getting the deed done as soon as possible.

When she'd told him in his office she didn't want to sleep with him, he'd of course had an equally visceral and enraged reaction. It had taken him every single day since to get a grip on that. And realise that giving in to their sexual chemistry would be a bad move—until he was in complete control of everything else about this arrangement.

But his hard-earned control had started to slip the moment she had appeared at the back of the chapel in a swathe of seductive silk, her wild, red hair tamed beneath the wispy veil.

His breath had backed up in his lungs and he'd been... Mesmerised. Enchanted. Bewitched. And angry—with himself most of all. Because the deep yearning squeezing his ribs had reminded him of that feral kid huddled in a doorway in the West End, watching the theatregoers stroll past him on their way to the Tube—rich, clean, well-dressed, beautiful people who'd had everything, while he'd had nothing.

Katie's wedding dress should have looked classy and demure—it was what he'd requested—but the shimmering fabric had hugged Katherine's curves like a second skin, sliding sensuously over her generous hips and those high, full breasts—made even more glorious by her condition.

The evidence of her pregnancy had horrified him that day in his office, but some aspects of it now only turned him on more—which made no sense whatsoever.

She'd walked towards him—her stride bold and determined—but then he'd seen the flicker of anxiety as she reached him. It had required a titanic effort to remain aloof and in command of his senses during the endless ceremony until the vicar had finally declared them man and wife.

But, when he'd heard the invitation to kiss his bride, he'd seen the note of panic and defiance in her expression. The answering tug of possessiveness—still tempered by the memory of that kid yearning for things he couldn't have—had made him determined to stake a claim. To prove to everyone—and Katherine most of all—she belonged to him.

And before he'd had a chance to think better of the impulse, he'd leaned in, inhaled a lungful of her provocative scent, seen the shocked arousal making the gold shards in her eyes gleam… And all hell had broken loose.

He'd stayed away from her precisely to avoid this uncontrolled reaction. Given their chemistry, he had no intention of having a platonic marriage, but he also had no intention of letting the hunger blindside him again, the way it had in Wales—and all those days ago in his office—until he figured out how to compartmentalise his reaction to her condition.

Distance hadn't worked, though, because his hunger for her had only become more insatiable, his desire more volatile.

Terrific.

He had a four-hour reception booked at an exclusive private members' club that he owned in Soho—entirely for the benefit of the press and his business associates.

Even better.

How the heck was he going to get through that, not to mention their first night together in the new house, without giving into this insane chemistry again?

Passion rippled through his body as he nodded to the vicar, who was watching them both with thinly disguised astonishment, his cheeks mottled with embarrassment.

'Cool, lead the way,' he said. He clasped Katherine's hand. The ring dug into his palm as he felt the tremor she couldn't disguise. He led her into the vestry to get the last of the ceremony over with. A ceremony that didn't feel nearly as pragmatic as it had when he'd originally planned it.

Katherine followed behind him, for once willing to be

led without an argument. Probably because she was still as shell-shocked by that damn kiss as he was.

This hunger wouldn't last. It couldn't. But he planned to treat it with extreme caution nonetheless, because he'd never experienced a need this intense or this unstable.

Controlling it completely obviously wasn't going to happen, but no way was he unleashing this fire again until he was absolutely sure he would not get burned—any more than he had been already.

Katie struggled to hold on to the ripple of reaction as Jack's warm palm settled on her back and he leaned close to be heard over the conversations buzzing around them in the sumptuous Soho club.

'We should head back to the house,' Jack said.

It had been her first assignment as Jack Wolfe's trophy wife and she felt as if she'd done her best. She'd made pointless small talk with a host of celebrities and VIPs, got besieged by photographers shouting her name as they'd entered the venue and had managed to appear calm and collected as Jack had introduced her and they'd received a ton of champagne toasts, good wishes and inquisitive comments laced with innuendo.

The decision had been made—according to Wolfe Inc's press secretary—not to announce the pregnancy until she was showing. Katie had been pathetically grateful for that, because answering all the probing enquiries from Jack's friends and acquaintances about their whirlwind courtship had been tough enough.

She supposed she had to thank Jack for that, too. He'd more than kept up his side of the bargain, playing the solicitous bridegroom with a predatory determination which had deflected anyone who got too close. As she'd struggled to adjust to all the attention, Jack's presence by her side had made her feel strangely protected, until she'd re-membered it was all an act. And, as the evening had worn on, fending off unwanted enquiries about their love affair hadn't been anywhere near as tough as stopping herself from dissolving into a puddle of need every time she'd got a whiff of his scent. Or felt the firm touch of his palm caressing her back.

Like now.

The effect he had on her had only got more intense and overwhelming as he'd remained diligently by her side through the champagne reception in the club's lavish atrium, a five-course meal of cordon bleu cuisine devised by the club's Michelin-starred chef—which she'd barely touched—and the never-ending parade of witty and heart-felt speeches.

She stiffened as his calloused fingers stroked her spine where the gown dipped, brutally aware of how addicted she had become to his clean, spicy scent. Surely that had to be the pregnancy hormones?

'Are you sure?' she whispered back, but had to stifle a yawn, the stress of the event and her struggle to keep her traitorous emotions in check—plus the fact she hadn't been able to have her usual nap this afternoon—finally taking their toll.

His lips quirked, but as his gaze raked over her the riot of sensations only intensified. How could he seem so de-tached? When she was burning up inside, both exhausted and on edge? Why wasn't he still struggling with the af-ter-effects of that wedding kiss the way she was? Was her constant awareness of him *really* just the pregnancy hor-mones? Because the thought of going back to the house, of being alone with him again for the first time in weeks, was not helping to keep those hormones in check—espe-cially after five solid hours of being the sole focus of his attention. Would he expect them to have a wedding night? And how was she going to resist him if he did?

He glided his thumb under her eye. 'Yes, I'm sure. You look shattered.' He glanced at her plate. 'You hardly ate a bite. Is it the nausea?'

She shook her head. 'No, it's mostly gone. I'm only sick occassionally now.'

Something she would have been a lot more grateful for if it hadn't made her even more aware of him. The morning—or rather, afternoon—sickness had once been a great way to dull this incessant attraction… Now, not a chance.

'Good,' he said, then lifted his hand to waylay one of the eager young assistants who had been hovering around them all day. 'Jenny, have the car brought round discreetly. Mrs Wolfe and I are leaving—with the minimum of fuss, if possible.'

'Yes, sir, Mr Wolfe.' The young woman, who had to be about the same age as Katie, bounced to attention so sharply Katie almost expected her to salute.

During the last few hours, she had noticed the deference with which all Jack's employees treated him, but also the fact he seemed to know all their names. She dismissed the sentimental thought, though—just because he was a good employer wasn't going to make *her* job any easier.

Despite Jack's request, it took a long twenty minutes for them to extricate themselves from the reception and the amused and ebullient well wishes of everyone from Jack's best man—an ex-rapper called Alphonse Parry who had been one of Jack's earliest business partners—to the hat-check girl, which only made Katie feel like more of a fraud.

A sleek black car was waiting at the back of the club. Jack dropped Katie's *faux* fur wrap over her shoulders while the driver opened the door.

'If you want to stay and chat, I don't mind heading

back on my own,' she managed, trying to disguise the shiver which had nothing whatsoever to do with the evening breeze pebbling her skin.

He let out a wry laugh, his scarred eyebrow arching. 'Don't you think our guests might get suspicious if I let my bride go home alone on our wedding night?'

Damn. Busted.

'Oh, right—yes, of course,' she murmured, feeling like a clueless idiot.

How could she forget this was all an elaborate charade to give her child a name, keep her business afloat and allow him to…? Well, she wasn't even really sure *what* he was getting out of this, given that she definitely didn't buy the excuse he'd given her in Wales three months ago. The wedding reception had been full of some of the most important people in the global business community, every one of them falling over themselves to be nice to Jack, and her by proxy.

How could dating, or indeed marrying, a lord's daughter make him any more of a big cheese in the City of London? The fact he hadn't bothered to invite her father—thank God—surely only confirmed that?

As they settled into the car's warm interior together, the smell of new leather went some way to covering the scent of him. She had to be grateful he made no move to close the distance between them once the car pulled into traffic.

She stared out of the window, the Ritz hotel's sign reflecting off the glass as the car turned into Piccadilly. Perhaps now would be a good time to press him more on his motivations. But did she really want to know the real reason he had been so set on this marriage? Wouldn't it only complicate things further?

'You don't have to be concerned, Katherine,' he said, breaking the uncomfortable silence.

Her head whipped round as the husky timbre of his voice had the familiar ripple shooting up her spine.

He was watching her with the same intensity he had been watching her with for most of the day, ever since she'd stepped into the chapel.

She had begun to wonder during the evening if he was keeping an eye on her—ready to correct her if she said or did something to give away the real circumstances of their marriage. But there was no judgement in his gaze, only an unsettlingly direct concentration.

'We'll sleep apart tonight. Consummation of this marriage is not part of the arrangement,' he murmured.

Why not?

The thought popped out of nowhere, making the ripple sink into her sex and start to glow.

'Good to know,' she murmured, trying to sound as nonchalant as he did. And to remember she didn't want to sleep with him, because this whole situation was already disturbing enough.

His lips twisted in that disconcerting smile, but his gaze only sharpened. And she had the awful feeling he could see right through her show of indifference.

'Although on the evidence of this afternoon's kiss and the one in my office a month ago,' he continued, the relaxed tone comprehensively contradicted by that focussed gaze, which was making sensation rush over her skin like wildfire, 'I doubt we'll be able to keep our hands off each other for very long.'

'I know,' she said.

He chuckled, but the sound was as raw as she felt.

'Good to know you know that,' he said, echoing her earlier statement.

She let out an unsteady breath, the bustier so tight around her ribs she was surprised she didn't pass out.

Clearly, pretending she could resist the insistent pull between them hadn't been such a smart move, because it felt as if he held all the power now that she'd been forced to admit the truth.

'So why aren't we having a wedding night?' she challenged, trying to grab some of that power back.

His eyes widened at the direct question and she felt the instant rush of adrenaline at the realisation she'd disconcerted him. For once. Instead of the other way round.

'Is it because of the baby?' she added, when he didn't reply.

He stared, then turned away. 'No,' he said.

On the one hand, she believed him. After all, he wouldn't have kissed her with such hunger if the pregnancy had been a turn-off. But she had touched a nerve without intending to. And the questions that had been burning in the back of her mind, the ones she'd been determined not even to think about, pushed to the front.

'Do you want to talk about it?' she asked.

'Talk about what?' he asked, turning back, but the confident smile had flatlined.

No, he definitely did *not* want to talk about the pregnancy. But somehow his stubborn refusal only made her more determined to press him on it, despite her own misgivings.

They'd both been knocked off-kilter by the pregnancy. She got that. But why hadn't she questioned the hasty arrangements that he had insisted upon, and which had unnerved her so much? The speed of her relocation to London, the lavishness of today's event, the opulence of the house he'd bought for her to live in, the attentiveness with which he had treated her during the ceremony and the reception and even the mysteriously opaque motives for insisting on this marriage in the first place. Because every one of those things had disturbed her in the last month. Had he rushed her into this commitment as an elaborate way to avoid having this conversation? Maybe even to avoid thinking about it?

And, if he had, why had she fallen for it so easily? She'd told him she'd decided to have the baby, and he'd accepted it without question. But she had no idea how *he* felt about it because she hadn't asked.

'Do you want to talk about becoming a father?' she asked patiently, aware she was tiptoeing through a minefield but not able to deny her curiosity any longer. No, this wasn't just curiosity about him and the kind of father he would make. It was much more fundamental than that. She needed to know if he would ever be able to think of their child as anything other than a mistake to be rectified, a debt to be paid. And, if not, why not?

'Do I *want* to talk about it?' he mused. 'No, not particularly.'

'Why not?' she pressed, refusing to be put off again.

His gaze locked on hers, the scar on his cheek flexing. 'Because I do not intend to be a part of its life.'

The dismissive answer and the brutal, brittle tone in which he delivered it had her heart contracting in her chest. It felt like a crushing blow. Which was ridiculous, really. After all, his response only confirmed what she had already suspected.

He was being honest with her. She didn't know him well, but what she did know—that he was ruthless, driven, and uncompromising enough to buy her cooperation to further his own business ends—probably meant it was a good thing he did not want to be involved in her child's life. After all, her own father had been physically present but emotionally absent throughout her childhood, and that had somehow been worse. Surely it was better not to have a relationship with your father than to have one that was so dysfunctional it made you feel unworthy, unwanted?

But, when his gaze flicked away again, she got the sense he wasn't telling her the whole truth.

The car glided to a stop outside the Mayfair townhouse, and he remained seated while the chauffeur got out and opened her door. As she slipped out of the vehicle, she couldn't help asking, 'Are you coming inside?'

'Do you wish to consummate the marriage tonight?' he countered, the ruthless demand in his voice shaking her to the core. And putting the power firmly back in his hands, as she was sure he had intended.

'Yes… I mean, no.' She scrambled to regain the ground she'd lost. 'Oh, I have no idea.'

His harsh laugh only made her feel more confused. And more powerless. A part of her *wanted* to lose herself in the sex, to take the physical pleasure he offered so she could forget about all the things this marriage would never offer her—security, companionship, maybe even love with a man who might one day come to care for her as well as her child.

But, with her emotions so raw, she knew giving in to that urge tonight would be a very bad idea. Because she wasn't sure she could avoid the intimacy with anything like the efficiency he clearly could.

'Which is it, Mrs Wolfe?' he asked.

'No,' she said with all the conviction she could muster.

'Then I think it's best if I return to the penthouse,' he said, but he reached forward and ran his thumb down her cheek with a possessiveness that stopped her breath. 'You know where to find me, when you're ready to stop running,' he added.

She drew her head back.

He signalled the driver. After she had stepped out of

the car, she watched it pull away, the traitorous desire still
pulsing in her core.

As she lay in bed half an hour later, her hand curled
around her stomach. She felt weary to her bones, the
odd feeling of dissatisfaction joined by the terrifying
thought her life had just taken an even bigger leap into
the unknown.

CHAPTER NINE

'WHAT THE HELL do you mean, the Smyth-Brown board still won't let us bid on the final share allocation?' Jack shouted. He'd had yet another sleepless night alone in his penthouse. The truth was he'd been tying himself in knots ever since tying the damn knot with Katherine three days ago.

He wanted his new wife to come to him. Wanted her to admit how much she needed him so he could forget about the devastated look in her eyes when he'd been straight with her about what he planned to offer this child.

He hadn't lied about that, but the sheen of sadness in her expression still managed to get to him. It made him feel guilty about something he had never promised and could not change. Which made no damn sense whatsoever.

And now this! The main reason he'd decided to go for this marriage—well, one of the main reasons anyway—was to finally get the old fossils on the Smyth-Brown board to agree to Wolfe Inc's bid for the controlling interest of the company. The original plan—way back when he'd first proposed to Beatrice—had been to use the marriage as leverage, to make them stop looking at him as a marauding corporate raider from the wrong side of the tracks and begin to see him as a settled family man they could trust.

His motives had become considerably more confused since then, thanks to his obsession with Beatrice's sister and the idiotic decision not to use a condom. But, if he couldn't even get this much out of the marriage, he was going to go completely insane.

'Jack, chill out,' Terry Maxwell murmured, completely unperturbed by his meltdown.

Terry was his right-hand man, his fixer, his *consigliere* and his chief financial strategist all rolled into one. Terry didn't do deference because he'd been in Jack's employ since Wolfe Inc had made its first million.

It had never bothered Jack before, but his temper surged when Terry added, 'Someone leaked the fact you're not living with your new bride. Daniel Smyth is not the only one beginning to question the authenticity of the marriage.'

'What?' Jack ground out the word, so furious and frustrated, he would not be surprised if steam began to pour out of his ears. 'Who leaked it? I want them fired immediately.'

How dared that son of a bitch question *his* integrity, especially with women, after what the guy had done to his mother?

But, before Jack could begin to work himself up into even more of a temper, Terry said, 'Jack, it could be anyone—you've been photographed coming and going from your penthouse. Perhaps the more cogent question is *why* aren't you living in Grosvenor Square with your beautiful wife?'

'That's none of your damn business,' Jack shot back, but he could hear the defensiveness in his voice as he strode to the windows of his thirty-fourth-floor office and glared at the view of the Shard on the opposite bank.

It wasn't Terry's fault he'd got into this fix with Katherine, allowing his libido and his pride to dictate his actions.

'Fair point,' Terry said, still not bothered in the least by Jack's temper tantrum. 'But, whatever your reasons, there might be a way to quash the rumours, thus fixing the problem with the Smyth-Brown takeover, while also giving the grand opening of Wolfe Maldives next month a huge publicity boost.'

Jack broke off his contemplation of the City skyline. 'Which is?' he asked, not particularly liking the sympathetic smile on his advisor's weathered face.

Terry didn't know about the true nature of his marriage, or Katherine's pregnancy, because Jack had kept all those details on a strictly need-to-know basis to stop any unwanted questions and ensure the smooth passage of the Smyth-Brown buyout. Or so he'd thought.

'The resort is already fully operational. All the staff have been hired and Wolfe Resorts' marketing division have been inviting journalists, travel bloggers and vloggers to try out the six-star experience over the last couple of weeks...' Terry began in a measured tone. 'But we can get rid of the media for a much better publicity coup.'

Jack turned round completely, to skewer his right-hand man. 'Get to the point, Terry.'

'Jack, the place is a prime honeymoon destination...' Terry stared right back at him.

'So?' Jack said, but he could already see where this suggestion was leading, because the familiar pulsing in his groin that had plagued him ever since he'd confronted Katherine on the limo ride back to the house in Mayfair on their so-called wedding night had gone into overdrive.

He had every intention of seducing his wife, and soon. He certainly didn't plan to wait much longer to settle that aspect of their relationship to his satisfaction. Especially as he knew full well her reluctance to welcome him into her bed had nothing whatsoever to do with a lack of desire. But spending any quality time with her was out. The last thing he wanted was to be subjected to another conversation like the one they'd had in the limo.

He hadn't married her to have an actual relationship with her. That had been the whole point of contracting her to *pose* as his wife—which she seemed to have conveniently missed. Of course, the pregnancy complicated that somewhat. But he didn't talk about his past, or his motives or feelings, with anyone. And certainly not with women he was sleeping with... Or intended to sleep with. Especially when they had the unique ability to blindside him with lust—the way Katherine did—and were also carrying his child.

'Jack, don't be deliberately obtuse,' Terry said, looking pained now. 'You've just got married. Wolfe Maldives isn't due to open for another month. A two-week honeymoon there with your blushing bride would garner the kind of organic global media reach your PR department would have wet dreams about for years.'

No way in hell.

That was what his head shouted but, even as he opened his mouth to tell Terry to forget it, the image of Katherine in a skimpy bikini, strolling out of the lagoon's glittering blue waters, those generous breasts bouncing enticingly as she moved, blasted out of his subconscious and sunk deep into his abdomen.

Damn.

He closed his mouth. And frowned.

As much as he hated to admit it, Terry had a point. The truth was, he didn't give a damn about the golden PR opportunity. But the chance to have Katherine all to himself—where he could seduce her in private—held some obvious advantages. Surely he'd already done enough to disabuse her of any sentimental notions she might have had about this marriage?

'Two weeks is too long,' he said, his voice dropping several octaves as more images of Katherine—wet and willing in a luxury beach setting—began to galvanise his resolve. 'I can't afford to spend that much time away from the business.' Which wasn't a lie.

Having Katherine all to himself in paradise—and making every one of the prurient fantasies he'd had about her since their first merry meeting come true—was appealing to all his baser instincts. But he wasn't about to push his luck.

'Really?' Terry looked sceptical. 'You haven't taken a proper holiday in the ten years I've known you.'

'I'm a workaholic, Terry. I like working. I can't spend a fortnight twiddling my thumbs just for a good photo op.' Not that he planned to be twiddling *his* thumbs, exactly.

Terry sent him a garrulous look. 'How about ten days, then?'

'A week,' Jack countered. 'We'll leave tomorrow night,' he added, the adrenaline rush surging at the thought he would only have to endure one more night—two at the most—without Katherine in his bed. 'In the Wolfe jet.'

He sat behind his desk, feeling more settled than he had in days. Hell, weeks. Make that four months ago. Ever since the first time he'd set eyes on his future trophy wife in her Little Red Riding Hooker outfit. He smiled. Maybe he could get her to bring it so he could peel it off her, the way he'd dreamed of doing ever since that night.

'That's great, Jack.' Terry rubbed his hands together with undisguised glee. 'I'll talk to Sully in the marketing division and the resort management team. And I'll let Gorinda know so she can rearrange your schedule. Do you want her to inform Mrs Wolfe of your plans?'

He looked up from his desk. 'Nah, I'll speak to her myself,' he said as the surge of adrenaline took on a fiercely possessive edge. 'Tell Gorinda I'll be eating in Grosvenor Square tonight.'

It was way past time he started laying down the law in this marriage—which was supposed to be for *his* convenience, not hers. He'd paid handsomely for the damn privilege after all. He'd been considerate—mindful of her delicate condition and the huge changes he was imposing on her life and her business. But she'd said herself at the reception that the sickness wasn't a big problem any more. He knew from his business manager's report that Cariad Cakes was now firmly established in its new premises in Hammersmith, and he had seen the way she'd looked at him on their wedding night. She was as hungry for him as he was for her. And he'd given her three long days and nights to come to terms with the way things were, which was more than long enough.

CHAPTER TEN

'JACK, YOU'RE HERE!' Katie stopped dead at the entrance to the dining room, a mix of shock and panic and exhilaration duelling in her chest at the sight of her husband sitting at the table where she'd eaten alone for the last three nights.

His white business shirt was open at the neck to reveal a hint of the tattoo across his chest, the sleeves rolled up tanned, muscular forearms, his hair mussed and his jaw darkened with a day's beard. The scene should have felt at least a little bit domestic. But it didn't. The possessive glint in his eyes echoed in her abdomen.

Yeah, right. Jack Wolfe is about as domesticated as his namesake.

'And you're late,' he said as his penetrating gaze glided over her flour-stained clothing and the weary set of her shoulders. 'You're working too hard.'

'Well, there's a lot to do,' Katie said a little defensively, disconcerted by the note of concern and the fact it made her feel cherished when she knew it wasn't real. 'I would have left earlier, though, if I'd known you were joining me for dinner...' she said, trying at least to *sound* like a dutiful wife. After all, it was what they'd agreed on. Although, she hadn't felt like a wife in the three days since their wedding. He hadn't even contacted her.

At first, she had fretted she'd somehow offended him by

being honest with him and not inviting him into her bed. His comment about the baby had upset her, making her feel uniquely vulnerable, but not seeing or hearing from him for three days had only made the unsettled feeling worse…not that it was exactly calm at the moment.

How did he manage to throw her for a loop simply by breathing?

'I didn't expect to see you tonight,' she added rather inanely as he picked up one of the freshly baked bread rolls laid out on the table by the kitchen staff.

'Last time I looked, this was my house,' he said as he buttered the roll, watching her intently as she walked to the place setting at the other end of the table.

'Are you planning to move in, then?' she asked, not entirely sure how she felt about the prospect. The twin tides of panic and exhilaration now danced a jig in her chest, and a few other places besides.

She couldn't avoid him for ever, and she really didn't want to. Surely getting to know him better had to be a good thing? Especially as she'd come to the conclusion—after three days of overthinking what he'd said about fatherhood—that perhaps she just needed to be patient with him.

He'd said he didn't intend to play a part in the baby's life. But maybe that would change. The pregnancy had to have been a major shock for him too—however good he was at hiding it. And he didn't have the same physical connection with their grain-o'-rice as she did. Of course, the baby would seem like a totally abstract concept to him at this point.

'Not tonight,' he said as a waiter arrived with the first course.

The exhilaration dimmed a bit as a beautifully prepared salad made up of crisp romaine lettuce, finely sliced radishes, carrots, apple and endives, and drizzled with a creamy dressing, was placed in front of her.

'Oh… Okay,' she said, trying to hide her disappointment. She tucked into the salad. Her appetite had returned full force in the last few weeks, despite all the tension over her situation with Jack but, as she wracked her brains to figure out what he was doing here, she couldn't swallow a bite.

'We're heading to the Maldives tomorrow night for a week,' he said. 'So you'll need to brief your team at the bakery and have the housekeeper arrange your packing.'

Katie dropped her fork onto the plate, so shocked by her new husband's bland pronouncement, she barely noticed the splatter of salad dressing hitting the table cloth. *'What?'*

He let out a gruff laugh, but his gaze remained locked on hers, more provocative than humorous. 'I believe it's the usual protocol after a wedding to have a honeymoon.'

'Except this isn't a usual wedding, is it?' she said. 'I haven't even heard from you in three days.'

He placed his knife and fork on the plate, before trapping her again in that blazing blue gaze. 'Have you missed me, Mrs Wolfe?'

Yes, you stupid…

She quashed the unhelpful thought before it could burst out of her mouth and give him even more power.

'I'm just saying, this isn't a normal marriage.'

He picked up his cutlery again, speaking in a conversational tone as he sliced through an endive leaf. 'Perhaps not, but I thought you understood the marriage has to appear to be real.'

'But… There was nothing about a honeymoon in the contract,' she floundered. She didn't want to go on some romantic getaway with him—for a whole week—even if it was only for the sake of appearances. She was having enough trouble sitting across the dining room from him without getting fixated on the way his shoulders strained the seams of his shirt, or recalling the rigid, resistant look on his face when she had asked him about his thoughts on fatherhood.

Getting to know him slowly, and carefully, with a full staff in attendance was one thing. Surviving a week of his focussed attention while battling her own insecurities was quite another. How would she be able to deny the insistent need with him right there? Sleeping with him would fundamentally change the parameters of their agreement in a way that could be dangerous if she wasn't emotionally prepared for the change.

'If you read the small print, it stated you would be required to travel with me,' he continued in that forceful, pragmatic tone that got on her nerves. 'This honeymoon is part of that commitment. You signed it, Red. Are you trying to renege on the deal already?'

'No, but…' She gathered her ragged breathing, forcing herself to remain calm. She'd known he would be dominant, demanding. She'd expected that. She must not lose her temper, because that would just give him the upper hand, especially as she was beginning to think he enjoyed provoking her.

'You said we could negotiate our work schedules. I can't very well leave my business for a week with less than a day's notice.'

He glanced at his watch. 'Our flight isn't leaving until eight tomorrow night, so you've got most of the day to brief your team.'

'Fine, but it's still too soon to relinquish—'

'There's an excellent Internet connection where we're going.' He cut her off, the prickle of impatience sending an answering prickle of irritation through her. 'You'll be able to check in with your team if necessary.'

Standing, he dropped his napkin on the table.

'But this isn't fair,' she said, annoyed when she heard the whiney tone of her own voice. 'I don't *want* to go to the Maldives.'

With you. Alone. On a fake honeymoon. Which will mean nothing to you and might mean something to me.

He strode towards her and tucked a knuckle under her chin to brush his thumb over her bottom lip.

She jerked her head back, but it was already too late. He had to have seen the awareness flare at the brief touch.

He planted his hands in his pockets, the smile as smug as it was predatory. 'I understand very well, Red. You think by avoiding each other this incessant heat will just go away. It won't.'

'But what if I'm not ready?'

His scarred eyebrow lifted, his cast-iron confidence completely undimmed by her declaration.

Damn him.

'I told you anything we do in private would be your choice. That hasn't changed.'

'Then why are you insisting on going to—?'

'However...' He interrupted her. *Again!* 'I did not agree to pretend the heat between us doesn't exist. Personally, I believe enjoying it for as long as your condition allows will make this marriage a lot more pleasurable for both of us. And trying to avoid it will only increase the problem. So I guess the battle lines are drawn.'

The tell-tale weight sunk into her sex as he returned to his seat and finished his salad. She sucked in a breath, too furious to speak.

Of all the arrogant, high-handed, conceited, overbearing...

She picked up her knife and fork again, ignoring the

tremble in her fingers. Fine, she'd go on his stupid honeymoon and show him he couldn't bend her to his will. But she'd refuse to be bulldozed back into his bed... By his hungry kisses, his addictive scent or that seductive promise in his cool blue eyes...even if it killed her.

Although it very well might.

After a frantic day spent running through recipes, answering countless emails, checking orders and getting her new business manager up to speed on all the commitments she was being forced to cancel for the next week, Katie was holding on to her indignation by a thread when her car arrived at Heathrow the following evening.

Instead of being dropped off in Departures, though, they were met by a passport official before being whisked through the airport, the lights of incoming planes shining in the night sky overhead. The car drove past the airport buildings to arrive at a huge private hangar behind one of the runways. A sleek silver jet took up all the available space as the car parked beside the metal steps.

She swallowed heavily as the driver opened her door then began unloading the luggage the staff must have packed earlier that day—*three* suitcases worth of luggage containing clothes she had never seen.

She frowned. Up until now, she'd really been far too preoccupied with the pregnancy, the wedding, the huge changes to her business and her constant panic about how to navigate the deal she'd made with Jack without losing her mind to think too much about the world of luxury she had entered. A world she'd been excluded from ever since she was a teenager. A world she'd left without a backwards glance.

But, as she climbed the steps into the jet, it occurred to her Jack Wolfe's lavish luxurious world was way, *way* more exclusive than her father's. She'd come from money and, although she'd never enjoyed the strings attached when she'd lived under her father's control, she knew how this world worked. Or at least, she had thought she did. But, even as the daughter of a British lord, she'd never travelled on a private plane—or had a passport official give her a personal service. Or had three huge suitcases full of clothes she'd never worn packed for her by someone else for a week-long holiday.

Except it's not a holiday, it's a honeymoon.

She puffed out her cheeks, the frustration that had been building ever since Jack's high-handed demand yesterday at dinner giving way to something a lot less fortifying and more disturbing.

She'd barely had time to think in the past month. Perhaps that was why it hadn't really occurred to her until this moment that *everything* about her new life with Jack Wolfe was way outside her comfort zone.

As she stepped into the plane's interior, she was greeted by a hostess uniformed in the red and black colours of the Wolfe Inc logo. The middle-aged woman smiled and took her coat, before directing her to the plane's interior.

'Mr Wolfe is seated in the lounge area, waiting for you, Mrs Wolfe,' she said.

Mrs Wolfe.

She'd been addressed by her married name several times since the wedding. But it had all seemed like an elaborate act until now. A knot formed in her stomach to go with the one in her throat.

She nodded, suddenly feeling woefully under-dressed in the worn jeans and plaid shirt combo she had been wearing all day to direct traffic in Cariad Cakes' industrial kitchen.

Jack sat in one of the large cream leather armchairs in the plane's lounge, typing something on his phone. The cabin was darker than she had expected, the lighting no doubt subdued for take-off. A single spotlight turned his short dark hair to a gleaming ebony and cast his handsome features into stark relief. He hadn't shaved all day, and the beginnings of the beard shadowing his jaw, together with the scarred eyebrow, made him look even more rugged and untamed than usual, despite the sharply tailored suit trousers and ubiquitous white shirt perfectly fitted to his muscular torso.

'Mrs Wolfe has arrived, sir,' the hostess announced behind her.

Jack's blue gaze locked on her face as he clicked off the phone. 'Good evening, Mrs Wolfe,' he said, the polite greeting loaded with a meaning that felt anything but polite thanks to the feral gleam in his eyes and the husky timbre of his voice.

She'd expected him to have his army of assistants with him on the flight but, as the hostess excused herself to prepare for take-off, Katie realised they were alone.

'Hi,' she said, but the word came out on a high-pitched squeak. Mortified, she cleared her throat of the rubble gathered there, and tried again. 'Hello, Jack.'

'Glad to see you made it in time for take-off,' he said, the slight edge suggesting he hadn't appreciated being kept waiting.

She hadn't arrived with only minutes to spare deliberately—she'd been extremely busy all day—but his tone still rankled.

'Did I have a choice?' she snapped.

A sensual smile—part arrogance, part amusement and yet full of approval—had her heartbeat leaping in her chest. She *knew* he enjoyed provoking her. But why hadn't she realised until now how much more he enjoyed it when she rose to the bait?

He chuckled. 'I can't very well go on a honeymoon on my own, now, can I?' he said, the mocking twinkle in his eyes making him look even more attractive.

The bastard.

Oddly—given her anxiety about what exactly they were going to be doing in the Maldives, and her indignation at the high-handed way he'd sprung this trip—she found her own lips twitching.

'I suppose not,' she conceded as she took the seat opposite him. She sunk into the soft, buttery leather, suddenly aware of how exhausted she was. The extreme fatigue of her early pregnancy had been replaced by a more manageable tiredness in the last few weeks, but she'd been on her feet most of the day—and coping with the inevitable sexual tension of being in Jack Wolfe's orbit didn't help.

'Although you may wish you had after a week stuck with me spinning my wheels,' she offered. 'I don't think I'm the "lying on the beach" type.'

It wasn't a lie. She couldn't remember the last time she'd taken a break, let alone been able to afford a holiday. She'd been working two or three jobs at a time ever since she'd left home—and even before leaving home she'd had a secret Saturday job because she'd wanted to be as financially independent as possible from her father.

'Neither am I,' Jack murmured. The approval in his gaze became hot and fluid, causing awareness to sizzle over her skin. 'I guess we'll have to find a way to keep each other occupied.'

The sizzle flared across her collarbone and rose into her cheeks.

His gaze narrowed on her burning face and the knowing smile widened.

If only she could conjure up a smart, pithy comeback,

but it would have been next to impossible to fake indifference, even if she hadn't been dead on feet.

The pilot's voice rang out over the intercom to inform them they had just been given a departure slot and would be taking off in ten minutes.

Katie fastened her seat belt as instructed and glanced out of the window, realising the plane was already moving and had left the bright interior of the hangar. The lights of the terminal building as they passed it illuminated the congested lines of passengers waiting impatiently at their departure gates.

She sighed and rolled her head back, only to get trapped once again in Jack's watchful gaze. But the sizzle dropped to a distant hum as fatigue settled over her like a warm blanket.

Her mouth cracked open in a huge yawn. 'Good to know there's at least one advantage to having a gazillionaire for my fake husband.'

His right eyebrow rose, drawing her attention to the scar, which had begun to mesmerise her. Curiosity and sympathy joined the potent hum of arousal.

Who *had* given him that scar? It must have hurt so much.

'Which is…?' he asked, the smile gone.

'No boarding queues,' she murmured, then shifted round in her seat away from that disturbing all-seeing gaze. Yawning again, she slipped off her shoes, snuggled her head into the soft leather and tucked her aching feet under her bottom.

She blinked at the red lights on the plane's wing tip flashing as they swung towards the runway. The jet engine's powerful rumble seemed to amplify the insistent hum in her abdomen but, as the plane accelerated down the runway, she couldn't seem to keep her eyes open. Eventually the flashing light dragged her into the darkness and she let herself fall under its spell.

Jack stared at his wife as the jet lifted into the night sky, not sure whether to be bemused or beguiled by the sight of her curled on the seat opposite, fast asleep.

Her russet hair haloed around her head, tendrils escaping from the practical ponytail to curl down her neck. Chocolate stains covered her well-worn jeans and the green and brown plaid shirt. She looked like a lush tomboy, the light flush on her freckle-dusted skin only adding to the spike in his groin. A few buttons had come undone on her shirt, giving him a tantalising glimpse of her cleavage as she slumbered, her body contorted into what looked like a very uncomfortable position.

She had been exhausted when she arrived. He had seen it in the smudges under her eyes and the lipstick that had been chewed off her lips hours ago. The stab of guilt joined the ache in his groin.

He shifted in his seat, visions of her soft, satiny flesh, that rich spicy scent of salted caramel, ripe apples and wild flowers permeating the cabin.

His gaze dipped and he imagined easing open the other buttons on her shirt, nuzzling the soft fragrant skin of her cleavage as it was revealed inch by tantalising inch, kissing the pulse in her collarbone, unhooking her bra, lifting her breasts free and sucking the plump pink nipples until they hardened against his…

He swore softly and swung his head away from her slumbering form to glare out of the aircraft's window. He gripped the arm rests as the inevitable wave of heat swelled. He sucked in a tortured breath. When had he ever been tormented to this extent by any woman? It was becoming ridiculous. Not to mention distracting.

Christ, if she knew the hold she had on him she would surely exploit it.

The carpet of city lights below them disappeared as the jet headed into cloud cover and began to level off at its cruising altitude.

The hostess appeared. 'Mr Wolfe, the bed chamber is ready for you and your wife,' she said, sending him a rather too amused smile.

'Right, thanks,' he murmured. 'If you could leave us, please.'

The woman immediately got the message and left.

He reached for his laptop, planning to work until Katherine awoke. But, as the minutes ticked past, he found it impossible to concentrate on the bids being put in place for the Smyth-Brown shares, something which should have had all his attention.

He sighed and closed the laptop. Hell, he'd have to check the contracts another day. It would be several months yet before the takeover was finalised and he could finally get his revenge on the man who had discarded his mother.

He had time.

His fervour for the fight would come back as soon as his new wife had become less of a distraction. Sun, sea, sand and lots of mind-blowing sex would cure this strange *ennui*.

His gaze landed back on Katherine, who had contorted herself into another uncomfortable-looking shape. He could smell her. The tantalising earthy aroma sent another unwelcome surge of arousal through his system.

She huffed and shifted, drawing her knees up and her chin down to snuggle tighter into the seat's headrest, almost as if trying to protect herself from something. Her eyelids flickered with dreams, her brows furrowed and her lips pursed into a tight line, her breathing becoming rapid suggesting, whatever the dreams were, they weren't happy or benign.

The shaft of guilt hit more forcefully. He dismissed it. She looked healthier than she had when she'd come to his office and told him of the pregnancy. A week in paradise would be good for her.

He tilted his head to one side to study her, while ignoring the tightness in his chest at the thought of what might be causing her unpleasant dreams.

Surely her nightmares had to be due to the uncomfortable position she was trying to sleep in? Nothing more disturbing than that. Even though it would be torture for him, she was clearly too tired for them to satisfy this hunger tonight.

He undid his seatbelt and approached her. Clasping her shoulder, he rocked her gently. 'Katherine, wake up and I'll show you to the bedroom.'

When she didn't stir, he tried again.

She shook her head, moaned and turned away from him.

'Damn,' he whispered. She really was shattered.

Unclipping her seatbelt, which had become tangled around her hips, he hooked one arm under her bent knees, the other across her back and scooped her up against his chest.

Her cheek nestled against his collarbone, her body soft and pliant and satisfyingly substantial in his arms, her warm breath tickling the skin under his chin. Heat gathered and throbbed in eddying waves in his groin, adding to the torture as he carried her through the darkened cabin and opened the narrow door to the master bedroom.

The hostess had turned down the bed, and a night light embedded in the headboard had been switched on, casting an eerie glow. But, as Jack deposited his cargo in the middle of the smooth satin comforter, Katherine's eyelids fluttered open. Trapped in her emerald gaze, her pupils dark and unfocussed, his breath squeezed his lungs. And his heart hammered against his ribs in hard, heavy thuds.

Thoughts of taking advantage of her drowsy, semi-conscious state bombarded his tortured body. He imagined joining her on the bed, stripping off her clothing, undoing his trousers to free the strident erection and thrusting heavily into the tight, wet heat.

But then her hand reached up to cradle the taut muscle in his cheek, the gentle touch soothing the rampant thoughts—as if he were a wild beast and she a fairy-tale maiden come to rescue him from his own depravity. Before he had a chance to make sense of the ludicrous notion, her fingertip stroked the jagged scar.

His heartbeat slowed, every part of his being focussed on that consoling, feather-light caress, and for one terrifying moment he almost believed it would cure the pain of his past.

'Does it still hurt?' she asked, her voice thick with sleep, her faced softened by the dream-like quality of someone who was not fully aware of what they were saying or doing.

He shook his head, but the relentless, insistent desire shifted, swept along by something a great deal more disturbing... Longing.

'Who did it?' she asked, still caressing the torn, ugly flesh, the symbol of how defenceless he'd once been.

'The man I thought was my father,' Jack said as the truth released from his chest in a guttural whisper.

Anguish shadowed her eyes, the glint of moisture reflecting in the half-light and making him aware of the gold flecks in the emerald-green. But then she blinked and a single tear dripped from the corner of her eye to roll down the side of her face. 'I hate him,' she said.

Shock washed through him like acid as his heart

clamoured and roared, the desire returning in a heady rush but driven this time by the brutal yearning.

He grasped her consoling fingers and dragged them away from the ruined flesh. He levered himself off the bed. Her gaze remained riveted to his, conveying emotions he didn't want to see, didn't even want to acknowledge, but could feel turning the weight in his chest into a ten-ton slab of reinforced concrete. 'Go back to sleep, Katherine. I'll see you in the morning.'

He left the room, closed the door behind him and headed into the other bedroom. Not caring any more about the torturous desire still throbbing in his groin.

Because he had a much bigger problem to deal with now. How the hell was he going to lift this concrete slab off his chest while spending a week in paradise with the woman who had dumped it there in the first place?

CHAPTER ELEVEN

KATIE SHIELDED HER EYES against the early-morning sunlight glittering on the turquoise blue of the lagoon. A lagoon which stretched for miles towards the horizon in every direction—literally a vision of paradise.

A salt-scented breeze moved through the palm trees that fringed the beach, adding a hushed rustle to the tranquil day. The translucent sea lapped against the shoreline in desultory waves. Standing on the bedroom terrace of the stunning steel-and-glass structure that was Jack's house on the island, she wondered where her so-called husband was.

Is he avoiding me?

She'd awoken yesterday, after eleven hours virtually comatose, when the private jet had touched down in Malé at midday. She and Jack had been driven by limousine from the airport through the colonial town to the port, where a motor launch had waited to whisk them across the water towards the Ari Atoll and Wolfe Maldives' private island.

One thing she remembered clearly was waking up in the plane's bedroom, alone, strange dreams still intruding on her consciousness—of Jack, his face tense, cautious and wary, shock and brutal sadness clouding his eyes. Even now, twenty-four hours later, she could still feel the texture of his scar against her fingertips, the warm skin ridged and torn. She gripped the balcony railing. Had she touched him in her sleep? Had he carried her into the plane's bedroom?

The man I thought was my father.

His gruff whisper murmured through her memory, as it had so many times on their strangely stilted journey from the airport to the island, and during the afternoon and evening she'd spent alone in the house after he had disappeared with some excuse about having to work.

Had he *actually* confided in her? The words had been full of bitterness but tinged with vulnerability—as if his answer had been wrenched from his very soul. Or had she imagined the dream-like encounter on the flight?

She had considered asking him about it during the limousine transfer to the port in Malé and the breathtaking journey on the motor launch across the vast blue sea. But he had been preoccupied ever since they'd left the airport, either talking on his phone, reading contracts or tapping out messages on his laptop. In fact, she'd barely exchanged two words with him since she'd walked into the jet's lounge area, feeling well-rested but still confused and on edge, to find him waiting for her, his watchful gaze holding so many secrets.

He'd been tense, brooding, the withdrawn quality telling her louder than words to keep her distance. And, even though she had decided any intimacy between them would be dangerous, she had missed the mocking, dominating—and impossibly hot—man who had invited her on this trip in the first place.

When they'd arrived at Wolfe Maldives—which had appeared like a tropical oasis in the midst of the never-ending blue, the main building a white wood-framed colonial palace which blended into the palm trees—Jack had disappeared with a team of his assistants and the resort's managerial staff.

So this was going to be a working honeymoon, then? Funny he hadn't mentioned that when she'd been freaking out about it at dinner three nights ago.

After he'd left her, she had ignored the pang of regret and concentrated on the tour she was given of the stunning facilities: two swimming pools, a fully equipped gym and several different dining areas, including one on a floating platform in the lagoon, draped in white linen that billowed in the breeze. There were tennis courts, a spa and a sea-sports area equipped with everything from jet-skis to paddle boards and snorkelling equipment, plus a dive hut where a diving instructor had offered to introduce her to the wonders of the reef that surrounded the island during her stay.

Then she'd been driven in a golf buggy to the Owner's Cottage on the other side of the island. Whoever had named it a cottage had clearly been delusional. Cariad was a cottage. The two-storey stone and glass structure perched on the edge of a white sand cove was nothing short of a palace.

After exploring the five-bedroom house and its grounds while the staff unpacked their luggage, she had been served a three-course meal on the veranda by the charmingly discreet staff...while Jack had been conspicuous by his absence.

After watching the sinking sun create a sensational light show of pinks and oranges and flaming reds from the jetty, she'd headed to bed, feeling anxious but also lonely.

Where was he?

Did Jack plan to join her in the master bedroom tonight? How would she feel if he woke her? Should she have stayed up to greet him when he finished his work commitments? What was her role here? Because she had no idea.

But, when she'd woken this morning, the bed beside her had been empty. And, after she'd checked the property to find another one of the bedrooms slept in but still no sign of Jack, the bewilderment and loneliness turned to agitation.

She frowned, the stunning, sun-drenched scenery doing nothing to dispel the knots in her belly that had been forming since yesterday.

Now she knew a little of how Mrs Rochester must have felt—the unwanted bride hidden away and going insane in the attic. Albeit this was a luxury paradise attic where every possible amenity waited to distract her from the fact her new husband wanted to have nothing to do with her...

Not that they were a *real* husband and wife, she told herself staunchly, but still it felt as if she'd been brought to the Maldives under false pretences. What had become of the man who'd teased and tormented her, who had insisted the heat between them needed to be dealt with? And what exactly was she supposed to do about the fact she was starting to want it dealt with too?

She breathed in the clean, salty air, the sun warming her skin. Was it possible that what had happened in the plane's bedroom hadn't been a dream? Was it behind his disappearing act? Was Jack running scared now?

And, if he was, what did she want to do about it?

Find him. Because avoidance clearly isn't working. It's just making me more insane.

They had six more days together in paradise and six months until the baby was born. She was tired of running—not just from the insistent desire, but the strange connection they seemed to share. She needed to discover if what he'd told her about the scar was true. Because that furious jolt of compassion for him, and the brutalised boy he'd been, was still there throbbing under her breast bone like an open wound.

Maybe the sensible thing would be to forget about what she thought he'd said to her. It would be horribly embarrassing if she'd conjured the whole scenario up from some desperate desire buried deep in her psyche. Always a possibility.

But she'd never been sensible when it came to relationships. She'd always been reckless, impulsive and passionate. It was how she'd survived on her own for years, especially after her grandmother's death. Why she'd been in Jack Wolfe's penthouse that night at her sister's request. And probably one of the reasons why she had agreed to this marriage in the first place.

Her decision to sign on Jack's dotted line had never been as simple or straightforward as she'd wanted to believe—it hadn't just been about the unplanned pregnancy or her desperation to get out from a mountain of debt and turn her business into a going concern. It had also been about that fierce, intense desire in Jack's eyes whenever he looked at her and the strange sense that he saw her in a way no other man ever had.

Maybe that intense yearning was simply about sex for him, but it was about more than that for her. And it was time she acknowledged it and found a way forward.

Striding back into the bedroom, she donned one of the designer swimsuits that had been brought for her. The one-piece had a fifties vibe, cut high on the leg with a crisscross design across her chest that lifted her breasts, while the vibrant letter-box-red matched the russet tones of her hair. Although the costume didn't show as much flesh as the bikinis, it flattered her hour-glass shape and gave her a confidence she needed.

She tied up the unruly locks of her hair in a casual knot, slathered all the places she could reach in sun lotion then added a pair of denim cut-offs, some beach sandals and a lose-fitting white linen shirt to her ensemble. She wasn't about to throw herself at the man if he didn't want her. But she refused to allow him to dictate all the terms of their marriage. He'd dictated enough already.

After downing a cup of mint tea and a bowl of the home-baked granola and fresh fruit laid out by the invisible staff on the stunning black quartz breakfast bar, she headed out onto the stone pool-terrace.

She squinted into the sunshine. It had to be getting close to ten o'clock. She'd been up for over an hour and Jack was still nowhere in sight.

He's definitely avoiding me.

Her heartbeat ticked into her throat, her breathing the only sound as silence greeted her.

A pair of sandy deck shoes had been left beside one of the loungers. *Bingo.*

The oval pool sparkled in the sunlight, fringed by large planters of exotic tropical flowers and shrubs. On one side of the beach beyond was the wooden jetty from where she had watched the sunset the night before, a gleaming motor launch and a couple of jet-skis docked at the end. As she scanned the cove, her gaze caught on a glimmer of movement about a mile out, coming around the point on the other side of the bay.

She shielded her eyes. Was that a dolphin?

But as the sleek shape drew closer she recognised it as a man swimming, or rather powering, across the lagoon in fast, efficient strokes, his dark hair and tanned skin contrasting sharply with the bright, translucent turquoise of the sea.

Jack! My invisible husband.

The knots in her stomach grew, and her thigh muscles quivered as he strode out of the water and onto the beach below the terrace. Dragging off a pair of goggles, he picked up a towel left on the sand and scrubbed himself dry in brusque strokes.

She stepped back into the shade of one of the flowering scrubs, the knots in her stomach tightening.

His muscular arms and wide shoulders glistened in the sunshine, the wet swimming shorts clinging to his thighs and hanging from his lean waist, displaying the ridge of his hip flexors. After rubbing the towel through the short strands of hair, he dragged off the shorts.

The last of her confusion and irritation dried in her throat, turning to something that felt uncomfortably like shock… And awe. It was the first time she'd seen him naked since he had disrobed in the grey, shadowy light of Cariad's storm-tossed bedroom.

Even though he stood a good twenty feet away, the bright sunshine made the view a lot clearer. The tickle of panic in the back of her throat—at the spectacular sight of Jack Wolfe stark-naked—was nothing compared to the flood of sensation working its way up her torso as she took her time devouring every detail—the tan demarcation line on his hip, the bush of black hair framing the long column of his sex before he hooked the towel around his waist.

Apparently Jack worked out… A lot. Something she hadn't registered the last time she'd seen him naked in the furore of need. During her lonely granola breakfast, Katie had rehearsed a script of all the things she wanted to say to Jack when she finally located him. But as he groped around on the sand, then picked up a pair of spectacles, every last word of those imagined opening gambits were whipped away on the breeze along with the last of her temper. And all that was left was the knot in her throat, the sultry insistent ache in her abdomen and the clatter of her heart beating against her ribs.

Jack wore glasses. How had she not known that?

As he headed towards the house with his head down, running his fingers through the cropped hair, she had a sudden vivid memory of the night they'd met and his un-focussed gaze as he'd glared at her. How myopic was he? Because it had seemed for a minute as if he'd had to use touch to locate his spectacles.

As he drew close, she stepped out from behind the plant. *Show time.*

His head rose and he stopped dead. Tension rippled through his body, but even behind the lenses of his glasses—which had darkened in the sun—she could see something fierce yet guarded flash across his face. Surprise and desire, certainly, but also a wary alertness.

And suddenly the last of her doubts disappeared. He *had* said those words to her about the scar in the jet two nights ago. It hadn't been a dream. Was that why he had been avoiding her?

Compassion blindsided her.

'Katherine,' he murmured, managing to temper his reaction sooner than she could. 'You're awake?' He sounded surprised as his possessive gaze took in everything, from her scarlet toenails in the open sandals to the damp tendrils sticking to her neck.

'I've been up for an hour,' she said, determined not to get sidetracked by the hum in her abdomen or the electrifying awareness that pulsed around them.

'Why didn't you come back last night?' she asked.

'I did,' he said, deliberately misinterpreting her question. 'You were asleep.'

'Don't lie.' She crossed her arms over her chest. 'You've been avoiding me, Jack. Why?'

'Because I've been busy.' Jack ground out the words, struggling to keep his voice firm and even when everything inside him was clamouring to touch her, to taste her, to scoop her into his arms, tear off the shorts that barely covered her butt, tug down the swimsuit peeking out from beneath her shirt and fill his mouth with the taste of salt and apples on her breasts.

Hell, how could he still want her so much after swimming for miles and burying himself in work yesterday to keep the hell away from her? Shouldn't this hunger have faded by now, or at least become a lot more manageable? Especially as she knew things about him now he didn't want anyone to know.

When they had arrived yesterday, he'd only planned to stay away from her for an hour or two, but the yearning had only become more insistent as the afternoon had worn on.

He needed to be able to control it, or he might blurt out something else. And he already hated that she'd caught him without his lenses in. The heavy glasses always made him feel weak, reminding him of the child he'd been, trying to dodge fists he couldn't see.

'Doing what?' she asked.

'Surely you can't be bored already?' he countered, damned if he was going to answer any more of her questions.

'We're supposed to be here on our honeymoon, Jack,' she countered right back. 'Don't you think the staff will find it odd if all you do while we're here is work…?' Her gaze dipped. 'And swim.'

Of course they did. He'd seen the confusion on the resort manager's face when he'd insisted on spending all afternoon and evening going over the specs for the press launch in a month's time.

'They're well paid not to question what I do,' he muttered, making the implication clear that she had also been well paid not to question him and not to confront him.

He was damned if he'd be found wanting by someone he'd paid to be his wife...

'Are you avoiding me because of what you told me about your scar?'

The gentle enquiry—and the astuteness behind it— shocked him so much, he couldn't hide his reaction.

Her gaze darkened, piercing the protective layer he'd always kept around his emotions.

'So you remember that?' he growled.

The sick nausea in his stomach was nothing to the surge of fury making his chest hurt. This was why he had never confided in anyone. Why the hell had he confided in her? Giving her ammunition against him? It made no sense, and the compassion in her gaze shook him to his core.

She nodded, the emerald eyes sparking with a sympathy he despised.

He didn't need or want her pity. He'd made a staggering success of his life, despite his squalid and violent beginnings—maybe even because of them.

'I hope he paid for what he did,' she said, her voice breaking slightly, as if she were holding back tears.

'He had his reasons.' He had no desire to talk about the man who he had feared and loved in equal measure until he had realised Harry Wolfe had never wanted him any more than Daniel Smyth had.

Her eyes widened, the shocked distress calling to something deep inside him that he had no intention of acknowledging.

'What possible reason could he have for mutilating a child?' she whispered.

'He discovered I wasn't his son,' Jack said, his thumb stroking the ragged flesh—until he became aware of what he was doing and dropped his hand.

Instead of ending the conversation as he'd hoped, Katie simply stepped towards him, invading the personal space he so desperately needed.

'That's not a reason, Jack,' she said softly. 'To hurt someone who loved him.'

'I didn't love him.' The denial scraped over the jagged boulder which had formed in his throat. 'He was a violent, abusive bastard to me and my mother for as long as I can remember. I was glad I wasn't his. It gave me an excuse to leave that place and never look back.'

Except he *had* looked back, many times, the brutal shame still lurking in some dark, unbidden corner of his heart. The picture he'd tried so hard to suppress flickered into his memory of his mother's face the last time he'd seen her. The once soft, beautiful skin had been strained and tear-streaked, puffy with exhaustion, desperation and the drugs she'd used to forget as the paramedics had arrived.

Don't tell them who did this, honey. Please don't, or he'll be even angrier.

Who had really been the monster? The man who had destroyed his mother, or the boy who had forced her into his arms then left to save himself?

Stepping closer still, Katherine placed her warm palm on his scarred cheek. 'I'm glad you got out.'

He jerked back, jolted out of the miserable reminiscence. Grasping her wrist, he pulled her hand from his face. 'Don't…' he said.

She stared at him, her eyes bold and unashamed.

Vicious sensation prickled across his sun-warmed

shoulders and sank deep into his abdomen, the need as swift and visceral as it had ever been.

To hell with it. There was no containing it. And he'd be damned if he'd even try any longer.

'Don't touch me,' he said, his thumb pressing against the inside of her wrist, feeling the rampant pulse, her instinctive response only making the swift, visceral need all the more brutal. 'Not unless you've changed your mind about sleeping with me.'

He expected her to retreat, to fall back on the lie she'd told him before they'd arrived on the island, but instead her expression remained open and unguarded, the hunger clear and unashamed. He dragged her into his embrace, until her soft curves pressed against the hard line of his body.

She didn't flinch, didn't fight him, her breath coming in ragged pants. Then she licked her lips and the fierce arousal turned to pain, his yearning flesh hardening against her belly. He breathed in a lungful of her smell, the rich, earthy scent beneath the aroma of sun cream and sweat sending his senses into overdrive.

'Admit you want me, Katherine,' he demanded. 'And I'll stop avoiding you.'

Shocked arousal dilated the vivid green of her irises to black. 'I want you.'

His raw groan echoed across the pool terrace as he lifted her into his arms. 'Wrap your legs around my waist.'

She grasped his shoulders and obeyed him as he captured her mouth, devouring her in greedy bites—the way he'd dreamed of doing for days. He thrust his tongue deep to capture her startled sobs and marched across the pool terrace and into the house.

All that mattered now was sinking into her again, driving them both to oblivion and claiming what was his so he could forget the things she'd wrenched out of him.

She didn't know him—not really. And he didn't want her to know him.

This was all he wanted from her, the only connection that mattered to him.

This is dangerous, and you know it.

Katie's brain tried to engage, but the rush of adrenaline and the swell of tenderness was unstoppable as Jack strode into the house and took the stairs to the mezzanine.

Her heart pumped hard, sensation spreading through her body like wildfire. He held her easily, as if she weighed nothing at all, while his kisses devoured her neck, her collarbone.

At last, he dumped her onto the huge, canopied bed where she'd slept alone the night before.

A glass wall looked out onto the bay, the diamond-white sand giving way to the iridescent turquoise sea. She lay dazed and disorientated as he dragged off the towel. His arousal jutted out from his belly, thick and long and aggressive, somehow. Her gaze lifted to the tortured expression on his face that matched the giddy, relentless desperation in her heart.

Why had she insisted on provoking him, even knowing the danger? But she couldn't look away from the tight, barely leashed need on his face and the thick jut of his erection as he joined her on the bed. Pushing her legs apart with one insistent thigh, he dragged her shorts off. Then he groaned, thumbing her turgid nipples through her swimsuit.

'A one-piece?' he murmured. 'Just kill me now.'

A chuckle rose up her torso at his look of consternation, but then strangled in her throat as he lifted the swollen flesh over the top of the suit and traced his tongue around one yearning peak.

'Tell me if it hurts…' He growled as he gathered the hardening peak between his lips.

'It doesn't!' she gasped as he suckled with unbearable tenderness.

She rose off the bed as the drawing sensation arrowed into the molten spot between her thighs, the ache intensifying.

She squirmed and writhed, the pleasure too much and yet not enough as he feasted on one nipple then the other.

She grasped his head to drag him closer and dislodged the glasses.

He swore softly and levered himself off the bed. 'Wait there. And take that damn one-piece off. I need to get my lenses in,' he said. 'I'll be damned if I do this blind.'

She lay on the bed, trying to gather her wits, or what was left of them. But her panting breaths only made her feel more light-headed, more disorientated.

She should call a halt to this—forget the harsh sadness in his eyes when he had told her about his past. But something stopped her, and she knew it was a great deal more than just the promise of having the desperate hunger finally fed.

She still lay there, the emotions churning in her gut, her heart pummelling her ribs when he returned. The glasses were gone—the intimidating erection wasn't.

She drew herself into a sitting position. 'Perhaps we shouldn't…'

'I think we both know it's too late for that,' he cut her off, then grasped her wrist and dragged her off the bed until they stood toe to toe. She'd lost her sandals on the way into the house, her bare toes sinking into the deep carpet, but his urgent erection was nowhere near as overwhelming as the turmoil in his eyes.

He cupped her cheek with a shocking gentleness that

weakened her knees. He threaded his fingers into her hair and the loose knot tumbled down.

'We need this,' he said.

She opened her mouth, wanting to deny it, but then he placed his mouth on the pummelling pulse by her collarbone. The protest lodged in her throat as he dragged off her shirt… And the words that would release her from the silken web imprisoning her refused to come.

He peeled the suit from her body in one forceful glide.

In the half-light of her granny's cottage at nightfall, her body had been sheltered, obscured, but here the glaring sunlight spotlighted every flaw, every imperfection. But he didn't seem to notice, his urgent hands stroking her to fever pitch.

At last he found her sex and began to torture and torment with insistent fingers.

He sank to his knees and cupped her hips before prising her legs apart. But a position that should have made him less dominant only made him more so as his gaze locked with hers and his tongue trailed up the inside of her thigh.

She shivered, sinking her fingers into his damp hair. She shuddered as he lapped and lathed, finally parting the curls hiding her sex to lick at her clitoris at last. The swell built, staggering in its intensity, shattering the last of her resistance and charging through her body on a tidal wave of stunned pleasure.

As the brutal orgasm subsided, she stood, shaking, exhausted. He rose to his feet to tower over her. 'It's too late to escape me, Red. You're mine now, in the only way that matters.'

She should reject the brutal cynicism, the claim of ownership. She would never belong to any man—but she no longer had the strength to resist it.

Pressing her back on the bed, he climbed over her.

Scooping up her legs, he lifted her knees, spreading her wide open for the brutal invasion. He anchored the huge erection deep in one slow, mind-altering thrust, impaling her to the hilt.

Her body contracted, struggling to adjust to the thick invasion, while dragging him deeper still as she clung to his broad shoulders. He began to move in a harsh, relentless rhythm, his breathing as ragged as her own.

The pleasure rose again with brutal speed; furious, overwhelming, rushing towards her on another wave. Her fingers dug into broad, sweat-slicked muscles, trying to concentrate on the physical. But the turmoil in her chest refused to subside as the tsunami bowled over her again, and she heard him shout out as he collapsed on top of her.

Katie lay dazed for what felt like an eternity, Jack's shoulder digging into her collarbone.

She drew in a shuddering breath and let it out again, waiting as the serene wave of afterglow faded into something hollow and deeply unsettling.

Groaning, Jack pulled out of her at last. She felt the loss of connection instantly. After gathering the last remnants of her sanity around her, the flight instinct that had deserted her so comprehensively minutes ago returned in a rush. She edged to the side of the bed.

He'd torn the swimming costume when he'd dragged it off her, so she scooped up the shorts. Embarrassment heated her cheeks as she tugged them on, forced to wear them without underwear.

'Hey, where are you going?'

The gruff voice behind her had her glancing over her shoulder.

He reclined in the bed, the white sheet lying low on his hips, one arm slung behind his head, the other flat against his stomach, a watchful, questioning light in those crystal-blue eyes.

Her thighs twitched and her sex pulsed, making her aware of the soreness where he had plundered her so convincingly.

'For a walk,' she said, desperate to get away from him and the brutal feeling of connection.

He wasn't the boy who had been scarred by a violent stepfather. He was a forceful, dynamic and scarily controlled man who was going to become a father himself but had no intention of becoming part of his child's life. Perhaps his past explained why he didn't *want* to be a father, but it also meant he was less likely to change his mind.

As she went to stand, he lurched across the bed and grasped her wrist.

She lifted her hand, trying to wrestle it free of his grasp. 'Jack, I have to…'

'Don't go,' he said, the request cutting her protest off at the knees. Her hand dropped to the bed, still manacled in his. 'Stay.'

'I don't think that's a good idea,' she said, but she could hear the foolish hesitation in her own voice. What was wrong with her? What was she hoping was going to happen?

And how could the yearning still be there? Now they'd fed the hunger?

Except it didn't feel fed…not even close. Her gaze lingered on the smooth contours of his chest, the bunch of muscle and sinew, the faded ink.

'Why not?' he asked, but then his lips twitched, as if he were holding back a grin. 'We're on our honeymoon.'

'Yes, but it's not a real honeymoon,' she countered, still trying to cling to what was left of her common sense.

Even as a niggling voice at the back of her head kept saying… *Why not stay and find out if there could be more?*

Hadn't they both been running for too long? Didn't she owe it to their child, his child, at least to try?

He fascinated her—his facets, his mood swings and all the carefully guarded secrets that lurked behind his eyes. She was attracted like a moth to a flame, the danger only making him more intriguing.

He had given her something this afternoon, a small glimpse of himself. How could that be bad?

'Right now, it feels real enough,' he murmured, his voice a rough burr of sound that seemed to scrape across her skin like sandpaper.

Sitting up, he turned her body until they sat together on the side of the bed, his thighs bracketing her hips, one large hand resting on the barely-there curve of her belly, his chest hot against her back. He hooked her hair behind her ear to expose her neck and nuzzled the sensitive skin over the galloping pulse.

'Come on, Katherine. We might as well make the most of this chemistry while it lasts,' he murmured. 'What have we got to lose?'

'But what if it never ends?' she asked, then realised how gauche that sounded when he chuckled.

'You don't have a lot of sexual experience, do you, Red?'

She shifted round, trying to see his face. 'I have enough,' she said indignantly.

He skimmed his finger down her nose, the gesture gentle and mocking, but also strangely approving.

'This won't last,' he said, his eyes flaring with fierce need. 'Nothing this good ever does.' The echo of regret made her heart pulse hard.

'But this wasn't supposed to be real,' she finally managed to blurt out as the heat gathered and twisted while his lips roamed over her skin, making her tender sex ache all over again. 'That was the deal.'

Did he know what he was asking of her? What he was risking?

His soft chuckle echoed across her nape before he bit softly into her earlobe.

'Deals can be renegotiated,' he said. 'If both parties are amenable.'

His hand drifted beneath the open fly of her shorts, his fingers delving, exploring.

She jolted as he found her clitoris, still wet, swollen and far too sensitive.

She gripped his wrist, trying to stop the devious, devastating caresses that were turning her into a mass of desperation all over again. How did he do that? So easily? How did he make her forget all her priorities, make her stop thinking and only feel?

His hand stilled, but his voice still held the hint of amusement and the purr of command as it whispered across her neck. 'Shh, Katherine. Let me prove to you how good this is.'

Her grip loosened, her head dropping against his shoulder as the last of her objections drifted away on the tide of pleasure, the pulse of emotion. He circled the slick flesh— tantalising, tormenting. Tortured sobs issued from her lips as a cloud covered the sun and she saw their reflection in the window glass.

His big body surrounded hers, his tanned hand working against the open fly of her shorts with ruthless efficiency. His mouth suckled and nipped at the pulse in her neck, but the sensation concentrated in her sex. His other hand covered one naked breast, moulding the round weight then rolling and plucking the engorged nipple, sending more darts to her core. She quivered and moaned as her back arched, pushing herself instinctively into the devastating caresses—wanting, needing, more.

'Please... I...' she whispered, begging him to take the ache away.

'That's it, Red. Come for me again,' he demanded, just as his fingers found the epicentre at her core. The ache exploded, the earthquake of pleasure too pure, too strong.

She flew again, bowing back, crying out, the climax overwhelming her. And knew, whatever came next, she couldn't run from him any more.

Later, much later—after a shared shower, an exhilarating ride out into the bay on the motor launch, a meal on the terrace delivered on mopeds by two waiters who disappeared as soon as they had served it and another tumultuous and exhausting lovemaking session—Katie lay in Jack's arms again and listened to the slow murmur of his breathing.

Somehow she'd agreed to make this a real honeymoon... Or rather, real enough.

The sun dropped towards the sea, the kaleidoscope of red and orange reflected off the dark water, but felt nowhere near as dramatic as the conflagration in her chest.

Had she done the right thing, giving in to her fascination with Jack? How could she not...? When she was so tired of fighting it? Tired of pretending the need didn't exist? And tired of denying the compassion she felt for the boy who lurked inside the man?

'Consider the terms of our contract renegotiated, Katherine,' he murmured against her nape, his hand absently caressing her stomach where their baby grew.

Her heart bumped into her throat.

But when he relaxed behind her, his breathing becoming deep and even against her back, it took her for ever to fall asleep too. Because she knew she'd just taken a step into unguarded, unknowable territory. A step into no man's land, despite all her best intentions. Just as she had done when she had left her father's house all those years ago.

On one level it terrified her. The only question now was, could she be strong enough, smart enough, patient enough, resilient enough to find out if Jack might one day take that step with her...or would it be another step she would have to take alone?

CHAPTER TWELVE

One month later

'WHERE IS MRS WOLFE?' Jack demanded of Katherine's housekeeper, Mrs Goulding, as he marched into her office in the basement. He'd searched the Mayfair house and couldn't find his wife.

'She had an appointment in Harley Street this afternoon,' Mrs Goulding replied.

The anticipation—which had been expanding under his breastbone and making it virtually impossible for him to concentrate on the endless conference calls he'd had that day to finalise the last of the Smyth-Brown takeover—popped like an overblown balloon.

'Is everything okay?' he asked, his impatience—because she hadn't been here when he had arrived, as she normally would be—turning into something else.

He'd left her in the early hours of the morning to return to his penthouse after spending most of the night ravishing her. She'd been deeply asleep, which wasn't like her at all. She'd been working hard recently on her new business after taking the decision to open a small shop in Knightsbridge to make her online bakery brand more visible.

It had been three weeks since they'd returned from their so-called honeymoon in the Maldives and the need hadn't abated one bit. If anything it had got considerably worse. But what was perhaps a great deal more concerning was the unsettled, agitated feeling that had begun to assail him whenever Katherine was out of his sight.

He had become obsessed with his trophy wife.

The rest of the week in the Maldives—after she had agreed to sleep with him—had been nothing short of idyllic. But not for the reasons he would have assumed.

She had been as eager as he to indulge their sexual connection. In fact, she had thrown herself into it with as much enthusiasm as he had. They'd made love on the beach, by the pool and on the power launch while anchored off one of the deserted islands on the atoll, after a morning spent snorkelling on the reef. And every night, every morning and many of the hours in between, when he'd woken dreaming of her, to find her body curved into his, wet and eager as he woke her.

She hadn't denied him once, had even initiated the contact on more than one occasion, her tentative, adorably artless attitude to sex becoming almost as demanding and adventurous as his by the time the trip had ended.

He'd remained living in the penthouse—to get the distance he needed—and she hadn't objected. He'd almost been disappointed when she had failed even to comment on his decision. While he still had his clothes in the penthouse, and despite his best intentions to ensure he continued to live his own life, he spent every night with her in Grosvenor Square before returning home, often in the early hours of the morning, to wash and change before heading to his office.

Keeping his belongings in the penthouse had become inconvenient, so he'd been forced to move some items into the house here. Again, she hadn't commented, hadn't pushed. She probed occasionally about his past, his childhood, but had allowed him to deflect those questions easily. And, when she had made offhand comments about the baby, the pregnancy, she hadn't pressed when he had failed to engage.

He should have felt fine. Their life was just as he wanted it, just as he had envisaged it when proposing this marriage.

So why wasn't he content?

Perhaps because it wasn't just the sex that had captivated him since they had returned. He also enjoyed the conversations in the evenings when he arrived from the office to find her in her study, video calling her team or strategising with her marketing manager, or in the kitchen, rustling up something delicious after giving the chef a night off.

During those conversations he had discovered exactly how smart, erudite and witty Katherine was, her intelligence and single-mindedness a match for his own. They'd argued about politics, culture and sport, and had talked at length about her business plans and her long-term goals. She'd come to him with queries, questions, hiring problems and strategy suggestions, and he'd been happy to help.

And she'd quizzed him about his own business. Because he had deflected any personal questions about his childhood, he had refrained from asking about hers, even though he was hopelessly curious now about *her* past. He wanted to know how she had survived after being kicked out of her home at seventeen. And how she had managed to retain such an optimistic and surprisingly naive attitude towards the generosity of the human spirit when he most certainly had not.

And why couldn't he stop thinking about her even now?

It would be pathetic, if it weren't so disturbing.

'I don't believe anything is wrong, sir,' the housekeeper said. 'It may be a scheduled appointment.'

It may be? What if it wasn't? Surely she would have told him if it was routine? She'd mentioned her antenatal appointments in the past. And he'd made a point of not engaging with the information. He didn't want to give her false hopes where his involvement with the child was concerned. But, even so, he knew she would have said something if she was going to be late home. They had a ball to attend tonight, which was why he had arrived home early... That and the fact he seemed less and less able to stay at the office when he knew she awaited him at the house.

Katherine had been tired last night, after returning from a concert they'd attended at the O2. He'd sourced the box seats because he'd caught her dancing to one of the famous band's songs a few weeks ago, and had watched her unobserved, charmed by the sight. He should have left her alone last night and returned to the penthouse after dropping her off, but he hadn't been able to stop himself, the excuse of ensuring she was okay having morphed into something urgent and unstoppable once they'd got to her bedroom.

The guilt that had been sitting at the back of his mind all day tightened its claws around his neck now like a malevolent beast.

Her subdued mood last night had left him holding her a little tighter as he waited for her to drift to sleep in the early hours of the morning. And it had been harder than ever to pull himself out of the bed and leave her to return to his own place.

Deepening their relationship was not part of the deal. And not something he wanted. Because it would only complicate things when he had to let her go. But perhaps he should have stayed with her last night.

'How was she this morning?' he barked, not quite able to keep the frantic urgency out of his voice.

Damn. If he'd woken up with her he would know the answer to this question. Why hadn't he stayed?

'She seemed tired, Mr Wolfe,' the housekeeper said. 'But then she had an early morning meeting, so she had to leave an hour ahead of her usual schedule.'

'She… What time did she get up?' he rasped, the malevolent beast beating on his ribs now.

'Six o'clock.'

He swore under his breath, the guilt and panic turning to anger. She hadn't fallen asleep until two a.m. Why hadn't she told him she had to be up so early? He wouldn't have kept her up half the night if she had.

'Is there a problem, Mr Wolfe?' the housekeeper asked.

Yes, there's a damn problem. My wife may be seriously unwell and it's my fault. And her fault, for not telling me to leave her alone.

His mind reeled, the unguarded feelings starting to overwhelm him.

'No,' he snapped. He headed back through the house towards the entrance hall, tugging his phone out of his pocket en route and speed-dialling Katherine's number. But as he charged down the hallway, intending to drive straight to Harley Street, an echo of his phone's ring tone sounded.

He stopped in the entrance hall to see his wife standing by the front door.

'Katherine!' He charged towards her and grasped her shoulders as the panic surged. 'Are you okay? What were you doing at the doctor's?'

'Jack?' Her eyebrows launched up her forehead, but he could see the fatigue still shadowing her eyes. 'What are you doing here so early?' she said, apropos to absolutely nothing.

'I asked first,' he said. 'What's wrong?' He forced himself to stare at the slight mound of her stomach, which he had noticed more and more in the last few weeks whenever they made love. 'Is it the pregnancy?'

'Nothing's wrong,' she said, but he could hear the weary note in her voice as she tried to shrug off his hold. His grip tightened.

'Jack, you need to let me go,' she said with strained patience, as if he were holding her for the fun of it. As if his head wasn't starting to explode. Why the hell couldn't she give him a straight answer? Was something seriously wrong and she didn't want to tell him?

'My phone's ringing and I need to answer it,' she added, cutting through the flash flood of disaster scenarios in his head.

He cursed, letting go of her with one hand, to fish his own phone out of his pocket and turn it off.

The confusion in her eyes darkened. 'Why were you calling me?'

'Why the hell do you think?' he shouted, frustration and fury pushing up his throat to party with the guilt and panic. 'You're always at home when I get here in the evening. You weren't here, and then Mrs Goulding told me you were at the doctor's and I—'

'It was a routine scan,' she interrupted.

The panic babbling stopped so abruptly, his fingers loosened.

She shrugged out of his hold.

His temper ignited. 'Well, that's just great!' he said, pushing the guilt back down his throat with an effort. 'Why didn't you tell me you had an appointment?' Had she planned to freak him out deliberately?

Was this some kind of dumb test? To push him into

admitting she meant something to him? Something more than they'd originally agreed on?

Because of course she did. Maybe this arrangement had no future, but he'd been sleeping with her every night for over a month—hell, he'd even started to neglect his business so he could spend more time with her.

The endless meetings and problems he had to attend to, being available twenty-four-seven to his managers and advisors, had become a chore over the last three weeks. He had turned down a ton of business trips—had even chosen not to travel to the product launch in Tokyo of a new tech company he'd acquired last year when it had clashed with the opening of Katherine's shop. Because he hadn't been able to bear to spend forty-eight hours away from her.

Of course, he could have insisted as per their original contract, that she travel with him. But he simply hadn't had the heart to tear her away from her business when she was clearly so excited about developing it.

And then there were their weekends, when he'd started to make excuses to be with her. He'd always worked at weekends in the past. But gradually, after they'd returned from the Maldives, he'd begun concocting reasons to contact her, spend quality time with her. And not just to coax her into bed. They had taken drives in the countryside, long walks in the park, watched movies in the house's basement cinema, or frolicked in the lap pool he'd had installed in the two-hundred-foot garden.

Yet another sign of how dependent on her company he had become.

He'd tried to convince himself it was still all about the sex—the quality time just an intriguing prelude to jumping each other. But this incessant need that never seemed to end—no matter how many times he took her, how many times they took each other—had forced him to realise that wasn't the whole truth. She meant something to him. Much more than she should. But instead of looking guilty or even contrite, she stared back at him now as if he'd lost the plot.

'Why would I tell you about the scan, Jack?' she asked with a weary resignation that made his ribs contract around his thundering heart. 'When you're not interested.'

She went to pass him, but he grabbed her arm. 'Wait a minute. What is that supposed to mean?'

'Why don't you figure it out?' she said, the sudden snap in her tone surprising him. He shook off the residual hum of guilt. *He* wasn't the one in the wrong here. She should have told him she had a doctor's appointment. So he hadn't had to find out from the housekeeper. End of.

'You think I don't care about your welfare?' he demanded, the turmoil of emotions making his anger surge. 'Of course I care. I care about you. A lot. *There.* Are you happy?'

But, instead of looking smug, her chin tucked into her chest as she sighed.

When her gaze lifted back to his, he could see the shocking sheen of tears. The sight punctured the self-righteous fury with the precision of a high velocity bullet, leaving shock in its wake.

'No, Jack,' she said, so quietly he almost couldn't hear her. 'I'm not happy.'

A single tear slipped from the corner of her eye before she could wipe it away with an impatient fist. And the shock reverberated in his chest like an earthquake.

She dug her teeth into her bottom lip to stop it trembling, her gaze bold and determined, but also somehow broken. The emerald-green, sparkling with all the tears she refused to shed, only crucified him more.

This was what he'd been determined to guard against—why he'd snuck out of her bed each night even though the desire to hold her, to keep her safe, had been all but overwhelming. Why he'd forced himself not to ask all the questions he wanted answers to about her father, her past, about the strong, clever teenager he wished he'd known back when they'd both been still too young to protect themselves.

And, because of that, he heard himself ask a question he knew he shouldn't want the answer to...but did.

'Why aren't you happy?'

Katie stared at her husband, her limbs saturated with exhaustion. The sight of him—strong and indomitable and hopelessly wary—was making sensation flutter and glow in her belly even now.

He'd taken off his jacket and tie, his short hair stuck up in spikes as if he'd run his fingers through it several times. His gaze roamed over her, his eyes searching and a little wild, as he pressed a warm hand to her shoulder then stroked his thumb down her arm.

The prickle of sensation which was always there when he touched her rolled through her. But with it came the fierce pulse of emotion she no longer had any control over.

She'd thrown herself into this relationship in the weeks since they had returned from the Maldives, forced the emotion down and let the heat take over so she could give them both time. To get to know each other, to feel comfortable. But as they'd begun to settle into a routine, the more Jack had let her see of that runaway boy who needed love the way she had, the harder it had been not to push, not to probe, not to beg for more.

Every time he made love to her with such fervour then left her sleeping alone. Every time they had a discussion about business, marketing or her latest cupcake recipe but he'd deflected any questions he deemed too personal. Every time she sent him an email with her latest schedule of antenatal appointments and scans but she got no response.

She blinked, the prickle of sensation turning to something deep, fluid and even more disturbing.

She didn't *want* to feel this way. Didn't want him to show her this side of himself. A caring, tender, nurturing side she was sure he didn't even realise he possessed. Because the more she saw of it, the more real their relationship seemed.

Like the time he'd caught her dancing in the kitchen and she'd seen the spontaneous, boyish smile curving his lips. Or the times he had suggested, more and more of late, that they do something together at the weekend, that he didn't need to work. Like the tension in his jaw she'd begun to notice whenever she yawned and he asked if she were okay. Or the leap of hunger and something more— something rich with relief and even joy—that turned his blue eyes to a rich cobalt when he came here each evening and found her.

And the moment last night, when she'd discovered he had paid a small fortune for tickets to a sold-out concert because he believed she liked the band that was playing. She hadn't even realised it was the same band who had done the song she had been dancing to several weeks before until he'd mentioned it oh, so casually. A part of her had been overjoyed. But another part of her had been devastated. How could he be so observant, so thoughtful, and yet not know how much it meant to her?

And how was she supposed to stop herself from falling hopelessly in love with that man?

But this afternoon had been the wake-up call she needed. The signal she had to start demanding more of him, or she would be lost. She'd seen her baby's three-dimensional image on the ultrasound equipment. She'd devoured the incredible sight of its tiny nose and mouth, the closed eyelids, its long limbs—just like its father's. She'd laughed at Dr Patel pointing out it was sucking its thumb, and shed a few stunned tears when she'd made the decision to find out the baby's sex after the doctor had told her she had a clear image of its sexual organs.

All those emotions had bombarded her—excitement, awe, wonder… And yet at the same time her heart had felt as if it were being ripped away from her chest wall. Because she'd experienced all those incredible, life-altering moments alone. Because Jack had chosen not to be there with her.

It hurt even more to see the stunned compassion on his face now, the wary confusion at her tears. And the defensiveness in his eyes. Because a part of her knew the words he had just flung at her like missiles, words which had stunned her, were true. He *did* care about her. Probably much more than he wanted to. But how could that be enough? For her or their baby?

'Why aren't you happy?' he'd asked her, as if he really didn't know.

Maybe he didn't.

She sucked in an unsteady breath, determined not to let another tear fall. She hated tears. They didn't solve anything. And she refused to be that woman who broke down rather than ask for what she wanted.

She'd been trying to have this conversation for weeks, and it had been like thumping her head against a brick wall, but he had given her an opening this time, and she would be a fool not to take it.

'You know, I saw our baby properly for the first time today on the ultrasound,' she said as conversationally as she could manage.

Something flickered in his eyes, something wary, tense and instantly guarded. But when he didn't say anything, didn't stop her or try to deflect the conversation as he always had before, the fragile bubble of hope expanded in her chest.

'Dr Patel told me what she thinks the sex is. Would you like to know?'

He stared at her, his expression unreadable.

'Of course, it's not one hundred percent, but Dr Patel was pretty sure. She said about eighty-five percent sure.' She was babbling now, but when his gaze shifted to her stomach, as she had seen it do so many times in the last few weeks as her bump had become more pronounced, the bubble grew. 'Aren't you even a little bit curious?' she asked.

His gaze lifted back to her face. He wanted to say no. She could see it in his eyes. So she blurted it out before he could stop her... 'It's a boy.'

His brows rose, the slash of colour on his cheeks hard to interpret. Was he pleased, surprised, indifferent? Why couldn't she tell even now? How did he manage to keep so much of himself back? Not just from her, but from their child? Would it always be like this?

Was this still all about that young boy he wouldn't talk about? The lost, brutalised child he'd given her a glimpse of in the Maldives and then refused to acknowledge ever since?

He looked away from her and she could see he was struggling from the tell-tale muscle twitching in his jaw. But what was he struggling with?

'I was thinking of the name Daniel,' she ventured.

His head swung back round. 'No. I don't like that name.'

'Oh, okay,' she managed, but her heart soared. It was the most he had ever given her. The first sign he cared enough about this baby to have a preference. Maybe this didn't have to be a lost cause. Had she given up far too soon? Allowed her own feelings for him to colour the progress they'd made? Feelings that perhaps weren't as unrequited as she'd assumed. Perhaps this wasn't so much about him but about her, and her own desire to protect herself. She was letting everything get mixed up in her head because she was scared too. Scared he would reject her the way her father had. But he'd already given her so much more, without even realising it.

'If you've got any suggestions, I'm all ears,' she managed, her throat thickening with emotion again. Did he know how significant this moment was?

The discomfort in his face was clear. Obviously, he did. But then he murmured, 'I'll think about it.' He glanced at his watch. 'We're supposed to be going to the Collington Charity Ball tonight.' His penetrating gaze searched her face, the wariness returning full force. 'You're tired. If you'd rather avoid it, I can make your excuses.'

Not on your life.

Her heart galloped into her throat, the stupid bubble of hope expanding so fast it was almost choking her. He'd said he cared about her. He'd clearly freaked out when he'd thought she was ill. And he had offered an opinion about the baby's name. And okay, it *had* been reluctantly, but after weeks of what had felt like no progress she was not about to let this shining, shimmering gift horse out of her sight.

'Give me an hour to dress,' she said, and left him standing in the hallway, the weary resignation lifting off her shoulders as she all but skipped up the stairs.

It wasn't enough, but it was enough for now. This didn't have to be about his past or hers. This could be about their future. A future she suddenly felt sure was so much brighter now than it had been an hour ago in the ultra-sound suite.

Jack Wolfe *could* be a father. All she had to do was let go of her own insecurities long enough to show him.

A boy?

The information reverberated in Jack's skull, doing nothing to deaden the fear that had been tormenting him for close to an hour as he paused in the doorway of his wife's suite.

She stood in the next room, checking out the fit of her dress for tonight's ball in the mirror, unaware of his presence.

His breath got trapped in his lungs.

The rich, red satin hugged her bold curves, lifting her full breasts, accentuating her lush bottom. The pale skin revealed by the gown's plunging back and the sprinkle of freckles across her bare shoulder blades were given a pearly glow by the room's diffused lighting. He wanted to put his lips at the base of her spine, trail kisses up the delicious line of her backbone to her nape.

He knew exactly how she tasted there, in the hollow beneath her earlobe. And how she would respond—first with surprise, then with excitement, exhilaration and a hunger which matched his own—holding nothing back.

He shoved his hands into his pockets and forced himself not to walk into the room and begin unravelling her outfit. Because in the last hour the flicker of joy, of belonging, of protectiveness which always assailed him when he returned to the house in Mayfair, seemed somehow threatening in a way it never had before.

She moved, revealing the compact curve of her belly, and the fear dropped into his belly like an unexploded bomb. The jumble of emotions which had been festering for an hour collided as he recalled the hope in her eyes. The last thing he wanted to do right now was escort her to the VIP charity event, to parade her in front of a load of other men like a trophy, an acquisition, even though that was exactly what she was supposed to be.

This arrangement had always had a sell-by date. How had he lost sight of that in the last month? After tonight he would have to re-establish the emotional distance he'd lost, or how else would he be able to control the deep pulse of regret, of longing, of loneliness which was already building when he was forced to let her go?

He cleared his throat and she swung round. The brief flicker of joy in her emerald eyes that he'd seen so many times in the past few weeks wrapped around his heart, scaring him even more.

'Jack?' she whispered, the sound raw. 'Is it time to go?'

He made himself walk into the room, aware of her appreciative gaze gliding over his figure in the tailored tuxedo. 'Yes, we should probably make a move,' he said, trying to keep his tone impersonal, to cover the emotions churning inside him and stop himself from blurting out what he wanted to say to her.

This isn't a marriage of convenience any more.

But even the thought of saying those words made him feel weak and pathetic and needy.

He placed a hand on her bare shoulder, felt her shudder of response. But, instead of placing his lips on the fluttering pulse in her collarbone, he slid his palm down her arm then lifted her fingers to his lips.

'You look beautiful,' he said as he kissed her knuckles and watched the leap of joy flicker again in her eyes at the inadequate complement.

He straightened and let her hand drop, the fear gripping his throat again.

'Jack, is something wrong?' she asked, pressing her palms against the smooth satin of the dress, her gaze far too astute.

'We need to go or we'll be late,' he said.

Her throat contracted as she swallowed. 'Okay.'

He didn't want to hurt her, but he knew he would, because he could never be the man she needed.

CHAPTER THIRTEEN

'How about Sebastian? Or Luca? I've always liked Luca,' Katie offered, excited as the chauffeur-driven car stopped in front of the ornate redbrick façade of the Drapers' Hall where the charity ball they were attending was being held.

Jack sent her a quelling look. 'We're here.'

She grinned back at him, refusing to be put off by his usual reserve when it came to talking about the baby. Talking about their son. The giddy hope had her beaming smiles and even waving at the barrage of press photographers as Jack escorted her into the hall. The smile didn't even dim as Jack led her into an imposing marble-columned ballroom, the gold leaf glimmering in the light of the chandeliers.

For once she didn't feel like a complete fraud as Jack introduced her to the array of VIP guests and business people who always gravitated towards her husband when they arrived at these sorts of events.

My husband.

Funny that tonight she actually felt like Jack's wife. And the mother of his child. Obviously this was still an arrangement, a bargain, a marriage with a sell-by date stamped on it. But they'd taken a huge step forward tonight. Not just when Jack had told her he cared about her, but when he had kissed her hand with such tenderness, such reverence, in her dressing room. She felt closer to him now than she ever had before.

She cupped her belly absently, excited about the pregnancy in a way she had never been before. What if they could do this together? What if she didn't have to do this alone?

She felt as if she were floating—with only Jack's stalwart presence by her side to anchor her to earth—as the evening sped past. She chatted enthusiastically about everything from how to bake the perfect brownie, with the French ambassador, to the wonder of Wolfe Maldives with an award-winning actress who was heading to the resort next month after her current film finished shooting. For once the small talk wasn't a chore and she didn't feel as if she was lying when she talked about her honeymoon or her husband.

But, after two hours on her feet, Katie began to flag.

'You look tired. Would you like to return home?' Jack asked but, just as she placed her fingers on his forearm for some much-needed support, about to give him a resounding yes, his muscles became rigid. His face hardened as his gaze locked on something over her shoulder.

She turned to see a tall, elegant, older man walking through the crowd straight towards them.

'Who's that?' she asked, concerned at the cold light that had entered Jack's eyes.

'No one,' he said, the bite in his tone chilling.

But, before she could say more, the man reached them. 'Mr Wolfe, I presume,' he said, the quirk of his lips doing nothing to dispel the hostile tone.

The man had a patrician handsomeness, the few lines on his tanned face making it hard to tell how old he was—probably in his mid-sixties, with his carefully styled hair more salt than pepper. There was something, though—

about the line of his jaw, the powerful way he moved, the brilliant blue of his eyes—which looked familiar.

Who was he? Katie was sure she had never met him, but she instinctively didn't like him, any more than her husband seemed to.

'I understand you are now our majority shareholder...' The man paused dramatically, the cold gleam in his eyes becoming laser-sharp, then murmured, 'Son.'

Jack jolted as if he'd been shot.

'I see you thought I didn't know,' the man continued, when Jack remained silent, the enmity thick in the air. Katie's skin chilled and her stomach jumped as realisation dawned—the physical similarities between them glaringly obvious now.

Was this man Jack's biological father?

The thought stunned her on one level, but horrified her on another, because there was no joy in the meeting—on either side.

The man gave a grim chuckle, both superior and condescending. 'My dear boy, did you really believe I would allow an upstart like you to own Smyth-Brown if I didn't want you to?'

Katie hated him, whoever he was, for treating Jack with such obvious contempt. She could feel the muscles in Jack's forearm flexing beneath her fingertips as he struggled to control his reaction.

'It won't make a difference,' Jack said, the words ground out on a husk of breath. 'I intend to destroy your legacy,' he added. 'For what you did to my mother.'

Katie's heart broke at the pain she could hear in Jack's voice, and the bone-deep regret she could see etched in the rigid line of his jaw.

But, instead of being cowed by the threat, the man—Jack's father—simply smiled, the tight line of his lips devoid of humour. 'Hmm, I see. Interesting you would blame me for her idiotic decision to marry that oaf,' he said as if he were having a conversation about the weather rather than an event that had robbed Jack of his childhood. 'Although it is a pity the brute maimed you.'

'You son of a...' Jack launched forward, his anger exploding as he grabbed the older man by his lapels.

Katie grasped his arm. 'Jack, don't. He's not worth it,' she pleaded, suddenly desperate to get him away from here. To protect him from the prying eyes of the growing crowd, riveted to the developing altercation.

She knew how much Jack valued his emotional control and his standing in the business community. Something he'd worked his whole life to gain. And she suspected a public fight was just what this bastard wanted—to expose Jack as a brute, an oaf, like the man who had scarred him.

What gave him the right to do that? When he had no part in Jack's life—or the phenomenal success he had made of it?

Jack's gaze met hers and she saw the flicker of confusion beneath the fury before the anger was downgraded enough for him to release his captive so abruptly, the man stumbled backwards.

'We should leave,' Katie said gently, touching his cheek, forcing him to look at her. Her heart yearned to tell him the words she realised she should have told him weeks ago. But she couldn't say them here, so she tried to convey them telepathically.

I love you. You matter to me. Whatever he did to you doesn't. Not any more.

He nodded, but as he gripped her hand, intending to lead them both out of the ballroom, the bastard stepped into her path.

'So this is the delightful Mrs Wolfe,' the man said, offering her his hand as if he hadn't just tried to emotionally destroy her husband. Katie ignored it.

'Daniel Smyth at your service, my dear,' he added.

Daniel.

Before she had a chance to register the name and what it might mean, his cold gaze skimmed over her belly then lifted back to her face, the satisfied smile even more chilling. 'Did you know, my dear, I required my son marry as part of the deal for him to acquire Smyth-Brown. I needed an heir, but I really didn't think he would be quite so accommodating as to provide me with two heirs for the price of one so soon.'

What?

'Get out of our way,' Jack snarled, shoving Smyth back as he strode past him and led her out of the ballroom, the click of camera phones and the man's cruel laughter following in their wake.

'Do you really believe you can destroy my legacy, boy?' he shouted after them, sounding vaguely mad. 'When you *are* my legacy?'

Katie felt stunned, shaky, disorientated, her mind a mass of confusing emotions as Jack led her to the waiting car and helped her inside.

'Jack… Why—?' she began as the car pulled away from the kerb, suddenly desperate to contain the fear contracting around her ribs and making it hard to breathe.

'I don't want to talk about it,' he cut her off, the tone rigid with barely leashed fury as the car drove down Piccadilly towards home.

Except it isn't his home.

Her body trembled as her hands strayed to her belly.

It's my home and our baby's home. Not his. Because he doesn't want it to be. Any more than he will ever want us.

Her mind struggled to engage with the thoughts careering around in her head. The emotions battered her as the hope she'd nurtured so diligently and so pointlessly for so long finally began to die.

He sat beside her saying nothing, offering no explanation, no solace, no comfort.

The hideous things that had happened to him as a child didn't give her a connection with him, she realised. They didn't have a shared pain after both having been rejected by their fathers. This was *his* pain. A pain he guarded so jealously, so relentlessly, he had married her just to destroy the man who had caused it.

The silence stretched, creating a chasm between them, until the distance felt like millions of miles instead of only a few feet.

The car pulled into the driveway of the Grosvenor Square house. Jack got out, dismissed the chauffeur and walked round the car to open her door.

She stepped out into the night, still dazed. His warm palm settled on her back to direct her into the house, the traitorous ripple only damning her more as he closed the front door and helped her off with her wrap.

'Thank God that's over with,' he said, his hands cupping her stomach as he dragged her back against his body, his lips finding the rampant pulse in her neck.

She jolted as ripples flooded her core at the feel of his already burgeoning erection pressing into her back.

His mouth devoured the spot under her earlobe he knew was supremely sensitive.

'Let's go to bed,' he suggested, but the raw, seductive command—one she had succumbed to so many times before—finally tore away the last of the fog until all that was left was the pain.

And the stark, gruelling light of truth.

'No,' she said, lurching out of his arms, wrenching herself away from the traitorous need.

'Damn it. I need you tonight, Katherine,' he said, his voice raw, his expression more transparent than she had ever seen it before.

She could see the hurt, the anger, the bitter confusion and the desperation the encounter with his father had caused. But she could also see in the rigid line of his jaw, in the anger sparking in his eyes, that this wasn't about her, about them, and it never had been.

She was nothing more than a temporary port in a storm, their marriage nothing more than a convenient means for him to get his revenge for everything he'd suffered in childhood. Her heart broke for that brutalised child…but there was another child now, one who needed her love and support more.

She steeled herself against the desire to soothe, to console, to take the pain away the only way he would let her. And forced herself to say what she had to say.

'I can't do this any more, Jack. You need to leave.'

'What…? Why?' Jack yelled, the stubborn refusal on Katherine's face—and the pulse of desperation swelling in his groin—all but crucifying him.

'Because it's not me you need, Jack,' she said, her voice breaking on the words and only crucifying him more. 'It's your revenge.'

The fury surged. The fury that had been building ever since Daniel Smyth had strolled towards him with that smug, entitled smile on his face and Jack had been forced to face the sickening realisation that the son of a bitch had played him all along.

He knew who I was. Right from the start.

Daniel Smyth had got the board to insist Jack marry

above his station so he could make the kid from a run-down council estate whom he had discarded before he'd even been born somehow worthy to become his heir. And Jack had eventually fallen right into the trap.

But that horrifying revelation, the cruel trick he'd allowed himself to fall for, wasn't nearly as gutting as the closed expression on Katherine's face now.

If only he could just lose himself in her. Forget about tonight, about his past, about the whole sick, stupid mess. He knew none of it would matter any more. After all, he hadn't really married her to get the shares. He'd married her for a host of other reasons. But as he lifted his hand to touch her cheek, to draw her back in, she stepped back.

'When you said you didn't like the name Daniel, I thought we were having a discussion about our son.'

He let his hand drop. So they were back to that. 'Katherine, I told you I can't—'

'But tonight I found out,' she cut him off, the quiver of regret in her hushed tone crushing him, 'I found out it had nothing to do with him. It was just another part of your past you won't allow me to see.'

'I told you on our wedding night what I can offer the child,' he said, even though it felt like a lie now. 'And what I can't.'

She simply stared at him, the gleam of tears almost more than he could bear. 'I know,' she said, so softly he almost didn't hear her. 'And I believed you then. But that was before I fell in love with you.'

'You…' The flood of need hit him square in the chest. But right behind it was the fear. 'No, you don't…' he said, locking away all the emotions he couldn't afford to feel.

One side of her mouth quirked in a sad half-smile, but the sense of hopelessness hovered like a dark cloud in the hallway. 'I spent the whole of my childhood trying to make my father love me. I can't do that with you, Jack. I won't.' Her hand covered her stomach where their child grew. 'I have to protect myself and my child. I don't want you here any more.'

She turned and walked away from him.

He stood, rigid with shock and anger for several seconds, desperate to chase after her, to make her want him, the way he had so many times before.

But the scar burned on his cheek, the agony real again, and so raw.

He'd begged Harry Wolfe to want him, to care about him, because he'd felt so scared. So desperate. And all it had done was left him more alone. He'd be damned if he'd make that mistake a second time.

She would come back to him. On his terms. And, until she did, he would survive without her.

But as he marched out of the house, and slammed the door behind him, it felt as if part of his heart was being wrenched from his body.

The bitter irony was, it was the part of his heart he thought he had killed a long time ago.

CHAPTER FOURTEEN

'GORINDA, I NEED you to speak to Dr Patel's office again. I'm paying the damn bills for my wife's care. I expect to be given regular updates on her condition and I've heard nothing in two weeks,' Jack announced as he marched past his PA into his office.

Two damned weeks Katherine had been sulking. And he was through playing nice, with her or the obstetrician who was charging a fortune for her care. He needed to know she was okay, that was all. Was it too much to ask he be kept informed?

'Mr Wolfe, I've spoken to Dr Patel's administrator several times already.' Jack glanced up from his desk to see his PA's harassed expression. 'I'm afraid she says they can't give you updates on Mrs Wolfe's care without your wife's permission. It's a matter of patient confidentiality.'

'She specifically asked I not be informed?' Jack demanded, the shock combining with the frustration and fury...

The last two weeks had seemed like two years. He'd waited for her to contact him, to call him, to ask him to return to the house in Mayfair.

But she hadn't.

He wasn't sleeping, was barely eating, the yearning to hold her, to make love to her, even to see the changes the pregnancy had made to her body, so intense he could barely function.

For two weeks he'd waited for the yearning to stop so he could return to who he had been before he had met her.

A man alone. A man apart.

But, as he stared at his PA's flushed face, the brutal stab of rejection made him realise that Katherine had destroyed that man—somehow—so comprehensively, he didn't feel like a success any more. He didn't even feel happy in his own skin.

The unfulfilled desire, the physical longing that woke him from fitful dreams—leaving him hard, ready, aching and groping for her in his bed, only to find it empty— was bad enough. But the emotions he couldn't control, the nightmares he couldn't contain, were so much worse. The thought of a lifetime without her smile, her quick wit, her passion, or her companionship, was destroying him from within. And he didn't know how to overcome it. Hell, he even missed her smart mouth and her absolute refusal to do as she was told.

'Apparently she did, Mr Wolfe,' Gorinda replied, sounding almost as weary as he felt.

So Katherine had cut him loose. She'd told him she loved him. But she'd lied.

Devastation hit him.

He thrust his fingers through his hair, only to become aware his hands were shaking. How had she come to mean so much to him when she was never meant to? And how did he make this pain stop now?

He got up from his desk to stare out at the City's skyline—the gothic splendour of Tower Bridge, the gleaming mirrored sheen of The Shard on the opposite bank. It was a view that had once had the power to excite and motivate him, to make him proud of how far he'd come, but today, like every day for the last fortnight, the view seemed dull and listless, ostentatious and unimpressive.

'Dr Patel's receptionist did mention Mrs Wolfe is going to be at the clinic this morning,' Gorinda added. 'Perhaps you could join her there? To find out how she is?'

He swung round at the tentative suggestion to find Gorinda watching him with sympathy in her warm brown eyes.

But I don't want to be a part of the baby's life...

The automatic thought echoed in his head. But even thinking it felt like a lie now. It wasn't that he didn't want to be a part of this baby's life, it was that he was scared to be. Sure he'd fail at fatherhood... The way he'd failed at so much else.

'Okay,' he heard himself say.

And suddenly it all seemed so simple.

He *had* to fix this. To hell with his pride, his fear of fatherhood, his fear of asking her—no, *begging* her—to take him back, his fear of letting her see the frightened boy instead of the man he had become... None of it meant anything any more without her.

Why had it taken him so long to realise she had always been what was missing in his life?

'Rearrange my schedule and text me the address,' he said as he charged back out of the office. Of course, he had absolutely no idea *how* he was going to fix it. Or even if he could fix it. He'd just have to wing it, he thought, with a great deal more confidence than he felt.

'Yes, sir,' Gorinda replied.

If Katherine didn't want to see him, he'd just have to deal with that when he got to the clinic. But he couldn't stay away from her... Or the baby... Not a moment longer...

'I'm sorry, Mr Wolfe, your wife is having a private consultation.'
'I don't care.'

Katie shifted on the bed at the shouted comments coming from outside the ultrasound suite.

'What on earth...?' Dr Patel murmured as she put down the tube of gel she had been about to put on Katie's stomach and clicked off the machine.

But before either she or Katie could do anything more the door burst open and Jack strode in.

'Mr Wolfe! I'm sorry, you'll have to leave...' The doctor began, but Jack marched right past her, sat down in the chair beside the bed and lifted Katie's hand.

'Let me stay, Katherine. I want to meet our son,' he said, his voice thick with desperation, his eyes wild with urgency and something else...something so naked and unguarded, she wondered for a moment if she was dreaming. If she had conjured up this moment from weeks of crying herself to sleep each night.

'Jack...' she finally rasped.

'Please,' he said, and the gentle buzz of his kiss jolted her out of her trance.

'Could you leave us for a minute?' she said to Dr Patel, somehow managing to remain calm while she struggled to sit up and place a sheet over her belly.

Dr Patel nodded and left the room.

'Jack, what are you doing here?' she managed around the painful lump in her throat.

He looked distraught, she realised. But beneath the wild intensity in his expression she could also see determination. And need.

He placed his palm on her belly and rubbed the sheet so gently, she felt tears sting her eyes. 'I want to meet him too,' he said. 'Please, let me.'

She placed her hand over his, but as the joy throbbed heavily in her chest right behind it was the brutal weight of sadness, the hollow ache she had struggled to come to terms with for so long.

'Okay,' she said.

She wanted Jack to be part of his baby's life. And whatever had made him change his mind, she would always be grateful for it. But she knew there was so much else she wanted from him that she could never have. And she couldn't let the hope back in again, or it would destroy her.

'Thank you,' he said, his head dropping down until his forehead rested on her belly. He caressed the bump, his shoulders shuddering with the release of emotion. 'I'm so sorry for being such a coward.'

'Jack, it's okay.' She touched a shaky hand to his head and let her fingers stroke the short silky strands, her heart shattering in her chest. 'I would never stop you from being a part of the baby's life. You can come with me to the scans from now on. And once the baby's born you can have all the visitation rights you want.'

He lifted his head suddenly, dislodging her hand. 'But I don't want visitation rights,' he said.

'Why not?' she asked, her throat so clogged with emotion now, she could barely talk.

He whisked away the tear that had fallen from her lid. 'Because I want us to be a family. I want to move in with you, have a real marriage, stop running and start building something that will last.'

'*Really?*' she said but, even as the balloon of hope expanded so much that it began to hurt, the insecurities she thought she'd jettisoned so long ago flooded back.

'Of course, Katherine,' he said, as if the answer she had failed to grasp was obvious. His face softened. 'I've been an idiot. Too much of a coward, to tell you the truth. That I was terrified of becoming a father. Because I didn't know how...'

'Having met your biological father,' Katherine said, the anger that still lingered after their encounter with Daniel Smyth sharpening her words, 'I understand why you might be wary. But you're not like him, Jack. You never could be.'

'I know,' he said. 'Which is why I told my broker to sell the damn shares on the way here. I don't want any part of his company. Not even to tear it to pieces.'

'You…you don't? But why?'

'Because you were right,' he said, his eyes shining. 'I don't need my revenge if I can have you instead.' His hand caressed the mound of her belly. 'And this fella too.'

His eyes met hers and she could see every single thing he was thinking for the first time ever… She saw sincerity, desire, fierce determination, even fear, but most of all desperate, unguarded hope.

'I need you, Katherine,' he said. He thrust his fingers through his hair, looking momentarily dumbfounded. 'Hell, I think I started to fall for you that first night when you were wearing that ridiculous outfit and I couldn't even see you properly. But I could sense your bravery and your boldness and I knew I wanted you, more than anything in the world.' He groaned.

'You…you do?' she croaked, so shocked by the heartfelt declaration, she could barely breathe, let alone think. But the insecurities were still there, asking… How could she trust him? How could she be enough, when she never had been for anyone before now?

'Yeah,' he said. His hand, trembling with emotion, gripped hers so tightly, it was as if he was holding her heart. 'I do.'

She shook her head but, despite the love that flooded through her, she tugged her fingers out of his. 'How can you be sure?'

'What? What do you mean?' he asked, his voice raw.

'How do you know I'm enough now, when I wasn't before?'

'Stop it, Katherine,' he said, looking desperate again. 'I'm telling you I love you. Why won't you believe me? Is this something to do with that bastard Medford? You think I'm like him?'

'No,' she said. 'But…' She stared at him, her heart breaking. But she couldn't back down again, couldn't just accept this at face value. 'Maybe it is. I always thought I'd got over his rejection. That it didn't matter to me. But maybe I never stopped being that girl in some ways. Because I want to believe you, but I can't.'

He took her hand again and held it, his gaze steady, direct, unbreakable. 'Tell me what I need to do to make it right.'

She eased herself onto her elbows until she was sitting up. 'Can you…can you tell me what Daniel Smyth did to make you hate him so?'

'I don't hate him. I don't even care about him any more. I told you that,' he said, but she could hear the defensiveness. And knew she needed to know all of it if she was ever going to put her doubts to rest. She needed to know he trusted her enough to let her in. All the way in. It was a big ask. She got that. And maybe this was about her insecurities as much as his. But she deserved to know or she would never be able to let go of the thought that she was still just a port in a storm, someone he might decide to discard again.

'I know.' She touched his scarred cheek, her heart breaking as she felt him lean into the caress instinctively. 'And I believe you. But I still want to meet that boy. To know him. To understand him.'

So I can love all of him, if he'll let me.

'You don't want to know him. Believe me,' he said, the bitterness thick in his tone. 'He was a little—'

'No, he wasn't,' she interrupted him. 'He was scared and alone, the way I was. What did he do to you, Jack?'

'Daniel Smyth tried to force my mother to have an abortion.' The words guttered out, making the anguish tighten in her belly. *Oh, no.*

'She didn't, obviously, or I wouldn't be here. But that's how she ended up with my stepfather. She wasn't self-sufficient like you are,' he said, his voice so quiet, it barely registered. But still she felt the jolt of pride at the approval in his tone, her doubts starting to drift away. He had always seen her for who she really was, had always admired the things about her her father had despised. How could she have forgotten that?

'Is that why you insisted on marrying me?' she asked, touched beyond belief. He had been showing her all along, who that boy was, and she hadn't even realised. 'Because he'd refused to help her?'

He stared at her, his gaze guarded again. 'Well, it's not the only reason.' He ran his palm over her belly again, caressing, sending the urgent desire through her body and making her smile. 'I wanted you. And… I needed you. But I didn't want to admit it. Not even to myself. Because it scared the hell out of me.'

'Oh, Jack.' She threw her arms around his neck, the happy tears flooding out—with no help whatsoever from the pregnancy hormones, for once. 'Yes. I love you. Let's be a family.'

'Wait a minute!' He drew back and held her at arm's length, his gaze confused. 'That's it? That's all you needed to hear?'

She nodded and grinned, despite the tears clogging her throat and rolling down her cheeks. 'I've been an idiot too. You showed me that boy. I just didn't see him. We're equals. That's all I needed know.'

'Thank God,' he said, then pulled her into his embrace and buried his face in her neck as she told him how much she loved him amidst watery kisses.

And when they finally got to look at their baby together for the first time, ten minutes later—and Jack bombarded poor Dr Patel with a ton of questions it would never even have occurred to Katie to ask—Katie knew for sure that neither of them would ever be alone again.

Because they had each other. Always.

EPILOGUE

Five months later

'WHAT BIG LUNGS you have, Master Wolfe.' Jack grinned down at the angry little face of the baby held securely in his arms as the tiny infant screwed up his eyes and launched into another angry, ear-splitting wail.

'All the better to drive us both mad with!' His wife grinned tiredly from the bed across the room.

'Shh, shh, little fella. It's okay. Daddy's here,' Jack said as he rocked the baby while crossing the room—to absolutely no avail. Young Master Wolfe was not happy. 'Sorry, Red,' he added, aware of how tired Katherine looked. 'I was hoping we wouldn't wake you.'

It was midnight. They'd only brought their son home this morning after Katherine had endured a twenty-two-hour labour. Jack adored his son to pieces, his awe and gratitude knowing no bounds when the baby had been handed to him after he'd cut the umbilical cord at the midwife's suggestion.

But no way in hell were they ever having another child. The labour had nearly killed him, and watching Katherine battle bravely through so much pain still had anxiety gripping his throat. He intended to wear condoms now for the rest of eternity.

If she ever wanted to sleep with him again, which was debatable. Because he wouldn't blame her in the slightest if she refused to allow him within ten feet of her naked body after what she'd been through less that twenty-four hours ago.

'It's okay,' Katherine murmured sleepily and sat up in bed—looking ludicrously serene and happy for a woman who had just survived what he considered to have been a major war.

Lifting her breast out of the feeding bra, exposing the plump nipple, she reached tired arms towards Jack. 'Give him to me,' she said, stifling a yawn. 'He probably just wants to feed.'

'Damn, seriously! He's done nothing but eat since we got home,' he murmured as he resolutely ignored the shot of arousal at the sight of his wife's glorious breast and handed her their precious little bundle of absolute fury.

The baby found the nipple, latched on immediately and began sucking furiously as if he'd been starved for hours, while his little fist finally stopped moving and settled against his wife's cleavage.

Another shot of arousal rippled through Jack's system…

What was wrong with him? Was he some kind of animal that he could get turned on by the perfectly natural sight of Katherine feeding their son?

'He's definitely a boob man, that's for sure,' Katherine said, her lips quirking in a cheeky smile that had his heart thumping his chest in hard, heady thuds. 'Not unlike his father.'

He chuckled, releasing the tension in his chest and letting go of the guilt.

God, but he loved this woman so much. How could she be so relaxed, so competent, taking this scary new experience called parenthood in her stride, when he was so useless? But he knew why. Because she was brave and smart and beautiful inside and out. And she had a wicked sense of humour that matched his own.

'Yeah, well, I hope he realises I'm gonna want those boobs back eventually,' Jack said wryly, joy bursting in his heart when she chuckled back.

'That may take a while, given how sore his mum is all over.'

'No worries,' Jack said, knowing if sexy banter was all he was going to get for a while it was more than enough. 'I can wait.'

She sent him a tender, welcoming smile as he climbed onto the bed beside her. He slung an arm around her shoulders and pulled her against his side, impossibly grateful for the companionship, the feeling of home she had created for him over the last five months...

He watched his son's cheeks gradually stop moving and the plump red nipple drop out of his mouth as he drifted back to sleep, as if by magic. Jack pressed a gentle kiss to his wife's temple while the wonder, the love—that was never far away when he watched his wife and child, his family—swelled in his chest, making it a little hard for him to breathe.

'Thank you, Mrs Wolfe,' he said softly.

'You're welcome, Mr Wolfe,' she whispered back. She lifted her head to smile at him. 'We really ought to give Master Wolfe a name, don't you think?' she said.

'How about Greedy?' he said.

She gave him a nudge in the ribs. 'I'm serious.'

'Okay, what do you want to call him?' Jack said, aware of a tickle of apprehension in his throat at the thought of this conversation. After all, the last time they'd discussed naming their son, he'd nearly torpedoed their whole relationship. 'I'm happy with anything you like,' he said, determined to make amends.

She gave him a patient, probing look. 'Okay, I like Aloysius.'

What the actual...?

'Okay,' he said, appalled and trying not to look it. 'Really?' he asked, when he spotted the mischievous twinkle in her eyes.

'No, not really... For goodness' sake, Jack. This is supposed to be a joint enterprise. I don't want to decide something so important on my own.'

'Okay,' he said carefully. But the apprehension still gripped his ribs. 'I just don't want to mess it up, like I did the last time.'

Katie stared at her husband and wanted to laugh and cry at the same time.

He'd been a wonderful father already. And an incredible partner over the last few months as they had navigated this stunning, life-altering and extremely scary experience together—of learning how to love each other, and how to prepare to become parents.

Not that there was really much you could do to prepare for something so momentous. She knew he was terrified of making a mistake, just like she was. She had seen how freaked out he'd been during the labour.

How much he already loved their son, though, and what an incredible father he was going to be, was plain to see. The mix of astonishment and tenderness on his face every time he held the baby with such care, talked to him in that deep, comforting and impossibly patient voice or even changed a nappy with a ridiculous amount of proficiency for a novice was both heart-meltingly sweet and stupidly sexy.

But he still had insecurities. She knew that. They both did. Insecurities which might take a lifetime to overcome. After all, neither of them had much of a blueprint for what a happy, contented, functional family life even looked like, let alone how to create it. She felt sure, though, that they would figure it out… But only if they figured it out together.

She sighed. 'You're not going to muck it up, Jack. Unless you let me call the baby Aloysius without an argument.'

He laughed and squeezed her shoulders. 'Point taken.'

His gaze drifted from her face and back to their son, who was now sound asleep in her arms. He touched a finger to the baby's downy cheek, cleared his throat and murmured. 'You said you liked Luca… Did you mean it?'

Her heart bounced against her ribs. 'You remembered that?' Why was she surprised, when he had always been stupidly observant, even when she didn't want him to be?

'Of course,' he said.

'Yes, I meant it. I love the name Luca,' she said.

He nodded. 'Good, because so do I.'

Kissing her tenderly on the lips—as her heart felt as if it were about to burst out of her chest with love—he held her securely in his embrace then murmured to their son. 'Hello, Luca Wolfe. Welcome to the family.'

* * * * *

CINDERELLA
IN THE
BILLIONAIRE'S
CASTLE

CLARE CONNELLY

MILLS & BOON

PROLOGUE

Six years earlier

'YOU AREN'T SERIOUSLY going out, Thirio?'

With his dark eyes rimmed with mirth and his almost too handsome face cocked at a curious angle, Thirio grinned. It was a grin that was known all over the world, certainly all over the tabloids and gossip blogs. 'Why wouldn't I?'

Constantina's lips pursed with obvious disapproval. And behind the disapproval, there was something more. Concern. She took a step into her son's palatial bedroom. 'Well, for one thing, tomorrow is your father's birthday. Hundreds of people are coming to spend the day, and he's going to expect—' She furrowed her brow. '*We* are going to expect you to be a part of the celebrations.'

'I'm not planning to miss it, Mother. Relax.'

Constantina moved deeper into his room, regarding her handsome boy—a man, now, really—through narrowed green eyes. 'Must you go out every night?'

Thirio turned, a petulant curl to his wide-set mouth. 'Does it really matter?'

'You're wasting your life.'

'What else would you have me do? Lie by the pool all day? Go and play golf? Sail about the Med in a yacht?'

'You could come to work with us,' Constantina pointed out, the position that had been created for him at Skartos Inc. one that had sat vacant since Thirio's eighteenth birthday. Thirio Skartos, born into one of the oldest, wealthiest families in Europe, did not *need* to work. The trust fund he'd been granted access to was filled with billions of pounds, and he intended to spend his way through each and every one of them. Hedonism felt good.

'I'm here, Mother. I came back for his party. Don't push it.'

Constantina sighed heavily. There was so much of her husband in their son. When she looked at Thirio's face, she could see Andreas. All his strength, pride and stubborn determination. She stood slowly, the sadness impossible to conceal from her delicate features. She didn't meet Thirio's gaze, so didn't see the answering hint of remorse that briefly creased the corners of his lips.

'I didn't come here to fight.'

'We're not fighting.' Remorse washed away, leaving a brilliant smile in its place.

'But, Thirio, you are off course. How can you live your life like this? Women, alcohol, parties. This is not how we raised you!'

'Isn't it?'

Constantina flinched, the accusation landing right in the centre of her heart. She thought of all the nights she and Andreas had gone out, or entertained, of the children they'd allowed to be raised by a mix of boarding schools, nannies and, in the holidays, a doting *yiayia*.

'You could be so much more.'

'How I live my life is none of your concern.'

Constantina pursed her lips. 'You are wrong, darling. And I *am* concerned.' She moved towards the door, innate elegance in every step. 'Please, do not infect your sister with this attitude. She is seventeen years old and thank God seems to want more from her life than the perennially low expectations you have set for yourself.'

'Heaven forbid Queen Evie should let her hair down a little,' he said with a heavenward roll of his eyes. 'If you ask me, she could do with a bit more fun—'

'Well, I'm not asking you,' Constantina denounced. 'Do not lead her astray, Thirio.'

'I'm here for Dad's party. I will talk to the guests, smile for the photos, and then leave. Happy?'

Constantina was far from happy. She had always adored Thirio. He had been the kind of little boy it had been impossible not to love: chubby and sweet with a ready smile and a delightfully bossy nature, even as a toddler. But at some point, he'd changed. Oh, he was still doted on. Feted, even. His good looks and natural intelligence made him popular socially, but his Midas touch had also made him arrogant and self-assured to a fault.

He will grow out of it, Andreas always insisted, with enough of a smile for Constantina to understand that her husband looked on their son's misdeeds with a far kinder eye.

'You are my child and I love you, Thirio. I always will. But there are times when I wish I could give you a healthy dose of reality. Can you not see what a gilded, privileged life you lead? Do you not wish to make something of yourself?' She shook her head sadly. 'You have all the opportunities in the heavens. You are smarter than anyone I know. You could change the world if only you would put your mind to it.'

Thirio's eyes narrowed. 'It's my life and I'll live it however I want.'

A spark of anger ignited in Constantina's belly. Thirio's wasted potential was a constant source of pain for the loving mother. 'Then let us both hope you start to live it better soon.'

She stalked from the room before she could say anything worse—though neither of them could have known those were the very last words she would ever speak to her son. Neither of them could have known that Constantina would not get the chance to see her son's life play out, her death, in the end, a tragedy of Thirio's making—a curse of sorts, that would haunt him for a great many years to come.

CHAPTER ONE

ON THE FEW occasions each year when Thirio absolutely had to leave the Castile di Neve, he always returned a foul-tempered beast. There was very little of the outside world that pleased him, and being forced to take part in it was an exercise that weighed heavily on his shoulders. Until finally he could fly his helicopter from whichever city he'd been obliged to visit, leaving civilisation behind, flying over the alpine forests for which these mountainous ridges were famed, drawing closer and closer to the castle he had, for the last six years, called home.

It rose from the cliff faces like a spectre of magic. On cloudy afternoons, the turrets of the towers appeared almost to hover, free-floating miles above the ravines that fell all the way to northern Italy, and, despite the romantic beauty of the centuries-old towers, Thirio felt an affinity with the ruggedness of their positioning.

They too did not belong.

And so here they stayed, two outcasts on the edges of civilisation. It was almost impossible to remember now the parties his parents used to throw here, the way the castle used to hum with life and joy.

As Thirio brought his helicopter lower, circling around the castle to the landing pad at the rear, he saw something that made him swallow a dark curse.

A car.

Small and black, parked right near the front door to the *castile*.

One of the things Thirio liked most about the castle was how inaccessible it was. Sure, there was a road, but it was narrow and winding and, with the *castile* the natural end point of the road, tourist traffic never went past. Out here, he was completely alone. Which was how he damn well wanted it.

He'd woken in a foul mood—the prospect of needing to travel always did that—and his mood had only worsened as the day went on. All he'd wanted was to get home and shower, to wash away the memories of other people, of his past, his history, his guilt.

He cut the rotor blades but stayed in the helicopter as they slowed, trying to bring his temper under control. He expelled a long, slow breath, his nostrils flaring, then pushed open the side door. It was crisp up here, despite the fact that spring was reaching through the rest of the northern hemisphere, bringing flowers, sunshine and optimism. At the top of the world, the clouds were grey, the trees heavy with fallen snow. He stepped out of the helicopter, slamming the door and stalking towards the steps that would lead to the back door of his palace.

He didn't know who'd dared to breach his sanctuary, but he would tell them to leave, in no uncertain terms. Thirio Skartos was not in the mood for being nice.

To say Lucinda Villeneuve was nervous would be an understatement. Not just because she'd arrived uninvited to the castle of a famously reclusive billionaire, proposal in hand, but because of what that proposal meant to her. If he agreed to hire her as the events coordinator for his sister's wedding, it would truly change Lucinda's life. The fee alone would be enough to secure a bank loan, so that she could finally buy out her awful stepmother and regain control of her late father's business. And more than that, it would prove to her doubters exactly what Lucinda was capable of.

She *had* to convince him that she was the woman for the job.

There wasn't a lot of information about Thirio Skartos on the Internet. Up to a point, there were tons of photographs: a young, handsome party-boy bachelor who seemed to go from one event to another—she was familiar with the type. But when tragedy struck and his parents were killed in a house fire, he disappeared from the public eye. For the last six years, he'd almost faded from existence, so it took some sniffing around for Lucinda to secure the address of his hideaway here in the Alps, on the border of Switzerland, France and Italy.

His younger sister, Evie, was easier to research. While she kept a low profile, she'd recently become engaged to the Prince of Nalvania, the fourth son of the reigning monarch, and so there'd been a spate of interviews. Lucinda had spent weeks analysing them, studying them, learning what she could about the soon-to-be Princess and weaving those titbits into her proposal. She *knew* it was good. Great, in fact. She just had to convince Thirio Skartos of that.

If he ever turned up!

Having arrived at the castle some hours earlier, she'd waited in her car a while, before moving into the foyer of the house and then, finally, going a little deeper, when the tea she'd had on the drive up had caught up with her and she'd needed to relieve herself. Only the search for amenities had taken her past the most stunning library, with triple-height ceilings and walls lined with ancient books. Was there really any harm in waiting for him there? She had decided not, and so it was here, in the library, curled up in an armchair with a very old copy of *War and Peace* in her hands, that Thirio discovered her.

Lucinda wasn't sure what she'd been expecting. His good looks were well established. She'd seen photographs of him online, taken years earlier, with his swarthy complexion, eyes darker than night, brows thick and straight, nose aquiline, jaw square—but the man who strode into the library looking as though he wanted to strangle something or someone was very, very different. Oh, his face showed the relics of that handsome young man, but his expression was so angry, so serious, that it was impossible to reconcile him with the smiling, carefree bachelor. And he was such a man—all six and a half feet of steel and strength; there was a darkness to his energy that was overpowering. Lucinda scrambled to her feet, thrusting the book guiltily onto the armchair, all professionalism forgotten in the face of Thirio's overt masculinity.

'Who the hell are you?' His accent was crisper than the temperature outside. His father was Greek, his mother Swiss, and he'd been educated between London and Vienna. He sounded as though he could pass for a member of the British royal family. But his voice was rough, thick and hoarse, as though he didn't use it often. As though he was angry to be using it now.

Lucinda swallowed past a bundle of nerves.

'Thirio Skartos?'

'You are in my house,' he said succinctly. 'Do you think you have any right to ask questions of me?'

She had not expected this degree of animosity. 'I have been trying to contact you via phone,' she responded haughtily, forgetting for a moment how badly she needed his business. 'You haven't returned my calls.'

'Most people would take that as a hint.'

'I'm not most people.'

His nostrils flared as he crossed his arms over his chest, staring at her wordlessly, so Lucinda's pulse ratcheted up without warning, without explanation. She bit down on her lower lip, then quickly stopped, when his very dark eyes dropped to the gesture, slowly appraising it, and then, her face.

'You are not welcome here.'

'I just need a moment of your time.'

Scepticism tightened his face. 'Do you not understand English?'

Lucinda flinched. He was not the first person to question her intelligence. Ever since her father had died, her stepmother and stepsisters had peppered her with insults, constantly undermining and taunting her.

What this man didn't understand was that Lucinda had learned to be strong in the face of put-downs, even when it took an immense effort.

'I appreciate what you're saying,' she conceded after a slight pause. 'But I don't intend to go anywhere until we've spoken. If you truly want to be alone, I suggest you listen to me. The sooner you've heard me out, the sooner I can leave.'

She'd surprised him. 'Who do you think you are to come into my home and start delivering ultimatums? I could have you arrested.'

'You could,' she confirmed with a slight nod, trembling inwardly. 'But that would take longer and involve more people. Whereas I don't intend to stay a moment longer than this conversation requires.'

It was very obvious that Thirio Skartos was not used to being challenged. If Lucinda's whole future and livelihood weren't hanging on his acceptance of her proposal, she'd have enjoyed the way his jaw was spasming with the effort of staying calm. It was fun to rile him, and she suspected he needed it. But this was too important—she couldn't go too far.

'I really won't take up much of your time.' She switched to a conciliatory tone of voice. 'It's getting dark and I don't much like the idea of tackling that road in the evening.'

'An excellent point,' he murmured, casting an eye towards the windows. 'And a storm is coming. If I were you, Miss—'

'Lucinda Villeneuve.'

He nodded once. Despite having prompted her for her name, he looked impatient at the interruption. 'I would leave while you still can. I'm going to take a shower.'

Lucinda's jaw dropped. Well, that had backfired spectacularly. She had very little information on this man, but one thing had stood out to her when she'd been doing her research. His sister spoke glowingly of him. She guessed their relationship to be close-knit.

'So you don't care what I came here to say?'

'Isn't that obvious?'

'Despite it involving your sister?'

Thirio paused. 'What about her?' Every word was sharpened like a bullet.

Lucinda took a step closer, then wished she hadn't, when a hint of his masculine aroma reached her nostrils. He wore a cologne that was all citrus spice, but beneath it there was a muskiness that was all him. This time, her response was unmistakable. Desire snaked in the pit of her stomach. She stopped walking and planted her feet firmly on the parquet floor of the library.

'Your sister is getting married and you're responsible for organising the wedding.'

There was a slight pause, as though he was going to argue. 'Did you come here to state the obvious?'

Again, a flicker of hurt lashed Lucinda. Not because of this man's words but because of words she'd heard far too many times in her twenty-five years.

'I believe I can give your sister her dream wedding.'

'You and every events coordinator from here to Sydney,' he responded with a curl of his lips that only made Lucinda more determined.

'The difference is, I'm right.'

She turned and walked towards a stunning carved table beneath a large window that overlooked a densely wooded forest. 'I know you'd agree if you'd take ten minutes to review my plans.'

'Wedding planning submissions are to be sent over email.'

'I know that.'

'So why are you here?'

Because I desperately need this job. 'My proposal is too big for email.'

'Then you should hone it further and submit it when you're done. I don't have time to read thirty pages of nonsense because you have difficulties being succinct.'

She gasped. 'You really are—'

'Yes?' he demanded, holding her eyes. Her heart thumped, and her knees felt all tingly.

She pulled back her own temper. 'What reason could you possibly have for refusing to listen?'

'How's this? I want to be alone.'

She flinched, curiosity and, strangely, sympathy washing through her. But this was too important for Lucinda to be put off.

'Okay.' She lifted her hands appeasingly. 'I promise, I'll leave. But first, let me describe—quickly—the dream wedding I've planned for her.'

'It's a wedding,' he growled. 'She'll wear a big white

dress, he'll wear a tuxedo, there'll be a band and food and alcohol and, at the end of it all, they'll be married.'

'Why the heck did your sister put you in charge if that's how you feel about these things?'

He opened his mouth as if to respond and then closed it again. 'That's not your concern.' He turned and walked towards the doors of the library. 'I presume you can see yourself out?'

Lucinda stared at him, open-mouthed. 'Will you at least promise to review the plan?' She held up the information, neatly collated into a booklet. Contrary to his implication, the data was succinct, the plans tightly worded to convey the effect of her intentions without getting bogged down in the minutiae of planning. That, after all, would be her job.

'No.' The single word reverberated through the castle and then he disappeared. His broad back fascinated her until he turned the corner and disappeared—taking with him all the hopes and fantasies Lucinda had created of Evie Skartos's dream wedding. Especially the freedom it would finally grant to her.

He stripped out of his clothes gratefully, as though each item he removed was also relieving him of the day's work, of the meetings he'd sat through, the deferential sympathy he'd endured, the curiosity, the watchfulness, the speculation. Did they think he didn't hear the whispering? Did they think he didn't know what it meant?

Naked in his bathroom, he let his eyes fall to the floor-to-ceiling mirror, inspecting his body slowly. At first, he'd hated the scars that started on his left flank and rose over his hip then bloomed beneath his arm to cover one pectoral muscle and the edge of his back, then higher, to his neck and the base of his throat. He'd hated them because they were a constant reminder, and now he relished them for that exact reason. His body bore the marks of his guilt, and he was glad.

The scars were a way of making sure he would never forget. Not that there was much danger of that—his mother's screams were embedded in his brain and could never be dislodged—but the scarring ensured he thought of that night often. Several times a day. He relived the trauma, and he replayed his part in it, the guilt he bore because he'd been a stupid, drunken fool.

He ran his fingers over the torn flesh, and, out of nowhere, pictured *her* fingers. The woman who'd dared to invade his space, to walk into his home and act as though he owed her anything. When she'd lifted that bloody folder, he'd noticed that her hands were delicate and pale, her nails short and rounded, her skin like porcelain. As his finger travelled the length of his scarring, the matted sensation familiar to him, he imagined her hands travelling the length, touching him like this, feeling the scar, her wide, amber-coloured eyes following the trajectory of the damage, her lips— He groaned, because her lips had been impossible to ignore. Perfect pillows of pink, with a Cupid's bow and a quickness to smile, even when he was glowering at her. He'd wanted to reach out and rub his thumb over them, to feel them part at his touch, and her warm breath escape, curling around his wrist. He'd wanted—

But he no longer deserved those pleasures. He had vowed never to indulge them again: celibacy was small penance, given his crime. He had stolen from his parents the chance to live their lives, he had no business taking joy in his.

For six years, he'd existed in self-imposed purgatory. He had not missed his old life, and the luxuries that came with it. He hadn't missed partying, alcohol, women, laughter. He hadn't missed anything except his parents, and the life he'd so foolishly taken for granted for so long.

When he thought of *that* life, and how spoiled he'd been, Thirio wanted to become a boy again, a boy who could curl up into a ball and cry in the corner, a boy who could scramble onto his mother's lap and be told that everything would be okay. But Thirio was not a boy and he knew nothing would ever be okay again. It was simply a matter of existing, for Evie's sake, and never allowing himself to forget all the reasons he had for turning his back on pleasure and life.

But he was still human.

He was still a man.

And he was still capable of feeling. Of temptation. Unbidden, his eyes strayed to the window. His legs followed, carrying him towards it, until his eyes fell on her.

He wouldn't have said he had a type of woman. Before the explosion and fire, Thirio had known only that he liked women—a lot. Tall, short, slim, curvaceous, blonde, brunette, he didn't much care. But instinctively he knew this woman was *not* his type. Oh, she was very beautiful, with her dark blonde hair that tumbled down her shoulders in luxurious waves, and eyes that were the colour of sunwarmed honey, clear, almost pearlescent skin and a slim, toned figure that he'd been unable to avoid noticing, given that she wore a form-fitting turtleneck and black trousers. Yes, she was beautiful, but she was also young, sweet and somehow fragile, so that even when he'd been barking at her to get the hell out of his house, he'd felt a strange desire to protect her.

Ridiculous.

Thirio was nobody's saviour, and she was, technically, a criminal. Breaking and entering was still considered illegal, wasn't it?

As he watched, she paused, turning to regard the castle, and the late afternoon sun bounced off her face, so she almost appeared to shimmer, like a fairy-tale princess. But there was no such as thing as fairy tales. Her eyes travelled the turrets, the wonderment on her features unmistakable.

He didn't move. In fact, he stood as still as an ancient statue, and yet, somehow, her eyes shifted quickly, as if drawn to his window, to *him*. It was impossible to know how much she could see. After all, these windows were old and rippled and the sun would surely be creating a reflection of the forest. And yet her eyes lingered. Inexplicably, he remained right where he was, his torn, broken body defiantly visible, as if challenging her to look at him like the wide-eyed ingenue she'd been downstairs.

Christos, she was beautiful.

The thought resonated through his brain so fast it was like a whip cracking, and a moment later, there was lightning—not inside his mind, though he felt that too, but beyond the ridge of the forest, cutting through the darkening sky like a blade.

The storm was approaching much faster than forecast.

Muttering a curse, he turned away from the window and grabbed his jeans, his lips a grim line in his face. She couldn't drive down the mountain in these conditions. For anyone, the road would be perilous, but for someone who wasn't familiar with the terrain, it was an accident waiting to happen, and Thirio had known enough of accidents and death for a lifetime.

CHAPTER TWO

THE ENGINE TURNED over with a delightful purr, so Lucinda closed her eyes and said a small prayer of gratitude. Mortification was heating her cheeks. Coming here had been a huge mistake. It had been bad enough to invade his personal space, but to *stare* at his half-naked—possibly even fully naked!—body? Unforgivable.

She flicked the car into drive, eager to escape. A quick glance in her rear-vision mirror and Lucinda was about to pull out, only a swift movement caught her eye.

Thirio.

Half dressed, still, his torso immediately drawing her attention. All of it. Every single iota of focus fell on his flesh, so sculpted and strong, so bronzed, and scarred on one side. Her heart thumped heavily against her ribs, making it almost impossible to breathe.

He stalked towards her quickly, a look on his face that was as thunderous as the clouds overhead.

As he approached the vehicle she forced her brain to connect to her body, and wound down the window. 'Yes?'

'You cannot leave.'

'Why not?'

'The storm will be here within minutes.' As if nature wanted to underscore his point, another bolt of lightning split the sky in two; a crack of thunder followed. 'You won't make it down the mountain.'

Lucinda's eyes slashed to the gates that led to the castle and, beyond them, the narrow road that had brought her here. Even in the sunshine of the morning, the drive had been somewhat hair-raising. She didn't relish the prospect of skiing her way back down to civilisation.

She turned to look at him, but that was a mistake, because his chest was at eye height, and she wanted to stare and lose herself in the details she saw there, the story behind his scar, the sculpted nature of his muscles. Compelling was an understatement.

'So what do you suggest?' she asked carefully.

'There's only one option.' The words were laced with displeasure. 'You'll have to spend the night here.'

'Spend the night,' she repeated breathily. 'Here. With you?'

'Not with me, no. But in my home, yes.'

'I'm sure I'll be fine to drive.'

'Will you?' Apparently, he saw through her claim. 'Then go ahead.' He took a step backwards, yet his eyes remained on her face and, for some reason, it almost felt to Lucinda as though he were touching her.

Rain began to fall, icy and hard. Lucinda shivered.

'I—you're right,' she conceded after a beat. 'Are you sure it's no trouble?'

'I didn't say that.'

His tone made her flinch. He was truly the most unpleasant man she'd ever met, despite his physical appeal.

'Maybe the storm will clear quickly.'

'Perhaps by morning.'

'Perhaps?'

'Who knows?'

The prospect of being marooned in this incredible castle

with this man for any longer than one night loomed before her. Anticipation hummed in her veins.

'Now, can we go inside before I freeze to death?'

Of course! He was shirtless and the rain icy. She nodded, putting her window back up and turning off the engine of the car. In those precious few seconds, Lucinda tried to pull herself together. Ever the optimist, she realised that a night with Thirio Skartos at least gave her an opportunity to make him listen to her proposal. She'd worked so hard on it; she was sure that if he heard what she had planned, he'd want her to organise the wedding.

But was that just a fool's hope? Because she could finally see a way to get rid of her stepmother and stepsisters and save her father's company. Nothing meant more to Lucinda than that. He had built it from scratch and she wanted to honour her father's memory. She'd finally take her place as his heir, and run things as he once had, restoring prestige to the company that was waning every day her stepmother was at the helm.

Evie Skartos's wedding was the key to that.

Determination fired through Lucinda, pushing everything else from her mind. Well, almost everything. It was hard not to acknowledge a tremor of sensual awareness when she pushed out of the car and came within a few inches of her unwitting host.

'Do you have a bag?' His tone could not be less welcoming, but the question itself showed a degree of thoughtfulness that surprised her. So too his concern for her safety, come to think of it. Maybe he wasn't all bad?

'No,' she said with regret. 'It's in a hotel in the city.'

His curt nod gave nothing away. He turned, striding back to the castle and holding the door open for her. She stared at it for several seconds, her throat inexplicably dry, before she stepped into the hall, almost brushing him as she passed.

He was warm. They hadn't touched and yet somehow she just felt it. Her skin seemed to be heating as if in response.

'Thank you,' she managed to murmur, then almost wished she hadn't offered the civility, for the way his face shifted, rejecting her gratitude.

'Follow me.' She wasn't sure how he managed to inject three syllables with so much disdain, but he did so with apparent ease. Little did he know, she'd had a lifetime of being treated like dirt by her supposed family—his behaviour didn't really phase her after that.

She fell into step just behind him, giving more attention to the castle now. The storm added a haunted, ethereal elegance to the rooms; the candelabras, while beautiful in the full daylight, were quite spectacular in the brooding, moody light.

'How long have you lived here?'

He stopped walking, but didn't turn to face her. His shoulders were tense. 'Rule number one. You are not my guest. You are not my friend. I have no interest in making small talk with you.' He turned slowly. 'And I certainly have no interest in answering questions. In case I have not made it obvious, you are here for one reason only: I do not want your death on my conscience.' The words reverberated with the strength of steel. 'The kitchen is through there.' He gestured to a pair of timber doors to his right. 'Eat whatever you want. But just…' He broke off, his eyes searching hers, the smallest of frowns arching between his brows before he seemed to rouse himself. 'Stay out of my goddamned way.'

She did exactly as he asked. For several hours, Thirio didn't hear a peep from his unwanted visitor. But he *knew* she was there. He could *feel* her in the castle, he could sense her. Vitally, he knew he wasn't alone, and being solitary was all he craved, particularly after the day he'd had.

His mind ran over the meeting he'd run, focusing on the details, but every few minutes a pair of amber eyes flooded his mind. So, some time after eight, he left the sanctuary of his office and began to stalk through the castle. He wasn't looking for Lucinda specifically, and yet, when he found her in the library, he was glad. Just to know what she was up to, to convince himself that she wasn't sticking her nose where it wasn't wanted. Thirio valued his privacy almost as much as he did his solitude.

'Hello.' Her voice was soft. Sweet. He ignored the tightening in his gut, the feeling that shifted through him that there was more to this diminutive, gentle woman. Curiosity was normal. Thirio didn't see many people. He even tended to speak to Evie on the phone or via WhatsApp, rather than face to face. He couldn't bear his sister's kindness, nor the sympathy that softened the corners of her eyes.

'Have you eaten?'

Her brows flexed together at the harshness of his tone. He told himself he was glad. Better that she be wary of him than look at him with sensual speculation. 'I grabbed an apple.'

'That's not dinner.'

'It's fine. I don't tend to eat much at night anyway. I'm usually so busy, I just have something quick.' She frowned softly. 'You don't have to worry about me.'

'I'm not,' he rejected that idea, but too quickly. The words didn't ring true. He expelled a rough breath. 'As I said, I don't want your death on my conscience. Come with me.' He stalked out of the room without checking that she was following. It had been a long time since Thirio Skartos was with people, but he still carried the belief that he would always be obeyed, always be followed.

'I don't think I'm going to die from starvation.' Her voice lifted in amusement and it did something strange to him. Something unwelcome, for the sheer fact of how good it felt.

'Probably not.' So why was he doing this? Why was he leading her to the kitchen, as though she were an invited guest rather than an opportunistic gatecrasher?

He pushed through the double doors, frustrated by the uncharacteristic behaviour. He supposed it was the novelty of having someone here. *And the fact she's as beautiful as an angel has nothing to do with it? The fact your libido is stirring to life for the first time in six years?* He ground his teeth together, wrenching open the freezer door and withdrawing two ready-prepared meals.

'Lasagne okay?'

She wrinkled her nose. 'I'm…'

'What?'

His curt interruption startled her. She visibly jumped and regret twisted his gut. He was all hard edges now, nothing soft about him.

'I'm a vegetarian.' The words emerged as an apology, and he felt even worse. For Christ's sake. He'd forgotten how to be around another human.

He replaced the lasagnes and removed, instead, a couple of portions of mushroom risotto.

'No problem.' He didn't look up to see her response, but instead busied himself with putting the contents into the microwave.

'Drink?'

She shook her head, her long, dark blonde hair shifting around her face.

Regardless of her answer, he removed a vintage bottle of wine from a special fridge and poured two glasses.

She eyed hers uncertainly. 'I really am sorry to have inconvenienced you.'

She hadn't. Not really. Her being here was a nuisance because he hated people—*all people*—but she hadn't personally done anything to exacerbate that.

'Why did you come here?'

'I told you. I wanted to talk to you about—'

'My sister's wedding. I don't mean that.' He lifted his wine glass to his lips, savouring the flavour before replacing it on the benchtop. 'Do you fly internationally to pitch for every event you want to manage?'

'This isn't just any event,' she pointed out, reaching for her own glass and taking a delicate sip, her full pink lips pressing against the glass in a way he found he couldn't ignore, her pale throat shifting as she swallowed. His gut tightened, muscles low down in his abdomen clenching with speculation and long-repressed need.

'I see. So my sister's reputation is why you're here.'

She hesitated, her eyes roaming his face for several seconds before she focused on a point over his shoulder. 'Actually, your sister is.'

'Do you know Evie?'

'Not personally, no. But there was something she said in her engagement interview that made me want to handle her wedding myself.'

'Not because she's marrying a prince and the budget is unlimited?' He couldn't help prodding, sure that the enormous chunk of money he'd pay out to the successful events firm had something to do with Lucinda's persistence.

'I mean, obviously that's part of it,' she agreed. 'To have a client for whom money is no object means the sky's the limit with the arrangements, but actually, no. That's not it.'

'So why, then?'

'Because I'm an orphan too,' she said, so softly he almost didn't catch the words. Her eyes were soft, her lips pursed as if she were lost in thought. 'My mother died when I was a baby. I never knew her. My father and I were very close, but I lost him when I was just fifteen.' She swallowed, and again, his eyes dropped to her throat, where the muscles bunched together. 'When your sister spoke of your parents, and how she wanted to feel them with her on her wedding day, I just knew I'd be the right person for this job, because I understand what that's like. I understand what it's like to live each day fully aware that there's this huge gap in your heart, that won't ever close over.' She lifted her slender shoulders, but Thirio was no longer looking at her. His ears were ringing with a familiar pressure, his breathing coming in short rasping spurts. Panic. He was on the brink of a panic attack. And this woman would witness it. He turned away quickly, staring at the microwave, focusing on his breathing. In, out. In, out. He closed his eyes but there were his parents, his mother's smile, his father's laugh. And then there were their voices, the screams his mother had made right up until smoke had filled her lungs and taken her away.

All because of him.

'I will consider your proposal with the others.'

His voice sounded surprisingly normal. The timer dinged; he plated their meals and placed them on the counter.

'Or...' she dragged the word out, her tone flirtatious without, he suspected, her intending it to be '...we could discuss it now. Pretty please. It won't take long, and I promise, you'll be glad. When you hear what I've put together, I know you'll be convinced this is a good fit.'

'You really don't give up, do you?'

'No. And that's another reason you should want me on the job.'

'Generally, I admire persistence,' he admitted after a beat. 'But I'm not in the mood tonight.'

'Or ever?' she prompted, watching carefully as he garnished their meals with a drizzle of olive oil.

'What does that mean?'

'You don't seem like the wedding planning type. Why did your sister put you in charge?'

It was a question he didn't feel like answering. 'Remember rule number one?'

She blinked, confusion on her features so beautiful and surprising that he wanted to take the words back. 'I'm not your house guest,' she said softly. 'Meaning you don't want to answer the question?'

'There is no question to answer.' His nostrils flared. 'You really are very inquisitive for someone who turned up on my doorstep uninvited.'

'Hey.' Her voice held a reprimand, which he wasn't expecting. 'You started this.' Her eyes were reproachful, and he felt that all the way to his gut. He hardened himself to her obvious charms.

'I feel I have the right to ask *you* questions,' he responded, spooning some rice into his mouth and glaring at her as he ate.

'You're wrong.' She jutted her chin out defiantly. 'You have no rights over me. The fact that I'm here doesn't mean I have to answer your questions, any more than you have to answer mine.'

'You don't think so?'

'No.' She pushed the risotto away. 'I've lost my appetite.'

He arched a brow. 'A hunger strike?'

Despite her obvious irritation, her lips quirked, a small smile slipping past her guard. His gut kicked. He liked seeing her smile. Danger sirens blared. He ate some more of his own dinner. 'Answer the question and I'll eat,' she bartered.

He moved the bowl closer to her, then crossed his arms.

'I'm good with details—wedding or otherwise.' And at this moment, he was noticing far too many details about the woman opposite him.

'So am I,' she said after a small pause. 'I've put a lot of work into the details for the wedding. I know it's what she'd want.'

Her confidence was seductive. 'And I'll consider your plan; I've told you that.'

'With the other proposals?'

'Did you seriously think turning up here in person, un-invited, would confer special privileges on your bid?'

Heat flushed her cheeks, so they were the exact same shade as her lips. He watched, fascinated, as the colour spread, imagining her strawberries and cream complexion beneath her turtleneck. Wondering if her breasts would be this same shade, and her nipples a dusty pink.

His groin strained against his jeans and he was glad then for the height of the bench. He really was out of practice if he was getting a hard-on just looking at a woman.

'Yes, actually.' She jabbed her dinner. 'Most people would appreciate the fact I've literally gone the extra mile.'

'I didn't ask for applications to be sent via email so that my request could be ignored. To be honest, the fact that you showed up here works against you. Big time. I'm not going to hire anyone who doesn't respect my requests. I'm not interested in arguing with the events company I hire. When I specify a way of doing business, I expect that to be adhered to.'

'You mean obeyed,' she quipped swiftly, sipping her wine, as though the drink could cool down her cheeks.

'Fine, obeyed. Is there a problem with that?'

'Well, how many events do you organise a year?'

He stared at her coldly. 'Your point?'

'That you don't know what you're doing.'

He resisted the strong temptation to point out that he single-handedly oversaw several multibillion-dollar enter-prises. 'I see. Is this how you usually go about ingratiating yourself with prospective clients?'

'I don't flatter anyone to gain work,' she responded swiftly. 'I'm honest. That's part of my charm.'

He didn't want to dwell on her charms, even when certain parts of his anatomy could think of little else.

'You need someone at the helm of this who knows what they're doing, and that's not you.'

He almost laughed at her assertion, but it had been so long, Thirio suspected he'd forgotten how. He drank his wine instead.

'How many events like this do *you* organise each year, then?'

For someone who'd been putting him in his place a moment earlier, she went very, very quiet.

'What? Cat suddenly got your tongue?'

Her cheeks went bright pink. He pressed his hands into the benchtop to stop from the sudden, almost irresistible urge to reach out and feel the heat for himself. What if she wasn't real? If he was going to conjure up someone to distract himself from his nightmare reality, then this woman would be exactly it.

'I—'

Her eyes dropped to the food.

Something sparked in his chest. Suspicion. Desire had muddled his senses but now instincts were returning. 'You're hiding something from me.'

Her eyes flicked to his, guilt obvious in their honey depths. Her hand lifted then, searching for something at her throat. She pulled down the rollneck of her sweater and found a small necklace—a diamond on a silver chain, pulling the pendant from one side to the other. A tell, if ever he'd known one.

He waited.

'Technically, I don't usually do this kind of thing at all.'

He stared at her, the admission catching him completely off guard. 'What kind of thing?'

'Any of this.' She took a long sip of wine, then placed the glass down, tinkering with the stem.

His eyes narrowed. 'Turn up at people's houses and walk in uninvited?'

'Well, that too.' She gnawed on her lower lip. Yearning spread through him like a tidal wave. He could barely remember what it was like to lose himself in a woman, her soft curves and undulations, to feel her warmth surrounding him. His groin tightened to the point of pain. His face gave nothing away.

'Technically, I'm not an events planner.'

His gaze narrowed. 'Then what are you?'

There was a plea in her eyes, one that very nearly weakened him. But Thirio wasn't interested in being this woman's saviour. It just wasn't within his skill set. He sipped his wine and waited silently.

'I'm an administrative assistant for an event management company.' The words were drenched in bitterness. She blinked, as if to clear whatever ungenerous thought had darkened her mind for a moment. 'The company I work at was my father's. I grew up in the office, learning the ropes from him. But when he died...' her voice faltered, and her eyes shifted away '...my stepmother took over.'

'And she hired you to do the administrative work.'

Her lips pressed together, as though she was biting back her first response. He didn't want that though. He didn't welcome secrecy.

He had no patience for lies. 'I deserve to know the truth.'

'Because I offended you by coming here in person?'

'Because you're lobbying to coordinate my sister's wedding. And if I was going to hire you, I'd need to know I could trust you.'

'You can.' Her eyes almost pierced him with their intensity. She appraised him slowly, as if evaluating him, and finally lifted her shoulders, as if in surrender. 'My step-mother gave me the administrative responsibilities because I'm good at that. I'm great at making our office run like clockwork. But I'm even better at people. I'm good at reading them, great at delivering for them. I genuinely care about our clients. She doesn't realise how much I do behind the scenes, how many events I've coordinated without her looking. I promise, I will deliver your sister the wedding she never dared dream of.'

He stared at her long and hard, wondering if she could feel the crackle in the air around them. Wondering if she was just very adept at ignoring it, and other things too, such as if she had a boyfriend, a lover, a husband? If Thirio hadn't sworn to abstain from pleasure, from anything that could bring him happiness he didn't deserve, he would have acted on the feelings that were rioting through him. He'd have leaned closer and let his breath brush her ear, his body lightly touching hers. He would have made it obvious that he was trying to inhale her sweet, vanilla scent, or fantasizing about throwing her over his shoulder and carrying her to his bedroom...

But Thirio had denied himself so much for so long that, despite the temptation that had walked into his home, he had no intention of weakening now.

'Please, Thirio. I need this.'

Despite the softness of her words, the sentiment cracked around the room like a whip, drawing him in. His name on her lips was an aphrodisiac. His control was in the balance.

And so he fought back hard now, while he still could.

'My sister's wedding is not a charity. I won't give you the job just because you beg.'

CHAPTER THREE

IT WAS IMPOSSIBLE not to regret her impetuosity in setting out for Castile di Neve in that moment. But ever since her father's death, she'd been told she wasn't good enough, even when she knew she was. For years, Lucinda had put up with the demeaning low-level jobs her stepmother had doled out, while watching her stepsisters attempt to keep the blue-chip roster of clients her father had cultivated. Didn't they realise how disastrous things would be if Lucinda hadn't kept intervening? If she hadn't made phone calls in the evenings to smooth over the mishaps? If she hadn't checked and triple-checked every detail until it was assured each engagement would run perfectly?

And now, for the first time in years, she could see a way out of this mess. If only Thirio would listen to her plans.

'I'm not asking you for charity,' she corrected with quiet strength. 'I just want you to consider my proposal.'

'I have said that I intend to.'

'I mean, now.'

'Before there's any competition from other companies?'

'There is no competition,' she said immediately, with more than bravado, because Lucinda knew that the wedding she'd planned was beyond spectacular. Exceeding a client's needs was her goal in life, just as it had been her father's. 'My plan is best. I'm only trying to save you time.'

'How magnanimous of you.' The cynicism was palpable.

'You really don't like me, do you?'

His dark eyes bored into hers, showing surprise at the honest question. 'Frankly, you're irrelevant. But I've made it clear, I don't look kindly on anyone invading my space as you have.'

She couldn't help but stare. She knew he'd been through a lot—losing his parents as he had—but that didn't give him a free pass to treat people like this.

She took a forkful of the risotto, and then another, and another, until her bowl was finished.

'That was delicious, thank you.' Her voice was stiff and formal, reminding her of how she interacted with her family. Not that they were her real family—just people she'd been thrown together with when her father had died. At fifteen, she'd been too young to be cut loose, but by eighteen, she'd been far too useful to let go.

So why hadn't *she* left? Why hadn't she walked away when her stepmother's treatment had become increasingly worse?

Because that would have meant leaving behind her family home, and her father's legacy, something she could never imagine. So she stayed and she toiled despite being treated like garbage day in, day out. But a flicker of something like rebellion ran through her now. Enough was enough.

'You know, I really didn't plan this.'

'I didn't say that you did.'

'No, but you're acting as though I came here looking to inconvenience you and I can assure you that's not the case. I had no idea you'd take my presence as some kind of insult, but if I'd known you'd feel this way, believe me, I would have avoided the trip.'

He pushed aside his own bowl, bracing his palms on

the counter and regarding her with that steady, dark stare. 'You're here. There's no point arguing about why now. If you've had enough to eat, I'll show you to your room.'

But anger was coursing through her. An anger that wasn't really his fault, an anger that didn't sit at his feet alone. It had been building inside her for years, and now, in this unexpected circumstance, it washed over her like a crushing tidal wave.

'Thank you,' she bit out, doing her best not to snap, not to argue, when her insides were churning at the injustice of his treatment. Okay, this clearly wasn't ideal. She shouldn't have come, she shouldn't have let herself in. She could see that was a misstep. But he was the one who'd insisted she stay. He was the one who'd chased after her and offered her his home for the night.

Yeah, to stop you driving over the edge of the cliff in the middle of a bad snowstorm. Not because he was yearning for your company. The heat of her anger faded, leaving her with a strange empty feeling in the pit of her stomach. It was far too reminiscent of the way she'd felt for years. Unwanted. Surplus to requirements.

As a teenager, she'd learned that disappearing into her room was best. She'd kept a low profile in the hope of avoiding conflict, and it seemed like the best course of action now. If only she knew where she'd be sleeping tonight.

'I—' She opened her mouth to pose the question, but Thirio beat her to it, speaking at the exact same moment.

'I will give you ten minutes to go through it,' he said with a darkness to his voice that made her insides squirm.

'Really?'

'Really.' He crossed his arms over his chest and despite the fact he was wearing a shirt now, she saw him without and, suddenly, she could hardly think straight. Her mind went fuzzy.

'Um, do you mind if I make a coffee?' There was so much at stake. She had to nail this.

His nostrils flared as he exhaled. 'How do you take it?'

'Just black.'

His lips curled with an emotion she couldn't place and then his magnificent back was to her, broad and powerful, as he brought a fancy-looking machine to life and began to brew two coffees. Hers was in an ordinary-size cup, his a short black, just the essence of coffee.

'Go.'

Nervous butterflies filled her belly. She took a deep breath, summoning her professional experience and the plan she'd been slaving over for weeks.

'Your sister has spoken about this castle often, you know. As a teenager, before the accident,' she offered with a sympathetic grimace, the pain of losing your parents one with which Lucinda was familiar, 'she was interviewed by one of those teen magazines and she mentioned family holidays here. I know it's very special to her.'

Thirio's expression was inscrutable but something in his eyes made the butterflies in her tummy double in number.

'And it's such a spectacular venue. I knew as soon as I saw a picture that it would be just perfect.'

Silence crackled around them.

'Perfect for what?' he asked, his casual tone forced, so she knew that tension underpinned it.

Okay. This was going to take work. 'The wedding.' She rushed on before he could argue. 'In my plan, I have overcome every objection you could make. The logistics of transporting guests from the town to here, the accommodation that could be offered, the caterers. I saw from some photographs online that there's a ballroom. Your sister and her fiancé have said they want an intimate—'

'No.' He held up a hand, silencing her with that one

word and gesture. But for good measure, he added, enunciating slowly, 'Absolutely not.'

She'd expected this. Not when she'd first arrived, certainly, but from almost the moment he'd returned home and greeted her like a bear with a hole in his head.

'The private areas of the house would remain cordoned off. We would only grant access to the ballroom indoors, and the chapel outside.'

'There is no chapel outside.'

'There would be, though, made from calico. A large timber floor with a lattice of fairy lights overhead, like a chandelier against the sky. The smell of pine needles filling the space. It will be so incredible. Just what Evie would want.'

His expression bore down on her like a freight train. 'No.'

'Why not?'

'There are one thousand reasons I could give you, but let's go with this one: I don't want strangers in my house.'

'They wouldn't be in your house,' she said slowly. 'I told you, we would keep guests to allotted areas. Your privacy would be protected.'

'No.'

She took in a deep, steadying breath. 'I understand your resistance, but…'

His laugh was short and sharp. 'This proposal is a dead end. If that's all you've got, then you've wasted your time.'

But Lucinda knew he was wrong. Oh, not about his personal wishes, but about what Evie would want.

'Do you agree your sister would want her wedding here?'

He hesitated. 'She would never ask it of me.'

His eyes darkened and he collected his coffee cup, stalking to the kitchen sink and placing it in the bowl, before turning to face her. Bare chest. Scar. Strength. She closed her eyes, willing the images away even when they seemed almost burned into her retina. They didn't help her in this moment.

And then he was walking again, towards the counter, then around it, to stand in front of her. So close she could almost feel the air reverberating with each breath he pushed out. His chest moved, and her stomach twisted. Desire stirred, heating the blood that gushed through her veins.

Focus. Charm him. Change his mind.

'I can show you how it would work.'

'But it won't work.' The words were chilling even when fire seemed to be ravaging her insides. She sucked in a deep breath and tasted him in her mouth. Her belly flopped and she had to clamp her lips together to bite back a soft moan from escaping.

'How do you know?' she challenged, but her tone was husky.

'I just do.'

'That's hardly an answer.'

'It's all the answer I care to give.'

'Even if you're wrong?'

'I'm not,' he snapped.

'I think you are.'

'I'm not sure I care.'

She frowned. 'Would you at least consider it?'

'Not for one iota of a second.'

'Not even to make your sister happy?'

'She's marrying the love of her life. You think the ceremony taking place here is what will make her happy?'

'She deserves the wedding of her dreams,' Lucinda insisted, her own heart heavy with all that she'd lost. 'She wants a wedding that will make her feel as though your parents are with her, watching over her, on this most special day in her life. This place is uniquely special to her. I know I can give her a dream wedding, and I promise to balance that with your need for privacy.'

'You don't know a thing about me or my needs,' he ground out, somehow closer to her, so now his chest brushed her breasts and her nipples tingled at the unexpected contact, aching against the fabric of her bra. Her eyes fluttered closed and she made a soft sound, a breath that was laced with all the feelings that were pouring through her.

Her own needs were tearing her apart, but they were needs she had no idea how to handle.

'And frankly, you don't know a thing about my sister, either.'

'I've done my research.'

'Apparently not, or you'd have known that this plan was doomed from the start. No wedding will take place at Castile di Neve. Is that clear?'

When she looked into his eyes, her face had to tilt upwards, and they were close enough to kiss. The thought came out of nowhere, impetuous and unwanted but impossible to let go of, so her lips parted and her eyes felt heavy with stars. Desire was a wind rushing through her, warm and inescapable.

'I want—' but Lucinda could barely finish the thought. What she wanted was impossible to articulate, and this man scared her to bits. Not the man himself, but the effect he had on her, and the fact they were here, in this stunning castle, in the middle of a snowstorm.

'What do you want?' The words were a growl.

Neither of them stepped back. It was as if some silent, invisible force had welded them together. She wanted him to kiss her. She wanted to feel his lips moving over hers, separating them, his tongue lashing hers. She wanted to forget about the wedding of the year, the fee, and what that would mean to her. Most of all, she wanted to forget about her stepmother and the mess she was making of the company, she wanted to forget about her pain and loneliness. She wanted to lose herself, just for one night.

His hand on her cheek seared her flesh. It was light and gentle, the tips of his fingers connecting with the skin beside her eye, at first, and then his whole palm curving around her cheek, while his thumb passed tantalisingly close to her lips. Stars burst through her.

'What do you want?' he repeated, his eyes holding hers, forcing her to stare at him simply because she couldn't look away. It felt as though he were looking into her soul, seeing all the things she usually kept so tightly concealed.

Instead of answering, she swayed forward, closing any gap that had remained between them, so his hardness pressed to her soft curves and something inside her—something vital and unknown—locked into place.

'Answer the question.' His lips were taut, almost white rimmed, and, despite the mask he wore that was carefully muted of emotion, she saw the torment in the depths of his eyes, as though even the hint of this conversation was making him feel things he wished he didn't.

'I don't know,' she whispered.

'Liar.' His response was swift.

'What do I want, then?' she volleyed back, eyes unflinching, heart pounding.

One side of his lip curled, derision unmistakable. 'The same thing I do.'

Dangerous delight soared through her. If she were standing on a precipice, she'd say he'd just given her a push halfway over.

'Which is?'

His eyes sparked with hers and she sucked in a deep breath, right as he dropped his head, his eyes still haunted as his lips covered hers, his mouth taking possession of hers in a way that stole her ability to think and breathe, that made her forget everything she was, everything she'd ever been. For one moment, that moment, there was only this.

'Thirio.' She said his name for no reason other than that he was there, and she liked the way it felt to say it like this, with his tongue sliding into her mouth, twirling with hers. A low, husky moan flooded her throat. She barely knew the man but this one kiss was evoking feelings in her that she'd never known, making her twist and turn with a desire she couldn't contain.

'Tell me what you want,' he commanded into her soul, before breaking the kiss, putting just enough space between them to look into her eyes, but not so much that his lips were far away. Her eyes clung to them, her breath coming in rushed little spurts.

But how could she verbalise it? How could she give voice to the cacophony of wants that were deafening Lucinda from the inside out? Heat spread through her, pinking her cheeks, darkening her eyes, until they were almost the colour of chocolate.

'I—'

Nothing made sense. She'd come here because her father's business's future depended on securing this job, and Thirio was the man in charge of hiring. Yet, at that very moment, Lucinda couldn't say she cared too much about whether her proposal was accepted or not. Other things were so much more important…

'You?' He gave her nothing. He wasn't helping her; he wasn't going easy on her. She closed her eyes, searching for sense, for calm, but, if anything, felt only a greater burden of need. For when her eyes were closed, her other senses were so much sharper, and his proximity set off a cascade of need she was powerless to resist.

'You,' she repeated, a whispered admission rather than a question. She peeked up at him, wondering at the heat that was stirring through her, wondering at the way her temperature was spiking. 'This.'

His own eyes closed then, as though it was the last thing he'd been expecting despite the way they'd just been kissing.

'It's not possible.' The words were heavy, final, and yet he didn't move, so she held her breath, grabbing hold of hope.

It *felt* possible. In that moment, everything she'd ever wanted seemed within her reach.

'You don't know what you're asking of me.'

But she did. Uncertainty with men, insecurity with the opposite sex, had always been a voice in the back of her mind—more often than not, that voice shouted so loudly it crossed over into the front of her mind, so that she never felt anyone would be interested in her. But there was something about Thirio Skartos that overrode those doubts and uncertainties. There was something about the way he looked at her that convinced Lucinda he wanted her right back.

'I think we're asking the same thing of each other.'

His eyes sparked, surprise obvious, and she felt a delicious lick of triumph.

His chest heaved with each breath, his eyes boring into hers, and she lifted a hand, pressing her palm to his chest, feeling the hard and fast rushing of his heart. More triumph flooded her veins.

'I didn't ask you to come here.' His fingers curled around her wrist, holding it right where it was. 'And I don't want to sleep with you.' He pulled her hand from his chest, holding it at their sides, his fingers still wrapped around her flesh, making a mockery of that statement.

'Don't you?'

His eyes closed for the briefest of moments and when he opened them again, she saw a battle being waged in the depths of his eyes. Desire warred with determination.

'No.'

Determination, apparently, won. Rejection seared Lucinda, making her feel like a fool for being so open about her wants, making her feel like an idiot for mistaking the chemistry between them.

'I see.' Pride, thankfully, came to her rescue. She wrenched her arm free and took a step back, somehow managing to summon a smile that was forged in ice. 'I must have misunderstood.'

CHAPTER FOUR

SHE HADN'T MISUNDERSTOOD, THOUGH. She'd read him like a book, and more fool him for not being able to control his responses to her.

After six years, he'd thought his libido had curled up and died. It wasn't as if he hadn't been around a woman in all that time, either. Though he rarely left the castle, when he did, he saw people. Flesh and blood people, beautiful women, who looked at him with the kind of interest he would have, at one time in his life, capitalised on. But Thirio wasn't that man any more.

He'd boxed away that part of his personality, those needs; he'd derived satisfaction from denying himself those pleasures.

And year on year, it had grown easier, so he no longer craved a woman's touch.

The scars on his body reminded him of why he had to abstain, of the loss and destruction he'd caused—not having sex was a very small sacrifice to make, when it came to penance. There was no penance, though, that would ever be enough.

He rolled over in his king-size bed, staring out at the rain lashing his window. It had intensified through the night, so he was glad of one thing: that he had not let her leave the castle.

Instead, the beautiful stranger was in a guest bedroom, just metres from his own.

If he'd had any choice in the matter, Thirio would have installed her on the other side of the castle, just as far away from him as was possible, but most of the place was closed off.

And so, Lucinda was barely twenty feet from him. He muted his breathing, closing his eyes and straining to listen. Was she still awake?

They had barely spoken after his rejection. She'd carried her plate to the sink, he'd muttered for her to leave it. She'd obliged without a word. He'd offered to show her back to her room and they'd walked in stony silence. But that hadn't changed the way the air around them had hummed when they'd crossed the threshold of her room. It hadn't meant he'd been able to easily ignore his body's yearning when he'd eyed the bed, and imagined drawing her into it with him.

And so he'd left before temptation could overpower him.

Thirio didn't deserve the pleasure he knew he'd experience in her arms, and he couldn't take it from her knowing that he would never offer more.

The sooner she left, the better. But for Thirio, the night stretched before him, long and impossible. He flipped onto his side, his eyes finding the silhouette of the pine trees, devouring it restlessly. Morning would come, as it always did, and then, he'd fly her away from here, into the town. Soon, he would be alone again, desire forgotten, opportunity lost, just as he wanted.

The noise was loud and woke her instantly. Lucinda sat up, disorientated and confused. Nothing was familiar. Not the four-poster bed, the renaissance art on the walls, not the view framed by the large bay window, and not the smell of pine and ice that hung in the air.

It took several seconds for Lucinda to remember where she was—and who she was under the same roof as! Just as that memory burst into her consciousness, a rush of ice wind encircled her, so she pulled the duvet higher, looking around. Her door was open.

A shiver ran across her spine. Thirio? Had he—?

Surely not.

The sound of howling wind called to her. She pushed back the covers and moved towards the door, the sweater Thirio had given her to sleep in soft across her body. It smelled so good. Freshly laundered with detergent that reminded her of lemons and vanilla. She paused at the door, noting the temperature seemed to drop by several degrees here.

Another noise, this time, the opening of a door. She turned on instinct, eyes landing on Thirio at the same moment her stomach twisted into a bundle of knots.

Holy crap.

Thirio was shirtless. Again. Only this time, despite the cool of the night, he wore just a pair of grey boxer shorts, so his muscular legs were visible to her very hungry, very fascinated eyes.

Her mouth went dry. Her gaze lifted higher, over his endlessly fascinating chest, marked and beautiful and broad and strong, to his throat, stubbled, and a square jaw that was set in a harsh line of disapproval.

'You should go back to bed.'

'I heard a noise.' Her own voice was barely a whisper. She swallowed to clear her throat.

'A tree came through the window,' he muttered. 'That's all.'

She looked again. One of the magnificent pines had

fallen, the tip slicing a path through the large window that she'd been admiring only hours earlier.

She grimaced, the destruction of a no-doubt ancient window a shame to see. 'What can I do to help?'

'Nothing.' His voice was commanding. 'Go back to your room.'

Even then, he was pushing her away, rather than taking her offer of help. She was tempted to argue, to insist on doing something useful, but the set of his jaw showed how little he would welcome argument. None the less, defiance spread through her.

'Rain's lashing the floor. If you get a tarpaulin, I'll help you secure it.'

'I said, go to bed.'

She ground her teeth together. For so long, she'd been told what to do, but with this man, it was different. She supposed her stepmother and sisters had come into her life at a particularly impressionable age, and then, the trauma of her father's death had made it feel impossible to go against her stepmother's wishes. Those habits were so ingrained now, she couldn't imagine fighting them. But with Thirio, everything was new and different and she refused to bend to his will. In fact, she got a thrill out of going against him.

'And I said, I want to help.' She crossed her arms, unaware of the way that simple action pulled the sweater higher, to reveal her slim, toned calves to his obsidian gaze. 'I'm not taking no for an answer.'

His breath hissed between his teeth. 'Fine. Have it your way.'

Pleasure—and power—spread through her.

'Stay here,' he muttered, stalking away from her, towards the wide staircase that led to the lower level. She moved instead to the tree, shivering a little, as the cold spread like icy tentacles through this level of the castle.

He reappeared quickly enough, holding a large blue sheet of plastic, flicking a light as he went, so the hallway filled with a golden glow. His eyes brushed over her and the frigid temperature in the air seemed to reverse immediately, bathing her in warmth that morphed quickly into lava-like heat. She looked away, face flushed, every part of her vibrating with an awareness that rocked her to the core.

'Grab this.' He held out a corner of the tarp, their fingers brushing as she took hold of it, so lava turned to electricity, bursting from nerve ending to nerve ending. Her eyes flew to his, to find him watching her, his gaze arrested as though he couldn't help himself.

He said something low and soft. A curse, she was sure of it, and then he turned away, taking the other corner of the tarpaulin, over the top of the tree, before approaching the broken window, peering through it.

'How bad is it?'

'The damage looks limited to this window. It could have been much worse.'

'Small mercies,' she agreed, taking a few steps closer to the edge.

'That's enough.' His voice held a warning, so she flicked a glance at him, curiosity shaping her features into an expression of interest.

'I'm just looking.'

'Do you remember why you are here? I do not want your death on my conscience.'

'Then it's just as well I don't intend to die, isn't it?'

'People rarely intend their deaths,' he responded grimly, taking his corner of plastic sheeting and lifting it up, standing taller and threading a piece of rope she'd only just become aware of around the top of the curtain rod. His movements were mesmerising. Steady and sure, confident with an economy of effort that spoke of lithe athleticism. She studied his hands first, capable fingers leading to tanned, smooth wrists and forearms. Then her attention moved to his bare chest and that scar again; she wondered at its origins before her eyes travelled lower, to the shorts that covered his rounded buttocks and muscular legs.

There was such concealed strength in his body, she wondered how he stayed fit. Did he run? Work out? Abseil? How did he spend his time? Their kiss haunted her. Staring at him, she relived the way his mouth had felt on hers, the way he'd tasted, the way he'd dominated her for those brief, beautiful moments, before he'd stepped away and denied them both what they'd wanted.

She wasn't aware of the tarpaulin falling from her fingertips. Her nerve endings were reverberating in awareness and need, but only of this man. The tarpaulin fell to the floor and Thirio angled a glance over his shoulder. Her eyes stayed locked to his fascinating, beautiful chest.

'Have you never seen a scar before?'

She flinched, jerked back to the moment by his darkly mocking words, her eyes finally shifting higher to his eyes, which studied her with barely concealed impatience.

'I wasn't looking at the scar,' she admitted, flushing to the roots of her hair.

'You're a terrible liar.' He pulled hard on the rope, checking it was secure, then strode towards her with a panther's grace and intent. He stood just two feet away from her, one hand on his hip—the side that was unmarked. 'There. Have a proper look. It's just misshapen skin.'

She flinched at his description. She wanted to look away, to tell him she had no interest in him or his scar, but neither was true.

Her eyes holding his, challenging him, she lifted her

fingertips, connecting with his marked hip, so his eyes clenched shut and his breath flew from his lungs in one rough exhalation. But he didn't move away. And he didn't ask her to stop. Emboldened, she crept her fingers higher, slowly, so slowly, as if by touching him she could understand, as if he were a sheet of music and she back at her piano, learning to play it. When she reached his ribs, she splayed her fingers wide, trying to capture all of his flesh. She felt the ridges beneath, but didn't stop there. Higher she went, towards his armpit, then detoured out, to his left pectoral muscle, and the hair-roughened nipple. Still watching him, she traced it, her mouth dry, her blood pounding through her veins at how daring she was being. This was so out of character, but it didn't feel at all strange—that was the weirdest thing of all.

'Lucinda.' The word was curt. Taken on its face, it was a warning. But his tone was gravelled and husky, and his heart was thumping, almost as hard as hers. She tilted her chin up, facing him, surprised by how close they stood, how near their mouths were.

'How did it happen?'

His expression was inscrutable, his face a mask that shielded his innermost thoughts. 'A fire.'

'Your parents—' She didn't finish the thought. The words hung between them, the question implicit. Had it been the same fire that had claimed their lives?

'Yes.'

It broke the mood. Thirio stepped sideways, bending down to pick up the dropped tarpaulin, carrying her corner to the other side of the window and reaching up to secure it. She watched his back as he worked, muscles rippling. Desire tightened the walls of her stomach.

'There.' He turned back to face her, his eyes guarded. 'Happy now?'

She wasn't. She was fighting a wave of frustration, and the more she fought it, the more it gnawed at her gut.

'You're wet,' she remarked softly, rather than answering his question.

He lifted a hand to his chest, pressing it to the rain-splashed skin. 'I'll dry.'

She couldn't look away. She wanted him. She wanted him to kiss her, to touch her, she wanted him to take her to bed and make her his in every way. The thought seared her like a lightning bolt. Never in her life had she known such immediate and impulsive desire.

'Thirio.' She said his name then frowned. What she wanted was to issue an invitation, but insecurities she fought so hard to keep at bay reared their heads. He'd already rejected her once, after all.

'Go to bed, Lucinda.' His eyes closed and, for the briefest second, she was sure she saw something strangling his features, something she suspected to be desire. Temptation. 'Now.'

She stood her ground, watching him to see what he would do next. He opened his eyes, realised she wasn't moving and then shook his head slowly. 'Fine, have it your way.' He began to walk, his stride long, and she held her breath, waiting, fingers crossed. But he walked right past her, down the hallway, and into his own room.

Disappointment was a physical ache in the pit of her stomach, the rejection thick and immovable in her soul.

There was nothing for it but to try to sleep, and somehow blot him from her mind.

'Christos.' Thirio tolerated his own room for all of five minutes before throwing back the covers in resignation. The whole level of the castle had been transformed into an ice box. In the time the window was broken, and un-

covered, every ounce of warmth had been sucked out, replaced by the arctic air that howled across the Alps. For his own part, he could live with it, but he was conscious of Lucinda in the room just across from his and, for many reasons, he didn't want to subject her to several hours longer in the ice-cold room.

He wrenched open his door, closing the distance between his room and hers, a scowl on his face. He hovered outside her room, strangely uncertain, until he thought of how frigid it was and how freezing she must be, and raised his hand to thump on the door.

'Yes?' Her voice came to him as if from far away. He hesitated a moment, hand on the doorknob, and that unusually tentative gesture brought something like a smile to his face. Since when did Thirio hesitate about anything?

'I'm coming in.'

'Okay.' Again, her voice was distant. When he cracked open the door, he could see why, and his instincts were immediately vindicated. She was huddled under the covers, so that only her eyes peeked out, her flaxen blonde hair like a messy crown. Something kicked in his gut, hard.

'It's too cold to sleep here. Come downstairs.'

'What's downstairs?'

'A fireplace, for one.'

She hesitated, but given the choice between a fridge-like room and the lure of a working fire, she wisely chose the latter.

She pushed back the cover, but when she stood, she drew it with her, wrapping it around her shoulders. The cape might have helped keep her warm but it did little to cover her legs, and it was impossible not to let his eyes flicker lower, just for a moment. It didn't help. Tension wound through him, building in the pit of his stomach, tighter than a spring. He had to conquer this.

Soon, she'd leave. He only had to be strong for a little while longer.

Almost as soon as he'd had the thought, a lightning bolt speared the sky. She flinched, her small gasp doing strange things to his insides. He glanced over his shoulder then wished he hadn't when their eyes met and the air between them charged with electricity.

So much for ignoring her.

He could tolerate her though, and the spark they shared. Just so long as she didn't start talking to him about Evie's wedding, and the preposterous idea of hosting it here. Just so long as she didn't look at him with those amber eyes, and pouting lips. Just so long as she didn't lean close, and breathlessly ask him to kiss her again.

CHAPTER FIVE

LUCINDA STRETCHED LIKE a cat, so warm and cosy that she smiled instinctively, blinking her eyes open slowly, fixing her gaze on the fire across the room, the flames low now, flicking the stack of wood lazily, no longer the frantic, tangling beast that had glowed red in the grate when Thirio had first built it. A different kind of heat built inside her now as she looked around the room, her eyes landing on him asleep in an armchair near the windows that framed another view of the enormous forest that surrounded the castle. The storm had cleared. The sky was still dark, but the rain had stopped, and in the distance she could just see tiny bits of blue peeking through.

Asleep, he was mesmerising. All the tension was gone from his face, so he looked so much more like the young man she'd seen photographs of on the Internet. Carefree and…happy. Her heart skipped a beat, her stomach swished. It felt wrong to stare at him in this unguarded moment, creepy to watch him sleep, and yet she couldn't look away.

Her eyes devoured his face, curiosity driving her actions. Had the fire done this to him? Or was it the death of his parents? Or something else entirely?

'Did nobody ever tell you that it's rude to stare?'

She startled, guilt heating her cheeks as her gaze burst

to his to see he was awake, watching her through eyes that were still half shuttered. The tension was back in his features, tightening them to the point of wariness.

'I wasn't staring,' she lied unevenly. And despite the fact the duvet was pulled up to beneath her chin, she felt exposed now, as though he could see right through the fabric and her clothing, to her naked body.

Lucinda had not led a particularly adventurous life. She organised events from behind the scenes and worked tirelessly to support her stepmother and sisters. She did not travel for work; she did not attend the glamorous events herself. This was easily the strangest encounter of her entire life.

'Yes, you were.' He didn't move, and yet he radiated tension, like a cat about to pounce.

'Fine,' she admitted after a beat. 'I was. Is that a problem?'

She'd surprised him. She *loved* surprising him. His eyes widened and his lips shifted, all so quickly it was easy to miss, but then he shrugged his shoulders and, despite the fact he was wearing a dark sweater, she could see him shirtless without any difficulty whatsoever. The image was burned into her retinas.

'I'm not used to it.'

'That's because you live like a recluse.'

A muscle jerked in his jaw. 'You've woken up in a very honest mood.'

'Honesty is my default setting.'

'Is it?' He skimmed her face, frowning, as if trying to understand if she was joking or not.

'You don't believe me? That's ironic.'

A flicker of a smile curved his lips and she realised she liked to see him smiling even more than she liked surprising him. Oh, heaven help her. She was actually *enjoying* being here with him.

It was just the novelty of it. Lucinda had been sheltered all her life. Not by choice—at least, not by her choice. She thought of the few times she'd dated in the past, and her heart was immediately heavy.

'It's also immaterial. After I take you off the mountain, I don't imagine we'll ever see one another again. What I think about you hardly seems to matter.'

Lucinda flinched. It wasn't just his summation of their situation, but his cold delivery. He clearly couldn't wait to see the back of her.

'Let's not forget, you came here under false pretences, so your claims of honesty seem a little far-fetched.'

'What false pretences, exactly?'

'That you work in event management.'

'I *do* work in event management,' she snapped, pushing the duvet off and sitting up, brushing her hair out of her face simply so she could have something to do with her hands. She had to make him understand.

'As an administrative assistant. That hardly makes you qualified to coordinate my sister's wedding to the Prince of Nalvania.'

Lucinda had been underestimated many times, but, for some reason, hearing that from this man was particularly goading. 'You're wrong. I'm uniquely qualified.'

'Because you are also an orphan?'

She winced. The words were cutting—intentionally so, she was sure of it. He was pushing her away.

'Why are you trying to insult me?'

His gaze dropped to her lips. 'I'm only saying what I've observed.'

'You seem to observe the world through a very cynical film.'

'Do I?'

'I think you know you do.'

One corner of his lips lifted, mockingly.

'I think you were determined not to like me, from the moment you saw me.'

'You had broken into my home,' he pointed out reasonably.

But Lucinda's nerves were stretched to breaking point. 'Not to steal anything,' she said sharply, resisting an urge to roll her eyes—but only just.

'You don't think privacy is a commodity that can be stolen?'

Her heart was thumping inside her chest. Lucinda hated confrontation. She always avoided it. It was one of her superhero skills, to be able to predict when someone's mood was turning and leave the room. She hated it, but with Thirio, she stood her ground regardless, even as her gut was churning and her blood felt as if a tsunami were pounding her from the inside out.

'I believed you'd prioritise your sister's happiness. I was wrong.' She stood, her fingertips tingling. 'I came here, in person, because I needed—' she pressed her teeth into her lower lip. How could she admit to him how much this job would mean to her? How could she explain? And why should she bother? It wouldn't change his mind. 'But that's beside the point.' She forced her eyes to turn to the window, grateful to see the sky was half blue now. 'The storm's clearing. I'll get out of your hair just as soon as I can. Excuse me.'

Her movements were jerky as she walked towards the door. 'You won't be going anywhere.' The words were thrown towards her, dark and commanding. She froze, staring at the door, her pulse in her throat. Slowly, with what she hoped would look like a sense of calm, she turned to face him.

'Oh?'

'The road will be icy, despite the clear sky.'

Lucinda's lips were pursed. 'Well, I can't stay here for ever.'

'Obviously.' His rapid rejoinder pulled at something in her chest. 'I'll check the roads after lunch. If they're clear, you can drive. Otherwise, I'll fly you out.'

Her pulse was hammering in her throat. She felt a thousand and one things, none of them easy to comprehend. How could she feel alight with desire even when she hated so much about this man?

'We can use the time to discuss the wedding,' she said after a beat, her arms crossed over her chest as she stared at him.

He stood up, frustration in the jerkiness of his movements. 'No. I've already told you, I'll consider your proposal with the others I receive. I don't want to discuss Evie's wedding now.'

'Why not? Let me show you what I'm thinking. I know—'

'You know nothing.' The words were loud, reverberating around the room. He closed his eyes and shook his head slowly from side to side, as if to clear their effect. When he looked at her, it was with a plea on his features. 'Just drop it, okay?'

No. It wasn't okay! She needed this! She needed him to listen to her, to be sold on the wedding. The idea of going back to her life in England, watching her stepmother destroy her father's legacy, year on year, was anathema. Lucinda had set out for the Alps with one goal in mind and she intended to achieve it. For her father, and for herself. She needed to pick up this client—her future and freedom depended on it.

'Why won't you even talk about it?'

'I do not want strangers at the *castile*. This is my home. Mine. I will not share it.' Again, his voice was raised, and

Lucinda felt the colour fade from her cheeks. He made a noise, a throaty growl, pacing from where he stood towards her.

He was so much bigger, but despite his obvious irritation, she wasn't afraid. Not even a little bit. The closer he got, the more her temperature spiked, the more aware she became of a thousand and one tiny details, like the stubble on his jaw and the groove to the side of his mouth, that formed a sort of dimple there. If he smiled, truly smiled, she imagined the effect would be quite breathtaking.

'It's your sister's too, isn't it?'

He was close enough that they were toe to toe. Lucinda argued with him for two reasons. She wanted to make a point and win it, but, more than that, she desperately wanted to argue, for the sake of it.

'Who the hell are you to come here and start interfering in my life?' he demanded. Rightly, she had to admit. What did she think she was doing? This wasn't at all like Lucinda. None of this was her business. Wanting the job didn't give her a right to speak to him like this, nor to judge him for his decisions.

Arguing was one thing, but Lucinda felt the high ground slipping away from her. 'My proposal—'

'I don't give a damn about your proposal!' he ground out. 'You think you've done your research? Maybe you have. But not on me. You don't know anything about me, or you'd understand that hosting my sister's wedding at Castile di Neve is never going to happen. Not ever.' He drew in a deep breath, visibly attempting to defuse his anger. 'Now, if you were to come back to me with a different proposal, with the wedding at a hotel or restaurant, or at a hired castle in the south of France, or the whole goddamned South of France, for all I care, then I would consider it.'

'But what if this is what she wants?'

'You don't know her.'

'But you do,' she insisted quietly. 'Which do you think she'd prefer?'

He pressed his lips together, regarding her for several long, charged seconds. His eyes were like black lagoons, so dark and deep she almost felt as though she could dive into them.

'It's not going to happen.'

'But—'

'Submit something else,' he ground out, lifting a hand between them, as if to placate her or reassure her. But then, his hand moved, falling to her shoulder and staying there. His eyes dropped, studying his fingers, moving them slowly and frowning, as if he couldn't quite believe that he was touching her. She held her breath, wanting more, but too gun-shy to show that. After all, he'd already rejected her: twice. 'Anything else.' The words rumbled out of his chest, wrapping around her, all gravelled and hoarse.

But Lucinda didn't want to come up with just any proposal. She wanted to nail this. And yet…a job was a job, and this job had the potential to change her life. She bit down on her lower lip, her eyes latched imploringly to his. She could work something else out. She was great at events. She'd grown up living and breathing this sort of thing. Okay, her next proposal wouldn't be as perfect as this, but it would still be better than anyone else's. She just had to go back to the drawing board.

'Okay,' she agreed softly, nodding slowly.

He expelled a slow breath, relief obvious on his features. His hand stayed where it was and a thousand little darts danced through her bloodstream, radiating from her shoulder to her limbs and pooling in her abdomen. Warm heat flooded her nervous system and, without her consent, her body swayed forward, her breasts brushing his chest.

His only reaction was a soft groan, just low enough for her to catch.

'But I don't want to send it via email,' she said quietly, finding it difficult to speak. 'Let me present it to you in person.'

'No.' The denial was immediate and fierce.

'Why not?' She tilted her face up to his, her eyes sparking with his, her lips parted expectantly.

'Because I don't want to see you again.' And yet, in direct contradiction of that sentiment, his lips brushed hers, so lightly it was almost as if she'd imagined it. Her stomach knotted tightly, and she went to pull away, but the hand on her shoulder tightened, and his other wrapped around her back, drawing her to him. This time, when he kissed her, it wasn't soft or light, it was demanding and desperate, the same kind of desperation that had been rolling through her since the first moment they'd met.

When they'd kissed before, she'd seen stars, but there'd been an element of caution within Thirio, as though he were holding back. She felt none of that now. It was, if anything, quite the opposite. His total surrender to their passion was obvious.

He swore into her mouth, lifting her easily, wrapping her legs around his waist as he carried her into the lounge room, kissing her as his hands fondled her bottom. She groaned softly, pleasure spreading through her at the madness of this. Somewhere in the back of her mind, the Lucinda she ordinarily was, the woman who would *never* behave like this, was screaming at her to stop being so careless and impulsive. But, heck, impulsive felt so good, how could she resist? He laid her on the sofa, his body over hers, his strength and weight sublime.

'Why did you come here?' It was a rhetorical question, asked as he pulled away, his fingers finding the hem of the sweater she wore and pushing it up, revealing her flat stomach as his fingers grazed her flesh. Goosebumps lifted, covering her skin, his touch like silk, torture for how light it was, and how much more she wanted. When he grazed the fabric of her bra she arched her back and a low whimpering sound formed in the base of her throat. Pleasure sparked like fireworks, just beneath her skin.

'I shouldn't—' he muttered, lifting the sweatshirt over her head and tossing it onto the floor beside them. He didn't finish the sentence. Instead, he straightened, staring down at her, the look on his face impossible to interpret.

She didn't know what he was waiting for, but she knew that she wanted him, come what may.

'Yes, you should.' She sat up and dragged him down on top of her, kissing him with her soul's desire, tongues lashing, hands roaming, feeling his back through the softness of his shirt. When she reached beneath it, to lift it off him, as he had done to her, he flinched, and pulled it back down with one hand, his kiss growing more desperate, more urgent. She moved her hands lower, curling them into the waistband of his underpants, curving around his buttocks and pinning him close to her.

She had never wanted anyone, or anything, more than she wanted Thirio in that moment.

'I'm not going to have sex with you,' he said darkly, almost as though he were speaking to himself. The words acted like a whip on her spine. She froze, shifting a little so she could see his face, then moved again, feeling the hardness of his arousal between her legs. Of their own accord, her hips lifted silently inviting him, contradicting him. His eyes closed, but when he blinked open, there was fierce determination in his gaze.

'I can't.'

He dropped his mouth to hers, then moved it lower, dragging his lips over her chin to her décolletage, flicking the sensitive flesh there so she whimpered. But that was nothing to the sensations she felt when he lifted one of her breasts from the silk bra, brushing a nipple with his thumb, so millions of sparks flooded her system.

'Thirio,' she groaned, still stuck on his insistence that he wasn't going to have sex with her. Until he'd verbalised that, she hadn't realised that was what they'd been building to. Not just from their first kiss, but from the moment their eyes had met and something had lodged deep in her gut. Desire of the most soul-changing type. For the first time in Lucinda's life, she wanted something for herself and was reaching out to take it. The idea of being denied stuck in her throat like a bone.

His mouth moved to her other breast and through the soft fabric of her bra he took it in his mouth, pressing his teeth to the outline of her nipple with just enough pressure to make her pulse throb hard and heavy in her body.

'Thirio.' God, she loved his name. She loved the way it sounded, the way it felt. She loved the way he reacted when she said it. She loved the way his mouth felt on her breast, the way his arousal pushed against the cotton of her underpants. When he moved his mouth lower, kissing her stomach, her breath became light and rasping, and when he lowered the elastic of her knickers, she almost laughed, a soft, throaty sound of disbelief and desire, choked from her throat. But when his mouth teased her sex, she didn't laugh. She couldn't. Flames leaped through her, made all the more urgent when his tongue flicked her clitoris, sending shock waves through her.

Never before had she been kissed there, in her most sensitive place. His mouth was magic, pushing away any doubts she might have, tormenting her, pleasing her, making her see stars.

Her fingers drove through his hair, clinging on as if for dear life, and then, she was arching her back as tension grew, spinning through her, until she couldn't handle it any longer and she exploded in a flash of blinding light, white hot and incendiary. He held her hips still as the waves rolled through her, moving his mouth back to her breast and flicking it lazily with his tongue, then pushing up onto his hands to watch her, to stare at her, as pleasure flushed her face and her eyes took on a fevered sheen.

Desire was weakening her and making her feel like a goddess all at once.

'Thirio...' This time, his name was a husky request, heavy with need. She lifted a hand to his chest, feeling the steady tattoo of his beating heart through the cotton fabric of his shirt. 'I want—'

His lips pressed together and slowly he shook his head.

She didn't understand. Was he really saying 'no', to more of this? She could feel how badly he wanted her; she knew she wasn't imagining his desire.

'I can't.'

Not 'I don't want to'. But *I can't.*

She frowned, her fog of desire making thought almost impossible. 'Why not?'

But he was pulling away from her, standing, his arousal pushing against the cotton of his pants, making it impossible to ignore.

She looked from his erection to his face, her lips parted, the loss of his physical proximity almost sucking the oxygen from her lungs.

'When you're ready, I'll fly you into town.'

Something inside her was spinning like a top, fast and out of control. A sense of helplessness gripped her. He was talking about sending her away. After what they'd just done. Or hadn't done. After what they'd just *started*, she amended, because the pleasure was building inside her even when he seemed to want to end their nearness.

Did he regret kissing her? Did he regret making her come? She sat up, straightening her bra, so her breasts were covered, her eyes probing his, trying desperately to understand.

'I have my car. I can drive.'

'The roads will still be icy.'

Then I can wait. The words died inside her. She stared at him, trying to comprehend, without wanting to ask the questions that were forming in her mind.

'Look.' He shook his head. 'That shouldn't have happened.'

She frowned. 'You didn't enjoy it.'

'That's a separate consideration.'

But he hadn't enjoyed it. Not as she had, and that knowledge brought a flush to her cheeks.

'I'll return your car when the roads clear.'

'Wait a second.' She lifted a hand to her forehead, trying to focus. 'I'm still on the "that shouldn't have happened" portion of the conversation. The car is kind of beside the point right now.'

His eyes bored into hers, but they were no longer fierce and cold, so much as almost…imploring. Her heart twisted sharply in her chest. 'I'm not in the habit of seducing beautiful, innocent strangers who seek shelter in my home.' A muscle throbbed in the base of his jaw.

'Are you worried you took advantage of me?' She raked his face with her eyes. 'Because you didn't. I mean… I definitely wanted that.'

'I know.' The gruff agreement didn't embarrass her as it could have. 'But I should have known better.'

'Why is what we did such a big deal?'

'You don't think sex is a big deal?' His cynicism was back, along with a healthy dose of mockery.

'We didn't have sex,' she pointed out.

'No, but we would have, if I didn't stop.'

'Yes,' she agreed quickly. There was no sense in lying.

'And that would be okay with you?' he pushed, his body language giving nothing away.

'Did you hear me asking you to stop?'

'*You're* in the habit of having sex with strangers?'

She frowned. She wasn't, but didn't particularly feel like having that conversation. 'You sound mighty judgmental for a guy who spent the better part of his early twenties with a different woman every night.'

Thirio's eyes narrowed, and for a moment he was unspeaking. But not silent. His eyes, his lips, the tension in his face, spoke volumes. She stood perfectly still, watching and waiting to see how he would respond.

'I'm not that person any more.' The words emerged darkly, each syllable clipped.

She tilted her head to the side. Something had happened to change him, and you didn't have to be a genius to guess what.

'Okay.' She nodded slowly. He clearly didn't want to talk about the fire, and she wasn't going to pry. But as for what had just happened between them? Well, it seemed only reasonable that they give it a bit more airtime. 'You're not. And nor am I, truth be told. That is to say, I don't seduce potential clients I happen to be stranded with no matter how hot they are.' His lips flickered a little, involuntarily, at her mention of 'hot'. 'Never. Not ever. But clearly there's something between us and I think we'd be stupid to ignore that.'

He didn't react. 'What do you have in mind?'

She frowned. A relationship? No. That wasn't what Lucinda wanted. And not with someone like Thirio. Right now, nothing mattered more to Lucinda than getting her father's company back in her name and returning it to its former prestige. Her dad deserved that, and Lucinda intended to deliver. A relationship would derail her from her goals. Besides, nothing about this man screamed 'happily ever after'.

'I don't have anything in mind,' she said after a beat. 'I just don't think you should act like we did something wrong.' For reasons she couldn't fathom, Lucinda didn't like the way he was sweeping it under the carpet.

'Fine.'

But his concession was meaningless. He was just trying to get rid of her. Anger bubbled inside Lucinda. How could he just brush her off like that?

Because it meant nothing to him.

And did it mean something to you?

She frowned, truly stumped by that question. Answers weren't within her grasp. She toyed with her necklace, staring at him, searching for something to say.

But he was withdrawing from her, his face a mask of disinterest.

'I'm not looking for a marriage proposal,' she said after a beat. 'But I enjoyed what we shared. I enjoyed kissing you and touching you, and I would have enjoyed getting to know you better. I would have enjoyed—' Heat flushed her cheeks. She shrugged, too shy to complete the sentence.

A muscle throbbed low in his jaw, making her wonder if he was grinding his teeth. Emotions emanated from him in waves, even when his body language was carefully controlled.

Silence beat between them, laced with tension. Lucinda could hear the throbbing of blood in her veins, washing through her ears, and she waited, but he said nothing for such a long time, she began to wonder if he didn't intend to speak. She took a step backwards, reconciling herself to that, when finally, his voice thickened the air between them.

'It shouldn't have happened.'

She opened her mouth to argue, but what was the point? Hadn't she learned how impossible it was to change someone's mind about you? Hadn't she learned the impossibility of getting someone to like you, love you, care for you, or even notice you? Her stepmother had given her a crash course in rejection, and Lucinda heeded those warnings now.

'Okay.' She shrugged as though his words didn't cut her to the quick. 'I'll get my things.'

She turned and walked away, head high, ignoring the strange sinking feeling in her stomach. He wasn't the first person to make her feel like crap, and he wouldn't be the last. But after the euphoric pleasure he'd given a moment earlier, the contrast stung.

CHAPTER SIX

THREE DAYS AFTER she left, he finally looked at it.

The goddamned plan. The wedding proposal she'd been so proud of.

It had sat in the centre of his kitchen counter since she'd handed it to him, and he'd wilfully, determinedly given it a wide berth, alternating between fury that she'd dare suggest he throw open his doors to a legion of strangers and an oversized sense of curiosity. She'd been so sure that her plan was worth the effort—the effort of coming to him, of waiting in his home, of getting stranded as a storm approached, of going toe to toe with Thirio, who no one ever dared argue with.

It was his curiosity that won out. Cracking the top off a beer, he regarded the document with a grim expression for several seconds before reaching for it and turning the cover page, slowly.

The first thing he noticed was her voice. Every word he read, he could hear in his head, as though she were speaking to him.

The next thing he noticed was the layout of the document. He employed tens of thousands of people worldwide and he knew what went into creating professional, easy-to-understand reporting. Lucinda had nailed this. There was a lot of organisation, costing, and alternatives to cater for different contingencies. She'd said she was an administrative assistant at the company, but this plan was by far the most professional he'd seen. If she'd put this together on her own, then it was clear she had a fair idea what she was doing.

The last thing that struck Thirio, as he neared the end of the document, was how right she'd been.

Evie would love this wedding. It would be, as Lucinda had said, her dream come true.

He drained his beer, eyes focused on the piercingly blue sky beyond the kitchen.

His actions had taken a mother and a father from Evie, and then he'd taken himself away too. He'd spent the last six years hiding out in a castle on top of the world, in self-enforced purgatory. Somehow, she'd grown into a beautiful, intelligent, happy young woman, who'd fallen in love with a guy who worshipped her.

And Thirio had the power to make all her dreams come true.

To give her the kind of wedding she would adore, at the castle that had always meant so much to their family.

He just had to get over his own issues and agree to make it happen. For Evie, he had to do that—she deserved nothing less.

'There's some ridiculously gorgeous guy waiting for you downstairs.'

Lucinda looked up from the filing cabinet at the sound of her stepsister's pronouncement. 'Who is it?'

'Beats me. I'm happy to interrogate him further, though.' Carina mimed fanning herself.

Lucinda frowned across at her stepsister. She was half tempted to agree. After all, the mountain of work that had built up while she was in Switzerland hadn't abated. Lucinda had been working even longer hours than usual to keep on top of it. Of course, that was an almost impossible task, given no one else in the business lifted a finger to take care of their own administrative work.

Why bother when Lucinda was there to clean it up?

She jerked the filing drawer closed with a clunk. The equipment needed upgrading. It all did. But her stepmother ploughed whatever profits the company made into funding her lavish lifestyle, rather than reinvesting in infrastructure or staff training. The company was stalling, and if Lucinda didn't act soon, all her father's work would be for nothing.

She spun around, skimming her eyes over Carina. Of the two stepsisters, she preferred Carina. She wasn't as interested in her appearance as Sofia, which was to say, she wasn't nearly as vain. She also made a point of being halfway decent to Lucinda, when Sofia and Elodie weren't around at least. And she had the added advantage of having never stolen Lucinda's boyfriend, unlike Sofia.

'That's okay,' Lucinda said with a tight smile. 'I'm due for a break anyway.' Besides, she was curious about the man asking for her.

As was Carina, apparently, because she walked behind Lucinda, down the stairs, so close she felt like a shadow.

Lucinda pulled the door to the reception area inwards, her caramel eyes scanning the space before landing on the very last person she'd ever expected to see again. Her gasp was involuntary. So too the flippy-flopping sensation in the pit of her stomach. He stood at the sound, their eyes locking and the air around them instantly sparking. It fired in Lucinda's veins too, and the whole world seemed to tip on its axis. She wasn't conscious of Carina, or the receptionist, or the sound of traffic whirring past the office.

There was only Thirio Skartos, his face, his body, the expensive suit that reminded her of the first day they'd met, his intense gaze, and memories of the way he'd touched her.

'Hello.' The words emerged soft and hoarse. She cleared her throat; he didn't look away. Her insides tightened.

'Lucinda.' Hearing her name from his lips flushed her skin with goosebumps. Her eyes flared and all she could do was stare.

His gaze shifted beyond her shoulder, his lips compressing with obvious disapproval before his attention returned to her.

'Is there somewhere private we can talk?'

Her heart skipped so many beats she wondered if it was going to give out altogether.

'Um…' She hesitated, merely because this turn of events was so completely unexpected. He lifted one thick, dark brow, his expression otherwise unmoving. But that was enough to jolt her out of her state of surprise. 'Of course,' she said with a quick nod of her head. She turned around, almost bumping into Carina.

Lucinda read the question in her stepsister's eyes, but pretended not to. She didn't want to introduce Thirio, and somehow she just knew that the reclusive man didn't want his name being passed around. Sure enough, as they left the front office, Lucinda heard the receptionist whisper, none too quietly, 'I don't know! He wouldn't tell me who he is.'

Lucinda's breath came in tight little spasms. She walked up the stairs, conscious of him behind her, at around the height of her bottom, conscious of his nearness, of the fact that if he reached out he could touch her waist, oh, so easily, conscious of how badly she wanted that.

'We can speak in here.' She pushed open the door to the filing room, ignoring the prickle of despair that ran down her spine as he regarded the space.

'You don't have an office?'

'Why would I?' she asked with a grimace, turning to face him slowly, because she needed that time to brace for this.

'Right. You're not an events planner.'

Something bristled inside Lucinda. 'Not technically.'

'No.' He was staring at her as though seeking answers, but rather than asking her any question specifically, he just continued to stare, until the tension knotting inside Lucinda became almost unbearable.

'So,' she said after what felt like hours. 'What can I do for you, Mr Skartos?'

That same dark brow lifted skyward. 'That's a little formal, isn't it?'

Given what we did. The unspoken words hovered in the air, making Evie's skin tingle. 'Fine, Thirio,' she brushed aside, her voice shaking only the slightest amount when she said his name. It still filled out her mouth in a way that made her nerve endings tremble. 'What can I do for you?'

'I came to talk about Evie's wedding.'

Lucinda's pulse ratcheted up a gear. 'I'm still working on another proposal,' she said after a beat. 'But I can get it to you by the end of the week.'

'No.' The word sliced through the air, thick and heavy.

Lucinda's brows drew together. 'Don't tell me you came all this way to ask me not to submit anything? This can't be because of what happened in Switzerland?'

He looked at her thoughtfully for several seconds. 'It's not.'

'Then why can't I offer a proposal? I have other ideas that I think your sister will love.'

He crossed his arms over his chest, and Lucinda had the sense he was fighting a war within himself. 'I doubt it,' was all he said, finally.

'Then why did you come here?' Frustration bubbled over into anger as Evie stared at the prospect of failure. This wedding had been her ticket to a better life, and she wanted, so badly, to be able to gain the account and know that the fee would enable her to buy out her stepmother.

'You misunderstood me.'

He took two steps, which, with his long stride, carried him to the wall opposite, then turned his back on her, his head tilted towards the top of the dark filing cabinets.

'I read your proposal,' he said after a beat.

Lucinda's brain scattered. It was the last thing she'd expected him to say. She couldn't even recall having left it. 'Did you?' she managed, eventually.

'Yesterday.'

She waited, her heart in her throat. She knew what he thought of it. He hated the idea. The castle was private. Lucinda had been so carried away in creating the dream event for Evie that she hadn't even stopped to consider how invasive her plan would seem to Thirio. Realistically, it had been doomed to fail.

'I'm sorry—' she said.

At the exact time Thirio turned to face her, and muttered, 'It's perfect.'

So Lucinda almost didn't hear him, and then she questioned if she'd *mis*heard him, because there was no way the same guy who'd refused to listen beyond the suggestion of turning his castle into a wedding venue for a weekend was now describing her plan as 'perfect'.

'I'm sorry,' she said again, with a different intonation this time. 'Did you just say—?'

He dipped his head in silent acknowledgement.

'But you hated the idea,' she blurted out, concern drawing her brows together.

'I still do.' His expression changed, flickering with a sadness she couldn't understand. 'But Evie would love it, and I want her to have the wedding of her dreams.' He took a step closer. 'You've created that. Or you will, once I authorise it.'

Lucinda's heart stammered and her eyes filled with stardust. 'You're serious?' For the first time in a long time, she felt something like relief cresting through her. Was it possible that everything might actually turn out okay? Well, not okay, because her dad would still be gone and that was a pain with which she'd never cope, but at least by buying the business, she could start running it as he would want.

'Yes.' He sounded as though he were preparing to have his teeth pulled, though, and, despite what this meant to her, hesitation crept into Lucinda.

'Listen, Thirio.' She moved towards him, lifting a hand and pressing it to his chest. Electricity arced through the tiny room, and yet it didn't feel strange to touch him. Quite the opposite. The second her fingers connected with his chest, something locked in place inside Lucinda. 'I can come up with something else. I've learned a heap about your sister from the research I've done. I know I can pull together a dream wedding scenario that doesn't involve the Castile de Neve.'

He held her gaze and yet it was as though he was staring right through her, fixating on something else entirely. 'When Evie was a child, she was badly bullied at school.'

Lucinda's brows knitted together. 'I didn't know that.'

He spoke as though she hadn't. 'It was very cruel. She was much smaller than the other girls, and she struggled academically. It took several years for my parents to realise she had dyslexia. By then, she'd been made to feel as though she were stupid. I remember one Christmas, when we were at the *castile*, I discovered her crying in her room. She'd found a note that had been stuffed into her book by a so-called friend, saying some pretty ghastly things. Evie told me that the *castile* was the only place she felt like herself, the only place she felt safe from the cruelty of other children.'

Lucinda shook her head softly. 'That's awful.'

He nodded once.

'I took her into the forest and, together, we fashioned a sled. It took us two full days, and while we worked I asked her questions about the children who were being cruel, the sorts of things they were saying. At first, she was tight-lipped, but the more we worked, side by side, the more she shared, so I came to understand how devastating their treatment was. I hadn't noticed before. My sister had been putting on such a brave face—that's something she does, you know.'

Lucinda nodded gently. She didn't know why he was confiding this, but she liked listening to him, particularly when speaking about his life.

'I haven't always been there for her. In fact, I've been a pretty crappy older brother, most of the time. But on that one afternoon, when I watched her ride the sled we'd made down the mountain, I saw her face glow with happiness, I saw her laugh for the first time in a long time, and I remember thinking I would do anything to know she was happy like that, always. And I can do that again now.' His Adam's apple shifted visibly as he swallowed. 'I want her to have her dream wedding.'

'But I can—'

He lifted a finger, pressing it to her lips, the colour of his irises shifting at the contact. 'You have already come up with the perfect wedding. Well, almost.' His lips twisted in a rueful expression that was almost a grin.

'Almost?' Her own voice was hoarse, the word whispering around his finger, her warm breath spiralling between them.

'There are some changes, mainly to the logistics. Considerations of which you could not have been aware. I also have some suggestions for the accommodation. Again, you are not familiar with the castle as I am, and therefore couldn't have known how many rooms could be made available to guests.'

'I wasn't sure if you'd want—'

'It makes sense.' His expression gave little away. 'My parents used to host enormous balls there every year, before they...' His voice trailed into nothing, and sympathy tightened her lips into a small frown.

'I'd love to talk logistics with you,' she said after a pause, fully aware that he wouldn't want to be drawn further on the tragic loss of his parents. 'Do you have time now?'

'I have another meeting to get to,' he said quickly. As if belatedly realising his finger was still pressed to Lucinda's lips, he dropped it quickly, his hand flexing by his side. 'What about tonight?'

Her heart stammered. 'Tonight?'

Something sparked between them. A silent understanding. A risk. A temptation. 'Purely business,' he assured her.

Only Lucinda wasn't assured. She felt thwarted. Every single cell in her body was reverberating with a need to kiss him, as strongly as ever. If not stronger, for the fact she hadn't seen him in days.

But she'd be crazy to push any kind of romantic agenda with him now. He was her saviour. This wedding was going to make all her dreams come true. Sure, she might desire him in a way that caused her heart to lurch and her pulse misfire, but she couldn't act on that. Not without potentially jeopardising this business arrangement.

Even as that occurred to her, she forced herself to grapple with an unappealing thought. 'Thirio, this isn't for any other reason, right?'

His frown was reflexive. 'Such as?'

Heat stained her flesh. 'Such as, what happened between us. This isn't some... I don't know...compensation for...'

'Do I need to compensate you?'

'No! That's exactly my point. As I said that morning, what we did was very mutual. Actually, it wasn't, but you know what I mean.'

His smile surprised Lucinda. It was the work of an instant, a literal flash across his face before darkness and cynicism returned. 'No, Lucinda. I'm here because I took the time to read your proposal, as you rather passionately advocated for me to do. And I'm not sorry, because you were right. The details you've thought of were very impressive. I know Evie will love it.'

Lucinda had been certain of that, and yet as she heard it from Thirio pleasure swarmed through her, warming her, his praise a balm she'd not known before. Despite all the work she did to keep the company going, she was never commended for it. Seeing things run smoothly was the only reward—and it had been, until recently, almost enough.

'There's one thing I don't understand,' she said after a small pause.

'Yes?'

'How come she's asking you to organise this? I mean, it's clear that weddings aren't your forte, and most brides are ridiculously invested in the details. Why not Evie?'

He opened his mouth but said nothing, then shook his head, just once. 'We will discuss that tonight.'

A *frisson* of anticipation ran the length of her spine.

'Okay. Where? When?'

He named an exclusive hotel in central London. 'Eight o'clock?'

'Fine,' she said with a small nod. 'It's a date.'

CHAPTER SEVEN

BUT IT WASN'T a date, it was business, she reminded herself and the butterflies that had taken up residence in her
stomach for the millionth time that night, as she walked
through the revolving glass door of the swish hotel foyer.
She was underdressed. Then again, how could she not be?
Lucinda didn't own anything even remotely fancy enough
for a place like this, so she'd relied on one of her favourite
outfits—flattering black trousers and an oyster-colour silk
blouse with a bow at the neck, teamed with black ballet
slippers and her trusty briefcase: a leather document wallet
that had belonged to her father. It was a good luck charm
for Lucinda, and how she felt that she needed luck tonight!

Not to land the job. She was sure she had that in the
bag. But to survive the next hour or so, discussing logistics
with Thirio. She looked around the foyer, but couldn't see
him. Frowning, she took a seat, knees trembling a little.
She opened her briefcase, pulling out her proposal, skimming it, re-familiarising herself with the details. She'd also
brought her secondary proposal, just in case he wanted to
see that too. Now that he'd agreed to go with her plan A,
she felt more than a hint of compunction at having talked
him into this. He valued his privacy and she wasn't sure
she was comfortable invading it any more.

'Miss Villeneuve?'

At the mention of her name, she looked up sharply, the smile on her face instinctive. Lucinda, though naturally beautiful, had been told for a great many years by her step-mother and stepsisters that she was plain and awkward, with unremarkable colouring and features, and their as-sessment of her had become a part of what she accepted as gospel. She therefore didn't notice the appraising glint in the man's eyes as he drew nearer, nor the appreciative smile that shaped his lips.

'Yes?'

'Mr Skartos will see you now.'

She blinked, wide caramel eyes flicking around the foyer. 'Will he? Because I can't see him.'

The man, aged somewhere in his forties with dark hair that greyed a little at the temples, smiled once more at her joke. 'He's in his suite. This way, please.'

'Oh.' She stood, darting the tip of her tongue out and moistening her lips nervously. The man led her to an el-evator, and pressed the button to summon it.

'Do you work for Thirio?'

'Yes.'

That interested Lucinda, and for reasons that went well beyond the professional. 'What do you do?'

The man's expression showed bemusement. 'I'm his personal assistant. Or rather, I am where it concerns his UK business.'

'Does he have much business here?'

'Enough to keep me very, very busy,' the man prom-ised with a wink as the lift arrived and they stepped into it. He swiped a card and the doors swooshed closed, the lift immediately beginning its ascent.

The answer gave little away. In fact, it only raised more questions in curious Lucinda, but they weren't questions she needed answers to. At least, not to be able to do her job. She needed to focus on the wedding, not all the little things she wanted to know about Thirio.

'I'm Lucinda,' she said as the lights indicated they were travelling higher and higher.

'Travis.' Did he know how nervous she was? The butterflies in her stomach wouldn't settle. She took a deep breath and exhaled slowly, trying to calm down. Was she nervous about the pitch and contracts? Was it adrenalin because of what this job would mean for her, personally and professionally? Or was it anticipation at seeing Thirio again, and this time in the privacy of his hotel suite? Definitely a combination, but mostly the latter.

The doors pinged open to a small carpeted foyer, with two doors coming off it. Travis led her to one, then knocked twice before pushing open the door, holding it wide to allow Lucinda to enter.

She knew the hotel to be exclusive, and everything about it had seemed quite grand, but, regardless of that, nothing had prepared her for what she'd find in this, the suite on the very top floor of the hotel. And she knew it was the top floor because of the skylights above the lounge area that would, in the morning, provide a delicious golden glow as the sun bathed Knightsbridge in gold. *Not* that she had any intention of still being here in the morning, of course!

'Enjoy your evening, Lucinda.'

Travis was already leaving, leaving her alone in this beautiful hotel living room.

She moved towards the lounge chairs on autopilot, running her fingers over the thickly stuffed arm of one, before taking several steps towards the floor-to-ceiling glass doors that opened out onto a small terrace. Just as she shifted her hand to the door to slide it open, Thirio did the same, from outside, so they stood, face to face, separated only by a piece of glass. Startled, Lucinda took several quicks step back, clutching her briefcase like a security blanket. It felt as though a frog had taken up residence inside her throat, her pulse was ticing so fast and hard.

He opened the door and the sultry night air breathed in, wrapping around her, so she inhaled deeply.

'I've always loved this time of year,' she said, out of no-where, then felt like an absolute idiot for saying the first thing that popped into her head.

Thirio, though, didn't look at her as though she'd said anything stupid. 'Why?'

'It reminds me of summer vacation.' She smiled, de-spite the tension radiating through her.

'Care to join me?' He gestured towards the balcony. She looked over his shoulder, nerves bursting through her.

'I won't bite,' he promised, after several beats of hesi-tation.

That's a shame. Her involuntary response almost brought a gasp to her mouth but she controlled the im-pulse—just. But the way his eyes held hers showed he'd heard her thoughts anyway, or perhaps had a similar thought himself.

Lucinda swallowed to clear the thickness in her throat as she stepped out onto the deck. It ran along the whole frontage of his suite, with thick white concrete railings and tumbles of geraniums spilling over the edges, coating the air in bursts of pink and red. Clumps of daisies sat in terracotta pots and there was a small plunge pool, illumi-nated by turquoise lights.

'Where did you go on summer vacations?'

Her hands squeezed the briefcase more tightly. 'As a girl, my father would take me to Cornwall every year. We stayed at the same little house. Nothing grand—close to a cove, covered in stucco with seashells pressed into every available surface. I used to dream that I was a mermaid,' she confessed with a soft laugh. 'I loved it there. The air smelled of salt and sunshine, and the night sky was so clear, you could see every star in the heavens.'

She tilted her face towards him, to find his eyes settled on her features in a way that made her stomach twist.

'What would you do on these vacations?'

'Nothing particularly special. At least, not to anyone else. It was just the little, everyday things. We'd get ice cream in the afternoon—two scoops for me—and walk until we'd finished it; my fingers would get all sticky. I remember the sound of seagulls hovering over the fishermen's boats, and the way fish would flip and flop in the nets. There was a black cat that belonged to the property, or lived there regardless of whether it belonged or not,' she tacked on wryly. 'Benedict.' The memory came back to her fully formed and immediate. 'He loved having the fur between his ears scratched. For dinner, we'd go to a little pub on the edge of the water: The Anchor and Grace. I'd get the same thing every night—fish with peas and gravy. I loved it.' Her smile was wistful. 'After losing my dad, all those memories took on a renewed significance.'

She didn't look at Thirio. She couldn't. She didn't trust herself not to give into the emotion that was tightening her throat, and the last thing she wanted to do was cry in front of him. If she had looked, she would have seen that he was frowning contemplatively, looking at the view of Knightsbridge, his handsome, symmetrical face silhouetted against the grey of the night sky and the darkness of Hyde Park.

'After I heard about Evie's wedding, I devoured every interview she'd done. I know that must sound creepy, but I wanted to be prepared, and weddings are so personal. From the first interview, I felt such an affinity with her and what she's been through. Or more specifically, what's missing in her life, because I feel that too.' Now, she turned to face Thirio, steeling herself against the emotional response that was softening her insides. His face remained tilted away, so she could only stare at his autocratic profile, the strength of his cheekbones, nose and brow quite remarkable. 'I feel it right here, you know?' She pressed her fingers between her breasts, staring up at him imploringly, not sure what she wanted him to say, only that it was suddenly vitally important that he understand.

Slowly, he turned to face her, the strength of his chiselled features almost taking her breath away, because there was such beauty in his face, and such sadness in his eyes, that she ached to comfort him. Evie's loss was also Thirio's. Where Evie had spoken quite openly about the deaths of her parents, and how it had affected her, Thirio had been resolutely silent. There had been no interviews, and he had disappeared from that day onwards. But none of that was confirmation that he didn't carry the same burden of grief. If anything, it was confirmation that he felt just the same, only he didn't know how to express that intense loss.

Would he discuss it with her? Would he let down that wall, if she prompted him to do so? Or would he withdraw, and turn right back into the beastly, angry man he'd been that afternoon at the *castile*?

'I can't imagine how hard it's been, on both of you,' she said softly, gently, giving him every opportunity to step slowly away from the conversation, to lead her in a different direction.

'Can't you? It seems to me like you can imagine perfectly. Your father's death must have tilted your world off its axis, given how close you were.'

So he was going to deflect. 'I felt very alone.'

'And your stepmother?' he prompted, his eyes tunnelling into hers. She felt exposed and seen, and Lucinda didn't much like that.

'What about her?'

'Did she fill a role for you, after your father died?'

Died. Not a euphemism, like most people employed. *Passed away. After you lost him. Went away.* Thirio was direct and to the point. He knew this grief, he carried its heavy burden also, and so he spoke as one survivor to another.

'You could say that,' Lucinda prevaricated, not naturally given to badmouthing anyone. Life was too short to carry grudges—how many times had her father said that? It was for his sake she'd forgiven her stepmother on so many occasions, for his sake she'd turned a blind eye and just kept her head down, focusing on the work that needed to be done for the company to prosper.

'But not a good one,' he pushed.

'I suppose you could say that,' she admitted uncomfortably after a beat.

'Yet you don't want to say it.'

Her lips twisted in something between a grimace and a smile. It was strange how he understood her so completely. 'I don't know if anything's served by trashing my stepmother behind her back,' Lucinda conceded. 'Besides, I think she's done the best she could, given...'

'Given?' he prompted, when she snapped her lips shut, mid-sentence.

'Her...personality,' she finished without meeting his eyes.

'It just kills you to say something negative about someone, doesn't it?' There was surprise in his voice, and it drew her gaze right back to his face.

'Well, that's not entirely true,' she murmured softly. 'I

seem to remember throwing some home truths at your feet when I was at your castle.'

His lips flattened. 'Nothing I didn't deserve.'

She angled her face upwards. 'Careful, Thirio. That's getting awfully close to an apology.'

His response was a short laugh, entirely lacking in humour. 'It's not.' But he brought his face closer to hers, their eyes remaining locked. 'Let's not forget, you were an unwanted houseguest.'

Unwanted. Just as she'd been all her life. The words were spoken with a hint of irony, so she couldn't tell if he was joking or not, but, either way, it didn't lessen the sting. It wasn't his fault, so much as almost a decade of conditioning. She cleared her throat, furrowing her brow as she tried to get a grip on things. 'Anyway, I came here to discuss the wedding, not my personal life.'

'And yet I find myself thinking a lot about your personal life,' he responded immediately, the words growled, his expression showing that he resented that.

'Oh.' She swallowed past her knotty throat. 'Do you?'

His nod was just one movement of his head.

'What sorts of things do you wonder about?'

'Are you single?'

She lifted both brows towards the heavens. 'Do you think I'd let what we did happen if I had a boyfriend?'

'I don't know anything about you,' he said slowly, each syllable spoken with care.

'You know some things.'

'Such as?'

'You know that I'm honest, remember?'

He nodded slowly, an intensity in his gaze that spread like wildfire through her belly.

'Also, you know that I can be pushy when something's important.'

His eyes seemed to spark with hers. 'And I know what you sound like when you are coming,' he added with a husk to his voice that made her pulse spin wildly.

'Thirio…' His name emerged as a gravelled admission—but of what?

'You are so beautiful.'

His words jolted her, because she knew they weren't the truth. 'You don't need to say that.'

His eyes narrowed, his thumb lifted, of its own accord, to her lower lip, rubbing across it, and his eyes hungrily chased the gesture, showing how badly he wished that it were his mouth in his finger's place. 'Why shouldn't I? It's the truth.'

Her eyes fluttered shut. True or not, his words were magical, weaving through her, so she tilted her head back slowly, just a little, swaying forward without intending to.

'I swore this wouldn't happen.'

She blinked, trying to focus on his face, but it was too close, so close that there was only a hair's breadth between them. 'Why?'

The simplicity of the question didn't change the fact the answer was complex and knotty. He hesitated, his face so close, his breath fanning her cheek. 'Does it matter? Apparently, I have no intention of taking my own damned advice.'

Adrenalin pumped through her, filling her body with steel. But she held her ground, pulling away ever so slightly, even when every fibre of her being was drawing her closer, making her want him with unmatched desire. 'It matters to me. You pushed me away last time. I think I deserve to understand why.'

Her insistence seemed to connect with him, and he straightened, a muscle twisting at the base of his jaw, the subtle action catching her attention, so her eyes dropped to it on autopilot. 'Did I hurt your feelings?'

He asked the question without a hint of sarcasm. In fact, there was genuine concern in his eyes, something that slowed her heart almost to a stop. 'Yes,' she said honestly, tilting her chin defiantly. 'Like I said that morning, I wasn't looking for a marriage proposal, but you totally shut me down. It made me feel...' *Unwanted. Cast aside.* But to admit that was to reveal too much of herself, and so she simply shrugged. 'Immaterial,' she finished eventually.

He made a small sound, rich with disbelief. 'If I thought you were "immaterial", I would have had sex with you.'

'What does that even mean?' she whispered.

'You're obviously sweet and kind and relatively inexperienced and I am not the kind of man who can be the Prince Charming you deserve.'

She furrowed her brow, even as his compliments ran through her like treacle. 'Who says I want Prince Charming?' She shook her head. 'Who says I even *believe* in such a thing?' After all, she'd learned the hard way that fairy tales were solidly the provenance of children and make-believe.

'Everything about you,' he ground out, but he moved closer again, putting a hand on her hip. It was nothing. The lightest touch, but it seared her skin and at the same time there was such sweet respectfulness to the contact, that her chest heaved with the weight of her heart's fullness.

'You're wrong.'

'About this?' His eyes dropped to her lips and her heart stammered; she wanted him to kiss her so fiercely it hurt.

Slowly, she shook her head, lower lip drawn between her teeth. 'Not about this.'

His eyes flared with an emotional response she couldn't understand. 'What is it about you?'

'I…what do you mean?'

'At no other time have I wanted—' He shook his head in exasperation. 'I shouldn't want—'

'But you do.'

He moved closer, his eyes glowing with intensity. 'I want things I promised myself I couldn't have. I want to make love to you, all night. I want to carry you over my shoulder, to my bed, to drop you down and pleasure you until you can hardly think, let alone speak. I want to taste you again, and feel your body tremble against my mouth.'

Lucinda closed her eyes, tilting her head back at the sensual imagery he was evoking. 'But what I want most of all is to resist this, even when desire is almost crippling me.'

It was the last thing she expected him to say. Her eyes flickered open. 'Why?'

One word, uncertain and confused, hovered in the balmy evening air between them.

'What do you want?' he responded, lifting his thumb to her lips and dragging it across the pillowy flesh there.

Lucinda drew in a sharp breath to quell her chaotic nerves. But for Lucinda, who'd been focused on one goal for so many years, and had barely allowed herself to have dreams or hopes of a personal nature, she struggled to verbalise her needs. Was it fear of rejection? That definitely played a part. But it was also just a lack of experience with going after what—or who—she wanted. Yet this was no ordinary situation, and Thirio Skartos no ordinary man. This demanded that she push herself outside her comfort zone, and find words for the desires that were causing the rapid spasming of her heart.

'Everything you've just said you want, I want too.'

CHAPTER EIGHT

HIS EYES CLOSED on her husky admission. 'And then what?'

'And then,' she said with a thoughtful frown, 'we plan the wedding.' His eyes sprang open and heat stole into Lucinda's cheeks. 'Evie and Prince Erik's,' she clarified. 'Obviously.'

'Yes,' he said, but still didn't move to kiss her. Frustration and impatience leaped through Lucinda, making her fingertips tingle. 'And after that?'

She narrowed her eyes. 'I've told you, I'm not looking for anything more. I don't believe in fairy-tale happy endings.'

'And yet you've planned a wedding that belongs in a Disney film.'

'Because it's what your sister wants,' she said after a small pause.

'And you?'

'Marriage is nowhere on my horizon,' she insisted. Nor, she wanted to add, was love. The idea of opening herself up to another person made her break out in a fine sweat. How could she ever allow herself to love and hope to be loved back? 'Until I met you, I didn't think any kind of relationship was,' she said with sincerity.

'Why not?'

She shook her head slightly. 'That's not important.'

'Isn't it?' He seemed to stare into her soul. She wanted to box away her feelings and hide from him. This was a part of her she didn't want to show!

'Perhaps it's better to say it's not relevant,' she murmured after a beat. 'Suffice it to say, what we both admitted we feel a moment ago is the beginning and end of this for me.' She forced herself to be bold and say it, to really strip things back to basics. 'Sex,' she rushed out, her cheeks flushing pink. 'And nothing more.'

'You really think you can operate that way?'

'Of course.' She jutted her chin out with determination.

He studied her for a very long time, but she held her ground, refusing to move away, or to admit that she'd never had a no-strings relationship. Refusing to admit that, in fact, she'd only ever had one boyfriend and that had ended spectacularly badly, when she'd walked in to find him in bed with her stepsister Sofia.

Oh, she wanted Thirio. And she would do almost anything to have him. The needs that were spinning inside her were no longer human, able to be contained by thought and will; they were so much bigger.

She'd been waiting for him to kiss her, needing him to do so with every cell of her body, and yet, it was only when their bodies connected that she remembered she had the power too. She could kiss him! Pushing up onto the tips of her toes, she didn't hesitate for even a moment before pressing her lips to his, moaning softly as they parted under her ministrations. He was very still at first but then, slowly, his hand came around her back, holding her to him, and he began to kiss her back, a guttural noise of his own thickening in his throat before bursting into her mouth. She felt it roar through her soul.

His tongue flashed into her mouth once, and then again, duelling with hers, dominating her as he had done in the kitchen of the castle. She pushed up higher, delighting in this feeling, relishing the prospect of what was to come, even as her body felt almost tormented by the strength of this desire. Her hands lifted, linking behind his neck, so her breasts were crushed to his chest and she was conscious of every single detail in that moment. Her nipples tingled against the fabric of her bra, the skin on her arms lifted with goosebumps and his breath mingled with hers, warm and frantic.

He swore—at least, she thought he did—in another language, Greek, perhaps, then moved, stepping forward and propelling her with him, away from the terrace railings, towards the wall of the penthouse suite. Her back collided with the cold stone and his mouth took hers again, so hot in contrast. His hands lifted the silk fabric of her blouse, separating it from her trousers, so his fingertips could brush her bare skin, running over her flat stomach with a sense of possession that was startling for how right it felt. Then again, it had been like this at the castle as well.

His hands roamed higher, his kiss grew deeper, but when he cupped her breasts she broke away, gasping loudly, because the sensation was so good that heat and moisture pooled between her legs, and suddenly, her impatience was almost ready to burst the banks of any kind of self-control she was trying to hold onto.

'Please, Thirio,' she moaned, pulling at the ribbon of her blouse and loosening the top button. He dropped his mouth to the flesh below her earlobe, his stubble grazing her sensitive skin there as he finished unbuttoning her blouse then removed it completely. His hands moved to her bra straps next, pushing them down her arms, then reaching between her back and the wall to unfasten the clip with impressive efficiency. The bra fell away, and she shivered at the sensation of the night air on her naked breasts.

He kissed his way south, dragging his mouth from the base of her neck to the top of one of her breasts, kissing the flesh there before moving lower, claiming a nipple, drawing it into his mouth and sucking on it then rolling it with his tongue, while a hand cupped her other breast and held her close.

She lifted a leg, wrapping it around his, drawing him closer, so his arousal was hard and strong against her womanhood. Lucinda had barely any experience with men. One boyfriend, what felt like eons ago, and some very unsatisfying attempts at making love—a first for both of them. But somehow, her body knew what she needed to do, and that was to try everything possible to be *closer* to him. They were welded together, and yet it wasn't enough. All she could think was that she needed *more*.

'Please,' she groaned, incandescent with desire. 'I want you.'

But suddenly, the magic stopped. His mouth pulled away from her breast; his head lifted and he stared at her as though only just seeing her for the first time. There was such confusion in the depths of his eyes that desire waned, making space for concern.

But, oh, she didn't want him to stop! She needed him—this—to keep going! 'Thirio, it's okay.' She didn't know why, but she sensed he needed reassurance. 'I want this to happen.'

'I know that.' The words rumbled out of his chest, as though dragged up from the depths of his soul. 'But I don't.'

She flinched, the denial stinging. Except she *knew* he wanted her. The proof of that was still pressed against her. 'Why are you fighting this?'

His eyes closed and he drew in a deep breath, as though trying to control his desire, to fight this—her—just as she'd said. Sure enough, when he opened them, there was clarity and determination in his features. He stepped back then crouched down, lifting her bra from the ground. Slowly, he began to slide the straps over her arms.

Lucinda stood there, letting him do that, but when he went to reach behind her and clasp the bra in place, she took advantage of his closeness and angled her face, kissing the base of his jaw, flicking the flesh there with her tongue. She felt his harsh intake of air.

'Lucinda.' Her name was both a command and a desperate, agonising plea. 'Stop.'

She could stand strong in the face of some rejection, but not much, and the strength of that word had her withdrawing immediately. Not just physically, but with all of herself.

'Why?' A plaintive whisper. She needed to understand—she deserved that, didn't she? 'I'm not made of glass. You won't break me.'

'No,' he agreed, lifting a hand and cupping her face, the kindness of the gesture somehow hateful. 'But I'll be breaking something else. Something important to me.'

'What? A vow of celibacy or something?' she joked, the words infused with angry spite.

But he tilted his face away, looking towards the lights dancing in the distance. 'Something like that.'

Her lips parted, confusion swamping her. 'But—are you serious?'

He looked down at her, his lips a grim line on his face. Mockery tinged his expression. 'Unfortunately, yes. And it means more to me than I can explain.' He stepped backwards, pulling away from her in every way now. 'Come inside when you're ready. We will discuss the wedding.'

Desire was not so easy to tame. She wished, more than anything, that she could simply switch off her feelings and focus on the plans she'd come to discuss. But where Thirio was completely himself again, looking as focused and calm as ever, Lucinda's nerves were still skittling around inside her, so she had to clasp her hands behind her back to stop them from visibly shaking.

'We will need more security than you've allowed for.' He turned the page, running the pen through the section pertaining to guest protection. 'Nalvania will send a contingent of guards for the royal family, but the other guests are also high profile. I will station checkpoints here—' he marked a cross on the aerial photograph she'd included in her proposal '—here and here, as well as drones in the valley, and obviously at all the entrances.'

'Are you really worried that the guests will be…attacked? It's a wedding,' she pointed out, shivering a little at the need for such defence.

'I am worried about press intrusions, primarily,' he said with a lift of his shoulders. 'But yes, there is also the concern of kidnapping.'

'Kidnapping!' she repeated, aghast.

'It never hurts to play it safe.'

Was that why he'd backed away from her? Was it some kind of safety concern? But she'd told him she wasn't made of glass. No, it had to be this vow of celibacy.

Unless that was just a particularly heavy-handed way to put her off. After all, it was almost impossible to imagine a man as virile as Thirio Skartos avoiding sex. And since when? She'd seen enough evidence of his hectic love life on the Internet.

But the accident. The fire. Her eyes lifted to his face, appraisingly, and her heart skidded to a stop. Was it possible that beneath this big, strong billionaire there was the broken heart of a young man who'd buried both his parents? She knew that he'd hidden himself away in the castle ever since, but had he locked himself away in every possible way, too?

'My sister is hopeful of keeping the guest list small. At this stage, she has said there will be around one hundred and fifty people in attendance. The ballroom can more than cope with this number.'

'I was hoping you'd say that,' she replied, her voice hoarse, and concentration scattered.

'Did you see it, when you were at the castle?'

She shook her head slowly. 'No.'

'Not when you were waiting for me to return?'

Her cheeks flushed pink. 'No. Contrary to what you might have imagined, I didn't go prowling through your private space. I came inside because my car was freezing and no one was answering the door.'

'Did it occur to you that I might not return home that night at all?'

She frowned. 'No, actually. It didn't. I think I was just so intent on presenting my plan to you that I didn't think about anything else.'

'Why did it matter so much to you?' He placed the pen down on the tabletop, stretching back in his chair and fixing her with a level stare. She wished she could channel some of his casual attitude, but she could still feel the ghost of his touch on her body, his kisses, and both memories were weakening her. 'It can't be just that you wanted to help out a fellow orphan.'

His perceptiveness no longer surprised her. 'When I read about your sister's engagement, and your parents' tragic deaths, I wanted to do what I could to give her the perfect, perfect wedding. That was my first thought. But...' She hesitated, wondering if the admission she was about to make would lessen her in some way. Nonetheless, she felt compelled to be completely upfront with him. 'I did have a more personal motive, as well.'

Silence crackled around them, and he waited for several beats before lifting a single dark brow and prompting, 'Which was?'

She sipped her water to buy time, then chose her words carefully. 'For years I have helped my stepmother and stepsisters from behind the scenes. I've dotted the i's and crossed the t's to make sure our events went off smoothly. When there were problems, I smoothed them over with our clients. But I have never had my own event to manage.' She toyed with her necklace thoughtfully. 'Frankly, I want the fee from this, all for myself.'

His surprise was evident.

'I know that must sound mercenary,' she said with a grimace. 'But it's very important to me. I need this fee, Thirio, and the acclaim the wedding will bring to me.'

'You speak like someone who intends to go out on her own. Are you opening your own company?'

'No,' she denied quickly. 'Not exactly.'

'Then what?'

She had hoped to avoid getting into too many details, but again, sitting opposite Thirio, the truth seemed to bubble out of her, almost without her awareness. 'My father died a year after they were married. He loved my stepmother very much and I think—I hope—she loved him. But I know now that before going through with the wedding, she insisted on a prenuptial agreement. It's ironclad. And my father paid very little attention to the terms. After all, he had no intention of divorcing her. She was very specific though about how his will should be updated.' Lucinda's voice cracked a little. 'So they married, and he got his affairs in order as required, with no thought that it would ever come to matter.'

'What were the terms of the will?'

'That everything would pass to her.' Lucinda's voice was blanked of emotion, but she felt it heavy in her heart. 'Our family home, my father's business—that I had spent all my spare time at growing up, because there was no one to look after me—and all his savings. I have nothing, Thirio. Everything became hers. I depended on her "generosity" after his death. I have ever since.'

Silence cloaked them as he digested this. 'And so this fee will enable you to start your own life,' he said, the words strangely thick.

She shook her head. 'I don't want my own life. I want the life I should have had. That business should be mine. My stepmother is only interested in using the database to find rich husbands for Sofia and Carina. She likes the income, and the cachet, but I believe she'd sell it to me—for the right price.'

'This fee surely wouldn't be enough.'

'No,' she agreed with a small nod. 'But it's a deposit. I've spoken to a couple of banks and I believe I'll be able to secure a loan.' There was doubt there, but she couldn't allow it to infiltrate her mind. She was living on hopes, and she had to hold onto them, or she might fall apart. 'It's all I've wanted, Thirio. For years. I decided so long ago that I would make this right. And then every time she—'

'Go on,' he urged, voice gravelled, when she stopped, mid-sentence.

Lucinda hesitated, running a finger around the rim of her water glass. 'Every time she was unkind to me, or mismanaged the company, or said something unfavourable about my father, I'd just hold onto the idea that, soon, I would fix it. That I would erase her from his business and my life.' She scrunched up her face. 'I know that must make me seem like a terrible person. She's my stepmother, after all.'

Thirio's stare was so intense it was almost unnerving. 'In what ways has she been unkind to you?' he asked, after several long seconds had stretched between them.

Lucinda's stomach looped.

So. Many. Ways.

She zipped her lips closed before the telling response could emerge, dropping her eyes to the table.

'What happened to honesty?' Thirio prompted. And though the words were soft, they had the cut-through of a sharp metal blade. She flinched a little, her eyes flittering to his before she could stop them.

'I—' She darted her tongue out, licking her lower lip. His eyes traced the gesture and her heart stammered. He had a point. An hour ago, she'd been wanting to sleep with Thirio, and yet she balked at revealing this information to him? It wasn't a secret. Her stepmother had eviscerated her publicly and openly, shouting at Lucinda in shopping malls and in front of staff at the office. 'I suppose you could say she never liked me very much,' Lucinda whispered. 'She hadn't really known my father all that long, then he died, and she was saddled with an extra child.'

He frowned. 'Were you difficult?'

'I was fifteen and in grief, so possibly.'

His eyes narrowed thoughtfully. 'Somehow, I doubt that.'

She flicked her glance back to the tabletop, running her finger over a knot in the timber surface. 'Me too.' She bit into her lip. 'I don't know why she hates me.' Lucinda shook her head, then squared her shoulders. 'But she does, and I've finally learned to stop trying to fix that. She'll never like me.'

'So why not walk away? Why does the business matter so much to you?'

'Because it was his,' she said immediately. 'I basically grew up there. As a little girl, I used to send faxes and open the mail. As I got older, I began to type letters and schedule bookings. By the time he passed away, I was already known to most of his clients and venues. The company's in my blood, and seeing the way she's running it into the ground makes me want to… I don't know…throw something at a wall!' She finished with an exasperated growl, then tried to bring herself back under control. 'I'm really good at this, Thirio.'

'I can see that.' He thumbed through the plan absent-mindedly. 'Your proposal is comprehensive and creative. I was very impressed when I read it.'

And despite having, only moments earlier, proclaimed her skill as an events manager, hearing him praise her felt like being dipped in delicious warm honey. Pleasure spread through Lucinda, almost ameliorating the sting of his earlier rejection.

'That's very kind of you.'

'Kindness is irrelevant. It's the truth. And your step-mother is a fool to waste an asset like you.'

More pleasure, so that her face felt as if it were glowing brighter than the moon. 'She doesn't want me to be good at this,' Lucinda admitted, as puzzled by that as Thirio was.

'You said she had children of her own?'

Lucinda's eyes darted to his and then away again. 'Daughters.'

'Close in age to you?'

'Yes.'

He nodded thoughtfully. 'So she's either jealous of you, threatened by you, or both.'

Lucinda's lips parted. 'Why in the world would she be either of those things?'

He stared at her as though she'd lost her mind. 'Have you looked into a mirror lately, Lucinda?'

She blinked at him, genuinely confused, and he swore softly under his breath.

'Do you truly not realise how beautiful you are?'

Lucinda's eyes widened in confusion. 'Thirio, I've already told you, I don't need to hear—'

'Why would I lie? We've already established I'm not flattering you to get you into bed.'

Her stomach knotted at the very idea.

'Let me guess,' he continued. 'They've insulted your appearance at every turn.'

Girls with your complexion can't wear that. It's unforgiving. Your waistline looks like a spaceship. Why are your legs so disproportionate?

'They're brutally honest,' she conceded quietly, hating to relive those moments.

'If they have been unflattering towards you, that's not honesty.'

For the first time, in many years, Lucinda wondered if perhaps he was right. Maybe they had been mean to her for the sake of it. And was it possible jealousy was at the root of that? Lucinda's heart was pure kindness and, therefore, such an idea had never occurred to her.

'Thank you,' she said unevenly, a smile crossing her face as she blinked up at him. 'That's very nice of you to say.'

Where her heart had turned to sunshine and smiles, his expression was a storm cloud suddenly. 'But I'm not nice, Lucinda. You have to remember that.'

'Why do you say that? Why are you determined to act

like this awful, beastly ghoul when, in actual fact, you seem like a very nice person?'

He flinched the tiniest amount, his expression shuttering as he looked down at the papers, effectively closing her off. 'Unfortunately, you don't know what you're talking about.'

Thirio felt like a top, spinning wildly out of control, and that was a sensation he hadn't known for a very long time. Not since the morning after the fire, when his body was broken and bandaged with a hangover threatening to split his head in two. And a gnawing sense of grief and disbelief that he had caused the explosion that had killed his parents.

But this loss of control was different. This was more elemental. He felt that his body was driving him down a road he didn't intend to travel. With every fibre of his being, he felt longing—longing for Lucinda, for pleasure, for laughter, for the obliteration and euphoria of sex. All things he had denied himself.

Beneath the table, he pressed a hand to his side, feeling the rough ruination of his skin through the fabric of his shirt, his touch a reminder, the scar a talisman to his guilt and fault, the reason he had forfeited his rights, long ago, to any kind of regular life.

But Lucinda's presence was dangerous.

She made him want to forget. And, worse, to forgive himself. Except, Thirio Skartos didn't deserve forgiveness. His parents' blood was on his hands, and he would have to live with that knowledge for the rest of his lonely life.

'There is one other factor we have not discussed.' He leaned back in his chair, hands hooked behind his head.

One other factor. Lucinda had been dreading this. The night had stretched, long and, she had to admit, the best night she'd had in a long time. Not for any specific reason. In fact, her nerves were all over the place. But sitting across from Thirio Skartos, she felt more *alive* than she'd felt in years. Only, *'one other factor'* spoke of an ending. Of goodbye. Of not seeing him again until closer to the wedding. The separation seemed like the dropping of a blade. He had stirred her body to fever pitch and then walked away, but those feelings hadn't disappeared. With every blink of her eyes she saw him, not as he was now but as he'd been on the terrace, face so close to hers. She felt his body, warm and strong, pressed against her, his hardness everything she'd ever needed.

'You've proposed a late summer date for the wedding, but it has to be sooner.'

'Why?'

His eyes probed hers, his hesitation only short. 'My sister is pregnant.'

Surprise shifted Lucinda's features into a broad smile. 'That's lovely news.'

He dipped his head in casual agreement. 'Her fiancé's a prince—albeit fourth in line—to a conservative country. Being visibly pregnant on her wedding day would draw the wrong kind of attention. They'd prefer to marry now.'

'I see.' Lucinda nodded thoughtfully, the change of date a hurdle she hadn't anticipated. 'How far along is she?'

'Six weeks.'

Lucinda nodded. 'Which gives us, perhaps, another six weeks.'

'Four, to be safe.'

Her eyes widened, then dropped to the comprehensive plan. It was an ambitious event. Not since her father had been at the helm had the company attempted such a thing. But this was what Lucinda wanted to do with her life, and, deep down, she knew she could pull it off—even with that tight deadline.

'Okay,' she said quietly, steeling herself for weeks of sleepless nights.

'You have asked, numerous times, why my sister asked me to organise the wedding for her. This is your answer.'

Lucinda blinked back up at Thirio's face, her heart tripping in her chest.

'She has been very sick. The pregnancy has her in bed, most days. The wedding must take place within a month, which left me to arrange it.'

Lucinda nodded slowly. 'But her husband's family? Surely they would want some say—'

'They haven't told the royal family that they're pregnant. Apparently, Erik's parents would not approve.'

Lucinda's jaw dropped in surprise and pique. 'What? How absurd. This is the twenty-first century.'

'Yes.' Thirio's eyes warred with Lucinda's. 'But they live by a different set of rules, according to my sister.' He placed a palm on the planning document, then slid it across the table to Lucinda, slowly and purposefully, but with a hint of dread, as though he were resisting what he was doing. 'I am the only person Lucinda could trust to manage the wedding planning and keep her confidence. No one can know about the baby. Understood?'

'You think I'm going to sell the secret to some tabloid or something?' she responded with a hurt grimace.

'No. But your company—'

'My stepmother,' Lucinda surmised. 'Don't worry. I don't plan on telling her about this wedding until it's over.'

Thirio considered that. 'Will that be possible?'

'Maybe not. But none of that is your problem. I will manage my stepmother, and the wedding, and I promise

I'll keep Evie's secret. You need only provide the venue, Thirio. I won't bother you again.'

The words hung between them, their finality undeniable. Lucinda's stomach twisted into a billion knots, her blood gushing through her body so hard she could hear it washing inside her ears.

'If only that were true,' he responded darkly.

Hurt cascaded through her. Rejection was a blade, pressed to her side.

'It's clear that you will need to tour the castle properly, to finalise these plans. The logistics can't be organised from a distance. I'm afraid there's no alternative: you will need to return to Castile di Neve.'

CHAPTER NINE

SHE HAD FALLEN in love with the castle the first time she'd laid eyes on it, but the second time was even better. Now, there was the anticipation of seeing Thirio again, a week after his trip to London. Secondly, there was the mode of her arrival. When Lucinda had come here before, she'd been anxious after navigating the goat track of a road that led to the secluded castle. Today, Thirio had sent a private jet to bring her from London to the nearest city, and then a stunning helicopter with caramel leather seats and walnut detailing. And she had a bag with her.

A suitcase.

Evidence that this was not going to be a daytrip, or even a single night, but two nights, so that she could lockdown as many details as possible.

The prospect of forty-eight hours with Thirio—and now as an invited guest—sparkled on the horizon like diamond water.

It didn't matter how many times she told herself not to want things that were clearly not going to happen. She *did* want. Her body, in fact, craved him. Far from missing him, since that night in London, she had been overwhelmed by him. Every moment of sleep was tormented by memories of the few times they'd kissed, and the passion that had sizzled between them. She tossed and turned, even touched herself in the hope she would wake and find his hands on her body. But always, she was disappointed. Always, she was alone.

She pressed her forehead to the window of the helicopter as it began to circle lower, to the clearing just west of the castle. From this angle, she caught many details she'd not been privy to earlier. Smaller turrets, with ivy scrambling up one side and jasmine another, the flowers in full bloom as spring took hold of the mountains.

The helicopter touched down, rotor blades spinning slowly, and a moment later the pilot had come around to her door, opening it with a friendly smile and holding out a hand to help her down. She placed hers in it, but her eyes were on the castle.

Where was he?

It was the wrong time of day to see through the windows. The afternoon sun was creating a golden reflection that meant she could see the forest mirrored back to her, but no hint of Thirio. Could he see her? Was he watching? The thought made her pulse thunder. She took a step towards the castle, and another, all the while aware of the loud clicking of the chopper's blades as they slowed down. The pilot removed her suitcase, carrying it easily a few paces behind Lucinda, leading her to a door at the back and opening it, before turning to leave with a polite nod.

Thirio was in there, somewhere. Would he continue to ignore the chemistry they shared? Or would he indulge it? And what did she want?

That was a question that didn't even need answering. She'd known what she wanted almost since the first moment she'd met Thirio, and she'd only grown more certain of her desire as they'd spent more time together.

Lucinda had only ever been with one man, and she'd been madly in love with him, or so she'd thought. Now, she wondered if she'd ever really known Beckett? Since him, there'd been no one. She'd been devastated after their relationship ended. Not because she'd lost him, but because of the manner of his betrayal. She told herself that had scared her off relationships, that it had been safer to throw herself into her work. But now, Lucinda was having second thoughts. Maybe she just hadn't met someone who was sufficiently tempting?

Thirio Skartos brought every single cell in Lucinda's body to life.

But she had other dreams. Other needs. What she wanted, more than anything, was to take back her father's company. Nothing could be allowed to come between her and that goal. No matter how consuming this crush was, it couldn't be allowed to steal her focus. This had to be the wedding of the decade. Everything needed to be perfect, and for that she'd have to concentrate on more than Thirio and his never-ending appeal.

She stepped into a room that was tiled in black and white, with pale blue cabinets against the wall. She rolled her suitcase along the tiles, stepping out of the mud room and into a larger hallway, looking left, then right, frowning, because she felt as though she'd been dropped in the middle of a forest without a map.

Just as she was wishing she'd brought a smoke beacon to signal for help, she heard footsteps on tile. Just the *sound* of his imminent approach was enough to send her pulse skittering wildly. She swallowed a groan and closed her eyes, sending out a silent prayer for strength, then opened her eyes to find Thirio filled them.

'Are you okay?' His concern was unexpected, and it did funny things to her equilibrium.

'Fine.' She forced a bright smile to her face to prove it.

'You looked like you were about to pass out.'

Was he standing really close? He occupied every single one of her senses. Even the air around them had changed, and was filled with Thirio. She breathed in and tasted him on the tip of her tongue. Her stomach dropped to her toes. 'I'm fine,' she repeated, a little less convincingly.

'Okay.' But he didn't move. Nor did she. It was as though a silent, invisible force were holding them right there. Every breath she took was mirrored back to her, his chest's gentle rise and fall drawing her gaze. She wasn't sure how long they stood like that, but eventually Thirio did what she could not, and broke the spell.

'Are you hungry?' He reached for her bag, their fingers brushing, so fireworks detonated just beneath her skin.

'Not really.'

'Then let me show you to your room.'

She fell into step beside him, her eyes scanning this new, unfamiliar part of the castle, while her body stayed resolutely focused on the man at her side. She was conscious of everything about him, and that was a form of torment.

'Where in the castle are we?' she asked, shaking her head a little, as he led them down corridors lined with ancient paintings, dimly lit and dusty smelling, that would have, at one time, or with a little care, been exquisite.

'The western towers.' He tilted her a glance. 'When the castle was first built, this outer wall was used for defence.'

'Really?'

'It was not like this then.' The smallest hint of a smile warmed his expression and her stomach lurched. She wanted him to smile more; she wanted to be the *reason* he smiled. 'Some time in the nineteenth century, the castle was overhauled. This large, open, relatively plain space was converted into a series of guest bedrooms, with some dining rooms. In the twentieth century, bathrooms were even added,' he said, his tone droll.

'I thought you'd like the view in here.' He pushed open a large timber door, gesturing for her to precede him into a room that was enormous, very old, and very beautiful. And yet, despite its perfection, Lucinda couldn't help feeling a wave of disappointment. The room she'd used last time had been so close to *his* room. She didn't have her bearings, but she couldn't help wondering if he was stashing her as far away as possible.

'It's very nice, thank you.'

She could feel his gaze on her face, watchful, intent, far too perceptive, so she turned her back on him, moving towards the window and inspecting the view. He was right—it was a stunning outlook. If she craned her neck, she could see all the way to the town at the base of the mountain pass, the little tiled roofs just specks from this distance, and in the foreground there was the magnificent forest that surrounded this castle. Though it hadn't always been this way. There were photographs on the Internet of the castle standing tall and proud, the forest trimmed back to allow the castle to draw the eye of any who cared to look. Now, it was grown over, the once grand gardens in disrepair.

And suddenly, now that she'd jumped the first hurdle and gained Thirio's permission for this plan, she began to wonder if she'd bitten off way more than she could chew. What if the castle was too run-down to be made ready for the wedding? What if the garden was too hazardous? She'd need to investigate Thirio's liability insurance before going too much further. Oh, her head was swimming with logistics, but in the midst of it all, there was a dangerous awareness of her host. Perhaps it was a good thing that he'd stowed her here, as far away from his room as the castle permitted?

Maybe it meant she'd actually get some work done?

'There is a bathroom, though it takes a while for hot water to get into the taps.'

'It's lovely,' she said quietly.

'Would you like a moment to freshen up before I show you the rest of the castle?'

Thump. Thump. Thump. Her heart was beating so hard she was sure the sound of it was reverberating around the old stone walls. He wasn't going to ditch her here. He was offering a personal tour.

'I'm okay to look around now.' She smiled up at him, her heart rushing.

His expression shifted, a mask slipping into place that kept her locked on the outside. 'Good. I need to make sure you understand which parts of the castle are off-limits. Follow me.'

Of course, it was about protecting his privacy rather than spending time with her. She shouldn't have let her hopes get raised.

Focusing on the business, she asked, 'Have you spoken to your sister about the plan?'

'Yes.'

'What did she say?'

Thirio slid her a knowing glance. 'She loved it.'

Lucinda expelled a sigh of relief. 'I'm so glad. I really hoped she would.'

'She said she could not have planned a more perfect wedding herself. She said you had thought of every detail.'

Lucinda's heart soared. It was exactly what she'd tried to do. 'And holding the wedding here? She's okay with that?'

'Why wouldn't she be?'

Lucinda considered that. 'I thought she might have doubts, because you're—'

'Ah.' He nodded slowly. 'Yes. She did. I have made no secret of the fact I like my privacy. Naturally she was concerned that opening the doors to the castle would be an inconvenience too great to bear.'

'And is it?'

'If it were, I wouldn't have agreed to it.'

'Even for your sister?'

His eyes bored into hers for several seconds, but he didn't answer her question. 'There are twenty-seven rooms in this western wing. I suggest we hold them for the royal family and their entourage. There are private dining rooms, sitting rooms, and areas where they can come to be away from the prying eyes of guests whenever they wish.'

'That's very thoughtful of you.'

'It was Evie's suggestion,' he added, something like a smile tightening his lips.

Lucinda considered him carefully as they emerged into the corridor. This time, she took in more of the details, from the ornate tiles to the delicate wallpaper, the paintings that were portraits of people who'd lived centuries ago, and brass lights that hung from the ceiling. There were not many windows, but those they passed framed a magnificent view, causing Lucinda to wonder why the renovation hadn't included making the windows bigger?

'The reason these rooms work is this private access,' he said, gesturing to the door through which Lucinda had arrived. 'It can be secured for their visit with their own people.'

'You've thought of everything.'

His frown was reflexive. 'No, Lucinda, you did. I'm only making it fit the areas of the house you didn't know about.'

The praise fanned the flames in her belly. She couldn't

help but smile at him appreciatively, her eyes twinkling and her cheeks pale pink in the dusk light. His eyes held on her face for a beat too long and then his focus returned to the home.

His tour was exhaustive. The ground floor had been modernised twenty years earlier. 'My parents,' he admitted after a small pause. But it was when he showed her into the ballroom that Lucinda realised how right she'd been to fight for this.

'It's perfect,' she whispered, reaching out and pressing a hand to his forearm quite by instinct. He stiffened at the innocent contact but she didn't withdraw her touch. She couldn't. She was too overwhelmed. This truly was the most beautiful room she'd ever been in.

The space was enormous—far bigger than she'd conceptualised—with ceilings that had to be at least ten metres tall. A string of chandeliers ran down the centre, crystal and ornate, with one in the middle of the room that was at least four times as large as any of the others. Here, there was no shortage of windows. One side of the room was filled with ancient, carved glass, fine and etched, that framed views of the valley, the forest, the sky and the town in the distance, with its medieval church spire just visible from here. At the far end of the ballroom was a set of beautiful timber doors, wide and grand.

'Where do they lead?' she asked, in awe.

'I'll show you.' Was she imagining the hitch to his voice? She couldn't take her eyes off the room, the shining parquet floor an artwork in and of itself. Her fingers stayed curled around his forearm as they moved. But it was a mistake, because all she could imagine was how it would feel to be here under different circumstances. Not as a paid contractor, but as a bona fide guest, invited by Thirio. Dancing with him beneath these incomparably beautiful chandeliers, the light golden and warm, as his hand pressed to her lower back...

She bit down on her lower lip, trying to calm her racing nerves, but his proximity only made the fantasy seem more real.

When they reached the doors, he pressed a hand to one, opening it with the slightest groan courtesy of its age.

'Watch your step,' he urged, dislodging her grip on his arm, but only so that he could use that exact same arm to curve around her back, drawing her closer to him as he shepherded her out onto the most exquisite balcony. It was large enough to accommodate perhaps ten people, and reminded her of the balconies at Buckingham Palace, where the royal family would gather to wave to their people.

'It's beautiful.' But her focus was no longer on the balcony, or the view, or the sublime sunset colours streaking through the sky, painting the forest in shades of deep violet and gold. She turned to face him slowly, bravely, but also with a sense of inevitability, to find his eyes resting heavily on her face, a frown marring his lips.

Again, her hand lifted of its own accord, pressing to his shirt front, her fingers splayed wide. She stared at her fingertips a moment, before lifting her eyes to his, almost blinking away again for the sheer rush of awareness that bolted through her at his nearness.

'Thirio.' She said his name without knowing what she wanted to ask him.

His features gave little away, but he made no effort to put space between them, nor to clear her hand from his body.

'Have you—?' She hesitated, embarrassed by the question she'd been about to ask.

'Yes?'

She swallowed past a bundle of nerves in her throat.

She had been silenced by uncertainty for a long time and didn't want that to be the case with Thirio. With him, Lucinda wanted to be completely herself, without fear of failure, without fear of anything. 'Have you thought about me, Thirio?'

His brows drew together, features darkening, as though her question was the last thing he'd expected. 'In what way?'

Her smile was lacking humour. 'Not the wedding planning kind of way.'

He made a noise of comprehension, his expression ambivalent. She waited, breath held, sure he was going to say 'no'. She braced herself for that disappointment, told herself it didn't matter.

But then his hand lifted, cupping her face, his thumb brushing the flesh at the side of her lips, as though willing himself not to kiss her. 'What do you think?'

'I truly don't know,' she admitted after a beat. 'I can't tell if I'm alone in what I'm feeling, or if you feel it too.'

'That's hard to believe.'

'What's that supposed to mean?'

'I've made my feelings evident.' His voice was little more than a growl. 'But I have also explained why I cannot act on them.'

She tilted her face towards his, an invitation in the parting of her lips and the gentle push of her body.

He dipped his head forward, not to be near her so much as to draw breath. But that didn't matter. The action brought his face closer to hers and Lucinda was sick of being pushed away. Maybe it was the magic of this castle, but she felt alive with temptation and need, and she *liked* the way that felt.

'Even when it's what we both want?'

'I'm sorry that you want me,' he admitted gruffly.

'I'm not.' She had to be bold, to make him understand. 'I've only ever been with one man before, Thirio, and I was never really into him, physically. Not like this.'

Thirio's expression was tortured. That was the only word for it. He stared at her, a plea in his eyes, disbelief etched around the lines of his mouth.

'I've *never* met someone and wanted them like I do you. That's not to say I *like* you, or even have a crush on you. I'm grown up enough to know that physical desire is a whole separate ballgame to love. You don't need to worry that I'm getting unrealistic expectations. But I do desire you, Thirio. I do want you. And I guess I'm not really in the mood to ignore that, given how rare this is for me.'

He stared at her, stricken and lost, and she waited, aware that she'd just dropped a bombshell on his lap.

When he spoke, it was slowly, with consideration behind every word. 'The fact that you are so inexperienced is simply another reason for us to avoid this.'

This. He wouldn't put a label on it, but it was there, between them, an actual feeling and need.

'Why?'

He compressed his lips.

'You think because I've only ever had one lousy boyfriend before—and believe me, he was lousy—I won't be able to sleep with you and keep a level head.'

He leaned down, his forehead pressed to hers, eyes pinched shut. 'Stop.'

'Why? I didn't come here intending to say this. In fact, I came here planning to focus on the job, and not you at all. But within one minute of seeing you again, all this bubbled up inside me. It's an uncontainable desire. If you don't feel it too, then tell me. I'll respect that. But if you're going as mad with longing as I am, then, please, put us both out of our misery.'

He groaned. 'I have thought of you.' His breath fanned her face. 'I have dreamed of you. I have wanted you.' He closed his eyes, as if seeking strength. 'But you don't understand what you're asking of me.'

'I know that you want to stay here, alone and cut off from the world. I'm not offering any kind of permanent reprieve from that. When your sister's wedding is over, we'll never see one another again, I promise. My life is wrapped up in my father's company, and that's just how I want it. But we have this small window of opportunity, Thirio, and I'm here, with you, asking you to stop fighting what we both want. Just for now.'

'Damn it, Lucinda.' She braced for his rejection. She knew it was coming. She was sure of it.

But then, to her surprise and delight, he scooped her up against his chest and carried her, through the lovely timber doors, across the parquetry dance floor, and straight into her wildest fantasies.

CHAPTER TEN

HER SKIN WAS like velvet, flawless and smooth, the palest cream colour all over, except for her breasts, which were peaked in strawberry-pink, delightfully full and round, the perfect size for his hands. He held them, felt their weight, massaged them until he knew he had committed every detail to memory, then he kissed her. Hard and fast at first, befitting his need. He'd thrown off all shackles, all hesitation, and given himself over to temptation completely. It was a betrayal of the pledge he'd made the morning after his parents' deaths, and he knew he'd regret this, even at the same time he suspected he'd always feel grateful for it, and her.

She was wrong about not being a reprieve. She was. For when Lucinda was in the room, she brought sunshine and warmth and somehow that pushed back the darkness, just for a while. He could never allow the darkness to go, though. He deserved to feel it. He needed to feel it. Only in submitting to that pain could he live with what he'd done.

But for tonight, there was this. Her skin, softer than a rose bud. His hands caressed her body, his mouth tasted hers, then ran lower, teasing each nipple in turn, flicking and rolling until she was a whimpering mess beneath him. Lower still, over her flat stomach and rounded hips, holding her to the bed, pinning her beneath him as his mouth roamed lower. Slowly, sensually, tasting her, nipping her with his teeth, until he reached the pale hair at the apex of her thighs and flicked her there with his tongue.

She cried out, arching her back, but his hands were firm. When she stilled, he relinquished the grip of one, moving it instead to her legs, separating them. He gloried in the feel of her femininity beneath his fingertips, parting her for his tongue, tasting her and pleasuring her until both were almost at breaking point.

He made a growling sound against her sex then shifted his mouth to her inner thigh, pressing his lips to the flesh there and sucking, unrelenting. This was less about pleasure and more about possession. Though it was something he'd never done before, Thirio wanted to mark Lucinda, here, in one of her most private places, so that she would see it tomorrow and know that he had touched her there.

When his work was complete, he moved lower, tasting his way down her leg, to her ankles, before standing at the foot of the bed and simply staring at her.

This was everything he had fought for six long years and yet he gloried in her presence, he revelled in his mastery of her body even while acknowledging she held a similar, if not greater, power over him. He wanted to make it last, but at the same time he needed to feel her, to bury himself inside her, to reassure himself that he wasn't dreaming.

It had been years since he'd slept with a woman, but certain instincts were ingrained. Such as needing to use a condom. That was something he didn't have here at the *castile*. Why would he? He swore under his breath in his native Greek, his heart ricocheting through his chest with disbelief.

She pushed up onto her elbows. 'Please don't stop this again.'

'I don't have any protection.' He dragged a hand through his dark hair until it spiked at strange angles. 'I haven't been with a woman in a long time. I'm out of practice.'

'You don't seem it,' she said with a soft, husky laugh. But Thirio wasn't laughing. He felt as if his body were being split in two. Could they risk not using one?

His eyes dragged up her beautiful body to her face, flushed pink to the roots of the hair.

'I—um…' She darted her gaze towards the window, where the trees sat verdant green against the dusk sky. 'I brought some.'

He wanted to scream *Hallelujah!* He wanted to laugh and praise the heavens, but, most importantly, he wanted to melt into the ground with the force of his gratitude. His reaction was proof—as though he needed any—that he really did want this to happen.

'Where?'

'In my handbag.'

'Which is?'

'In my bedroom.' She groaned, and he understood why. He'd intentionally put her in the room farthest away from him, in an attempt to prevent exactly this.

He reached for her hand, lacing their fingers together, pulling her naked form against his own. 'Come with me.' The words were a gruff command, one he hoped she wouldn't question.

She didn't.

On his own, the walk to the western towers took perhaps five minutes, but with Lucinda, it took twenty. They kissed the whole way, their hands tangling, running over one another's bodies, relishing the sensations of being free to do this, at last. It was a form of torture. By the time they finally reached the room he'd allotted for her use, his blood was raging in his body, so fast and hard he could barely hear over its thundering torrent.

'Where?' he ground out, pulling his mouth away just long enough to ask the question. She spun around, looking over her shoulder, and he followed her gaze to the bag. He moved, long strides, picking it up and tipping it onto the bed, ignoring the jumble of lipstick, pen, notepad, phone, and landing on a strip of four condoms with a bubble of relief and amusement, all rolled into one.

'Thank God for your forethought.'

'God had very little to do with it,' she quipped in response. 'It was all wishful thinking.'

He spun around to face her, holding out the condoms. 'Care to do the honours?'

Her eyes flared wide and she nodded, her fingers trembling as she took the foil square from him. She used her teeth to open it, and his eyes hungrily chased the gesture, staying on her full lower lip, right until she liberated the rubber from its wrapping and came to stand in front of him.

When she knelt down, he almost regretted suggesting this. He hadn't been with a woman for more than six years and he seriously thought he had the stamina to stand still while she touched his arousal with those beautiful hands of hers?

When her mouth connected with his fractured, ruined skin on his hip, he startled. It was not what he'd expected. Her caress was so gentle, like silk, and on a part of his body that he had long ago associated with loss and guilt and self-flagellation; it was impossible to feel her kiss and not want to recoil. It was his scar. Burned, broken skin that spoke of horrors and had no place here in this moment of unimaginable pleasure. But it was a part of him, the truth of his soul, and he could never ignore it, could never forget what he'd done. And most vitally, he could never allow himself to hurt another soul.

Her lips moved sideways, slowly, as he had done to her, and he realised the cruelty in that torture now, for he yearned for her in a way that was immediate and wild, which could barely be contained by this slow, cautious exploration. But then, her lips kissed the base of his erection, her tongue flicking at the taut flesh there, before running over him, following a dark, throbbing vein to his tip, where a bead of pleasure shimmered. She lifted her eyes to his, confusion in the depths of hers as she darted out her tongue and tasted him, moaning softly as he filled her mouth. There was nothing soft about the sound Thirio made. His response was an eruption in the room, a loud, guttural groan that bounced off the walls, filling his ears with his own surrender.

'Don't,' he ground out, reaching for her shoulders, drawing her attention to his face.

'You...don't like it?' The uncertainty in her eyes was his undoing.

'I like it, too much. I haven't slept with a woman in six years. If you do that again, this will be over.'

'For now,' she responded impishly, grinning up at him.

'For now' was a phrase that held such promise. He had to hold himself back from reminding her that this was not the beginning of a relationship, so much as...what? He couldn't answer that.

'Yes, for now,' he agreed, after a beat. 'And I want to lose myself in you.'

Her eyes widened and her hands lifted, holding his arousal, as if committing him to memory as he'd done with her, and then she was reaching for the condom and stretching it down his length. The slow procession was torture. At several points, he wanted to take over, but his own hands were shaking and he wasn't sure if he'd be able to achieve the result any faster.

Finally, he was sheathed, and their passion threatened to engulf them completely. He reached down, lifting Lucinda to standing, kissing her lips, parting her mouth and warring with her tongue as though his life depended on it, as their bodies meshed once more, arms tangled with arms in an effort to get closer, legs pushing between one another's legs, as they stumbled and tumbled to the bed, finally falling onto it, pens and lipsticks beneath his back as she rolled on top of him, her kiss taking over, dominating, as she straddled him hungrily.

'Hang on,' he muttered, reaching behind his back and pulling out her keys, pushing them to one side, then freeing up as much detritus as he could, swiping it from under him, uncaring when it hit the floor with a loud succession of clunks.

She laughed but only for a moment. When he settled back on the bed, she moved her mouth back to his, kissing him and tasting him, lifting her hips and bringing her womanhood closer to his arousal, teasing him with her nearness, until, finally, she wasn't teasing so much as taking him, all of him, inside. Slowly, slowly, her muscles stretching around his size, inch by inch, until, finally, he was buried deep within her, so tight and spasming that his control was almost completely shot. A sound hissed from between his teeth as he closed his eyes and let the feelings explode through him.

Hell, he wasn't going to last long. Apparently, taking care of his needs with his own hand was no substitute for actual sex.

He pushed up, rolling Lucinda to her back, staring down at her with a sense of frustration. He needed to control this. He had to be able to pleasure her without losing himself.

His pride was at stake here. Thirio was not a selfish lover; he never had been. He loved making women feel good, and that hadn't changed.

Watching her face, he moved, slowly at first, then faster, all the while concentrating on the nuances of her expression, seeing what she liked most, bringing her to the edge of pleasure slowly, building it within her before pulling back, kissing her gently, relieving the pressure, then building it up again, until, finally, she tipped over, exploding in a loud, frantic, sudden wave, her muscles tightening around him until, control be damned, he was coming too, his own release almost in synch with hers, his body racked by the force of his release as he held himself above her, staring down at Lucinda without seeing her, for the brightness of the shooting stars darting across his eyelids.

He felt as though he'd run a marathon; he felt as though he were king of the world! Everything was bright and shiny and delightful. Now when he stared at Lucinda, she came back into focus, her beautiful face flushed and watchful, those full, angelic lips pouted into a natural smile, her bare décolletage begging for his attention. He dropped his head and kissed her there, feeling the frantic racing of her pulse beneath his lips, tasting her salty perspiration and finding that even that was an aphrodisiac. His arousal jerked inside her, and she made a rasping sound.

'I appreciate your enthusiasm,' she whispered into his ear, so he tilted his face and found her watching him with the most angelic expression.

His gut twisted. This was a betrayal in every sense of the word. And yet, he'd made himself clear to her. She wasn't expecting anything from this, besides sex. How could either of them resist this? Why had he bothered trying? Not for six years had he been tempted, but there was something about Lucinda Villeneuve that had turned his pledge on its head. It went beyond the fact she'd arrived here unannounced and gone toe to toe with him. This was more complicated, more elemental. Completely unavoidable.

'That was amazing.'

He lifted a single dark brow. 'There's room for improvement,' he conceded, though his body felt pretty bloody great.

'Oh, really?' She ran a finger down his cheek, towards his lips. 'What would you change?'

'For one thing, I'd have the stamina to give you more than one orgasm.'

'Not just one orgasm,' she corrected. 'A mind-blowing, life-altering orgasm.'

'Ah.' He nodded with mock seriousness. 'Then at least three of those.'

'Three?' she repeated incredulously. 'I can't even imagine.'

'You won't have to imagine.' He turned his head quickly, capturing her finger between his teeth and biting down on it, so she laughed. 'Next time.'

The words floated between them, a silent promise that lifted her skin with goosebumps.

'You certainly know how to set the bar high,' she said after a moment.

It felt so good to be lying naked with her. He wanted to stay there all evening, until he was ready to take her again, but that was all the more reason he had to move. Oh, he'd succumbed to this, absolutely, but he wasn't ready to lose all of himself. There still had to be an element of control and separation.

He pulled out of her with regret, standing and turning his back so he could dispose of the condom in a wastepaper basket, before coming back to the side of the bed. She was still lying where he'd left her, completely spent. He studied her, delighting in his effect on her, knowing he should pull her to standing and draw her away from the bed, return to the business she'd come here to do.

But greater forces were at play, and instead Thirio flopped back beside her, albeit with a good two feet of space between them. He propped onto his side, facing her, and a moment later Lucinda did the same thing, echoing his body language. It was almost impossible to lie there and not reach out to touch her, but Thirio wanted to challenge himself, and so he stayed where he was, with all the appearance of being at ease even when a coil was beginning to wind inside his belly, tighter and tighter, building pressure as though he hadn't just had the mother of all releases.

'Have you really not slept with a woman in six years?'

'No.'

Her lips quirked downward. 'I'm surprised.'

And though he could understand her surprise, he shrugged and said, 'Why? You shouldn't believe everything you read on the Internet.'

'Well, pictures don't lie,' she said quietly, mulling this over. 'And there are a lot of photos of you with a lot of different women.'

Yes, that was true. 'It was another life.'

Sympathy darkened her amber eyes. Damn it. He didn't want to do this. He didn't want Lucinda, of all people, to feel sorry for him. He was so sick of the way people looked at him, and to have her turn into one of *them* was the last thing he wanted.

'My sex life is not interesting,' he said darkly. 'I would much rather discuss yours.'

'Or the lack thereof?'

'Yes,' he agreed. 'That is a much greater mystery. How

is it possible that a woman like you has not had more than one boyfriend?'

She lifted a hand to her throat, as if looking for something. He remembered the necklace he'd seen on the first day, diamond on a fine silver chain.

'I can't say.'

'Because it is a secret?'

'No, because there's not really any particular reason.'

His eyes narrowed. 'What happened to your claim that you are always honest?'

Her lips parted in surprise. 'I'm—I am being honest.'

'No, you're hiding something from me.'

She looked as though she was about to deny it and he waited, his expression giving nothing away. But then, she sighed softly and focused her gaze on the bedspread between them. 'It was not a good breakup. I guess I lost a lot of confidence when he left me. And relationships are hard, you know? You have to put yourself out there and be vulnerable to another person. You have to trust someone else not to hurt you, and, after Beckett, I just wasn't able to do that again.'

Thirio had a burning curiosity. He wanted to understand everything about this Beckett, including how he could be so stupid as to treat a woman like Lucinda badly enough that she'd be gun-shy of all relationships.

'What did he do to you?'

The tone of his voice drew her gaze. She furrowed her brow, adding complexity and interest to a face that was already far too mesmerising. 'He fell in love with someone else.'

'Someone you knew?'

Wariness flashed in her eyes. Surprise too. 'Yes.'

'Someone you trusted?'

Her lips pulled sideways. 'I wouldn't say that.' Lucinda's long, elegant fingers moved between them, plucking at the bedspread. 'One of my stepsisters, Sofia.'

'The woman I met at your office?'

'No, that was Carina. She's not—quite as bad as Sofia.'

Thirio had run the gamut of emotions in his life. He'd known delirium and joy as a boy, and careless, giddy happiness as a teenager and then the flipside to that, incomparable loss and grief as a young man, but he wasn't sure he'd ever known an emotion quite like the one pummelling him from the inside out. It was a mix of protectiveness and angry disbelief. 'Tell me about these women, *agape mou.*' The endearment slipped out before he could stop it, words he'd never said to a woman in his life, for the simple reason he'd heard his father say them to his mother so many times, they seemed almost to belong to his parents.

She opened her mouth, then closed it, sighing softly. 'What do you want to know?'

'You have said your stepmother mistreated you. I gather your stepsisters were just as bad?'

'No, no one could be.' She responded quickly and with no artifice, so he knew that whatever torment her stepmother had put Lucinda through must have been truly awful. 'I can't blame my stepsisters. They're by-products of their upbringing and my stepmother is not a kind woman. They were never taught to see the goodness in the world, nor in people. They perceive life through a prism of what they can get, not what they can give.'

Her words spoke volumes about her own outlook, but then, he already understood this facet of Lucinda. From the moment she'd arrived, she'd lobbied hard to give Evie her dream wedding. She'd fought hard for a woman she'd never met, because of the connection of being without parents. How deeply did this experience define Lucinda?

'Whereas you prefer to make people happy.'

Her eyes widened. 'What's wrong with that?'

He put his hand over hers, staring at the visage they made. 'Nothing.' His voice was hoarse. He cleared his throat, focusing the conversation back on less tenuous ground. 'Did you love this man?'

She bit down on her lower lip and his abdomen tightened. 'I thought I did. Looking back, I think I was just desperate to be in love, and, more importantly, to be loved by someone in return.'

'After your father died, was there no one besides your stepmother who could have raised you? Grandparents? Aunts and uncles?'

'No. No one.'

'I'm sorry,' he said with sincerity.

Lucinda's smile was uneven, a failed attempt at the gesture. 'I didn't really want to move out, anyway. It's the only home I've ever known, and to think of my stepmother and stepsisters living there, without me, without Dad.' She shook her head, her eyes shifting as though searching for words. 'It was like a bomb had gone off right in the middle of my life,' she said quietly, with no idea that she was speaking to someone who'd lived through an actual explosion, and knew exactly what a detonation sounded like, smelled like, tasted like. He tried to push away the memories, seared into his brain, and focus instead on her words. She'd invoked an expression, that was all. 'One minute it was just Dad and me. The next, he'd fallen madly in love and was getting married.'

'And you supported him in this.'

'Of course,' she responded instantly. 'He was my father and I wanted him to be happy. I thought she'd make him happy.'

'And did she?'

Lucinda hesitated. 'I don't have enough experience of

relationships to say for sure. Perhaps it was a different kind of happiness. More complex, maybe more rewarding? I don't know.'

He lifted his hand to her cheek, pushing some hair behind her ear then returning it to her hand. Just the simple contact stirred heat in his veins, renewed desire. 'Did they argue?'

'Not really. They just didn't seem to "click". Maybe I had romanticised ideas of what a great relationship should be like. I was only fifteen and, to that point, had watched a heck of a lot of Disney movies and read my fill of romance novels,' she said with a soft smile. 'I thought he'd stepped into a fantasy and that our life was going to be everything I'd always wanted. A real family, at last.' She shook her head. 'But instead, I kind of...'

'Yes?' he prompted, when she tapered off into silence.

'I sort of just lost my dad, from the moment they were married. All of the little rituals we had stopped overnight. My stepmother seemed to resent anything that he and I shared. I wanted to include them, but she preferred to start new traditions.'

'That's insensitive.'

'Yes.' Lucinda's features tightened, her face showing pain, so he wanted to ease it, to push it away for her. He'd known enough of those torturous inner feelings to wish to free her from them for life. 'I don't know what happened to my stepmother to make her the way she is. I used to want to try to know, to understand her and even help her, but...'

'She pushed you too far.'

Her eyes flared wide at his perceptive comment. 'Yes,' she agreed softly. 'Now I just want her out of my life.' She flipped her hand over, capturing his, her fingers brushing the skin between his thumb and forefinger. 'I wish her well. I want her to be happy. I just don't want her to be anywhere near me.'

'And your stepsisters?'

'Them too.'

He could imagine what it took for a woman like Lucinda, who was all kindness and goodness, to express such feelings about anyone. 'How old were you when this man left you for your stepsister?'

'Nineteen. It feels like a lifetime ago.'

'Did they stay together?'

She shook her head. 'It was never really about that. Sofia seduced him just to take him away from me. I had something good in my life, I was happy and felt loved for the first time in a long time, and I guess she didn't like that.'

He bit back the curse that came to mind. 'What about him?'

'He was…not the man I thought him to be. He didn't even fight for what we shared. I meant nothing to him,' she added, the last words said so calmly and yet he felt the tension emanating from them, the importance of that phrase to her being, in some way.

'And so you swore off men and relationships?'

'It wasn't so dramatic as that.' A smile tugged at her lips and something in the region of his heart glowed warm. 'More than anything, I just couldn't imagine getting close to someone, only to have them leave me again. So I focused on the business.'

'And that became your life.'

'Yes,' she agreed. 'And it's enough for me. It's all I want, Thirio. It's all I'll ever want.'

CHAPTER ELEVEN

THAT HE'D SET up a state-of-the-art office for her shouldn't have surprised Lucinda. He had told her, right from their first meeting, that he was detail-orientated. But it was beyond her expectations to have these facilities at her disposal.

It was the perfect space to work, and yet there was one problem.

She was distracted. For every ten minutes she spent emailing contractors and tying down details of the wedding, her mind wandered to Thirio, and the way they'd come together the night before, as though driven by forces much greater than they could understand. Passion had hummed and zipped around them like a cord, tying them together. There had been no escaping their lovemaking. It was inevitable. And perfect.

A smile touched her lips and she leaned back in her chair, running her eyes over the computer screen without really focusing. She'd been at it for hours, and, though she hadn't achieved as much as she'd wanted, she was confident the wedding was on track. The biggest items had been ticked off—the caterers were world class, the menu she'd selected carefully put together to appeal to all palates and tastes. The musicians had been booked and the photographer she'd spoken to had set aside a photoshoot for *Vogue* magazine to come and capture the wedding. Everything was going to be perfect.

A smile pulled at her lips, a true smile, born of absolute, untouched happiness. And hope. Because this wedding was the gateway to her dreams—she was so close to being able to buy the business. But it was more than that. She felt hope because of what she'd shared with Thirio. She wasn't stupid enough to think that sleeping together was the start of a meaningful relationship, and yet it *had* meant something to her. It was the breaking down of a wall she'd built around her heart. She didn't trust Thirio in the sense that she wanted to spend the rest of her life with him, but she had put her faith in him for this short while, and that was a big step for Lucinda. Maybe she wasn't as closed off to relationships as she'd come to believe.

His intrusion was not unwelcome. Nor was it really a surprise. It was as though she'd manifested his arrival.

'I brought you coffee.' He placed the cup on the edge of the desk, remaining where he was, arms crossed, eyes skimming her face in that intense way he had. Her heart trembled.

'Thank you. Coffee is always welcome.' She reached for it, inhaling the fragrance before taking a deep sip. After they'd made love the night before, they'd eaten dinner—toasted sandwiches—then gone back to bed. Lucinda hadn't slept much and she was tired now. She stifled a yawn then sent him an apologetic smile.

'How's it going?' He nodded towards the computer screen.

'Everything's on track.' She ticked off the list of professionals she'd hired. 'Our firm's worked with all of them previously. They're the best in the business.'

'I trust you.'

She startled—the words expressing so perfectly the thoughts she'd had moments earlier—then blinked away. He only meant that he trusted her to manage the wedding.

'I've prepared a brief note, to update you as to my progress.' She reached for the printout she'd made only half an hour earlier. 'Ordinarily, it would go to your sister, but as you're handling all the logistics...'

'I'll email it to her,' he said, taking a photo of the document, clicking a couple of buttons then returning his focus to her face. 'She's been a bit better the last couple of days. She'd love to see it.'

'Has she been able to organise a dress?' Lucinda enquired sympathetically.

'There is a designer attached to the Nalvanian palace,' he said with a nod. 'That's taken care of.'

'Of course.' Lucinda's eyes drifted to the view beyond the window. It was such a beautiful castle. What a shame that it should be a prison rather than a home. She frowned, the thought coming to her unprompted, and yet she realised that it was accurate. That was how Thirio used this place: the walls kept him locked away from the world, and the world locked away from him.

The idea of that propelled her to stand and move to him, to press her hands to his chest and stare up at his face. The air around them grew thick, their awareness impossible to fight now that they'd been together. Their bodies were in sync, hearts beating in unison.

'Have you worked enough for now?' he growled, arms behind her back, drawing her closer to him, so she felt the stirring of his attraction through the fabric of her dress.

Her eyes widened, lifting to his in time to see a mocking smile on his lips. 'The coffee might have been a ruse,' he said with a non-apologetic shrug.

'Ahh...' She grinned right back at him. 'But an excellent one.' She moved one hand to reach for the cup, taking two big sips before returning it to the edge of the desk. 'I'm quite tired after last night.'

'Are you?' He scanned her face. 'Do you need to go back to bed for a bit?'

Heat spread through her like lava. 'Yes.' She nodded slowly. 'But not to sleep.'

Thirio had travelled in helicopters since he was a young boy. He was intimately familiar with the *thwop-thwop-thwop* noise of the blades, and particularly when they drew close to Castile di Neve. But in his drowsy state, it took him a moment to place the noise, and then to realise what it meant. He shifted, dislodging Lucinda so she woke, blinking at him as if from a very deep dream, then smiled, happiness and contentment so obvious on her beautiful face.

'Someone's here,' he explained, nodding towards the window of his room, which now showed a dark speck growing closer.

'Maybe it's just flying overhead.'

'The trajectory is wrong for that.' He squinted a little, recognising the golden emblem on the side of the aircraft. 'It's my sister.'

'Your sister?' Lucinda gawked, her perfectly relaxed aura disappearing. 'Coming *here*?'

He stayed where he was, bemused by her reaction. 'It does happen, from time to time. As you so wisely reminded me the day we met, this is her home too.'

'I should never have spoken to you like that,' she muttered apologetically, pushing out of bed and hurriedly pulling on underwear. The helicopter blades grew louder.

'You were right,' he said. 'And what is the matter?

You're acting as though you've been caught with your hand in the cookie jar.'

Her fingers trembled a little as she slid into the dress he'd enjoyed removing hours earlier.

'She's my client.' Lucinda pulled a face.

'Technically, that's me.'

'Well, yes, *technically*,' Lucinda agreed, rolling her eyes. 'But really, it's Evie I want to impress.'

'Because I'm already impressed enough?'

She laughed. 'You're incorrigible.' She was fully dressed, but it didn't change the fact that she still looked as though she'd been being ravished for hours. A conclusion she evidently came to herself when her eyes landed on their reflection in the mirror. 'Oh, gawd,' she squawked, bending down and grabbing his jeans then tossing them across the room at him. 'Get dressed.' When he didn't move, she pushed her hands together. 'Ple-e-e-ease.'

His laugh surprised them both. It was a natural, deep rumble, true mirth in its tone. 'Relax.' He shook his head. 'She doesn't bite.'

'I just don't want her to think this is how I got the job.'

'I'll happily tell her that you broke in and refused to leave until I'd acquiesced.'

'Thi-ir-io-o-o-o…' she moaned, finger-combing blonde hair over her shoulder with one hand, while the other licked her thumb then wiped clean the smudges of make-up around her eyes. 'Please don't.'

'Relax,' he repeated. 'It's going to be fine.'

'Easy for you to say,' she said with a shake of her head. 'Your whole future isn't riding on the next fifteen minutes of your life.'

'And neither is yours. You'll get paid no matter what my sister thinks of you.'

Lucinda's eyes widened, and hurt showed in their stunning amber depths. 'This isn't about money,' she said stiffly. He frowned, because, actually, it was. She needed money to buy her father's business back, and money was no issue for Thirio. In fact, he was tempted to give it to her now so she could get the ball rolling.

'Then what is it about?' he asked, gently, not wanting to scare her off.

'This is my first proper commission. I've done the hard yards on a lot of events in my time, but this is the first job I've landed on my own, the first job I'm solely responsible for. Your sister's happiness is a huge part of the success criteria. I want her to be happy—no, thrilled—with what I've arranged. It's important to me.'

Then it was important to him too. He didn't say the words. They felt wrong, and as if they might give her a misleading impression about their relationship, and yet he felt them, deep in his bones.

'Okay, okay,' he said instead, shaking his head ruefully. 'But you'd better go and choose a different dress if you don't want her to know how we've been spending our time.'

Lucinda frowned then turned to the mirror, her fingers lifting to her neck where the edge of a love bite was just visible. 'Thirio!' she squawked again. 'You are...'

'Incorrigible. You've already said that. But by my estimate, you've got five minutes before Evie walks in the door, at most.'

'Argh!' She turned and ran towards the door, in such a hurry that she jammed her hip into the bedpost as she passed it. She pressed her fingers to the spot.

'I'll kiss it better later,' he called, half laughing, to her retreating back.

At the door, she turned to face him. 'You'd better,' she

muttered, smiling. And then, 'Thank you for everything. That—' her eyes fell to the bed '—was wonderful.'

Evie arrived alone, which, given her status, was very rare these days. 'I gave my guard the slip,' she said with an innocent blink of turquoise eyes. 'They fuss even more than you do.' At just over five feet tall, Evie had to stand on her tiptoes to kiss her older brother's cheek. 'How are you, darling?'

He didn't dare answer honestly. In that moment, he felt as if he were on top of the goddamned world. But if Evie knew the reason for his unusual ebullience, she'd obsess over keeping Lucinda in his life, and that wasn't possible. Thirio was already breaking the pledge he'd made to himself. But at least it was temporary. In a matter of days, or weeks at most, things would return to normal, and for the rest of his life he would be alone, grieving his parents, paying penance for his role in their deaths. And that penance would be even more meaningful if it meant denying himself Lucinda.

'I'm fine,' he responded, his tone suitably glowering as the recollection of his guilt brought a storm cloud over his newly cheery mood.

'You look well.' She nodded her approval. 'Shall we sit on the terrace?'

'Why are you here?'

She laughed. 'Charming. Can't I come just to visit my big brother?'

'Of course you can.' He waved away her joke, trying to tamp down on his impatience. Wanting to be alone with Lucinda didn't give him the right to be rude to his sister. He softened his tone. 'How are *you* feeling, more to the point?' She looked slim, and pale. He met her concern with his own.

'Actually, I'm okay. I've eaten breakfast these last four days, so that's something. Still just a piece of toast and half a banana, but that's better than nothing.'

'It's not enough.' He frowned. 'Is your doctor any good?'

'Apparently, she's the best in Nalvania.'

'Then let me find you the best in the world,' Thirio insisted. 'Nalvania is a small country—'

'With excellent healthcare,' she assured him, shaking her head affectionately. He'd blinked and suddenly his younger sister had grown into a beautiful, confident, self-assured princess-in-waiting. 'I'm okay, Thirio. The doctors are not worried.'

'You're too thin.'

'Gee, thanks,' she muttered. 'What's got into you? You're even grouchier than usual.'

He glowered, unable to answer her question honestly. He'd been wrenched out of bed with a beautiful woman—the first lover he'd taken in six years. Damned straight he was cranky at the intrusion.

'The reason I came is to discuss this.' She brandished her phone.

He focused on the screen, recognising Lucinda's wedding details. 'Is there a problem?'

'Far from it. I'm overjoyed. Everything here is so perfect, Thirio, I can't believe it. It's as though this woman has tunnelled right into my subconscious and pulled out my innermost thoughts and wishes. The wedding is going to be everything I could ever want.'

And despite the fact he had absolutely no right, pride puffed Thirio's chest. Not personal pride, but a sense of pride for Lucinda, and for the work she'd done. Now that he knew more about her, and understood the adversity she'd faced to accomplish what she had, he was even happier that she'd been able to so perfectly anticipate Evie's needs.

'I'd like her number so I can call and thank her.'

'You can thank her in person.'

'What do you mean?'

'She's here.'

'Here?' Evie stared at him as though he'd said something quite ludicrous. 'At the *castle*?'

Thirio laughed, her incredulity not hard to understand. 'Well, she does have to organise rather a major event.'

'Yes, but still,' Evie said with a small shake of her head. 'I didn't realise you'd be...'

'Yes?'

'I thought—' Evie laughed, then mock-punched Thirio's arm. 'Stop making fun of me. You know what I'm getting at. You *hate* people. You particularly hate having people in your personal space.'

'And yet I agreed for your wedding to be here.'

Evie was quiet, chewing on that a moment. 'Why *did* you agree to this?' Her eyes probed his. 'I know you must hate the idea.'

He nodded slowly. 'My first reaction was to say no. But then I read the plan and I knew how happy it would make you. There is nothing I want more than your happiness, Evie.' What he didn't add, but they both understood, was that he felt an obligation to deliver that happiness to her, after what he'd taken away.

'But at what cost?' she murmured. 'I don't want you to suffer.'

'I'll cope,' he drawled. 'It's one night.'

'But two days.'

'I'll cope,' he repeated firmly. 'Stop worrying and start enjoying.' His edict was followed by a knock on the door jamb of the living room and, a moment later, Lucinda ducked her head around. He stood very still. In fact, it was as though his body had been turned to rock. All he could do was stare at her. Gone was the woman he'd just been making love to. In her place stood a stunning, confident, smiling professional, wearing a silk blouse and knee-length skirt, her hair braided over one shoulder.

'Hello. You must be Evie.' Lucinda barely looked at Thirio.

'And you must be my guardian angel!' Evie responded with a soft laugh. 'Honestly, I don't know how you did this.'

'It's my job.' Lucinda shrugged modestly. 'But I'm very happy that you're pleased with the progress.'

'Pleased? I'm in awe. You've thought of everything, right down to your suggestion that guests make donations to the Nalvanian Childhood Literacy fund rather than giving us presents. After all, what more do we need?'

'I know it's a cause that's close to your heart.'

'But *how* do you know?' Evie responded with obvious disbelief. 'It's as though you're living in my mind.'

'I read a lot of interviews,' Lucinda confided with a hint of pink in her cheeks. 'That might seem a bit creepy, but I find it's the best way to get to know a client and work out how to help them.'

'On the contrary, I think it's genius. On other occasions, I've had to spend days being questioned and going over proposals and I just couldn't stomach it this time. Which is why I handed the tedium to Thirio. You've saved us both a lot of effort.'

'It's my pleasure,' Lucinda promised, her eyes briefly flicking to Thirio, who met her response with a small grin. He couldn't help it. Inwardly, he corrected her: it was *both* of their pleasure. 'Would you like me to go through it all with you?' Lucinda offered.

'That's exactly why I'm here!' Evie clapped her hands together, glowing with happiness and vitality. That brought joy to his heart, but it was immediately followed by a rush of guilt, because their mother deserved to see her like this. He'd deprived them all of so much. 'Shall we start in the ballroom?'

'Absolutely.' Lucinda turned to face him. 'Thirio? Did you want to join us?'

He was frowning, and not listening properly.

'Thirio?' Evie waved her hand in his face. 'Are you coming?'

'No.' His response was quick. Panic was rising inside him, the familiar rush of adrenalin something he'd become used to over the years. It always happened when he thought of their parents. 'You go ahead. I have work to catch up on.'

'It's a weekend, you know,' Evie reminded him, but good-naturedly, so he offered a tight smile.

'You'll have more fun without me. Go. Enjoy yourself.'

'Is he being unbearably rude?' Evie asked, when they were alone.

Lucinda jerked her gaze to Evie. 'Who?'

'My brother,' Evie said gently. 'It's okay, you don't have to protect him. I know what Thirio's like.'

Lucinda contemplated that. The first day she'd met Thirio, he'd been beastly, but it had been a long time since she'd seen that side of him. 'He's okay, actually.'

'You're very tolerant. Or perhaps very polite. Probably both.' Evie smiled. 'In any event, thank you for putting up with him. He's got a heart of gold, deep down. It's just *very* deep down, and not many people ever get to see it.' She frowned. 'In fact, I'm probably the only one who believes that.'

I believe it, Lucinda added inwardly, while nodding politely. 'A marquee will be erected over there.' She stopped walking and pointed towards a window. There was a large flat area of grass, with a stunning view of pine trees and wildflowers. 'A carpet, made locally from recycled wool, will cover the ground, preserving guests' shoes. The chairs will be sourced from the attic—did you know there's over two hundred chairs from the early twentieth century there?'

'I forgot. How did you find them?' Evie said with obvious surprise.

'I went exploring yesterday,' Lucinda said, glossing over the fact that Thirio had given her a tour of the castle. 'They're so beautiful. Classic art deco, they'll look wonderful.'

Evie's smiled was tinged with nostalgia. 'My parents used to host New Year's Eve parties here. Those are the chairs they used.' Her eyes were suspiciously moist, but she blinked quickly then smiled. 'It's good you found them. I really do want to avoid the appearance of extravagance,' Evie said as they continued their progress towards the ballroom. 'That's what I loved about your proposal. Everything is thoughtful, repurposed, meaningful, with just enough special touches to reassure traditionalists that it's a royal wedding.' She pulled a face as she said the last two words.

'I imagine there's a lot of pomp in your life?' Lucinda enquired thoughtfully.

'It's not so bad. As the fourth son, Erik has no expectation of becoming King. It's the media that intrudes, and we cannot appear ungrateful for their attention, so it's a delicate balance.'

They entered the ballroom and Evie sighed heavily. 'I've always loved it here.'

'And yet, you don't come often?'

Evie turned to look at Lucinda, appraising her for a moment before shaking her head. 'No. It's my brother's home.'

'I get the impression you two are very close.'

'We love one another a lot, but that isn't the same thing as being close. I don't think Thirio will ever let anyone close,' she added, then shook her head. 'But that is not your burden. I shouldn't have said anything.'

'It's okay,' Lucinda said gently, a hint of guilt in the words, because the last thing she wanted to do was pump Thirio's sister for information about him. 'Anyone associated with your wedding has signed an ironclad confidentiality agreement, so whatever you say will stay between us.'

'Oh, in that case, we should grab a couple of chairs, we could be here for hours,' she joked. 'I don't mean to make it sound so bad. Thirio and I message often. I know he has my best interests at heart. But you've probably gathered from the way he lives that Thirio is a recluse. He closes himself off from the world, and that includes me. I come here when I can. Once or twice a year. But I know he is only tolerating my company, and I can't quite bear that.' Sadness made the words husky. 'I don't overstay my welcome.'

'I'm very sorry to hear it,' Lucinda replied, her own heart heavy with grief at the picture Evie was painting.

But wasn't it the exact same picture Lucinda was at the centre of? True, Thirio had been very accommodating on this trip, but that was temporary. Lucinda felt the same as Evie, in many ways: chiefly, that she could not overstay her welcome. Having already been subjected to Thirio when he was cold and dismissive, she hated the thought of being on the receiving end of that treatment again. And invariably she would be, when he decided that the time had come to end their fling.

Which was why she had to keep it light and leave as

soon as her work was completed. She would take a page from Evie's book, and leave Thirio before she'd overstayed her welcome.

And just like that, all her old insecurities were back, curdling in her belly, so she found it hard to concentrate. But she forced herself to focus, enough to complete the tour, and to ask Evie the handful of questions she had to ensure she'd checked off her list.

'The seating plan is mine to worry about,' Evie said as they concluded their discussion. 'Protocol has to be observed, so someone from Erik's staff will oversee the guest list and work out the most diplomatic place to seat everybody.' She tapped her pen against the edge of the table. 'As for Thirio, there's someone I'd like him to meet.' She flashed Lucinda a conspiratorial grin. 'A girlfriend of mine, from Nalvania. He hasn't been seeing anyone for— well, a long time, but I think he might be ready. After all, he's agreed to host the wedding here, which is a huge step forward for him.'

Lucinda smiled kindly, used to concealing her innermost thoughts, and particularly used to concealing any hint of pain she was feeling. But the truth was, Evie's casual mention of a friend she wanted to set up with Thirio was like a knife in Lucinda's heart. Why should it be? Thirio wasn't her boyfriend. They'd made no promises to one another. And yet the idea of him being with another woman was anathema to Lucinda. She couldn't even contemplate it.

'Will you come to the wedding, Lucinda?' Evie asked, clear eyes on Lucinda's face, reminding her in that moment of Thirio and his very direct stare.

'I will be coming,' Lucinda responded with a professional smile. 'I'll be in the background, making sure everything runs smoothly.'

'Surely you have staff for that? I meant for you to attend as my guest. It feels like the least I can do, after the perfection you've accomplished.'

'It's my job,' Lucinda responded softly. 'And believe me, I'm much more comfortable fading into the background.'

Evie frowned, but didn't push the point. 'Well, if you change your mind, please do come. I'd love to have you there.'

'That's very kind.' Lucinda knew she'd never accept the invitation. Thirio might have made her feel as though she were on top of the world, but she was well aware that it was temporary.

When she returned to London, and the office, reality would swallow her whole again, and her stepmother and stepsisters would be reminding her of her flaws and faults as reliably as day followed night. This weekend was a fantasy. A small bubble separate from the rest of time and place, her own little nirvana on earth, but it would not last. All bubbles burst eventually.

CHAPTER TWELVE

SHE HAD TOLD herself she wouldn't ask, but as they lay on the rooftop terrace of one of the turrets, limbs entwined, the softest blanket beneath them, a spider's web of stars twinkling against the black velvet of the dawn sky, Lucinda was driven to throw caution to the wind. She kept her head pressed to Thirio's chest, listening to the steady, heavy thudding of his heart, as her finger chased the texture of his chest, feeling every knot.

'Was this from the accident?'

It was impossible not to feel how he stiffened, his body radiating tension.

'You don't have to answer. I didn't mean to pry.'

'Your curiosity is natural,' came his clipped, closed-off response. And it was such a harsh reminder of the way he'd been that first day they met that she felt as though she were teetering on the edge of a very tall building. She tried to steady her breathing but the truth was, after the intimacies they'd shared, and the way she'd relaxed with him over these past two days, going back to that cold, closed-off man was the last thing she wanted.

'But you don't want to talk about it.' Already, Lucinda was pulling her barriers back into place, telling herself she didn't care if he rejected her, because he wasn't the first person. But the truth was, her heart was heavy and she couldn't imagine being in the same room with Thirio and having him treat her with the coldness of a stranger.

'No.' The word was gruff, torn from his chest. 'But as I said, your curiosity is natural.'

She stayed very still.

'It wasn't an accident.' The words dropped like stone between them.

They made no sense. 'What do you mean?'

'The night my parents died. It was no accident.'

'I've read the papers. They all say—'

'My parents were very rich, with powerful friends. They made sure the fire was reported in a specific way. But it was not an accident.'

She kept her ear to his chest, running her fingers over the flesh again, slower, as though she could heal his hurt and heart with her touch. 'Then what happened?'

'Are you sure you want to know?'

'Only if you want to tell me.'

He expelled another deep breath and this time, she pushed up to look at him.

'It is not a matter of wanting to tell you,' he said after a long pause. 'But it is a part of who I am. Somehow, I don't mind you knowing, even when it will change everything.'

She waited, without speaking.

'It was the night before my father's birthday. I should have stayed home—my mother begged me not to go out. But that was what I did back then. Pointless, indulgent, selfish existence. I partied as though there were no to-morrow. I blew through tens of thousands of dollars a night. I drank too much, had indiscriminate sex, shallow friendships. I had no responsibilities and used to think I was glad.'

'I can't imagine you ever behaving like that.'

'I am not the same as I was then.'

'No.' This she'd already gathered.

'I came home in the early hours of the morning, wasted and famished. I decided to cook some bacon and set the stove going, emptying my pockets out on the bench beside it. I went upstairs to take a shower, then fell asleep. The next thing I knew, the earth beneath me was shaking.' He spoke without stopping, the words tripping over each other to get out, as though he had to relive them in this order, without a break, now that he'd started. 'There had been an explosion. It woke me, and Evie. I stumbled downstairs, to find the whole level engulfed in flames. I could hear my mother crying out. She was still alive. I just had to get to her. But there was Evie, too, and in that moment, I needed to make a decision. Evie was terrified of fire. She was crying upstairs. I ran back and got her, carrying her out, before returning to my parents. I was still drunk, Lucinda. I wasn't thinking straight, it was instincts alone that were making me act. I ran into the fire, a shirt wrapped around my face, trying to get to them. A beam fell on me. I was trapped, flames were everywhere, but somehow, I managed to push it off me and keep going. But there was too much fire. By the time I got to their room, it was hotter than the sun. I couldn't go in. I wanted to. Even now, recounting this to you, I wonder if it was really so bad. If I couldn't have pushed through and got to them. But they were already dead. I will never forget the sight of my mother on the ground, Lucinda. And all because I had to go out and get hammered, like every other night of my pointless goddamned life.'

'Oh, Thirio.' Her cheeks were wet. 'That's still an accident.'

'I put my cigarette lighter on the edge of the stove. I basically created a bomb. Yes, it was an accident, but it was also entirely my fault. This was preventable.'

Sadness welled in her chest, for so many reasons. 'And all this time, you've lived with this guilt?' she asked, pushing up so she could see him better. He stared straight ahead, his eyes fixed on the stars above them. 'All this time you've blamed yourself?'

'Who else is to blame?'

She shook her head. 'You didn't mean to cause the fire. Accidents happen.'

'And if I had broken a vase or even crashed a car, I might see it your way. But I killed my mother and father. I deprived Evie of her parents. I destroyed our family. For years I wished I had died too. It was only Evie that kept me going. I couldn't leave her.'

'Oh, Thirio, don't say that. You have so much to offer. You parents would want you to live your life.' She hesitated, not sure if she was going to ruin everything, but judging that it was more important to help him than to preserve their status quo. 'And not like this. They would want you to live your life properly and fully, to find a way to be happy. You cannot keep yourself in stasis for ever, and, what's more, you don't deserve that.'

'I deserve to rot in hell,' he muttered. 'If you could only know the kind of person I was back then. Selfish, spoiled, entitled—'

'And young,' she said quietly. 'You were still a boy, Thirio, in your early twenties.'

'It doesn't matter. Nothing you say will change this. I killed my parents, and I will live with that knowledge for as long as I live.'

'And you will stay here, away from people and fun and friends, hidden away, miserable, soaking in your grief?'

'What would you suggest as an alternative? Draw a line in the sand under my parents' deaths and kick up my heels as though it never happened?'

'Don't be facetious,' she said softly, reproachfully, so his gaze slid sideways to hers. 'I'm not saying you can ignore your pain, nor that you should. But you have to find a way to live with it, as a part of you, rather than shutting down completely.'

'Thank you for the advice.' There wasn't a hint of gratitude in the words. 'But this is the approach that's working for me.'

'Is it really working?' She quietly reflected on that, pulling apart his sentiment. 'And this is why you've pledged not to have sex?'

'Why should I get to enjoy my life when I deprived them of theirs? When I deprived Evie of her beloved mother and father? Going without sex and companionship is a small price to pay, given what I did.'

'Thirio,' Lucinda groaned. 'I'm so sorry you feel this way.' She struggled to know what else to say. 'You couldn't have known that would happen.'

'No,' he agreed, voice grim. 'But the way I used to behave, it was only a matter of time.'

She thought about the photos she'd seen of him on the Internet, the lifestyle he used to lead. 'You aren't the only twenty-something who's enjoyed going out and partying, who's then done something stupid because they were drunk, and young.'

'It killed my parents.' His eyes were haunted. 'Would you forgive yourself?'

'Listen to me.' She put her hand on his cheek. 'You have to, for one reason. Your parents would want you to. Do you think your mother and father would wish you to sacrifice your enjoyment in life as some kind of price for their deaths? Of course not. If they loved you at all, and I'm sure they did, they would want you to live your life *for* them. You should be ringing every moment of delight, and feeling it on their behalf. Make your life a tribute, Thirio, not a torment.'

'Beautiful words,' he said, his tone showing that he had heard them without intending to listen. 'But this is how it needs to be. It's the only way I can live with myself.'

Sadness filled her chest. His grief was palpable, so too the tragedy of what had unfolded.

'Would you tell me about them?' she asked, nestling her head back on his wounded chest, knowing now that the outward scars were nothing compared to the marks he carried on the walls of his heart.

His chest rose with his intake of breath, then fell as he expelled slowly, a little unevenly. 'What would you like to know?'

She put her arm over his chest, holding him tight, reassuring him and caring for him. 'Anything you want to tell me.'

And as the dawn sky gradually permitted more light, Thirio spoke of his parents. He told stories of his childhood vacations, travelling, laughing, having fun. He spoke of his mother's love of Christmas, and how she'd infused that time of year with so much magic, right up until that last year. He spoke about the runs he and his father would go on, miles and miles of silence and then how they'd stop, and talk about nothing in particular. How his dad always made him feel as though he could do anything he wanted, and his mother made him feel as though he wasn't doing enough. He talked about how time had changed his perspective. He used to hate the way his mother hounded him but now he understood how frustrated she must have been by his choices, how desperately she was trying to shake him out of the lifestyle he had chosen. And he spoke of the arguments they'd had, in the last few years, when his life had been off track and he hadn't wanted to go home and listen to his parents.

'After they died, Evie and I inherited everything they owned, equally. Right down the middle. But Evie was still a legal minor, not to gain control of her share of the family's companies for another four years. They were mine to run. I dedicated myself to that. My father had been so devoted to his work, and I'd always neglected that side of our life, not wanting to know anything about the corporate world. I immersed myself in it, so that I could understand and take over.'

'All while you were recovering from your own injuries?' she asked gently, as the sun pierced the forest with a single beam of golden light.

'It was the perfect opportunity. I was bed-bound in hospital for over a month.'

She gasped softly. His injuries must have been very severe.

'When I was released, work became my life. It has been ever since.'

The rest, she knew. Part of her research had told her that Thirio Skartos had taken the already magnificent family fortune and at least trebled it in the last few years. He regularly topped rich lists around the world. But he was also known for his social conscience. His investment in the infrastructure of developing countries had funded schools and highways, and their family foundation had contributed billions of dollars to refugee causes.

'And your charitable work?'

'I donate money.' He brushed it aside.

'You do good, Thirio. A lot of good.'

Silence crackled around them. She yawned, though she wasn't tired. Her mind was wired, even if her body wanted to sleep.

'I do what I think they would want me to. I try to live up to the person they wish I'd been.'

Her heart shattered for him. His pain was so intense.

'"If only" is the most useless phrase in the world, Thirio.' She stroked his chest tenderly. 'You can't go back in time and follow a different course.'

'I know that.' The words were ripped from him.

'But all the things you've just told me about your parents, that's what you need to think about. Remember how much they loved you, even when they didn't agree with you. Remember how your mother tried to fight to get you to find your potential, and how your father tolerated and supported the phase you were in. They adored you, Thirio. If they were here, they'd put their arms around you and hug you and tell you that it's okay, that they forgive you, and want you to be happy. For them, for Evie, for everyone who's ever cared about you.' Her voice cracked and her own heart gave a little stumble, as feelings she couldn't decipher jumbled through her. Suddenly, her own fate seemed tied to his happiness. This was a temporary union, and yet she couldn't imagine going back to her life and leaving him here, carrying this weight all on his own.

She couldn't imagine leaving him at all.

The sun crested higher, dousing the valley in gold, spreading light across the land just as her heart finally woke up and made itself heard.

Lucinda had sworn she'd never love another person in her life. The fear of rejection was paralysing, and had made it impossible. She'd *chosen* to be alone, without realising that love wasn't really something you had any say in. By spending time with Thirio, she'd opened the door to a world that was inevitable, from the moment they'd met.

She loved him.

But she *couldn't*. She must be mistaken. It was sympathy that was tearing her apart, making her pulse race and her heart thump. It was grief for him, that was all. Once she was back in London, she'd feel differently. Then, everything would be normal.

The cost of loving someone like Thirio would be way too high for Lucinda. She closed her eyes, shutting out the world, Thirio and, most of all, her awakening feelings, simply trusting that things would be different and better when she woke.

After his parents' deaths, he'd been urged to speak to therapists, counsellors, psychologists. He'd been urged to *talk about it*, as though saying how wrong he'd been, over and over, would help at all. He'd never taken that advice. He hadn't wanted to speak to anyone about his complicity in the accident. He hadn't wanted to feel better.

His conversation with Lucinda was a first, and yet, strangely, he didn't regret it. Somehow, it was right that she should know about this part of him. He couldn't explain why, but he suspected it had something to do with the way she looked at him. As though he were perfect.

When he wasn't, and he needed her to know that. He didn't want her to think he was some kind of hero after what he'd done. He didn't deserve the admiration or respect of anyone, let alone a person as wonderful and decent as Lucinda.

He was glad she was leaving today, even when he acknowledged that her departure would be a wrench. In the space of a few short days, he had become used to her presence. He'd liked not being alone. He'd liked knowing she was working in the office he'd made for her. He'd liked walking past and hearing her hum or her fingers clicking over the keyboard.

But it was a fantasy, and now, it was time to get back to reality.

He flicked the coffee machine to life, lining up two cups as he looked out at the same view he'd been staring at for years. There was something about the age of the forest that comforted him. Hundreds of years of growth, these trees had weathered everything, and they'd seen much. Death, destruction, grief, loss. They were the witnesses to humanity's failings, and its successes. His own grief would seem inconsequential to the forest.

But it wasn't to Thirio. Nor was his guilt. Absent-mindedly, he ran his fingers over his chest, feeling the knotted flesh beneath his shirt, the gesture one he did often, reminding himself of his failings.

He needed that reminder particularly this morning, when the pleasures of this weekend threatened to blank out the pain he deserved to feel.

'Good morning.' Lucinda's voice was soft and croaky as she padded into the kitchen behind him. Thirio turned, and his whole body exploded in an unwelcome, automatic response to her appearance. She was so beautiful and so sexy. Her hair was dishevelled about her heart-shaped face, and she wore a shirt of his, long and oversized, only the three middle buttons done up so his eyes dropped to the swell of her cleavage first then the sweep of her shapely legs next. But it wasn't just desire that was making his heart hop and skip. It was the look in her eyes.

As if he were perfect.

Even after what he'd told her.

Even after what he'd done.

He ground his teeth together, instinctively pushing away her kindness and acceptance. He didn't deserve either.

'Coffee?' His tone was brusque and before he turned

back to the machine he saw the hurt that lined her eyes and wanted to fix it, to take back the rough question.

'Oh.' The soft sound of disappointment tightened something in his gut. But he told himself he was glad. He wasn't perfect and she needed to understand that. 'Yes, please. What time is it?'

'Eleven.'

'Eleven?' She moaned. 'Why did you let me sleep so late? I have to leave soon.'

And that was why. Coward that he was, Thirio couldn't bear to spend more time with her. Not much more. There was danger in her company, danger in their conversations.

'We were up all night. I presumed you'd be tired.'

'I was,' she agreed. 'But still...'

'Are you comfortable with what you've achieved this weekend?' He pulled the cup away from the machine and turned, handing it to her, watching as she took it. A small frown was on her lips.

'Honestly?' Her eyes searched his, probing, pushing. 'I'm tempted to say no, so you'll invite me back next weekend.'

She was sounding him out, trying to work out what he wanted. Was there more here? Would he offer her more? He couldn't lead her on, no matter how much he wanted to see her again. It wasn't fair to Lucinda. She deserved more than he could ever give.

'If you need to organise anything else, you're welcome to come back. Just let Travis know the details and he'll organise a flight.'

He saw the businesslike words hit their mark. She stood her ground but something in her expression seemed to recoil. Just as he'd wanted, he told himself.

'If this is about last night, Thirio, please don't beat yourself up for talking to me. I'm glad you told me about what happened. I like that you shared that with me.'

His gut twisted. He'd liked it too. But that was the problem. He didn't *want* to like anything about his life.

'We both knew this was a weekend thing. You're leaving in a few hours. What more do you want me to say?'

Even as he spoke the words, he heard them as she must and wanted to take them back. He'd gone too far. They were too cutting. Too cold. Too careless. *So fix it.* But how, and, more importantly, why? She needed to leave and to forget about him. What had started out as a harmless, inevitable fling was now edged with danger, because he knew her better. He knew her softness and vulnerability and he felt a strange yearning to protect her, to keep her safe and make her smile. But these were not skills he had. He couldn't be trusted.

'Nothing.' She sipped her coffee, looking away from him, and he had the terrible, awful feeling that she might be about to cry. But a second later, she faced him, her expression composed. 'I've coordinated everything I need.'

It was the answer he wanted to hear, so why did his gut sink like a stone, all the way to the tiled floor at his feet?

'So you won't need to come back again?'

Hurt lashed her features but she sipped her coffee, using those few seconds to hide that pain. 'No.' Her throat muscles bunched. 'I mean, yes, but not until right before the wedding.' She hesitated. 'If that's okay with you?'

He didn't want her to feel as though she had to ask him for permission! He wanted to tell her she was always welcome here, but it was all too hard, too fraught. He closed his eyes, pushing back the doubts he felt, and focusing on the well-worn path he'd chosen. Six years of loneliness were behind him, a lifetime in front.

'Of course. I expected as much when I hired you.'

She flinched, right before she turned away. When she placed the coffee cup down on the bench, it was with too much force, all of the emotions she was containing coming out in the splash of dark liquid that landed on the countertop.

He wanted to apologise. He could taste the word in his mouth, he could feel the explanation forming, but to what end? He had to let her go. A curse had fallen on him the night his parents had died, and he couldn't draw Lucinda into it. He couldn't let her get any closer. He couldn't let her care for him, maybe even love him. He couldn't let her put her life in his hands. How could he live with himself if he made another mistake and she paid the price?

He had to let her go.

And so he did exactly that, watching her retreating back without moving, even when every cell in his body demanded that he follow.

CHAPTER THIRTEEN

EVEN AFTER THEIR DEATHS, he hadn't wallowed. Thirio had been full of purpose. He had focused on the businesses, on learning everything he could about his parents' work, and then, he'd thrown himself into being alone. Isolated. Sober, so that he could feel every single thread of remorse and guilt and responsibility, so that he could hate himself without the softening effects of alcohol. He had avoided the phone calls of his friends until they'd stopped calling, giving up on him completely.

But he hadn't wallowed.

Even his guilt had been directed and ambitious—he had given himself a lifelong sentence and set about observing it.

But this was different.

Lucinda was everywhere in the castle, even when she was, now, nowhere. He felt her here, most of all, in the room they'd first made love in. His fingertips brushed her bed and memories jerked through him. He walked past her office and heard her fingertips on the keyboard, but when he looked inside, the computer was abandoned, the space empty. Her fragrance, just a hint, lingered, so he stepped inside, breathing in deeply. She was in his bed, in his shower, on the terrace, in the kitchen. Her hands were on his coffee cup, his chest, his scar, his face. Her lips, oh, her lips. He felt them everywhere, memories cutting through him, heating him and destroying him even as they gave him a strength he hadn't known for a long time. Something bright caught his eye and he bent down, digging his finger into the gap between the floorboards, feeling something sharp. Frowning, he pushed at it harder, loosening it, pulling it free as a thousand memories exploded through him. Clutching it in his hand, he closed his eyes, remembering this, her, everything.

The world had shifted. Something fundamental was changing, but he fought that. He'd known he was playing with fire. He'd tried to resist her. He *had* resisted her, for as long as he could, but in the end, it was impossible. Yet even as he'd succumbed, he'd known it would have to end, and now she was gone. This was just something he'd have to deal with.

Still, the wedding loomed, not for the event it was, not for the fact it was his sister's day, but because it would bring Lucinda back to the *castile*—for the last time. He would need to be strong and he would need to remember: nothing good came from wanting what you could never have.

Anxiety was a tangle in the pit of her stomach. After all her hard work—and the last two weeks had involved twenty-hour days, hours of conference calls, flights to meet contractors, making contingency plans for any event, any unforeseeable crisis—and finally, she knew, beyond a shadow of a doubt, that everything was in place. This wedding was going to be spectacular—so much as she could control—and Evie was going to have the time of her life.

And Thirio?

How was he feeling about the impending arrival of one hundred and fifty of Europe's elite at his hideaway castle?

If she'd known then what she knew now, would she have pushed this plan on him? Would she even have dared suggest it? The castle was his sanctuary, and he deserved that. But didn't he also deserve to be made to face reality again? Did Evie know how shattered he was by their parents' deaths? Did Evie understand why he hid himself away?

So many questions had clouded Lucinda's mind since leaving the *castile,* but she had reconciled herself to the fact she would never have these answers. It wasn't her place to know.

Thirio had made that abundantly clear.

Even his name sent a shiver of anticipation down her spine, but she quelled it. An expert at concealing her feelings, Lucinda knew, nonetheless, that this weekend would test her as no other time in her life ever had.

As the plane lifted off the tarmac, she forced herself to focus on the acquisition of the company—being handled through a third-party broker. She didn't want her stepmother knowing that she was behind the purchase until the ink was dried on the contracts. Despite the amount of money she'd offered, she worried that Elodie would refuse to sell, just to be unkind to Lucinda. Again.

But so far, everything looked in order. Lucinda was going to get everything she'd worked so hard for. She should have been delirious. But where she'd expected joy and contentment to finally fill her heart, there was only a dull, throbbing ache of emptiness. Somehow, her dreams had shifted, and her father's business was no longer the pinnacle of what she wanted in life…

He had intended to install Lucinda in the staff quarters, with the caterers and housekeepers who'd been brought to the *castile* to manage the logistics of the weekend. Over eighty workers filling a dormitory-style wing of the castle, just as they had in the past, when the family had travelled here for Christmas vacations and his parents had put on lavish parties that had drawn half of Europe—or so it had felt to a young Thirio. But as the wedding approached, he'd found himself giving instructions for the room she'd occupied on her first night at the *castile* to be made available for her. It was close to his. A test, if ever he'd known one. But it was a test he intended to pass.

And yet, he also wanted to be near her. To see her smile. To help her if she needed it. He was no one's knight in shining armour but that didn't mean he didn't care about Lucinda. He wanted this weekend to be perfect. For Evie, but also for Lucinda, who had so much riding on it.

And he wanted to see her, as much as he could. Even from a distance. He just needed…to look.

Would that really be enough?

She refused to take it as an omen that her luggage was lost on the flight. If anything, Lucinda convinced herself that that was her little piece of bad luck for the weekend, already got out of the way. Now, there would only be good luck! Besides, the luggage would turn up within a day or so, the airline had promised.

Closing her mind off to the suggestion that it was a bad omen, she stepped out of her hire car with a look of assumed calm. She wasn't going to think about Thirio. She wasn't going to wonder if he was watching. But, just in case he was, she wasn't going to let him see how shredded her nerves were!

She walked to the front door with head held high, smiling when it was drawn inwards by a housekeeper in a black dress and pale grey apron.

'Good morning,' the woman said with an efficient nod. 'Miss Villeneuve?'

'Yes.' She held out her hand in greeting.

The older woman with her golden hair pulled back into

a bun extended her own hand. 'I'm Vera. Come this way. Do you have a bag?'

Lucinda recounted the story as they walked, noting with pleasure how many of her instructions had already been implemented. The florists had been busy, and arrangements of bright flowers stood all through the common areas, huge bunches that were fragrant and meaningful—the national flower of Nalvania was the star of the group, with its pale pink and yellow blooms dominating the centre—surrounded by peace lilies and laurel leaves to represent Greece. There were also pale pink hydrangeas—believed to bring luck— peonies for prosperity and long tendrils of rosemary for remembrance. Each arrangement perfectly matched the illustrations Lucinda had sent. She paused to inhale one as they passed, tears touching her eyes.

Evie was going to love it.

She was so caught up in the details that she didn't notice Vera leading her up a very familiar set of stairs, past a window that had been broken four weeks earlier and which was now perfectly restored, so that no one except her and Thirio would know that a tree had crashed right through it.

But when Vera led Lucinda to the door of the room she'd been sleeping in that night, her heart leaped into her throat and her feet refused to move.

'There must be some mistake,' she said with a small shake of her head. 'I'm to stay in the staff quarters.'

'There is no bed available,' Vera said apologetically. 'Mr Skartos suggested this room instead.'

Lucinda's lips parted in consternation. The last thing she wanted was to be difficult, but she'd purposefully placed herself with the staff, to avoid any blurring of lines between herself and Thirio. Whatever they'd shared was over. She was just someone who worked for him now.

'It doesn't seem appropriate.' She clutched at straws. 'Is there nowhere else?'

Vera's laugh was soft and kind. 'The castle will be overflowing with guests, Miss Villeneuve. Every room is spoken for.'

Resignation hit Lucinda between the shoulder blades.

As Vera began to walk away, Lucinda spun on her heel. 'Will you let me know when my suitcase turns up?'

She asked the question at the exact moment Thirio prowled from his room, head bent, hands in pockets. She knew then that he hadn't been watching for her, because he looked genuinely surprised to see her. Almost as if he hadn't remembered she was coming a day ahead of the ceremony.

'Lucinda.' His voice was deep, wrapping around Lucinda's whole body, drawing her towards him even when her feet stayed firmly planted on the ground.

'Thirio.' She dipped her head in a polite greeting.

'Did your suitcase get lost?'

Vera smiled curtly and left.

'The airline lost it.' Lucinda's words were clipped. She looked towards her bedroom door. 'I didn't intend to sleep here. The staff quarters would have been fine.'

'They get draughty.'

She tried not to let it warm her heart to think that he had made this choice out of concern for her comfort. She stared at him, completely off kilter. It was as though they were strangers, and yet they weren't. She *knew* him. Not in an encyclopaedic way, where she could quote every single fact about his life, but in a true and meaningful way. She knew what made him tick. She knew what mattered to him. And most of all, she knew what he was afraid of and excited for. And more than that, she loved him.

Pain lanced her as she forced herself to fully face the

truth for the first time, to stare down the hopelessness of loving him, knowing he would not—could not—love her back.

'Excuse me,' she said with quiet resignation. 'I'm going to freshen up before I check in with the caterers.'

'Have dinner with me tonight.'

It was not a question. But nor was it at all expected. Heat rushed into her cheeks. She forced herself to meet his eyes, as her stomach rolled and flipped and tightened with uncertainty.

'I don't think that's a good idea.' *Have dinner with him,* her heart pleaded. Regardless of the damage that would be done to that very organ, she didn't want to take the safe road. She wanted as much of Thirio as he was willing to give to her, even while acknowledging that it would never be enough.

'Perhaps not.' He drew closer, his eyes probing hers. 'Do it anyway.'

Wasn't that just what her heart had said?

She stared up at him, lost, destroyed, hopelessly wanting. She breathed in, searching for words, and tasted him in her mouth. Her knees went weak. 'Thirio—'

'It's just dinner.' But he lifted a hand and caught her cheek, touching her as though he couldn't bear not to.

'Is it?' she pushed, forcing him to be honest.

His lips curled in a derisive smile. 'No.'

'Then what is it?' She was surprised by the bold question, but she was also glad she'd asked it.

'One more night,' he said simply.

'And then what?'

He frowned. 'And then you go away again.'

'For ever?'

A muscle jerked low in his jaw. His nod was slow. A surrender to the necessity of that. But was it really necessary?

'It has to be that way.'

'Why?'

'You know the answer to that.'

She did. At least, she knew what he believed. But he was wrong. How could she make him see that? And how could she possibly fight for him to understand?

He would say no.

He would reject her.

Thirio would become just another person in her life who didn't care for her. Someone else she loved who wouldn't love her back. Just like after her father had died and she'd turned to her stepmother and stepsisters, expecting consolation and receiving cruelty. Just like when she'd fallen in love with Beckett and he'd chosen her stepsister.

Thirio would be just the same. He would choose not to be with her.

And she couldn't bear it.

How could she fight when the outcome was already ordained?

Perhaps this would be all they'd ever have. Snatches of time with no hope for a future.

Sadness cloyed at her throat. She wished she could refuse him. She wished she could tell him to go to hell. But she loved him, and she would take whatever time they had, before the real end game.

'Dinner,' she agreed finally, her voice uneven.

His relief was obvious, but so too his concern. This wasn't easy for either of them.

He had planned to avoid her. Simply to know she was here and be near her without touching, without speaking more than was necessary. But as soon as he'd seen her, the plan had crumbled around him and he'd reached for her as a drowning man would a lifeline. He'd clutched at more time together. More of Lucinda.

It ran contrary to everything he'd planned.

He actually felt nervous. Thirio Skartos! A man who'd

dated hundreds of women in his life felt as though his legs were going to fall out from under him as he waited for Lucinda. The only advantage to having his castle overrun by staff was that he'd been able to have the terrace set up like a restaurant. One single table stood in the middle of the space, covered in a white cloth with a candle at its centre. Strings of fairy lights ran overhead, and soft jazz music played through the speakers. The air was heavy with the scent of food covered with sterling silver lids. Brightly coloured cushions had been scattered on the far side of the terrace, as well as a picnic rug. It looked perfect.

Too perfect.

It looked like a night of promise, but this was no such thing. There was nothing Thirio could offer Lucinda. Would she mind? Would she hate him? He almost hoped she would.

'Wow.' The word curled around him, so he closed his eyes before turning, needing to rally his strength before he saw her.

He spun slowly, bracing himself, but there was nothing he could do to stop the wave of awareness that cascaded through him.

She was beautiful.

More beautiful than she'd ever looked.

It was ridiculous. She was wearing the same thing she'd been wearing earlier, but her long hair was out now, loose down her back and tumbling over her shoulders, and her feet were bare. That small detail sent his nerves into overdrive. It was so intimate. So…at home.

The phrase gripped him like a noose.

This was his home; not hers.

'Please.' He cleared his throat, gesturing to the table. She walked towards it without sitting down. Her fingers shook visibly as she reached for the bottle of red wine and poured herself a glass, then moved around the table and poured him one. Her fingers were still shaking when she picked both up and walked slowly, purposefully towards him, extending a glass. He reached to take it, his fingers closing over hers without regret. The contact seared his skin, sending arrows of awareness darting through him.

'You hurt me.'

The raw admission was like a punch in the gut. She pulled her hand free at the same time she took a gulp of her wine, eyes fixing on the view, the silhouette of hundreds of pine trees against the dark night sky.

He didn't ask what she meant. He knew the answer.

'I was abrupt,' he admitted. 'I hadn't expected things to go so far between us.'

'I know that.' She nodded softly, her kindness the last thing he wanted and deserved.

'I thought it was just physical. I thought we could sleep together and then I'd be able to move on. I didn't know you'd get under my skin, Lucinda.'

She flinched a little. 'And you don't want me there?'

'I don't want you to care for me,' he said automatically. 'I don't want you to hope that you can change me, and what I want in life.'

'Which is to be alone.'

'Yes.' He stared at her, to convince her, even when doubts were flicking through him.

'What if I want to help you feel better?'

He shunned that. 'I don't deserve it.'

'Says who?'

'Anyone who can see clearly.'

'An eye for an eye? Is that it?'

He took a drink of his wine, barely appreciating the excellence. 'Something like that.'

'What about what's right for Evie? What about what's right for me? What about the people who care about you, who want you to be happy? Don't we deserve some consideration?'

Ice flooded Thirio. 'I've been honest with you from the start about my…limitations.'

'But you weren't honest,' she countered angrily. 'You told me you wanted to be alone and yet you reached for me with both hands. You do it every time we're together.' He ground his teeth. 'But you didn't tell me why you were fighting this, until it was too late. If you had, I would have known that you'd made the decision from a place of fear.'

'You can't possibly understand.'

'Maybe not.' She sighed. 'All I know is that you're denying us both something really great because you're living in the past.'

'Only it's not my past,' he ground out. 'It's my present, my future, my waking nightmare. Every time I look in the mirror I see the evidence of what I did. You're asking me to forget—'

'Not to forget. But to forgive yourself.'

'And I'm telling you, I can't. I never will.'

'Even for me?'

'I don't deserve—' He shook his head. 'This has no future.' He forced the words to ring with certainty. 'I don't know how else I can say it to make you believe…'

'Tell me you don't want me,' she said quietly, stoicism in the words.

He tried to shape the words, but couldn't. 'I want you to forget me after the wedding. I should have been strong enough to end this before it started.'

Sadness washed over Lucinda's face, but her lips twisted into a smile that was ghostly, bittersweet. 'I'll always be glad you didn't.' She angled her face away for a moment, drawing in a shuddering breath. 'Let's eat, Thirio. Tomorrow's a big day. We both need a good night's sleep.'

Regret clawed through him. He wanted—with all his heart—things he could never have. But that didn't stop him wanting.

CHAPTER FOURTEEN

AFTER HER FATHER had died, Lucinda had learned a lot about the circles of control. There were some things in her life she could control, and into those things, she poured her energy. The circles that were beyond her ability of influence, she had to make her peace with.

Her suitcase not arriving was beyond her control.

The weather too.

So when she woke and saw the hint of storm clouds on the horizon, she didn't put her energy into worrying about them. She'd planned for this. There were wet-weather contingencies for miles. She pushed out of bed, trying not to think about the fact Thirio was just across the hallway as she moved to the window. Despite the fact it was still early, an army of staff was positioning canopy tents to form a walkway from the makeshift car park to the entrance of the castle. There were also, she noted with pleasure, dozens of umbrellas in a basket, by the door. The umbrellas had been printed with Evie and Erik's monogram, and the date of their wedding—a keepsake for guests, albeit a practical one.

As she'd predicted, the day was busy. There were checklists upon checklists and, despite the fact the contractors worked like a well-oiled machine, Lucinda was kept so busy overseeing the preparations that she could only devote about half of her brain power to Thirio, and wondering where he was. Wondering *how* he was. Opening his doors to hundreds of people was Thirio's idea of hell, and yet he'd done it, out of love for his sister. And guilt too? Because he blamed himself for their parents' deaths?

She pushed the thought away. It was crippling in its intensity, so too her desire to run to him and kiss him until that guilt ceased to exist. She hated that he felt that way. Their deaths were a curse from which he would never escape.

But what if love was the answer? What if love would break that curse?

She stopped what she was doing, causing the housekeeper to look at her with concern. Lucinda stared straight ahead, her heart thumping hard against her ribs. What if she told him? And suddenly, it wasn't a question of whether or not she would, but *when* she could. The knowledge that she loved him was like an oppressive weight, and only revealing it to him would lighten that.

Doubtless, he would reject her, but that didn't change the fact that she wanted him to know how she felt. She needed him to understand that she saw him as he was, she knew about his past, about the act for which he hated himself, and she loved him regardless. She needed him to understand that she loved him enough for both of them. And if he rejected her, it would hurt, but at least he would know that he was worth loving.

She continued with her work, her brain now almost fully engaged in thinking about Thirio, until about an hour before the wedding, when one of the Nalvanian palace staff came up to her.

'Excuse me, madam, but Miss Skartos is asking for you.'

'Is there a problem?'

'No. She's this way.'

Lucinda followed behind as the servant led her to the old family quarters. Thirio had gestured to it without entering and Lucinda understood now. This part of the palace was alive with his childhood. Photographs hung on the wall of a young Thirio, his parents, his sister. She paused, looking at one with eyes that were misted over. Any doubts she had flew from her mind.

She loved him, and he had to know that. He'd lost so much when his parents had died and instead of allowing himself to grieve, he'd thrown himself into his guilt instead.

When Lucinda entered Evie's room, she gasped. 'You look so beautiful.' Evie was a picture of elegance and glamour, in a white silk dress with a pale blue sash crossed diagonally over one shoulder. Her blonde hair had been secured into a bun and a diamond tiara sat atop her head.

'Thank you.' Her smile was loaded with pleasure. 'I'm so excited.'

'That's exactly how a bride should feel.' Lucinda nodded encouragingly. 'Everything is organised. Can I get you something while you're waiting? Tea? Something to eat?'

'No, I actually have something for you.'

'Oh?'

'Follow me.' Evie smiled serenely as she sashayed across the room, to a walk-in wardrobe. It was only a quarter full, with the clothes Evie had brought for the wedding. But at the end, there was the most stunning dress Lucinda had ever seen. Silver, with wide straps and a sweetheart neckline, and a structured skirt that fell to the ground. There were tiny diamantés all over the bodice, so that it gave the impression of sparkling, just like the fresh snow on treetops.

'That's stunning.'

'I'm glad you think so. I got it out for you to wear.'

Lucinda's eyes were enormous when she turned to face Evie. 'For *me*?'

'I understand your suitcase went missing, and I won't hear any of this business about you not attending. You should get to come and enjoy your handiwork.'

'That's not really how this works,' Lucinda insisted.

'Please? I don't know why, but I really feel like you should come. Think of it as a wedding present.'

Lucinda stared at her client, the woman she'd sworn she'd move mountains to give the perfect wedding day to. 'It really is a beautiful dress.'

'It was my mother's,' Evie said quietly, moving towards it. 'She had the most incredible taste. Her wardrobe is classic.'

'I can't possibly wear it.' Lucinda was stricken.

'Nonsense.'

Lucinda moved closer to the dress, running her fingers over the bodice. 'So many diamantés,' she said with appreciation for how they were stitched into the fabric.

'They're not diamantés.'

Leaning closer, Lucinda, heart pounding, realised that Evie was right. The bodice was covered in tiny diamonds—and some not so tiny. 'Evie, this dress is…'

'Please.' Evie waved a hand through the air. 'It will be perfect on you. Let me help you get ready.'

'I—'

'You asked me if I needed anything earlier? It's this. I want to pass the time. Would you oblige me?'

How could Lucinda say no? As she stepped into the dress, then sat while Evie styled her hair into a crown of braids, Lucinda felt as though *she* were the princess, going to the ball, and Evie her fairy godmother. Thirio was right, though. He wasn't Prince Charming. But did it follow that they couldn't have their own Happily Ever After?

Thirio—along with every red-blooded male in the marquee—saw her enter and watched as she moved gracefully towards an empty seat and slid into it, eyes forward. Not looking around. Not looking for him.

But he couldn't look away.

Lucinda was always stunning. He'd seen her in many guises now, and he found her beautiful no matter what she was wearing. But in this dress, she was some kind of untouchable fantasy, her swan-like neck on display courtesy of the hairstyle.

'She looks lovely, doesn't she?'

He turned as his sister joined him, and a lump formed in his throat. Because Evie was so beautiful, so like their parents, and he loved her so damned much. He put his arms around her, aching for the fact they weren't here, aching for what he'd taken from Evie, but also feeling gladness that he could give her this day, this wedding, at the *castile*. Lucinda had been right about how much this would mean and he was glad he'd listened.

'You look lovely,' he corrected.

'Thank you.' She pulled away, blinking back tears. 'Don't make me cry.'

'What did I say?'

'You didn't say anything. It's the expression on your face.' She pressed a kiss to his cheek. 'I love you, Thirio.'

He squeezed her hand rather than saying it back. The words jammed inside him.

'Are you ready?'

'I was ready three years ago.'

'You met Erik three years ago,' he pointed out.

'And I've known ever since then.' She smiled up at

him, the certainty in her features shifting something in his chest. She loved her fiancé. She knew beyond a shadow of a doubt. He didn't analyse that thought any further.

The ceremony was long, repeated in Nalvanian after the English vows, but he focused on the bride and groom the entire time, standing with them, only letting his eyes stray twice to where Lucinda sat, her eyes fixed on Evie, a soft, contemplative smile on her face.

He felt as if he'd been punched in the gut.

'Would you dance with me?'

It was late into the night. Everything had gone perfectly. Lucinda was glowing. And when Thirio approached her, asking her to dance, she spun, her heart thumping, certainty forming a shield of courage.

'Absolutely.'

His eyes held hers as he took her hand, then turned and led her onto the dance floor, drawing her close to his chest, holding her against him as they began to move, slowly.

'Everything went well,' he said after a moment, the compliment weaving through her.

'Yes.'

'When will you fly back?'

Her heart twisted painfully. The prospect of leaving— and for good—filled her mouth with acid.

'Tomorrow.' She pulled back a little to see how he reacted, but his face was angled away. Was she imagining a stiffening of his frame?

'And you'll buy the company?'

'It's already in motion,' she agreed with a nod, wondering why that now left her with an empty feeling in the pit of her stomach. It was as though she was putting down firm roots, but in the wrong place.

'I'm glad. You deserve that.'

He was wrong. She deserved so much more. She deserved to be loved as she loved. She deserved what she'd been denied for years. She hadn't always thought so. Before meeting Thirio, she'd believed the answer was to bury herself away from the possibility of love, not to take a gamble lest she got hurt. But Thirio had changed her. She realised now that love was worth fighting for. Even when there was a risk of loss, rejection and pain.

'Can we go somewhere a little more private?' she asked, putting a hand to his chest and drawing his attention.

His reluctance was obvious, but so too his yearning. He was afraid of what he felt. He was afraid of what they shared. He was afraid he wouldn't be able to say 'no' to her. 'Please.'

His eyes closed and he nodded, a muscle jerking in his jaw. 'Come with me.' He laced their fingers together and pulled her with him towards the entrance of the ballroom, then through the wide doors, past the candelabras that were weaved with long strands of ivy, then out onto a terrace, this one far enough away from the revellers that they could only hear the strains of the music.

'Private enough?' he asked, warily.

'Yes.' She had to do this. A thousand nerves fired through her but she didn't change course. 'I will leave tomorrow, if that's really what you want,' she said. 'And I will never contact you again. You made a choice six years ago to live your life alone, to pay for what you see as your crime.' Sadness washed over her. 'But I would stay if you asked me.'

His eyes flared wide.

'I would stay, and I would live here with you, a part of you, just like you're a part of me.'

His lips parted.

'I love you.' She said it simply, in the end, because her love for him was simple. Brick by brick, it had been placed inside her heart, and it would always be there.

He groaned, catching her face in his hands, holding her steady. 'Don't say that.'

She felt the ping of hurt. She'd expected his rejection, and thought she'd protected herself against it, but she was wrong. It stung. She blinked quickly.

'I love you, with all my heart,' she pushed on regardless. 'You are worthy of that love. You are deserving of it. And more than that, you are deserving of happiness. I want to be with you. I want to love you. I want to be loved by you. All you have to do is open yourself up to that future. Step away from the darkness, Thirio.'

'It's not that simple. The darkness is inside me.' He pressed a palm to his chest. 'I can't escape it.'

'You can choose happiness.' She lifted up onto the tips of her toes and brushed her lips to his. 'You can choose me.'

'No.'

She ignored his rejection. 'You will always feel that pain. You will always feel grief and guilt and regret. But you can feel other emotions alongside it. Your life can be a tribute to your parents, the sort of life they'd want you to lead.'

'No,' he said again, but she understood: he was rejecting her because he was scared. He wanted her to leave, only that wouldn't solve anything for either of them.

'Whenever we get close, you push me away,' she said gently. 'Does it ever really work?'

He stared at her without speaking.

'Do you ever actually forget about me?'

His jaw shifted, teeth clenching.

'I didn't think so,' she said softly, reaching for her throat, for the necklace she always wore. Except she'd lost it, weeks ago. Instead, she tapped her finger to her pulse, hoping for calm.

'What is your point?' he asked after a moment.

'Fighting this is futile. You won't win. I love you, and

I'm almost certain you love me too. You're going to be miserable if you let me go.'

His lips tightened into something like a grimace. 'I'm used to that.'

She shook her head sadly. 'So you're going to use what you feel to punish yourself some more? Denying us both what we want in life because you're so hell-bent on this prison sentence you've created?'

'I told you from the beginning—'

'But everything's changed since then! Hasn't it?'

He stared at her for several beats.

'Answer me.'

He expelled a rough sigh. 'Some things have changed. Some things haven't. I can't click my fingers and alter my past. I can't change the fabric of who I am.'

'I'm not asking you to.'

'Yes. You are.' He ground out the words with frustration. 'You don't get it. I don't want to be loved. I don't want anyone to love me, to trust me, to put their faith in me.'

'Because you think you don't deserve that? Or because you're worried you'll do something that will hurt me?'

'I killed my parents, Lucinda.'

'It was an accident.' She lifted up and kissed him again. 'An accident.' She whispered the words against the corner of his mouth. 'An awful, tragic, unforgettable loss, but an accident nonetheless. I can't promise you that I'll never get hurt or sick or even die. I know better than anyone how cruel and unpredictable life can be. But I do know I'd rather live every day I possibly can with you. My heart is full of love for you—it always will be—whether I'm here or in England or anywhere in the world.' She breathed in deeply. 'I know you're angry. You have every right to be. You lost so much that night, and you haven't let yourself feel that loss.

Guilt is different from grief. Perhaps it's better for you to feel guilt as there's an element of control in it, I don't know.'

'Psychoanalysing me doesn't change a thing,' he said gruffly.

'Perhaps not.' Her smile was a bitter twist of her lips. 'Only, I wasn't sure if you knew what you were doing. You think staying here, hiding out from the world, is penance? It's cowardly. You're giving in to guilt, rather than facing your grief. You're hiding from it, instead of learning to walk alongside it. You will miss them every day of your life, but you still deserve to have a life.'

He stared down at her, his expression unmoving. Sadness welled inside her. She'd known this would be his response.

'I needed you to know how I feel. Before I met you, I was afraid too, Thirio. I was scared of love and loss. I was hiding as well. I avoided friendships and relationships, any closeness that might lead to me being hurt, and I don't want to live like that any more. You've woken me up and now that I've seen the beauty of closeness, I want to feel it every day. Even when it makes me achingly vulnerable.' Her lips twisted to one side. 'Even when I know that walking away from you will be the hardest thing I've ever done.'

'God, Lucinda. I didn't ask for this!'

She blinked up at him. 'Neither of us did, yet here we are. The question is, what are you going to do about it?'

He stared at her for so long, she thought he wasn't going to answer. And then, slowly, his voice rumbled between them. 'You're wrong. I grieved. I was saturated by it for a long time, and, out of that grief, I made a decision that I could live with. I made a choice to sacrifice certain things to fix what I'd broken.'

'But how does it fix it?' As she asked the question a blade of lightning cut through the night sky, illuminating his face in shadow.

'It means I can live with what I did.'

'By hating yourself?'

'Yes.'

'You deserve so much better, Thirio. Your parents would want—'

'You don't know them.'

'I know what you've told me. I know what I saw in the photos near your sister's room. I know Evie, and how she loves you. I know that you are a good, kind, decent man. And I know that I love you.' She stared at him, willing him to believe her, to say it back. There was only the distant grinding of thunder. 'But I also know how stubborn you are. If this is truly what you want, I'll leave.'

She waited, nerves stretched to breaking point.

'You'll never hear from me again,' she promised, saying the words to herself as much as to Thirio.

'I'm sorry.' The words were a tortured admission that this pain weighed heavily on him.

'Don't apologise to me,' she said with a tilt of her chin. 'This hurts like hell right now, but I'm a better person because of what we shared. You changed me in the best possible way. You drew me into the light, Thirio. I just wish I could have done the same for you.' Her heart cracked into a thousand pieces. 'Please, never forget that I love you. Whenever you are here, alone, ruminating on the past, know that there's someone out there who's seen the parts of you you're ashamed of, and loves you with all her heart.'

She turned and walked away, head held high, managing to keep her tears at bay until she was alone in her room. Only then did she give in to them, and face the reality of the life she would be returning to. A life without Thirio.

CHAPTER FIFTEEN

IT RAINED THAT NIGHT.

All night.

Thirio watched it fall from his bedroom window. He stared out at the rain and forced himself to remember another night, a clear, sunny night, dry and hot, when his arrogance had forced him to fight with his mother, and his selfishness had pushed him out of the door.

He remembered the smell of smoke and the taste of ash. He remembered the sound of death and the knowledge of fault. But as the rain fell, and his heart groaned under the burden of his memories, he felt something else.

Doubt.

Doubt about this path he'd chosen. Doubt about the wisdom of spending his life like this, in his parents' names. Lucinda had said they wouldn't want this for him, and, alone in his room, he admitted to himself that she was right. His parents would have wanted him to forgive himself, and move on.

More than that, for the first time in six years, he allowed himself a fantasy he'd never dared indulge: he wondered if they'd have been proud of him, and the man he'd become. Would his father admire the work Thirio had done with the company, and for their favoured charities? Was he the version of himself his mother had longed to see? Would she smile now to know how different he was? Or would she judge him for making more decisions she didn't agree with, for pushing away Lucinda?

He had reconciled himself to the fact that this was temporary, and yet, as the sky lightened and the moment of her departure approached, he doubted everything.

Most of all, he regretted words he hadn't said, words she deserved to hear. She'd overcome her fears to tell him how she felt—didn't he owe her the same? Regardless of what the future held, shouldn't he show the same courage she'd demonstrated?

It rained all night and he watched every drop, until the sky was wrung dry, and only then did he breathe in deeply and turn, walking towards her before he could change his mind. Walking towards her because, in the end, it was the only thing he could do.

Her bedroom was empty.

Panic laced his veins.

He'd left it too late. His rejection had been too final. She'd left.

He swore into her room, true desperation flooding him. As a weak dawn light filtered into her bedroom, he felt with clarity what he'd lost, and this time, it was the hardest loss he'd ever known. Because it wasn't a drunken mistake. He'd pushed her away. Again and again and again, when she'd been brave enough to face up to what they shared, he'd shut her down, building a wall around himself, fighting for this solitary existence.

He dropped his head, his breathing ragged, the reality of his choices burning through him.

'Thirio?' Her voice was soft, edged with worry. 'Are you okay?'

'Lucinda.' His eyes pierced her. 'You're still here.'

She stepped out of the en suite bathroom, wearing a T-shirt and briefs. He barely noticed her state of undress. He could only stare at her face, her beautiful face, so grateful to see it again when seconds ago he'd been sure she was gone for good, just as he'd asked her to be. 'What did you think?'

It felt foolish now. After all, the logistics of leaving the *castile* in the dead of night, particularly a stormy night, were almost insurmountable.

'That you'd left,' he said with a small shrug of his shoulders.

'Not yet, but soon.'

He hadn't come here to hide from the truth any more. He needed to face up to this. No more delays. 'I don't want you to leave.'

The words filled the room, expanding and contracting until they occupied every space. She stared at him, her features giving nothing away.

'I see.' She hesitated. 'No, actually, I don't. What exactly do you mean?'

Good point. He hadn't exactly made himself clear. 'I knew the moment I met you that you were dangerous to me. You were different and perceptive and kind, and you didn't let me get away with anything. You challenged me from the moment you got here, and I needed that. I needed you.' He still wasn't getting this across. He reached into the pocket of his trousers, withdrawing the small jewel he'd found.

He carried it towards her, his hand closed into a fist until he reached her, then he flatted his palm to reveal what he held.

'Where did you find this?' She reached for the diamond necklace, touching the stone gently, then moving to his palm, pressing a finger to his flesh and closing her eyes.

He did the same, inhaling, tasting her on the tip of his tongue. He pulled away, watching her as he unfastened the chain. 'After you left, I spent a lot of time in your room. No matter what I was doing in the day, I was drawn to that space, as though by being there I could be close to you. I found it in a gap in the floorboards.'

'Oh.'

He lifted it, placing it around her neck, moving behind her so he could fasten it.

'It was my mother's. It's all I have of hers. It means so much to me.'

'I should have returned it before now,' he admitted. 'But I held onto it, because it was a part of you, and I liked having something of yours near me. I knew I was addicted to you, but I thought I could conquer that.'

'I see.' Her voice was soft.

'You have lost so much, and yet you offered me your love. I can't let you go without telling you how I feel.'

Silence cracked, heavy with expectation, but also anxiety. Thirio knew this was a watershed moment, and, after six years of walling himself away, it took concerted effort to step over this threshold. But for Lucinda, for the life his parents would have wanted him to grab, he knew what he had to do.

'You are not just under my skin, *agape mou*, but you are a part of my soul, the owner of my heart—lock and key. You are the other part of me, a part that I have been missing all my life, a part that I hunted for before the accident, and that I have badly needed ever since. I did not think I was broken. If anything, I thought my decision to remain here was a mark of strength.' What a fool he'd been!

'But I was wrong. I was shattered by what happened—splintered into a thousand pieces—but meeting you—loving you—has made me whole again. I love you,' he said, simply. 'And it is a love that has given me the strength I need to face the world, regardless of what I did. You were right when you said I must learn to walk alongside my grief. And I will. But I would much rather do that with you at my side.'

Her back was to him, but he felt her shoulders tremble and spun her gently in his arms.

'I love you,' he said again, his eyes showing the truth of his heart. 'I am yours, Lucinda, in every way, for all time. I can never thank you adequately for being brave enough to admit how you felt, even when I gave you no reason to think I would welcome your admission.'

'You gave me every reason,' she denied tenderly. 'You love me. I could feel it. I knew it. And I hoped, more than I have ever hoped for anything in my life, that you would know it too, one day. I was willing to wait for you, Thirio, but I'm so glad I don't have to.'

His laugh was a deep rumble. 'No. No more waiting.' He pressed his forehead to hers. 'Do you think the priest could be persuaded to perform another ceremony today?' he asked, only half joking.

She smiled against his lips. 'Sadly, no. There's paperwork required. But perhaps he'll come back in a month?'

Thirio blinked. 'Are you—do you actually mean—?'

She laughed. 'That depends. Were you seriously asking?'

'Lucinda Villeneuve, I want, more than any person has ever wanted anything on this earth, to spend the rest of my life with you. I want to wake up with you, to kiss you, to taste you, to make you smile and to see all your dreams come true. I want to love you as you deserve to be loved, to worship you, to support you and hold you, for as long as we both shall live. You are my other half,' he said simply. 'Will you marry me?'

She nodded. 'In a heartbeat.'

And their hearts *would* beat, both perfectly in synch, for as long as they lived.

Three years later

'Are you absolutely sure about this?' Thirio scanned the paperwork, before passing it to Lucinda.

'One hundred per cent. It's been an amazing ride, but I've achieved what I wanted. Besides, the purchase price is too good to refuse,' she joked, because Mrs Thirio Skartos hardly needed any more money. For this reason, she'd decided to donate the proceeds from the sale of her father's company—which she'd spent three years building into an events powerhouse, with Thirio's support—to a bereavement support charity.

'I know the business will be in safe hands,' she added. 'Much safer than it was before. Reflecting on things, that's what I really wanted. It wasn't that I needed to follow in my father's steps, it was just to stop my stepmother from destroying his legacy.'

'And you have done that, ten times over,' he said with satisfaction, thrilled that the grasping, unkind Elodie and her equally displeasing daughters had disappeared completely from Lucinda's life. Whatever thoughts Elodie had entertained of their marriage being a pathway to billionaire husbands for Sofia and Carina had been swiftly shut down by Thirio, who wasted no time confronting Elodie with his feelings about her cruelty, and telling her she would never be welcome in their home.

Perhaps he'd gone too far, but there was nothing he wouldn't do for his wife. Besides, they had each other, and they had Evie and Erik and their twins, and a small, loyal group of friends that made them feel blessed every day.

'So long as you know I would have supported you working at this company for as long as you wanted.'

'I know that.' She grinned across at him. 'You've been wonderful. But I have something else I'd like to work on now, and I think it's going to take a lot more of my time and energy than rebuilding Dad's business.'

'Oh?' He watched his wife with sheer admiration. Anything she decided to take on, she could accomplish. He had seen that first-hand. 'What is it?'

She stood, walking around the table, placing a hand on his shoulder. 'Haven't you noticed, Thirio? Is that really possible?'

He frowned. Always detail orientated, he struggled to think what he might have missed.

Lucinda chuckled. 'Look.' She took his hand in hers and pressed it to her flat stomach. He stared at it, her meaning obvious, even when it didn't compute.

'Lucinda.' He jerked up to standing, his heart pounding into his throat. 'You can't be serious.'

'Oh, I am.' He grinned.

'But…you haven't been at all sick.'

'I know. I've felt wonderful.'

'But Evie—'

'Every pregnancy is different.'

'How long have you known?'

'Only a couple of weeks,' she said with an apologetic smile. 'And then I decided to wait until I was twelve weeks, just to be absolutely sure.' Her kindness was so typical of Lucinda—to try to spare him from the pain of a possible loss. 'But I had another scan yesterday.'

'Your mystery appointment!' he accused with a grin. 'I did notice you were being quite vague about your schedule.'

'I just desperately wanted to know for sure before I told

you. Everything's fine. In six months we will have a lovely baby…do you want to know?'

'Not that it matters, but yes, I want to know.'

He waited, and Lucinda stepped up onto her tiptoes, whispering the gender into his ear. He pulled apart, grinning down at his wife, feeling as though the world had blessed him with a goodness he didn't deserve. Except Lucinda told him every day that he did, and Thirio was just starting to believe it.

'I hope she has your goodness, my darling wife.'

'And your heart.'

A year later, they held their six-month-old daughter in their arms, little Connie, named for his mother, as they eyed the memorial garden that had been created in the grounds of the *castile*, for his parents. Evie and Erik stood a little to the side, the twins weaving between their feet, Evie's hand pressed to her rounded stomach. Erik held her close as tears fell down Evie's cheeks. It was a poignant moment, but a necessary one. At last Constantina and Andreas Skartos's memories were brought into the light, where the good times could be remembered with joy, the gifts they'd given their children honoured daily. Grief was still a part of Thirio's heart, but it was a grief he was determined to learn from.

Life was short. Unpredictable and precious, and he was determined to make every moment of his count, just as he intended his children would.

He kissed his wife's forehead and he smiled.

He was exactly where he was meant to be, with Lucinda by his side, and life was truly, wonderfully good.

* * * * *

COMING SOON!

We really hope you enjoyed reading this book.
If you're looking for more romance, be sure to
head to the shops when new books are
available on

Thursday 21ˢᵗ
July

To see which titles are coming soon, please visit

millsandboon.co.uk/nextmonth

MILLS & BOON ®

Coming next month

HIS DESERT BRIDE BY DEMAND
Lela May Wright

"Can you explain what happened?" Akeem asked. "The intensity?"

Could she? Nine years had passed between them—a lifetime and still… No, she couldn't.

"My father had a lifetime of being reckless for his own amusement—"

"And you wanted a taste of it?"

"No," he denied, his voice a harsh rasp.

"Then what did you want?" Charlotte pushed.

"A night—"

"You risked your reputation for a night?" She cut him off, her insides twisting. "And so far, it's been a disaster, and we haven't even got to bed." She blew out a puff of agitated air.

"Make no mistake," he warned, "things have changed."

"Changed?"

"My bed is off limits."

She laughed, a throaty gurgle. "How dare you pull me from my life—fly me who knows how many miles into a kingdom I've never heard of and turn my words back on me?" She fixed him with an exasperated glare. "How dare you try to turn the tables on me?"

"If the tables have turned on anyone," he corrected, "it is me because you will be my wife."

Continue reading
HIS DESERT BRIDE BY DEMAND
Lela May Wright

Available next month
www.millsandboon.co.uk

MILLS & BOON

THE HEART OF ROMANCE

A ROMANCE FOR EVERY READER

MODERN

Prepare to be swept off your feet by sophisticated, sexy and seductive heroes, in some of the world's most glamourous and romantic locations, where power and passion collide.

HISTORICAL

Escape with historical heroes from time gone by. Whether your passion is for wicked Regency Rakes, muscled Vikings or rugged Highlanders, awaken the romance of the past.

MEDICAL

Set your pulse racing with dedicated, delectable doctors in the high-pressure world of medicine, where emotions run high and passion, comfort and love are the best medicine.

True Love

Celebrate true love with tender stories of heartfelt romance, from the rush of falling in love to the joy a new baby can bring, and a focus on the emotional heart of a relationship.

Desire

Indulge in secrets and scandal, intense drama and plenty of sizzling hot action with powerful and passionate heroes who have it all: wealth, status, good looks…everything but the right woman.

HEROES

Experience all the excitement of a gripping thriller, with an intense romance at its heart. Resourceful, true-to-life women and strong, fearless men face danger and desire - a killer combination!

To see which titles are coming soon, please visit

millsandboon.co.uk/nextmonth

LET'S TALK

Romance

For exclusive extracts, competitions
and special offers, find us online:

- facebook.com/millsandboon
- @MillsandBoon
- @MillsandBoonUK

Get in touch on 01413 063232